# Scythian Trilogy
# Book 3:
# Funeral in Babylon

## By Max Overton

Writers Exchange E-Publishing

http://www.writers-exchange.com

Scythian Trilogy Book 3: Funeral in Babylon
Copyright 2013, 2015, 2025 Max Overton
Writers Exchange E-Publishing
PO Box 372
ATHERTON QLD 4883

Cover Art by Julie Napier www.julienapier.com
from an original concept by Ariana Overton

Published by Writers Exchange E-Publishing
http://www.writers-exchange.com

ISBN **ebook**: 978-1-922066-96-1
**Print**: 978-1-925574-53-1 (WEE Assigned)

# Contents

# Prologue

The body of warriors rode casually, relaxed, as they moved along the broad dirt roads of northern Persia, heading south and west into the late afternoon sun sinking in a cloudless sky. Lengthening shadows stretched out behind them, rippling on the clouds of acrid dust churned by their horses' hooves. As the road wound slowly down from the mountain fastnesses of the borderlands toward the central plains of Persia, the land slowly took on a richer, more verdant aspect. The loose scree slopes and stunted vegetation gave way to austere pasture dotted with clumps of willow, poplar and alder; fresh new leaves burgeoning on spreading branches.

From time to time, even in these desolate hinterlands, the group passed men on foot or in rough-hewn carts drawn by resigned oxen. Peasants for the most part, dressed in ragged clothes, they gazed with stony-faced indifference at the armed horsemen confronting them. Few merchants found worthwhile opportunities in the northern mountains; those that passed that way kept a carefully neutral expression as they nodded a greeting. Without exception, the people of those parts deferred to the riders, recognising the tacit authority of armed men, pulling to the side of the road to let them pass.

Curious eyes followed them as the riders moved down from the mountain passes of the north into the rich fertile plains. Two men in particular watched from a stand of poplar trees atop a low hill several hundred paces from the road.

The smaller of the two men, slight of build and with a narrow, pinched face twisted by virulent emotion, shaded his eyes against the setting sun.

"That is the Greek. The one in front," he snarled.

The other man glanced across at the speaker. His deep-set brown eyes stared without expression for a moment before turning back to the road. "You have good eyes," he replied. "At this distance and against the sun, all I can see is a body of riders."

"I tell you it is he," repeated the thin man. "I would know that man if it were darkest night." The man's body shook with rage and his right hand clutched convulsively at the sword in his belt. "I will kill him now. I will avenge my lord Areipithes."

The other man raised an eyebrow. "Avenge?" he queried. "I thought you said it was the Massegetae noble Parasades, who killed Areipithes. Doesn't he even now rule as king over your tribe?"

The thin man swung round, his sallow face twisted with anger. "The Greek is responsible, you fool! I told you.." His eyes met the taller man's stare and he took a step back, his face paling at the murder in the other's eyes. "Your...your pardon, Scorpion," he stammered. "I meant no offence."

The man called Scorpion stared at the thin man a moment longer then turned his hooded eyes away from the smaller man. "You would do well to remember you are no longer in Scythia, Scolices. In these parts, my name carries more weight than the name of any Scythian king, alive or dead."

Scolices scanned the distant road and the figures of the riders silhouetted against the setting sun. He loosened the collar of his felt jacket, feeling sweat trickle down his back. "Is it always this hot?" he whined. He fanned his face against the warm breeze from the south.

Scorpion grunted. "You think this is hot? Wait until summer. You will long for the high cool plains of Scythia."

"What will you do?" asked Scolices. "About them, I mean," he added, gesturing toward the road. "You promised my lord Areipithes."

"I shall keep my word," Scorpion flatly replied. "Even though your lord is dead, I will keep my promise, made in the name of a friendship we once had."

"Good!" snarled Scolices. "His ghost will welcome their deaths."

Scorpion turned toward his companion again, his face expressionless. "Why such hatred? I can understand wanting a man's death, but not this consuming hatred. What has he done to earn this?"

"He is a barbarian Greek," spat Scolices. "He..."

"A Macedonian," interrupted the other man. "Nikometros, son of Leonnatos. An officer in Alexander's army and quite cultured, I hear. Hardly a barbarian."

Scolices shot the taller man a venomous look. "He seduced both our chief and the priestess Tomyra. He weakened our people..."

Scorpion smiled. "Your chief made this Nikometros a blood-brother quite freely. There was no coercion involved. As for the priestess, well yes, a seduction took place. By all accounts they are lovers."

"She was a virgin priestess of the Massegetae. To touch her is death. It is our law. She whored with the Greek and deserves death too."

"My spies tell me the Mother Goddess has not cast her off, despite her indiscretions," observed Scorpion. "Do you presume to tell the Goddess her business?"

3

"Of course not!" grunted Scolices. His hand flicked out, palm downward, in the sign of appeasement. "But sentence of death was pronounced on her and her barbarian lover."

"By a man now dead."

"He is still my king," said Scolices quietly. "I will follow his last command."

"The command of a man consumed by hate." Scorpion shook his head and turned back to scan the road sinking now into shadow as the sun dipped below the horizon. "I don't recommend hate as a way of life."

Scolices squinted into the growing darkness as the last of the riders vanished from view. "How will you do it?"

"Do what?"

"Kill them, of course."

Scorpion laughed. "I shan't kill them." He held up a hand as Scolices swung toward him, anger again twisting his features. "I'll cause it to be done by others."

"Why?" snarled Scolices. "You have the men. You outnumber him five times over. Do it now that I may wash my hands in his blood."

"This is Persia," observed Scorpion. "A land of law, even under Macedonian rule. If I were to kill travellers upon the Royal Road I would find myself hunted down and exterminated. I have seen other...seekers of profit...destroyed by their greed and arrogance. Even my position as a prince of traders and supplier of the Macedonian army would not save me. I won't risk that."

"Then how?"

"This Nikometros assumes he'll be able to pick up his life and his duties where he left them before he disappeared into the northern plains. Others, however, may suspect his motives and present purpose." Scorpion laughed again and strode over to his horse. He took the reins in his hand and swung the beast around before looking back at the smaller man. "A word or two in the proper ears and our purpose is accomplished."

Scorpion swung himself up onto the horse's back and guided it carefully down the slope through the evening shadows. With a muttered imprecation, Scolices hurried to his own mount and followed, leaving the warm wind from the south swaying the poplars.

# *Chapter 1*

T he small villages along the Royal Road relied for their survival on a constant stream of travellers. Early spring brought merchants and farmers down from the snowy fastnesses of the mountains of northern Persia, carrying goods and produce to the markets in the south. Less often, bodies of armed men stayed at the villages, even in these troubled times. The wars of conquest, as Alexander crushed the Persian Empire, had largely passed by these northern lands. Macedonian officers, backed more by Alexander's reputation than force of arms, governed with a light hand for the most part, leaving local officials in place unless they proved untrustworthy.

The elder and headman of the village of Abyek, however, lived in almost constant fear. Smugglers and brigands infested the region and more than once Macedonian forces had investigated rumours that he, Algoas, knew more of such business than he admitted. When a party of armed men, led by a Macedonian officer, rode into Abyek on a cool spring afternoon, his first thought was flight. Hastily grabbing a small sack of gold, he hurried out the back door and into a rickety stable attached to the back of the house. With trembling hands, he started to set the bridle on one of his mules.

A screech of anguish rattled the door of the stable. "Where are you going, husband? Will you leave me for the soldiers?"

Turning quickly, Algoas held up his hands. "Wife," he implored, "please be quiet. You will bring the soldiers down on us."

"You're leaving with all our gold. You'll leave me destitute. What will become of me?"

Algoas gave the thin-faced woman standing at the door a sour look. He forced a smile onto his worried face. "Molatta, my honey cake, I'm only taking our gold to a place of safety until the soldiers are gone. How can you think I would leave you?" He glanced beyond her to the shadows, glimpsing the rounded form of their young servant girl. A brief regret flitted across his face. "I'll be back in two or three days, as soon as the soldiers have left."

Molatta stamped her foot. "The soldiers aren't here for you, you fool," she snapped. "You're just using them as an excuse to rob me of my gold."

"Of course they're here for me, wife. Why else would soldiers...why do you say that?"

"Would soldiers on duty bring their women? You must think I'm a fool..."

"Women?" Algoas dropped the bridle and gripped his wife's arm. "What women?"

Molatta shrugged her bony shoulders and screwed up her face. "How should I know? One is richly dressed and she has a few others in attendance. A Macedonian officer leads them but the men are not Macedonians or locals."

"Where are they now?" asked Algoas.

"The officer and the lady went into the inn. His men remain outside."

Algoas sighed. He thrust the bag of gold into his wife's arms. "Put it back, my beloved. If they aren't looking for me then I must make sure they are well looked after." He pushed past Molatta into the house and hurried out the front door into the street.

Turning to his left he saw a number of townspeople milling around the entrance to the inn, gawking at the strangers. Shouldering his way through the crowd, Algoas bustled up to the door of the inn. A swarthy young man, sweating in layers of felt and leather, stopped him, barking unintelligibly in his face. Algoas grinned weakly and tried to push past.

The young man jabbered again then threw up his arms and turned in exasperation to a burly man behind him. "Speak to him, Timon. This fool does not seem to understand."

Timon nodded and stepped forward, blocking Algoas' way. "Easy, Tirses. Not everyone knows Scythian." He turned to the pale villager and switching to a mixture of Persian and Greek, addressed the man. "Who you?" He jabbed a finger at the man's chest.

Tirses chuckled. "Very subtle, Timon. Your command of the local language astounds me."

Timon glowered and flushed. "You could not do better," he rasped. "Who you?" he repeated, tapping the villager on the chest.

Algoas stepped back, flicking an alarmed look at the ring of strange faces. "I am Algoas," he stammered. "The elder of this village. I have come to welcome you to Abyek." He looked toward the inn door. "There is a lord and lady with you? I was told..." Algoas let his voice trail away.

Timon stared back at Algoas for a few moments through a great bush of eyebrow and beard. "Aye," he growled. Then, "Niko!" he shouted through the door, "Somebody to see you."

Metal gleamed in the doorway as a tall sun-bronzed man in cavalry armour emerged. He brushed back his long fair hair with one hand, his grey eyes appraising the scene in front of him. With a cool smile that came nowhere near his eyes, the man cocked his head at the villager standing with Timon and Tirses.

"I...I am Algoas, elder of Abyek. I welcome you, my lord...er..."

"Nikometros," said the tall man softly. "These are my men."

"Then you are indeed welcome, my lord Nikometros. Perhaps I can offer you such hospitality as our poor village can afford?" Algoas gestured toward the inn.

"It seems not," replied Nikometros. "All the rooms are full."

"Oh, I am sure that cannot be so," exclaimed Algoas. He bobbed his head and scurried into the darkness of the inn.

Timon raised an eyebrow at Nikometros then grinned as the sounds of a violent argument poured into the street. A few moments later, Algoas came out with a huge smile on his face.

"As I thought, my lord. A misunderstanding. Rooms will be made available to you at once. Perhaps while they are readied you will have some refreshment?"

Nikometros smiled. "Thank you. Perhaps some wine to wash the dust from our throats." He turned to the sweating Scythian. "Have the horses stabled then join us, Tirses." He looked back at the village elder and gestured. "Lead on, Algoas."

The interior of the inn was dim after the bright sunlit street. The air lay heavy and still, redolent with the odours of smoke and cooking. Several trestle tables sprawled in haphazard abandon through the room, each with a candle flickering and guttering, making its own small contribution to the soot-filled air. Stairs at the back of the room led up into darkness. Several men and two women stood in a huddle near the stairs arguing with a burly man who was ordering a string of servants. Bags were hastily thrown down and the burly man started ushering the group toward the door.

As the men passed Nikometros and Timon they flashed them a surly look, muttering imprecations. One of the women swore loudly and colourfully before being hurried out by her companions.

The burly man hurried over, nodded to Algoas and turned to Nikometros.

"My apologies, lord." He flashed a gap-toothed grin and bobbed his head deferentially. "A misunderstanding. Those misbegotten sons of whores..." he gestured toward the now-empty doorway, "...could not pay." He glanced toward Algoas and hurried onward. "Some wine, my lord? Not of the best, I'm afraid. It's been a bad year. Brigands are everywhere now that the Great King has fallen..." The inn-keeper's voice trailed off and he paled visibly in the darkness. "I...I'm sorry, my lord. I didn't mean..."

Nikometros nodded. "These are troubled times. The new Great King will restore order, I'm sure. Now, you spoke of wine?"

The innkeeper snapped his fingers and bellowed into the dim recesses of the inn. A young boy scampered out, bearing an earthenware jug and several wooden cups in a bag. He set the jug and cups on a table, his wide round eyes darting everywhere. The innkeeper cuffed the boy and sent him back to his work with a growl.

"If there's anything else, my lord, you have only to say. I'll see to your dinner." The innkeeper backed away.

Nikometros peered around the dim room. "Where are the ladies," he enquired, "and the old man?"

"They are upstairs, my lord, inspecting your rooms. They'll be ...ah, here they come, my lord." The innkeeper gestured toward the dark stairs then, grabbing Algoas by one arm, dragged him toward the kitchens.

Two figures appeared in the gloom, carrying guttering candles that accentuated the shadows rather than banishing them. A tall, dark-haired young woman in a flowing robe walked sedately toward Nikometros, threading her way through the tables. Behind her stalked a tall warrior in jacket and trousers, a sword belted at the waist and rich enamelled gold ornaments hanging around a slim neck. Only the lack of facial hair and the low swell of breasts betrayed the warrior's gender. An old, bent man, wisps of white hair clinging to an otherwise bald head tottered behind them. Thin arms crossed over his chest sheltered a black cat that inspected everyone in the room with yellow-eyed suspicion.

Nikometros grinned. "How are the rooms, Tomyra? To your satisfaction?"

The robed woman grimaced. "Dirty. And with holes in the walls." She set the candle down on the table and sank onto a stool. "However, I'm too tired to worry about it." She glanced up at the tall figure behind her and grinned. "Bithyia wants to force the inn-keeper to clean the rooms himself. At sword point if necessary."

Timon snorted with laughter then embraced the slim figure. "I'd wager good money he never had to deal with a Scythian warrior woman before." He kissed the tall woman before ushering her to the table. "Come, Bithyia. We have wine and the promise of a meal." He poured the thin wine into cups and passed them around.

Nikometros stepped around the women and guided the old man to a bench and passed him a cup of wine. The grey head shook his head and motioned the cup away. "Water," he muttered. "And some milk for Bubis."

"The water is not safe in the plains, Ket. It will give you the flux," replied Nikometros gently. "At least add some wine to it. Enough to take the ill from it." He scratched the black cat behind the ears and smiled as it butted his hand. "I'm certain we can find some milk for Bubis though."

Tirses arrived from stabling the horses and threw off his jacket with an oath. He slumped onto a bench and drained a cup of wine, spilling some of the thin red liquid onto his chest and shirt. He belched loudly and grinned.

11

"Apologies, my lady. But I really needed that." He refilled his cup and sipped. "The men are settled in the stables, my lord. Meat has been provided, and wine."

Nikometros nodded. "Good." He paused before carefully putting down his cup. "What is the mood of the men, Tirses?"

"Mood? What do you mean, my lord?"

"We've been traveling a month. A month away from their native Scythia. How are they holding up? Do they want to turn back?"

Tirses shrugged and glanced away. "One or two speak of their homes with longing."

"Malcontents!" growled Timon. "Do they imagine Parasades would leave them alive if they returned?"

"Such is the way of the world," muttered Ket.

"Yet they allowed Agarus to remain," pointed out Tomyra. "I really thought he was coming with us. But when he turned back at the last minute..."

Bithyia nodded. "Parasades will do anything to retain his mastery of our people. Those who followed the lord Nikom...Nikometros..." she stumbled over the pronunciation, "...would die as soon as they crossed the borders."

"They know this," Tirses quietly replied.

"Then why do they grumble?" barked Timon. "Give me their names. I'll teach them loyalty."

Nikometros gripped Timon's arm. "It doesn't matter who they are, Timon. Didn't you long for Macedon when we were captive?"

The meal arrived, ladled from the steaming kitchen cauldron into large earthenware bowls. A thick lamb stew, reeking with herbs and spices, set their mouths watering then rapidly satiated their hunger. Freshly baked bread, hot from the ovens, soaked up the juices of the meal. At last, they pushed their bowls back and stretched, watching Bubis delicately lick the last traces of gravy from the tabletop.

"Now that was a meal," grunted Timon.

"A bit too spiced for my taste," observed Bithyia, "But quite acceptable." She stifled a belch and took another sip of wine.

Tomyra yawned and pushed her bench back. "I think I'm ready for my bed. Will you join me, Niko?"

Nikometros smiled and rose. "Presently, Tomyra. I must talk to the men first. Timon, Tirses, will you join me?"

Bithyia watched her man leave the room with Nikometros and Tirses before turning to her priestess with a smile. "As soon as we reach the army I'm going to insist we're married."

Tomyra grinned. "Does he know what a firebrand he's getting?"

Bithyia curled her tongue and licked her upper lip. "Oh, he knows." Her eyes sparkled then flicked across at Tomyra. "And you, my lady? What of you and Niko?"

Tomyra's grin faltered. "I don't know."

Ket looked up sharply from where he sat, cradling Bubis in his lap. "You haven't told him yet, child?"

Bithyia shook her head. "My lady, you said you were going to days ago."

"It isn't easy to tell the man you love that you carry another man's child."

"Tell him," Ket gently admonished. "Tell him. He knows the circumstances; he'll understand."

"Of course he will," growled Bithyia. "Dimurthes forced you and he's now dead by his own hand. The Mother Goddess forbade you to rid yourself of it, so there must be a reason for you to carry it."

"Still, he's a man..."

Ket leaned forward and gently held Tomyra's wrist. His wise gaze searched her face. "How far gone are you, child. Three months?"

"Near enough, Ket."

"Then it will show soon. Do you mean to let him believe it is his own? Will you found your marriage on a deceit?"

"If you don't tell him, he'll never know it's not his," snapped Tomyra. "Niko is an innocent in some things."

Ket shook his head. "I won't tell him, child; that is for you to do. However, I've known him longer than you. He's no fool and he will find out."

"How can you say you've known Niko longer?" interjected Bithyia. "You were a slave of the Jartai when we found you. Niko and my lady were already close."

"Have you forgotten I was a priest at Siwah in Egypt, girl?" asked Ket. "I was there on that golden day when the pharaoh, Alexander, son of Ammon-Ra, came to the oracle. His half-brother Ptolemy was there, as was a certain youth in his entourage, scarcely more than a boy. Nikometros, illegitimate son of Ptolemy and nephew to Alexander." Ket lifted his cup and sipped his well-watered wine. "Oh yes, I have known Nikometros a long time."

Tomyra sat silent with her head bowed. For several minutes the only sounds in the room were the muted purring of Ket's cat, the clatter behind the kitchen screens and the ever-present drone of flies. At last, Tomyra raised her head and pushed back the black locks of hair falling over her eyes. She nodded.

"I'll tell him tonight."

"Would you like me there?" Bithyia nervously eyed her friend. "I can at least give you some moral support."

Tomyra opened her mouth to reply then shut it with a snap, whipping her head round as a volley of shouts and the clash of steel resounded from the street. She leapt to her feet and darted toward the door, Bithyia on her heels. Bursting into the street, the two women halted, staring in horror at the scene outside.

The narrow street overflowed with armed men. Greek soldiers in armour and clutching long spears stared belligerently over tall shields at Nikometros and Timon who crouched by a body lying in the dust. Behind them, Tirses and his men stood with drawn swords, uncertain as to their next action, waiting for a word of command.

The ranks of the soldiers parted and a tall man in full parade armour strode out to confront the two men crouching over the body of their fallen comrade. Scarlet plumes on his gleaming helmet bobbed as he advanced and the glint in his dark eyes matched that of the drawn sword. Fixing Nikometros with a steely glare, his voice rang out in the silence.

"Nikometros, son of Leonnatos. You are under arrest for treason."

# *Chapter 2*

The small stone cell sweltered in the noon heat. Nikometros lay on a thin straw pallet, feeling sweat trickle down his body. He shifted and scratched at the vermin bites scattered over his torso. A bar of sunlight, golden and rippling in the heat, lay across his legs. His eyes roamed the cell then gazed up to follow the light to the window high on the southern wall, where a thin sliver of blue sky taunted him, speaking of the wide, grassy plains of Scythia. His mind, unlike his captive and supine body, raced free, recounting over and over the events of the last three days.

Outnumbered and confronted by the lawful authority of the land, Nikometros surrendered his sword to the tall Macedonian officer in Abyek. His men, bewildered but ready to fight and die in his defence, unwillingly put down their arms. Nikometros argued for their release as envoys of the Massegetae people but to no avail. The most he could secure for them was the freedom to accompany their captive leader to Kharmsar, the headquarters of the local Macedonian garrison. At least they had retained their weapons and hence, some measure of honour.

Tomyra and Bithyia were treated well and with honour, as was the old Egyptian, Ket. Nikometros grinned despite his discomfort as he remembered the old man querulously insisting he be addressed by his full title and name: Holy Priest of Ammon-Ra, Beloved of the Gods, Keeper of the Oracle at Siwah, Ketherennoferptah.

Timon was taken captive. Though clearly an enlisted man and under the orders of a superior officer, he was named in the arrest warrant as an accomplice. He and Nikometros were bound and, under strict security, transported to the garrison town of Kharmsar, to await trial and sentence.

Footsteps sounded on the stone flagging outside the cell. Nikometros stood up, brushing down his tunic and running fingers through tangled hair. The bolt rattled and the heavy wooden door swung open. An armed officer stepped into the cell, flicking his gaze around the bare stone before settling on the unkempt and unshaven figure before him. After a moment's scrutiny he stepped back, letting an unarmed soldier enter.

The soldier thrust a wooden bowl at Nikometros then stooped and set a jug and cup on the floor. Rising, the man stared at Nikometros, scratching his chin.

"Say your prayers, traitor," he grated. "This will be your last meal."

"Enough, Demos," the officer quietly remarked. "Leave the gentleman alone."

The soldier shrugged and sidled out of the cell. The officer stared at Nikometros a moment longer. "My apologies, sir," he said. He paused. "I would try to collect my thoughts, sir. I'll come for you within the hour. A brave showing may mean the difference between a quick death and a lingering one."

Nikometros glanced down at the bowl he held then tossed the stale bread within it onto the pallet. He cleared his throat and took a deep breath. "I am condemned then? There's to be no trial?"

The officer shook his head. "You're under Macedonian law now. You'll be heard, of course; though the evidence against you is clear enough."

"What evidence...?"

"In due course," interrupted the officer. "For now, eat, prepare yourself." He stepped back, dragging the door shut behind him. The bolt rattled home and the sound of footsteps diminished.

Nikometros slammed the empty bowl against the wall with a curse. He stared around the small stone cell, his hands clenching impotently at his sides, his nostrils flaring. Taking a deep breath, he uttered a few choice epithets, describing the ancestry and desired fate of the officer and his superiors. After a few moments contemplation, Nikometros sighed and shook his head. He straightened his tunic and ran a hand over the stubble on his chin and then, shrugging at the impossibility of making himself presentable under the present circumstances, he picked up the crust of bread and lay down on the pallet. Chewing absently on the bread he looked toward the barred window far above. The tiny strip of blue sky beckoned to him and he lost himself in memories--for a while he roamed the open plains of Scythia with Tomyra by his side.

The shaft of sunlight was a hand span higher on the wall when they came for him. Nikometros heard the tramp of boots outside the cell and shouted commands. Footsteps resounded in the passage and the cell door crashed open. The same officer beckoned to him.

"Nikometros, son of Leonnatos, it is time."

Nikometros smoothed down his tunic and stepped past the officer into the corridor. Two burly soldiers took hold of his arms and started to hustle him toward the exterior door. A sharp command from the officer and they released him, standing back against the walls of the corridor.

Nikometros nodded toward the officer. "Thank you."

He turned and walked toward the open door, flanked by the guards. He stepped into an open courtyard surrounded by low buildings of wood and stone. Squinting into bright sunshine, Nikometros made out a large building at the opposite end of the courtyard. Scarlet pennants flew from poles affixed to the roof and armed guards stood at attention outside the broad doors. He started across the dusty ground toward the building.

The officer fell in beside him and several more soldiers followed with hands on sword hilts. To one side, several soldiers lounged around a rough wooden stake set into hard-baked earth. One or two rested, leaning on slender javelins. Others hefted them or practiced casting them at a pile of rags. They fell silent as the small party walked by, turning to look at Nikometros with curiosity.

One man laughed. "Ho, traitor! I'll enjoy killing you." His fellow soldiers guffawed and turned back to their practice. Nikometros paled slightly but lifted a hand in a half salute and marched on.

"Bravely done!" muttered the officer.

Nikometros inclined his head. "What is your name, sir?" he asked.

"Dymnos." The officer paused. "I met you before, sir. Well, sort of. After the battle at the Granicus River. I was in Nicanor's infantry. You were wonderful." Dymnos flushed. "The Companion Cavalry, I mean, sir. You swept all before you."

"I must admit I don't remember you, Dymnos."

"No reason to, sir. We were plundering the enemy camp when the cavalry returned from chasing Darius. I handed you a flask of wine. Men pointed you out as one destined for great things."

"I'm sorry, Dymnos, I don't remember, but it was a kindness all the same. I do remember a great thirst and being surrounded by good comrades."

"Aye, sir," said Dymnos. "It saddens me to see it come to this. Never fear, if all goes ill I will do what I can to make sure your death is a swift one." He looked up as they approached the guards at the door.

When the doors swung open, Nikometros' first impression was of being in a garden. A small portico led into a large tiled room. The centre of the room opened to the sky and a fountain sprayed high into the air, splashing and tumbling into a rippling pool. Sun flecks shimmered and danced, reflected into the farthest recesses of the room. Flowering and fruiting trees of all descriptions sat in great earthenware pots around the pool, filling the air with a delicate perfume.

A heavyset man at an ornate table sat to one side of the pool, out of reach of splashes. The man, dark and bearded, wore a drapery of rich robes and an indefinable air of command. Across the dark polished wood of the table lay scattered papers, one of which the man intently studied. At a smaller table sat two men whose duties could only be that of secretaries as a profusion of pens and scrolls lay around them and one scribbled furiously while the other dug through a mound of papers. Dymnos and Nikometros marched up to the table and halted, saluting.

"Sir," said Dymnos. "The prisoner, Nikometros son of Leonnatos."

The heavyset man looked up, scrutinised Nikometros briefly then resumed reading. Nikometros waited in silence. At length the man put down the paper, sighed and looked up again.

"You stand accused of treason, soldier," drawled the man in a weary voice. "The evidence is overwhelming but as you're a Macedonian, I'll hear what you have to say before you are executed."

"Whom have I the honour of addressing, sir?"

"Alcimenes, son of Leanndros, garrison commander of the Macedonian army at Kharmsar and the surrounding provinces," the man replied. "If you entertain some hope of appealing to a higher officer, know that I have full authority to punish wrongdoing and will do my duty."

"What is my supposed crime, sir?"

"Treason." Alcimenes leaned forward. "Are you hard of hearing, soldier, or do you need an interpreter?"

"No, sir. I meant only that treason could be many things. What precisely am I accused of?"

Alcimenes waved a hand toward his secretaries. "Read him the list of charges, Druon."

A short balding man dropped the pen he was scribbling with and searched through the papers in front of him. "Yes, my lord," he muttered. He cleared his throat and read from a scroll.

"First, that last spring, with foreknowledge, you did lead a troop of Macedonian auxiliaries into an ambush, resulting in the deaths of ten of your men.

"Second, that you did enter..."

"I didn't lead any troop into an ambush, sir," interrupted Nikometros.

"You deny the incident?" Alcimenes furrowed his brow. "It's a matter of public record. The bodies of most of the soldiers were recovered for burial."

"Then you must know that Eumenes captained our troop. He was in command. I only took over when he was killed in the ambush."

Druon sifted through his papers. The other secretary handed him a list that he swiftly scanned.

"A Eumenes is listed sir, but not his rank."

Alcimenes made a notation on a piece of paper then signed to Druon. "Continue reading the charges."

"Yes, sir. Second, that you did enter into a treaty with the enemy."

Alcimenes raised an eyebrow at Nikometros. "You wish to answer that charge?"

21

"Indeed, sir. I entered into no treaty. I recognise I don't have the authority. What I did do, to preserve my life and the lives of my surviving men, was to become a blood brother of the chief of the Massegetae Scythians."

"You have proof of this, or do I only have your word?"

"Send for my man Timon and the priestess Tomyra. They were both present. Where are they anyway?" Nikometros dropped his voice to a whisper. "Sir, what has become of my companions?"

Alcimenes leaned back and examined his nails. He nibbled at the side of one and spat delicately to one side. "Your women are safe. We don't make war on women. As for the Scythians with you, they'll be detained, quite comfortably I might add, until word arrives from Ekbatana as to their disposition."

"And Timon?"

"He's been found guilty of treason. After a bit of persuasion, he admitted to making arms for the Scythians. He'll be executed by stoning this evening."

"Sir, that admission is taken out of context." Nikometros stepped forward as he spoke, waving his arms in agitation. The guards drew their swords and Dymnos put a restraining hand on Nikometros' arm. He allowed himself to be pulled back. In a calmer voice he went on. "Call him back or question Tomyra. They'll give you the truth of it."

Alcimenes stared coldly at the unkempt man in front of him. "I'll consider it." He waved his hand vaguely at the secretaries. "Continue reading the charges, Druon."

"Third, that you waged war on the loyal allies of Alexander and, by extension, on your fellow Macedonians."

Nikometros gaped. "What allies? I know of no allies."

Alcimenes leaned forward. "Do you deny you invaded the lands of..." He pushed a few papers aside and picked one up, scanning several lines of writing before continuing. "...the lands of the Serratae. Not only did you carry war to this people but also you caused the death of their chief Dimurthes."

Nikometros shook his head weakly. "That's not how it was," he muttered. "How did you come by this information?"

"That isn't your concern. The facts speak for themselves. You stand condemned." Alcimenes pushed his chair back, gripping the arms as he started to rise to his feet. "Guards, take this man..."

Nikometros took a pace forward, shrugging off Dymnos' hand. "Sir, may I not at least confront my accuser."

Alcimenes collapsed back into his chair and stared. "What a novel idea!" He gave a short bark of laughter and waved away the guards. "Why would you want to do that?"

"The man is lying. I am sure that he's one of the former chief's men. I could easily show that he seeks my death, by any means, not the truth."

"I thought you said you were some sort of a blood brother to the chief. Why would he want you dead?"

"That was the father, sir. The son, who succeeded him, wanted my death."

Alcimenes shook his head and picked up a delicately wrought silver cup of wine from the table. He sipped, looking thoughtfully at Nikometros over the rim.

"You cannot confront your accuser."

"Sir, I beg of you..."

Alcimenes put down the cup and held up his hand. "He's no longer available. His name is Parates, a merchant of some distinction in these parts, and one who has served the King before. He made a sworn statement before me, accusing you of these crimes. Do you know the man?" he asked.

Nikometros frowned. "I don't know the name, sir."

"Then why should I delay?" Alcimenes cocked his head. "Should I take the sworn statement of a reputable merchant, or that of an accused man who will say anything to escape death?"

Nikometros stared stonily at the garrison commander. "I am a loyal soldier of my king, sir. I fought bravely against his enemies and would do so again. Let me call witnesses to speak on my behalf."

"Who would you call? Don't think to buy time by naming distant witnesses."

Nikometros shook his head. "They are here, sir. My companion Timon and the young woman Tomyra."

"I already know your man is loyal. He took some persuasion to admit his own crimes but refused to implicate you." Alcimenes sipped his wine again. "Why the woman? What is she to you?"

"She is a priestess of the Mother Goddess, sir. Sacred to the Scythians and Greeks alike."

Alcimenes pursed his lips. "This deity of theirs...she has a name?"

"Tabiti, sir, though they rarely invoke her by name. I'm convinced she's the goddess we know as Artemis."

Alcimenes leaned back in his chair and stared at and through Nikometros. He tapped a finger against his lips, his brow furrowed in concentration. After many minutes, he nodded.

"Very well, I'll question your witnesses."

# *Chapter 3*

The doors to the commander's residence crashed open, the heavy oak panels shivering with the force of the impact. Timon, his arms bound behind him, rebounded from one door and kicked out at his guards. One fell to the tiled floor with an agonised howl, clutching his groin. The others fell on Timon, wrestling him to the floor and landing a series of heavy blows with their fists.

"Enough!" Alcimenes leapt to his feet, violently pushing back the table. His wine cup toppled and the secretary Druon made an unsuccessful grab for it. A purple puddle seeped into the papers.

"Get that man up," hissed Alcimenes. "Dymnos!" He whirled on the officer standing by Nikometros. "If you cannot control your men I'll find someone who can."

Dymnos saluted and strode across to the struggling guards. He tossed one away, pushed another aside and hauled Timon upright. Ignoring the bellowing man's attempts to kick him, Dymnos cocked a fist and drove it into Timon's face. Blood spurted and Timon staggered back then sat down hard on the tiled floor. He stared up at the figures standing over him.

"Fonf of whoref," Timon mumbled through the blood pouring from a swollen gashed lip. "I'ff already told you the truff." He shook his head, wincing and peered past Dymnos. "Niko? If ffat you?"

Nikometros stepped forward, past Dymnos. "Yes, Timon." He dropped to one knee beside his friend and gently wiped the blood away with his fingers.

"Godff, Niko," mumbled Timon. "Tell thefe baftardf the truth of it. They accufe me of making weaponf for the enemy."

"I know, my friend. They believe we both conspired to betray our fellow countrymen." Nikometros half turned and gestured behind him. "The commander here wants to ask you some questions." He got to his feet, wiping the blood on his tunic.

"Sir, allow me to tend to this man's wounds before you question him."

Alcimenes stared coldly at the blood-spattered man on the floor. "He has already been condemned and I don't intend to waste any more time on this than I must." He walked around the table and stood over Timon. "Tell me about the patrol you were in that was ambushed by the Scythians."

Timon spat on the floor, bloody saliva dribbling into his beard. "North Sogdian province, near the Oxus River. There had been raids on the farms." He shrugged. "We rode out to find the raiders. What more do you want me to say?"

"Who commanded you? This man?" Alcimenes pointed at Nikometros.

Timon shook his head and groaned. "No, some stuck-up prig by the name of Eumenes." He glanced up at Nikometros. "Sorry, Niko. I know he was your friend but he shouldn't have been leading us."

"And when did this Eumenes die?"

"In the first volley." Timon thought for a moment. "Things happened fast."

"What did this man do?"

"Niko? He saved our miserable carcasses. Half of us were dead already and nobody knew which way to turn. We were cut off but he led us over the hills and down the other side." Timon shook his head again, wincing. Drops of blood spattered the tile. "I couldn't have pulled the men together like that; none of us could. But Niko did. Just bad luck we ran into a Scythian raiding party."

"Then what happened?"

"They cut us to pieces. Only three of us were captured."

"Three? Who was the other?"

Timon shifted uncomfortably on the tiles, pulling against his bonds. He cleared his throat and spat again. "Mardes, son of Oxartes. He was a Persian auxiliary recently enlisted."

"And where is he now?"

Timon shrugged. "Nikometros sent him south with dispatches about four, maybe five months ago. He was to report to the local commander."

Alcimenes pursed his lips and stood for a moment looking down at Timon before turning back to the papers on his table. He picked up a wine-stained list and scanned it. Abruptly he signalled to Dymnos.

"Send riders out immediately to the garrison commanders at Nesapur, Dezi and Semnan." Alcimenes began to pace as he fired out the names. "See if this Mardes has turned up. If he has, bring him to me, together with his report."

Dymnos saluted and strode from the room, his shouted commands cut off when he closed the doors behind him.

"I can tell you what was in the report, sir," Nikometros quietly responded.

"No doubt," snapped Alcimenes. "However, the existence of this Mardes or the report will verify your account of the ambush and what followed." He pulled up his chair and sat down then picked up his wine cup.

Finding it empty he slammed it down on the table and gestured irritably for it to be filled. Druon hurried over with a jug.

"You there, on the floor." Alcimenes pointed at Timon then hesitated. "By the gods, Druon, what is that fellow's name?"

"Sir," interrupted Nikometros. "His name is Timon, I elevated him in the field to junior officer rank. I would remind you sir, that even though he stands condemned by you, he's a brave soldier and comes from a good Macedonian family." His voice grew steely and he drew himself up as he spoke. "He does not deserve your discourtesy."

Alcimenes stared at Nikometros in silence for several moments. Abruptly he snorted with laughter and signalled to the guards by the door. "Pick him up. Put him in a chair." He waited while Timon's handlers placed him in a chair.

"His bonds, sir?" inquired Nikometros.

Alcimenes nodded and a guard cut the ropes around Timon. The big man flexed his arms and looked speculatively at the commander.

"Now, Timon," Alcimenes stared at the big man. "...Please tell me how you survived capture by the Scythians. By all accounts they usually take no prisoners."

Timon nodded. "Aye, that's right..." He caught a finger signal from Nikometros and appended a reluctant "...sir."

"They're a superstitious lot...sir," went on Timon. "They saw an old armband of Niko's and thought it was a sign from their Goddess. They spared us, intending to sacrifice us."

Alcimenes silently and intently inspected Timon. After a few seconds, he shifted in his chair. "And...?"

"They sent Niko unarmed against a fully armed Scythian." Timon grinned, wincing as his split lip gaped. "By all the gods, that was a fight! Disarmed the bastard and killed him with his own sword."

Alcimenes raised his eyebrows. "Indeed? Then what happened?"

Timon raised the hem of his tunic to his lips and gently pressed them. He eyed the bloodstains, his tongue probing the wounds. "The priestess said it was a sign from the Goddess. She talked her father, who was the chief, into sparing our lives. He made Niko a blood brother."

"So, we come to it." Alcimenes leaned back with a sigh and sipped from his cup.

The door to the courtyard opened and Dymnos slipped into the room.

Alcimenes gestured him to one side. "What was the nature of this oath?" Alcimenes fixed on Timon again. "What were the terms? What obligation was placed on you?"

Timon shrugged. "To fight for one another. His enemies were our enemies, his friends our friends."

"Scythians fought against our troops," the commander quietly replied. "It cannot have been pleasant being forced by your oath to take arms against your countrymen."

Timon grinned again, one hand leaping to his lip. "Not us, sir! Niko here thought that might arise so made it a term of the agreement that we never be forced to fight Macedonians or their allies."

"Yet you fought against the Serratae?"

Timon furrowed his brow. "What of it?"

"The Serratae signed a treaty with the Empire. They are our allies."

Timon paled, his jaw hanging slack. He swallowed and glanced up at Nikometros. "That cannot be," he gasped. "Can it, Niko?"

Nikometros stared at Alcimenes. "When was this treaty made, sir?" he asked.

Alcimenes waved his hand vaguely through the air. "A few months, I think. Maybe more."

"Then we fought them before they became allies." Nikometros turned and smiled encouragingly at Timon.

"Is one of your titles 'Lion of Scythia'?" Alcimenes abruptly asked, fixing on Niko. He nodded. "Yes, I see from your face you know the title. Well, the chief of the Serratae, one Sparses I believe, mentioned you specifically as aiding their enemies the Massegetae."

Alcimenes rose to his feet and signalled to Dymnos. "There is no answer to that, Nikometros son of Leonnatos, you are proven guilty of warring against an ally of King Alexander. The penalty is death. Dymnos, the sentence will be carried out immediately."

# *Chapter 4*

T he guards stepped forward, hands on sword hilts, and flanked Nikometros and Timon.

Dymnos turned to Alcimenes, hand outstretched. "Sir," he implored. "Hear the priestess. She waits outside the door."

Alcimenes hesitated and Nikometros spoke quietly into the gap. "She's Scythian royalty sir. As well as priestess, she's daughter of the old chief. There's no one who knows the circumstances of the war with the Serratae better."

Alcimenes scowled and signalled the guards back against the wall. "Very well." He stabbed a finger at Nikometros. "You will not speak. I wish her words to be hers alone." Slumping back into his chair he picked up his cup and drank. "Send her in."

A guard opened the outer door and stood aside to let two figures slip past. Tomyra glided softly into the sun-flecked room, her eyes flicking over the figures seated and standing around her. Behind her strode the athletic figure of Bithyia, hand resting on the handle of her dagger while her gaze took in the situation. She caught sight of the bloody figure of Timon and a

31

look of fury welled up into her eyes. Bithyia strode over to Timon and laid a hand on his shoulder, her other sliding the dagger from her belt.

"Who has done this, beloved?" she whispered. "I will have his life."

Alcimenes nodded and two guards levelled their spears at Bithyia. "What is your name, woman?" he grated.

"Bithyia. Handmaiden to the priestess of the Great Goddess and daughter of the Massegetae," replied Bithyia. "Who has done this to my man?"

"Then I don't need to speak to you. Stand away or die. It's nothing to me." Ignoring the anger on Bithyia's face, Alcimenes turned to the other woman. "You must be the priestess."

Tomyra glanced at the silent figure of Nikometros then toward the bearded man. She inclined her head in a gracious nod. "I am Tomyra, daughter of Spargises, chief of the Massegetae. I am also priestess of the Great Earth Mother." She paused, inspecting him. "And you, sir?"

"Alcimenes, son of Leanndros. I am commander of Alexander's armies in these parts." The garrison commander stood and gestured to the chair in front of him as Timon and Bithyia were ushered to one side. "Please be seated, lady. Some wine?"

When Tomyra shook her head, Alcimenes reseated himself. "I must ask you some questions, lady. Do you speak Greek well enough or must I find an interpreter?"

Tomyra settled herself onto the chair before replying. "I can speak your tongue and will answer your questions. But before I do so, Alcimenes, son of Leanndros." Her gaze hardened. "I would know why I and my escort are kept captive. We came in peace, bringing greetings and gifts from our king to yours."

"An unfortunate set of circumstances, my lady." Alcimenes avoided Tomyra's eyes. "I'm sure we can quickly settle this matter and let you continue with your mission."

"And my escort?" Tomyra looked across at Nikometros then turned toward Timon. "They seem to be ill-used."

"There lies the problem, my lady. These men are soldiers of our king, Alexander. They are accused of capital crimes." Alcimenes leaned forward and stared at the young woman. "Your words may shed some light on the issue."

Tomyra paled but held herself still. "Ask on then, my lord Alcimenes. What do you wish to know?"

Alcimenes leaned back in his chair and steepled his hands, resting his chin on upturned fingers. He silently regarded the young woman for several minutes. "What is this man, this Nikometros, to you?" Alcimenes asked at last.

Tomyra paused, her eyes flicking sideways toward Niko. "He is...was, a general in my father's army and protector of the priestess. Now he is an interpreter and envoy from the king of the Massegetae to the court of Alexander."

Alcimenes smiled thinly. "Nothing more?"

"What do you mean?"

"I have a report that he's your lover."

Tomyra flushed and shrugged. "What of it?" she asked.

"I was led to believe that priestesses were virgins." Alcimenes' scrutiny sharpened on her face. "Does this mean you're no longer a priestess?"

Tomyra's eyes flashed and she drew herself upright. "The Mother Goddess accepted me when I offered my virginity to her. She accepts me still."

"Why did the Massegetae take in this Nikometros when the custom was to kill captives?"

"The Goddess willed it. Nikometros bested my champion in the ritual sacrifice. Also, my father, the chief, wished it."

"So, he was made a blood brother." Alcimenes nodded then he snapped, "To what purpose? To war on your enemies?"

Tomyra shook her head. "Is that what all this is about? Nikometros did not war on you, even though we Massegetae have always raided the farms and villages of these lands. Niko stipulated that his friendship did not extend that far and my father accepted it. Furthermore, we left for the north within days and never saw another Greek."

Alcimenes leaned toward Druon and held a short, whispered conversation with him. Druon scribbled on a piece of paper for a few minutes then filed the piece carefully in a small stack.

The garrison commander turned back to Tomyra. "Do you deny the Massegetae and your lover Nikometros waged war against the Serratae?"

"No!" snapped Tomyra. "And if I had my way I would exterminate every last one of them."

"The Massegetae fought and killed Serratae people?"

"Yes."

"And Nikometros?"

"Yes. Why do you ask?"

"The Serratae are allies of the Macedonians. To wage war on an ally is treason."

Timon groaned from his position near the wall.

Alcimenes glanced up. "You will keep silent," he grated.

"If Greeks are allies to the Serratae," whispered Tomyra. "You must truly be barbarians."

Alcimenes exploded to his feet, his face going scarlet. "You call us barbarians?" he shouted. "We, who have brought civilisation to the known world?"

"How civilised is it to kill by treachery? To slaughter innocent women and children? To rape a consecrated priestess of the Mother Goddess?"

"No Greek would do such a thing!" Alcimenes blustered, his face becoming redder. "You are making this up."

"No." Tomyra shook her head. "Would that I was. The chief of the Serratae, Dimurthes, invaded our lands though we were at peace. He killed my father, killed my maidservants and carried me off for his pleasure." She glanced at Nikometros, who stood against the wall, a wooden expression on his face as he stared off into the distance. "He raped me, knowing I was a priestess."

"And all this was witnessed?" Alcimenes asked.

"Ask any who are here today. Every Massegetae here knows the truth of Dimurthes' treachery and the killing of our women and children."

"And the rape?"

Tomyra shook her head. "Only Dimurthes. And he is dead by his own hand."

"So, we only have your word for this charge?"

Tomyra sat silently, head bowed.

The fountain splashed and gurgled in the open courtyard, filling the silence. Armour creaked as the guards shifted, eyes and ears avid for the unfolding story.

"My lady?" Alcimenes interrupted. "You have no way of proving the charge of rape, do you?"

"I bear his child."

"Eh?" Alcimenes' eyebrows lifted. "What did you say?"

Tomyra raised her head and defiantly stared into the commander's eyes. "Dimurthes raped me. As a result, I carry his child." She blinked, and turned toward Nikometros.

He stared back at her, his face pale and rigid with shock.

"I am sorry, Niko," Tomyra whispered. "I wanted to tell you before but...."

Alcimenes gaped then chuckled as a grin spread across his face. "You didn't know, soldier?" He shook his head and clapped his hands together. "Pleasured her this last year by all accounts then she ups and has another man's baby."

"My lord Alcimenes," Tomyra pleaded. "I would ask you to be civil. This isn't a situation for mirth."

Alcimenes dismissively waved a hand. "Your pardon, lady. But the expression on this man's face..." He leaned forward. "Why didn't you simply get rid of it? I know you women can do such things."

Tomyra paused. "I considered it, but the Goddess forbade me. I don't know why."

Alcimenes leaned back in his chair and picked up his wine cup. He slowly turned it, examining the rough outlines of men and beasts carved into the wooden rim. "So, what do I do with all of you?" he mused. He sipped the wine then put the cup down before rising.

"My first thought is to just execute the men." Alcimenes nodded at Nikometros and Timon. "It's a tidy solution. However..." he went on, "...if the Serratae are fomenting war then the policy makers in Babylon need to hear about it firsthand." The commander paced, ignoring his audience. "The first charge can probably be dismissed," he muttered, "depending on the report of this Persian auxiliary, Mardes. The second, aiding the enemy, needs further investigation. The third and most serious, that of waging war against our allies, hinges on the testimony of the priestess."

Alcimenes halted and looked at Nikometros and Tomyra, then Timon and Bithyia. He turned toward the guard. "Dymnos. You will escort the prisoners and their Massegetae companions to Ekbatana. You will carry dispatches addressed to the lord Hephaestion as commander of the Companion Cavalry. Let him decide on their fate."

"Yes, sir!" Dymnos snapped to attention and saluted. He turned and hesitated before turning back to face his commander again. "Er, sir?" he queried.

"Yes, Dymnos, what is it?"

"There are twenty er...prisoners, sir. Or rather, nineteen after the death in Abyek."

"So?"

"If I am to guard them sufficiently, sir, it'll deplete our forces here in Kharmsar. It wouldn't be wise..." Dymnos' voice trailed off uncertainly.

Alcimenes grunted, the corners of his mouth turning down. Then he looked at Nikometros, his eyes measuring the man. "Nikometros, son of Leonnatos, do you count yourself a gentleman?"

Nikometros inclined his head.

"If I send you to Ekbatana with no more than a nominal escort, will you undertake, on your honour, to present yourself to the commander there?"

Nikometros considered for a moment then, "I will, on my honour, sir."

Alcimenes nodded and turned back to Dymnos. "Take no more than a squad. You pick them. I'll prepare the dispatches tonight and you'll leave at dawn. If the Persian soldier or his report turns up I'll send it after you. I'll also send a rider ahead of you to alert the army of your coming."

Dymnos saluted then shouted commands to the guards. The armed soldiers, wary of the glowering Timon, ushered their charges from the building and into the barrack rooms. They began to prepare for the long journey south to Ekbatana, to the summer palace of the Persian kings and the court of the emperor Alexander of Macedon.

# *Chapter 5*

The King's Road lay broad and dusty, running straight and true to the south. For many days it wound between mountains, over high passes, along narrow defiles and through gorges bursting with freshly melted water. Now the hills were softer, more rounded, flattening out into broad and fertile plains. The dusty air, once acrid and sour from the thin mountain soil, became softer, redolent with the odours of living things. Though still early spring, the noonday sun beat down from a cloudless sky, rippling the air and obscuring the now distant horizon. Spilling out into the plains, the road gathered itself for the final push south through the civilised lands of Persia to the hills that bore the great city of Ekbatana.

Tomyra rode her grey mare near the front of the company, seeking to avoid the clouds of pale dust thrown up by the horses' hooves. She squinted up at the sun and sighed, pulling the stopper from her flask. She sipped tepid water, flavoured with just enough wine to counteract any possible flux in the plains water. Turning to the rider alongside her, she grimaced and desultorily waved her free hand at the monotonous landscape.

"I thought you said Persia was a beautiful land, Niko. These fields and farms are colourless and boring."

Nikometros grunted. "Boring maybe, but productive. Besides, we'll be entering hill country again soon. It will be cooler and I can promise you glorious sights."

They rode in silence for a while. Each village and town they passed brought an increase in traffic. The column of horses picked its way through herds of animals moving to and from pastures, caravans of traders bringing commodities from the farthest reaches of the empire, and gaggles of common people caught up in the excitement of the king's presence.

Tomyra sipped from her flask. "Niko," she said in a small voice. "I couldn't prevent it."

Nikometros did not answer. He twitched the reins of his stallion, Diomede, guiding him around a particularly large pothole.

"Would you rather I had killed myself, Niko? I considered it."

Nikometros jerked around. "Gods, no!" He smoothed back unruly blond hair and sighed. "I'm sorry Tomyra. I'm finding it difficult to...to accept..."

"To accept that your woman bears another man's child?" Tomyra bluntly asked. "I'm not a piece of property Niko, neither yours nor any man's. I was raped, taken against my will. The fault was not mine. Why do you blame me?"

"I don't, Tomyra," exclaimed Nikometros. "Before the gods, I..." he fell silent when a group of merchants passed close by, heads turning in curiosity. "In my homeland I would have the man's life for what he did. He dishonoured me...and you, and his blood would have cleansed us of the shame."

Tomyra stared at the man riding beside her. "I feel no shame," she snapped. "If you think I enjoyed the experience, you're a fool. Dimurthes died by his own hand. He felt the shame, not I."

"Forgive me, Tomyra, that was not well put." Nikometros slapped his thigh with frustration. "I wouldn't willingly hurt you but..."

"No," sighed Tomyra. "But you're still a Greek barbarian for all your experience of my people. What any Massegetae would accept as meaningless has taken over your mind. Get past the injury, Niko, whether real or imagined. My love for you is unchanged."

"You shame me, my love," Nikometros whispered.

Tomyra uttered a sharp cry of frustration. "Forget shame! I don't feel it, nor should you. Just live your life as the Goddess sends it. Love me as you once did and all will be well between us."

Nikometros bit his lip, his sunburned face darkening. "And...and the child?" he enquired, nodding his head toward her belly.

"I bear it but I shall not mother it," she quietly responded. "The Goddess requires me to have it, for some purpose of Her own, but I shall not rear it. I'll give it away." She pulled back on the reins, bringing her mare to a halt before turning to face him.

"If you can put all this behind us and love me as before then come and see me tonight. For now, I'll ride with Bithyia. I have need of the company of women." She pulled her mare around and trotted back to where the warrior woman rode.

Nikometros rode on at the head of the column, his face burning and his mind in turmoil. Presently, Timon, dislodged from his place beside Bithyia, came alongside his friend.

"What in Hades did you say to her, Niko?" Timon asked with a puzzled look. "I've seldom seen her in such a mood."

Nikometros shrugged. "Nothing special," he muttered.

"Ah!" Timon nodded with understanding.

The two men continued in silence, threading their horses through the gaggle of humanity that crowded the Royal Road near the towns. They passed by a small hamlet on the left, bustling with life. It reeked of noise and the odours of a farm community. The land gently rose before them, presaging the hill country that surrounded their goal.

A small family group of farmers approached, the man pulling a cart laden with vegetables. A woman pulled an unwilling goat on a short tether, while several children ran and played around them.

Timon jerked his head at the children as they passed. "See that boy?"

Nikometros grunted in reply and gave the farmers a cursory glance.

"Strange isn't it?" Timon glanced at his friend. "The others are so dark haired and swarthy, yet he's fair haired."

"Not so strange. An army went through here."

The blond child fell and set up a howl, while stubbornly sitting in the middle of the road. Passing the care of the goat to an older boy, the woman hurried over. The man stopped and turned, exchanging a few words. The young boy ceased crying and limped over to the cart. Once there, he stood smiling as the man gently picked him up and deposited him among the produce.

"The man, who is plainly not his father, appears to love him, doesn't he?"

"All right," Nikometros growled. "I get the point."

Timon grinned. "What point is that, Niko?"

Nikometros scowled and kicked his heels into Diomede's sides. They thundered away, Niko's back stiff with anger.

With a laugh, Timon urged his horse forward, matching the other until he slowed once more to a walk beside them.

After a short silence, Nikometros turned and gave his friend a weak smile. "And how is Bithyia?" he asked.

"Fretting. She hates not being in control of the situation. I had to dissuade her and Tirses both from overpowering our escort and setting out on their own."

"Not a good idea. I gave my word we wouldn't escape. Our lives would be forfeit on sight if we tried anything like that."

"I know. But really, how do you rate our chances when we get to Ekbatana?"

"Hephaestion is a fair man by all accounts," Nikometros carefully replied.

Timon snorted. "And what are our chances of getting to see him? Far more likely we'll end up with some self-important mid-level official like that bastard Alcimenes." He fingered the nearly healed scar on his lip.

Nikometros smiled. "I think you're overlooking our novelty value. Do you think anyone at Ekbatana has seen Scythian horsemen up close? That alone should get us noticed."

"Aye, you could be right." Timon yawned and eyed the afternoon sun. "Getting on," he remarked. "Maybe we should stop at the next town." He turned and looked back down the road at the column of Scythian horsemen and Macedonian cavalry. "I'll go and suggest it to Dymnos."

"I will," Nikometros said while wheeling his stallion around. "I need to talk to him anyway." He trotted back down the road. As he passed the two women he smiled and nodded but did not stop.

Dymnos, dressed in full armour, sat astride a grey stallion that walked sedately beside the small Scythian pony of Tirses, the leader of the Scythians. He looked up as Nikometros approached, breaking off his conversation with the other man.

"Greetings, Nikometros," Dymnos said when Niko came close. "Tirses was telling me of your exploits among the Massegetae. By the gods, you made your mark there." He laughed and smacked his stallion on the flank, causing it to shy and whicker with annoyance.

Nikometros guided Diomede alongside, pulling his stallion's head away as it tried to nip the other horse. "Don't believe everything you hear.

Scythians love a good tale and will make one up if they cannot think of a true one." He grinned at Tirses. "Not that I'm calling anyone a liar, of course."

Tirses snorted. "Any other man I'd call out if he called me a liar. Not this one though. I value my life too much."

"Indeed," Dymnos chuckled. "I heard about your combat with the priestess' champion. Unarmed, yet you defeated a fully armed warrior?"

"The gods smiled on me," Nikometros replied with genuine humility.

"Or goddess, more like, from what I hear." Dymnos smiled. "I would be honoured if you addressed me by name, Nikometros. I think my rank will only be higher for a short while." He caught the puzzled look on the other man's face. "This trial will be but a formality. When the lord Hephaestion hears how you secured the trust and goodwill of the border tribes, I would be very surprised if he didn't promote you."

"Well, we shall see...Dymnos." Nikometros leaned back to catch the eye of Tirses. "I would have a moment alone, my friend."

Tirses saluted and slowed his horse, falling back to join his tribesmen.

Dymnos said nothing but cocked a quizzical eye at Nikometros.

"Timon thinks we should stop for the night, perhaps at the next town," Nikometros stated. "I agree."

"This required you speaking to me alone?"

Nikometros glanced away. His gaze settled on nearby groves of fruit trees, the branches laden with green buds of unidentifiable fruit. "Er, no. I was hoping to find, well...a jeweller or a goldsmith..."

"Ah! A token for the lady." Dymnos grinned. "All is well between you then, Nikometros?"

"I think so, Dymnos, though I would find some present for her. She likes gold ornaments."

Dymnos nodded. "I find gold is always acceptable to women."

Nikometros glanced at the rider beside him. "That brings me to my problem," he muttered. He cleared his throat before continuing. "I have no money." A flush creeping into his face, Nikometros hurried on. "Scythians don't use it and I had no need. My army pay for the last year should...if and when I get it..."

"You need a loan," Dymnos replied. He grimaced. "You're welcome to what I have, Nikometros," he said, fingering a small leather purse at his belt, "But I fear all I have would barely buy a jug of wine at an inn."

Nikometros shook his head. "Never mind. I thank you for your offer."

"Even if I had money, it would be useless to you. There are no towns between Ekbatana and here. I thought to push on to the city. We could reach it not long after dark."

"And miss the sight of the great walls? I would rather come in sight of the city in daylight."

Dymnos laughed. "Yes, that would impress a lady used to open plains and small towns. Very well, Nikometros, I'll look around for a place to camp for the night."

"Perhaps Tomyra will be content with the sight of Ekbatana until I can afford a jewel." Nikometros smiled.

Dymnos pursed his lips, forehead wrinkling in thought. "Why not give her something beautiful in the meantime? A flower perhaps?"

"A flower? Are you serious, Dymnos?"

"Have you never given her a flower, Nikometros?" Dymnos grinned and shook his head. "You still have much to learn about women. Believe me, she'll like it."

Nikometros looked around at dusty farmland slowly giving way to pasture and groves of trees. "Where would I find a flower?"

"Go and look. I'll have the men make camp at the next clean stream." He smiled at Nikometros' ardent search of the surrounding area. "Go and find your flower, Nikometros, then take it to your lady."

# *Chapter 6*

"Did I not say it is a spectacle worthy of the gods?" Nikometros' eyes sparkled with awe and joy. "There lies Ekbatana, summer palace of the Persian kings."

The Scythian horsemen drew rein and sat stock still in the middle of the road, staring at the city that rose up before them, sparkling in the early morning light. The Royal Road from the north crested a low line of hills before dipping to a great flat expanse of pasture. Beyond the open plain the hills rose again, increasingly dotted with buildings of stone and wood. The houses clustered in groups, gathering together and shrinking beneath the enormous edifice that reared in their midst. A great white wall dwarfed the nearby buildings as if the hills ended in a colossal cliff face. Tiny figures of men could be seen atop towering battlements, the sun glinting on burnished armour and spear points as they moved along its walkways.

Behind the white wall rose another, but this one gleamed black, a wedge of darkness that seemed to soak up morning light as if night had fallen once more. Rising above it, another wall, this one crimson in colour. Then successively great rings of blue and orange-painted stone layered beyond.

High atop the hill, encircled by these five huge rings of stone, lay two smaller concentric walls. Beaten sheets of silver plated the stone of the outer ring, sending blinding shards of light flashing across the countryside. Within it lay the brilliant but mellow glow of gold, spread over the innermost walls; precious metal that proclaimed the richness of the kingdom for all to see.

"Impressive," Ket muttered as he stared at the artistic scene before him. "Though it is still small and insignificant beside the grandeur of Thebes in my beloved Egypt."

Tirses grinned then turned back to view the city again.

The Macedonian escort clattered up. The men gave the city a cursory glance then sat and talked quietly while they waited for their leader to command them.

Dymnos guided his horse to the knot of Scythians. He leaned toward Tomyra and Nikometros. "Incredible, isn't it? I admit I just sat and stared when I first saw it. The palace itself lies within the seven walls." His gaze lingered on the walls. "The innermost one contains the residence of the king and the treasury...not that I've seen either. I'm told there are beautiful gardens, fountains and orchards there too. The court, many officials and guards occupy the lower levels."

Tomyra shook her head, eyes wide, slowly absorbing the sight. "And the people?" she asked.

"In the city below," Dymnos replied with his gaze still fastened on the sight. "Nobody enters the walled city without the express permission of the officials."

"So where do we report?" Nikometros asked.

Dymnos pointed across the plain. "The army is encamped over there, near the river. We will find an officer in the Companion cavalry and have word carried to Hephaestion."

"I hope this matter is resolved swiftly," Nikometros said with a note of irritation in his tone.

"Perhaps, though undoubtedly there will be many layers of officials to get through." Dymnos grimaced then looked Nikometros in the eye. "I must ask you and your men to be more circumspect now, Nikometros." A tiny smile tilted his lips at the corners. "I must at least appear to be in charge of this unit."

Nikometros nodded, his attention distracted by an excited shout from Bithyia.

"There, Timon, see?" the warrior woman cried. "Is it a battle?"

To the far left, on the opposite side of the Royal Road from the army encampment, lay a great level area. Dust rose into clear summer sky, churned up by the hooves of countless horses. Glimpses of armour and weapons pierced the dust clouds and the cries of men wafted faintly on the breeze.

Nikometros shaded his eyes and studied the mass of cavalry below them. "Not a battle," he decided. "What would you say, Dymnos, manoeuvres?"

"Let us ride down and see. The road carries us in that direction anyway."

Dymnos urged his horse forward and led his troop and the band of Scythians down the road at a gallop.

Nikometros rode on Dymnos' heels, the wind pulling his cloak out behind him.

As they drew close to the mass of milling horsemen, the apparent confusion resolved itself into several distinct groupings. A body of riders was involved in intricate manoeuvres, but the majority were merely onlookers, standing around the perimeter of the large field. Heads turned as Dymnos and Nikometros approached and a detachment of armed men rode out to intercept them.

An elderly officer with a grizzled beard brought his men to a halt in front of Dymnos and raised a weather-beaten hand. A large scar over his right eye showed pale in his tanned skin. "Your business, sir?" the officer demanded.

Dymnos saluted. "I bring dispatches for lord Hephaestion. Where might I find him?"

The officer grunted. "He's over there with the king." He jerked his head in the direction of a small group of observers. "I doubt he'll see you now but I'll send word."

Tomyra sidled her mare up alongside Nikometros as the officer spoke. She gasped and sat up straight, staring at the men the officer indicated. "The king? Alexander?"

The elderly officer looked Tomyra over carefully and with evident pleasure. "Aye, lass," he replied with a smile. "Alexander, no less. And who might you be?"

Tomyra turned to the officer. "I am Tomyra, daughter of Spargises of the Massegetae Scythians. I accompany my lord Nikometros." She gestured. "We seek an audience with lord Hephaestion."

"Scythians, eh?" The officer stared at the horsemen behind her for several moments then at the accompanying Macedonian cavalry. He nodded and pointed to one side, addressing himself once more to Dymnos. "Wait over there. I'll send word to Hephaestion that you await his pleasure. If anyone asks your purpose, tell them my name...Agisthes." He watched as Dymnos led his men at a walk to the indicated area then called up a soldier. A few hurried words and the man galloped off towards the royal party.

The Scythians and accompanying escort spread out along the edge of the field and watched the action.

Nikometros stared at the riders as they wheeled and pranced in the open field. The riders advanced toward Alexander and halted just short of a group of tall, muscular women around Alexander. The women raised their voices in a high-pitched paean.

"Those are women!" Nikometros exclaimed. "Who in Hades are they?"

Tirses smirked. "Shapely ones, whoever they are. I can see breasts."

Agisthes rode up, overhearing the remark. "Amazons. They are supposed to be fine fighters," he said. "The local satrap found them and knew Alexander would be interested. Always interested in new things, is the king."

Tomyra gave a cry of derision. "Amazons? Nonsense." She gestured at the troop, now dismounted and bowing prettily to the king. "My Massegetae women archers would cut them down before they could use those little axes."

"Still," Dymnos replied, "They could be Amazons, couldn't they? Herodotus describes them as having their right breasts bared and being armed with axes."

Tomyra snorted again. "My mother was a priestess of the Sauromantians by the Euxine Sea. The tribes thereabouts called my mother and her women Amazons but they were modest. They never exposed themselves like that and always carried bows." She sneered as the women on the field clambered onto their ponies again. "Those are soft women playing at being warriors."

A body of horsemen rode out from the Macedonian cavalry and formed around the women, escorting them from the field. As they left, heads turned once more toward Nikometros and the Scythians.

"Which one is Alexander?" whispered Tomyra. "That tall one on the grey horse?"

Dymnos shook his head. "No, that is Hephaestion. The king is shorter. See, he rides the black stallion."

"Surely you are mistaken," Tomyra said. "The tall one is more kingly in his bearing."

"Many make that mistake, lass," interrupted Agisthes. "When Alexander first captured the harem of the Persian king Darius, he went with Hephaestion to pay his respects to Darius' mother. The old lady, being used to tall kings--Darius was a giant--thought Hephaestion was the king and bowed to him."

"What happened?"

"Alexander laughed. He said Hephaestion was also Alexander." The officer shook his head. "They were always close like that, even as boys. Well, some men like boys. For myself, I always take my pleasure with women..." His voice trailed off and his face flushed beneath his tan. "Your pardon, lass."

The figure of Alexander could be seen leaning over in earnest discussion with the taller man. Abruptly, Alexander wheeled his horse and led a detachment of men galloping toward the city. Hephaestion followed at a more sedate pace, angling back toward the main army camp. A rider trotted out to meet Agisthes. The officer listened then nodded, bidding the man stay close. He turned to Dymnos.

"Lord Hephaestion will see you immediately," said Agisthes. "This man will take you to his tent. I'll escort your companions and see to their comfort."

"Thank you," Dymnos replied, "But my dispatches concern my companions and they'll be needed as witnesses."

"Very well then," Agisthes crisply retorted. "If you would follow me, I'll take you there myself." He pulled his horse around and trotted off in the direction of the army camp.

The Scythians followed in a knot, whispers and comments humming through the air as they rode.

Nikometros turned to Tirses and barked a command. "Tirses, remember your training. Do not let the army see us undisciplined."

Tirses nodded and rode into the mob of tribesmen, shouting and pushing. Rapidly, their training reasserted itself and a tight body of cavalry followed the Macedonian escort into the heart of the army camp.

The muted roar of thousands of men busy with their everyday duties rose about Nikometros and his friends. They passed a horse line where hundreds of mounts stood beneath great canvas awnings, attended by dozens of grooms and stable boys. Clouds of flies rose from the mounds of dung being collected for transport to the middens. The familiar stink of an encamped army assailed their nostrils, a mixture of excrement, cooking food and the rancid odours of unwashed bodies. Tents lined their passage, stretching away in orderly rows, each with a group of men standing or sitting by the entrance, mending tackle or sharpening weapons.

Heads turned, shouts arose as scores of men ran from tents and cooking fires to watch the newcomers. Old campaigners merely leaned on their spears and watched with interest while younger soldiers scurried to get closer.

Nikometros led his men through an avenue of armed men to the shade of a grove of poplars by the riverside. They dismounted and surrendered their horses to a swarm of grooms who led the beasts away to be fed and groomed.

Nikometros, with Timon, Tomyra and Bithyia close behind, entered a tattered tent guarded by watchful young men. Inside, the tent displayed none of the ostentatious finery that might be expected of a man of Hephaestion's rank, but gave the impression of a rough bivouac set up on a campaign in enemy territory. A large table scattered with maps and documents dominated, with several chairs and stools virtually the only other furniture. In the far corner sat a small truckle bed and an open wooden chest.

Dymnos stood at attention in front of the table, with Agisthes standing alertly to one side, his hand on the hilt of a sheathed sword. Hephaestion stood behind the table, reading the dispatches handed to him by Dymnos. Tall, with swept back blond hair streaked with grey, he looked up unsmiling when Nikometros and his friends entered the tent.

Hephaestion gestured toward a group of chairs. "Be seated. I'll talk with you in a moment." He continued to read. When he finished, he stood lost in thought for a moment then walked around the table to stand in front of Nikometros.

"What was your unit, lieutenant?" Hephaestion demanded.

Nikometros stood and saluted. "Companion Cavalry sir, fourth squadron."

Hephaestion's pale eyes searched Nikometros' face. "Your commander was Philotas, later Cleitus," Hephaestion stated in a flat voice.

Nikometros caught his breath then nodded. "Yes, sir. At the time I was transferred to garrison duty, Cleitus commanded, but Philippos was my immediate superior."

"You are unlucky in your commanders. First Philotas is executed for treason and now Cleitus is dead by the king's hand. Philippos fell in battle." Hephaestion's mouth twitched in a wry smile. "I'm not sure I should welcome you back under my command." He glanced down at the dispatches. "The garrison commander at Kharmsar is adamant that you're guilty of treason, lieutenant." Hephaestion held out the dispatches. "Read them. Tell me if they are accurate."

Nikometros accepted the papers and scanned through them. He read the charges carefully and the listed facts then handed the papers back to the commander. "Substantially correct, sir. I would argue with the findings, however. I am, and always have been, a loyal Macedonian soldier."

"Well said." Hephaestion nodded then turned back to the table and pushed the maps and papers aside. He found a blank piece of paper and scribbled on it for a few moments before holding it out to Nikometros.

"Take this and present yourself to the commander of the fourth squadron. For the time being you're reinstated in your position and may draw army pay...including any back pay owed. You will hold yourself and your man Timon in readiness to answer these charges should a decision be made to follow up on them."

Nikometros flushed. "Yes, sir. Thank you, sir."

"Don't thank me," Hephaestion dryly replied. "I hate to see a talented man wasted. You will be put to use."

"Yes, sir." Nikometros glanced round at Tomyra and the men he could see standing outside the tent. "And the others, sir? The men are Massegetae Scythians, here as envoys for their tribe. Further, this lady is a priestess of Artemis." He nodded at Tomyra.

Hephaestion acknowledged Tomyra with a nod and raised an eyebrow. "Indeed? Artemis, you say? Well, be that as it may, in the meantime, they'll be housed with other embassies in the city."

Tomyra rose to her feet and smoothed her robes while nodding her head at the commander. "My lord," she said. "I ask that I and my companion handmaiden be allowed to remain with Nikometros and Timon."

Hephaestion shook his head. "This is an army camp, lady. No place for women such as yourselves. You'll be housed as befits your position within the city." He forestalled Tomyra's protest by raising his hand. "This is not open for discussion." Turning to Agisthes, Hephaestion issued a stream of orders before she could protest. The officer saluted and ushered Nikometros and his companions outside.

"I'll see that your friends are comfortably housed," Agisthes reassured them. "In the meantime, I suggest that you and your man report at once to your unit." He beckoned a nearby soldier and gave him detailed instructions. "Say your farewells quickly, lieutenant. No doubt you will see your companions again within a few days."

Agisthes waited while Nikometros and Tomyra quietly talked, looking discreetly away when they embraced. He signalled, nodding in satisfaction as Tirses and the Scythian horsemen remounted and stood waiting. At last, the women finished their goodbyes and Nikometros and Timon stood and watched as their entourage disappeared toward the towering seven-fold walls of Ekbatana.

Nikometros turned at the sound of a soft cough and saw a young soldier standing awkwardly behind him.

"Sir," the young man said. "If you would be so good as to follow me, I'll take you to your squadron commander."

# *Chapter 7*

"**B**y the gods, it's Nikometros. What in Hades are you doing here?" A young man, slim and of medium height in resplendent armour, pushed his way through the milling throng of onlookers around the tent of the Fourth Squadron commander. Black hair framed a soft, almost effete face; softness belied by the flinty fire of piercing dark eyes.

Nikometros looked round and for a moment struggled to recall the man's name. "Peithon? The Cretan? I might ask you the same. I thought you dead." He grinned and embraced the young man then stepped back and stared. "You fell at the Granicus, didn't you? I saw you fall myself."

Peithon grinned back and swept his dark hair to one side, revealing a jagged scar that lay pale on the sun-darkened skin of his neck. "If you'd turned back you might have seen I was still alive."

Nikometros frowned. "I could not. The squadron..."

Peithon waved a hand dismissively. "Of course not. I didn't expect it of you, nor of any man. We all take our chances in battle."

"What happened to you?"

"Oh, I survived long enough to be found by the doctors after the battle. It was some months before I could rejoin the squadron but by then you were languishing in some Sogdian hell-hole with a head wound." Peithon smiled and clapped Nikometros on the shoulder. "It's good to see you again."

"Thank you, Peithon." Nikometros looked at the commander's tent with the surrounding guards. "I must see the commander." He hesitated. "Still Kerros I suppose?"

Peithon nodded. "I wouldn't keep him waiting. I doubt he likes you any more now than before." He half-turned away, and then looked back over his shoulder. "Come and find me when you can, Nikometros. You can buy me a drink and tell me what happened to you."

"Where will I find you? Are you still a junior in the Third Squadron?"

Peithon smiled. "Gods, no. I'm a staff officer at the court now. Under Perdikkas. In fact, as a colonel I outrank you now." He winked then strode off through the crowd.

Nikometros approached one of the guards and introduced himself and his purpose. The guard thrust his head inside the tent flap for a few moments then turned back to Nikometros, bidding him enter.

The inside of the tent was more sumptuous than that of Hephaestion. The heavy walls and hangings muted the sounds and smells of the surrounding camp. A large bed occupied the rear of the tent, strewn with thick blankets over a billowing mattress. The spoils of campaign lay everywhere, scattered over a richly patterned carpet. A small table stood to one side, lit by a bright oil lamp. A burly man lounged on a carved chair behind the table, his fingers wrapped around a jewelled cup.

The man looked up as Nikometros entered, strode across to the table and saluted. Putting his cup down, the man suppressed a belch and heaved his large body upright.

Nikometros held out the paper from Hephaestion. "Commander Kerros. Lieutenant Nikometros reporting for duty as ordered, sir."

Kerros stared at the paper then, with obvious distaste, took it from Nikometros with the tips of fat fingers. He unfolded it and scanned the writing. His mouth puckered into a moue of disgust.

"Nikometros. I heard a rumour you were back but hoped it wasn't true. Now you're ordered back to your squadron by Hephaestion, no less." Kerros turned his back on Nikometros and poured himself some more wine. "Your position has been filled, but I dare say I can find something for you to do." A smile creased his pudgy face. "Something suited to your talents."

Kerros barked out an order and one of the guards hurried in. "Take this man...this officer," he sneered. "...to the cells. His first duty is command of the punishment detail." Kerros lifted his cup and drank deeply, the wine spilling over his chin. "Nikometros, you will oversee the execution of one Lymnos, found guilty of uttering traitorous comments." He grinned. "One of your old comrades from your squad, I believe."

Nikometros maintained a stony expression and snapped off a crisp salute. "Yes sir." He turned on his heel and left the tent with the guard on his heels.

The man plucked at the sleeve of Nikometros' tunic and pointed across the camp. "This way, sir." He hurried off.

Nikometros followed with a sick expression on his face.

Timon joined him from a group of old soldiers standing near a campfire. "Not a bad lot, sir," Timon muttered with a grin. "Met a couple of fellows I knew from way back. They were telling me..." He broke off and looked askance at his commander's sour expression. "What happened, Niko?"

"Kerros is still squadron commander. I believe I may have mentioned him once or twice."

"Bad sort, is he?" asked Timon.

"The worst," muttered Nikometros. "Cruel and greedy. He was a good officer once, before Philotas promoted him. Now he seeks only his pleasure, not the welfare of the men."

Timon grunted. "I've known a few like that. Still, stay out of his way as much as you can and he'll forget about you."

The guard strode on through the camp with Nikometros and Timon, passing rows of tents with soldiers lounging around campfires, tending to their weapons or mending ragged clothing. Several local Persian women, from the lower levels of society to judge by their dress and behaviour, sat with the soldiers. Some looked up as the three men passed, making lewd comments.

"Kerros won't forget me," stated Nikometros. "He's hated me for years. He'll degrade me with the worst of tasks until he tires of me and then he'll probably arrange for my death."

The city of tents gave way to an open arena on which dozens of men ran, jumped or wrestled. All were naked, their bodies gleaming from liberally smeared oil.

Timon grinned. "I wonder what Bithyia's reaction to this will be? Scythian women are not used to such public nudity."

"I dare say she'll get used to it, Timon." Nikometros tapped his friend on the arm. "I think we've arrived."

Timon looked around at the walled stockade with alert guards at the gate. "He's putting you in prison again?" growled Timon. "He cannot. Lord Hephaestion just freed you."

Nikometros shook his head. "No, Timon. I'm to take charge of an execution. Kerros ordered me to kill a man I once knew."

"Fornicating bastard!"

"Careful, Timon. That could be judged insubordination. You risk a flogging."

Timon scowled and spat on the ground but kept silent. He followed Nikometros and the guard into the stockade and across a bare patch of ground to where a young officer stood with a squad of soldiers. The men leaned on javelins, watching as the trio approached. The guard saluted the officer and passed him the note from Kerros. The officer read the note, looked at Nikometros then snapped off a crisp salute. When Nikometros returned the salute the man relaxed and ventured a cautious smile.

"Glad to see you, sir. I wasn't looking forward to this detail."

"I imagine not," Nikometros replied. "No man likes to kill in cold blood but it sometimes has to be done." He beckoned the man aside, out of earshot of the soldiers. "This prisoner uttered traitorous remarks?"

"Yes sir. Though why the commander should take such drastic measures against a fool like Lymnos..."

"A fool who may be a traitor," interrupted Nikometros. "I remember this Lymnos. Straight talk may be valued in his native Sparta, but he should know when to keep his mouth shut."

"No, no. Not the Spartan, sir. Who said the Spartan? It is Lymnos the Macedonian who is condemned."

Nikometros stood nonplussed. "The stable hand? But the man is a halfwit. Dropped on his head or some such when he was a baby. How can he be a traitor?"

The young officer shrugged. "The commander interrogated him. He made some comments about Alexander and how he'd offended the gods."

"I cannot believe it," muttered Nikometros. He ran nervous fingers through his tousled hair. "Fetch the man. Let us see what he has to say for himself."

"Judgment has already been passed, sir. You cannot..."

"Do it." Nikometros stared the officer down then watched while the man hurried into one of the cells, emerging a few moments later with a middle-aged man, thin and balding.

The prisoner shuffled along in front of the officer, his head cocked to one side with watery eyes squinting in the sunlight, his hands twisting and turning in agitation. He stopped in front of Nikometros and gaped up at him.

"Lymnos," Nikometros said. "Do you remember me?"

Lymnos stared uncomprehendingly.

"My name is Nikometros. Do you remember?"

Lymnos gave a weak smile and nodded. "Big golden horse."

"Yes, Lymnos." Nikometros nodded. "I have a big golden stallion called Diomede." He lowered to a squat, pulling Lymnos down beside him. "Do you know why you are here?"

"Here?" Lymnos asked uncertainly. "Want to go. Horses need me. I go now?" A smile broke out over his face.

"Lymnos, listen carefully. You said some things about Alexander...about the king. Do you remember what you said?"

"The king..." Lymnos' forehead wrinkled in concentration. "He thinks himself a god but he will be struck down for his hoo...hoob...I cannot remember the word."

Nikometros rocked back on his heels. "Hubris? You said the king would be struck down for his hubris?"

Lymnos grinned. "Yes, yes. That is the word the man used."

"What man?"

Lymnos shrugged. "A man." He frowned. "I had not heard the word before and I forgot it. What does it mean?"

"It means he was too proud and that the gods would punish him for it," muttered Nikometros. He got to his feet and called the officer and Timon over. "This man doesn't even know the meaning of the words he spoke. He was just repeating them."

Timon snorted. "He could be punished for repeating them, I suppose, but it would be unjust for him to die for it."

"Nevertheless," stated the young officer. "The commander ordered his death. I have the signed warrant here."

"I'm not going to execute him for merely repeating another man's words," Nikometros replied with a frown.

The officer stubbornly clenched his jaw. "I won't disobey my commanding officer. If you won't carry it out, I will." He turned and shouted to the squad of soldiers. They hefted their javelins and ran into a semicircle around the stable hand.

Lymnos straightened and stared around him. "What is happening?" he whispered.

"By almighty Zeus," Nikometros swore. "The man isn't even aware of what's happening to him."

"Stand aside," warned the young officer. "Or I'll have you removed and placed under arrest."

"Better do it, Niko," muttered Timon. "The poor fool is not worth your life."

Nikometros swung round and gripped Lymnos by the shoulders. "Lymnos," he yelled. "Look at me." When he was sure he had the man's attention he lowered his voice. "Say this, Lymnos. 'I appeal to the king'. Say it."

"Stand aside," the officer said again. He snapped an order and two soldiers leapt forward, grasping Nikometros by the arms.

Timon grappled with them and was restrained in turn by other soldiers.

"Lock them up," grated the officer. "I'm sorry, sir, but you leave me no choice."

"Say it, Lymnos!" Nikometros bellowed as he was dragged back.

Lymnos looked bewildered. "I...I appeal to the king," he muttered.

"Louder! Say it louder!" Nikometros shook himself free and headed back toward the condemned man.

A soldier leapt in front of him and levelled a javelin at his chest.

"I appeal to the king," Lymnos repeated, louder. "I appeal to the king."

Nikometros relaxed. "There," he said to the officer. "You cannot deny him his request."

"What do you mean? He's condemned already. I intend to carry out the sentence."

Nikometros pitched his voice to carry over the open area so all present could hear his words. "A Macedonian soldier, accused of any crime, may appeal directly to the king for judgment. It is the Law."

"Nonsense," barked the officer. "Besides, he's not even a soldier."

"He is still a Macedonian and has appealed to the king," Nikometros said stubbornly. "By law he has a right to be heard by the king."

"He is condemned already. It does not apply."

The soldier in front of Nikometros lowered his javelin and turned toward the officer. "Beggin' yer pardon, sir, but it does." He called over to the other soldiers. "Don't it lads?"

Amid a chorus of agreement, the soldiers grounded their javelins, falling back into rough lines again. "It's his right, sir."

"Aye, sir."

"Could be any of us, lads. 'Tis the law."

The young officer stuttered, looking unsure, and then he capitulated.

"V...Very well, then. Lock him up again. I'll send word to the commander."

"To the king," Nikometros ordered. "He appealed to the king, not the commander."

The young man looked around at his squad, noting the determined looks on their faces. He nodded and turned on his heel before stalking to the nearby barracks.

Nikometros beckoned the nearest soldier over to him. "Take word of this to the city, soldier," he said quietly. "Make sure the king hears of it, or someone close to him."

The soldier nodded and saluted. "Aye, sir...and thank you."

# *Chapter 8*

Autumn rains, borne on chill winds from the north, swept through the Macedonian camp, beating out a staccato rhythm on the tent sides, finding the smallest gaps and worn areas in the cloth. Clothing became damp, bedding mouldy and the earthen floors beneath the carpets softened. Outside the ground became a sea of mud, churned by countless feet and the sharp hooves of the cavalry detachments.

Morale fell. The land was at peace and no campaigns or wars beckoned. Men sat around listlessly, tending their equipment or gossiping. Food was cold or half cooked, the fires smouldering fitfully at best in the humid atmosphere. Discontent grew.

Nikometros sat on a padded chair in the officers' mess tent, apart from the other officers, talking quietly to Timon. He nursed a cup of watered wine, sipping from it absentmindedly, listening to snatches of argument and conversation drifting across from the other off-duty officers.

Timon jerked his head in the direction of the other men. "Sooner the Caspian Expedition starts the better, if you ask me. Listen to them, Niko.

Much more of this weather and it wouldn't surprise me to hear talk of mutiny."

"Winter's no time for campaigning, Timon. Not in the north anyway." Nikometros shrugged and pulled his damp cloak tighter about his shoulders. "It'll be spring before anything happens." He shivered. "Gods, I wish I knew how Tomyra is."

Timon nodded gloomily. "Aye. Two weeks since they were taken to the city and no word from them. And no leave to visit either."

"I'm sorry, Timon. I shouldn't have involved you in my...disagreement with the commander."

"That bastard?"

Heads turned at Timon's outburst, the conversation faltering. Timon dropped his voice and leaned closer. "That son of a whore has it in for you and no mistake, Niko. Keeping you here under virtual camp arrest and giving you no duties. Can't you appeal to the king too?"

Nikometros smiled. "For what? I'm not accused of any crime." He sighed and sipped his wine. "No, this is the reality of army life Timon, as you well know. You keep the favour of your commander or you suffer for it."

"It's the sitting around that kills me, Niko. I need to be up and doing something." Timon got up and grabbed the wine flask, pouring more of the ruby liquid into their cups. He splashed water in after and sat down again, turning his face to the tent flap.

The rain drummed on the sides of the tent, splashing and dripping into the sheets of water that slowly ran between the tents, down to the swollen river. Sounds of the army camp came muted to Timon's ears, the murmur of discontented men, the distant whicker from the horse lines and the measured stamp and splash of the dejected but ever alert guards. He listened absently, his mind churning with thoughts of Bithyia. He sipped from his cup then paused, the cup at his lips. Slowly he lowered it and cocked his head.

"Something's up, Niko. Listen."

Nikometros raised his head and stared toward the tent entrance. The barely heard babble of thousands of men swelled into a low roar of interest as the sound of many hooves ploughing through the mud grew in volume. Nikometros got to his feet and moved to the entrance, lifting the tent flap with one hand. He ignored the cold rivulet that ran down his uplifted arm and stared out into the rain.

A column of horsemen in the colours of the Bodyguard rode slowly down the lines between the tents. As they passed, crowds of men, drawn by the presence of something new, moved after them, wrapping themselves tightly in already wet cloaks. The column approached and came to a halt outside the officers' mess of the Fourth squadron.

A young man, fresh faced and alert, called out to Nikometros as he stood in the tent entrance. "Please tell Nikometros, son of Leonnatos of Pella that I wish to speak to him."

Nikometros folded his arms and leaned against the tent pole. "Who shall I say wants to see him?"

"Iolatos, equerry to the king," the young man replied. "Please call him, there is some urgency."

The other officers crowded behind Nikometros in an eager babble of questions. Timon pushed through to his side, ignoring the protests from the higher ranked officers. Nikometros stepped out into the rain and stood looking up at Iolatos.

"I am Nikometros," he said.

A look of annoyance flitted across the young man's face. "Why didn't you say so at once?" His eyes flicked toward the tent. "And your adjutant Timon?"

"Here," growled Timon. "What does a young pup like you want with us?"

"Not I, you fool," said Iolatos. "The king requires you. Immediately." He gestured and two of his men rode up, leading two fine horses. "Come."

Nikometros glanced down at his wet and muddied tunic, his frayed cloak and scuffed boots. "I should change," he muttered.

Iolatos looked down at Nikometros and casually flicked a spot of mud from his cloak. "Yes, no doubt you should but one doesn't keep the king waiting. Mount up, lieutenant. Now!"

Nikometros nodded and beckoning Timon, grasped the mane and reins of one of the horses and swung himself up on it. Iolatos barked a command and the squad swung about, enclosing Nikometros and Timon in their midst, before breaking into a trot.

The rain eased by the time the squad entered the city and stopped altogether as they approached the first gate into the great citadel of Ekbatana. The guards at the gate obviously expected the squad, snapping to attention and saluting as they passed through. Seen from within, the outer wall was still impressive, towering above the riders and a warren of buildings and streets. The next wall, though seeming to reach high above the outer battlements, now betrayed that height as owing to the rise of a hill within the citadel.

The horses slowed to a walk as the road climbed upward, circling toward the second gate. The exertion of the climb, combined with the weak heat of the sun struggling through a dissipating cloud cover and a freshening breeze, dried their clothing. Wisps of vapor rose into the rain-washed air, mingling with the smoke of renewed cooking fires.

The road continued upward, passing through successive battlements, the intervening buildings becoming fewer but more spacious and sumptuous as they ascended. Nikometros and Timon craned their necks, overcome with curiosity after their prolonged detention in the camp.

Iolatos noticed their interest. "You haven't seen the citadel before, lieutenant?" he enquired.

"Once," replied Nikometros. "But only to the second level. I came to purchase a new sword from the armourers. Who is housed in these other levels?"

"General tradesmen, army suppliers and such in the lowest level. Armourers as you know, in the second, together with goldsmiths." A faint smile marred Iolatos' calm features. "If you need jewellery for your lady I can recommend a good smith. The third belongs to the court servants, minor chamberlains and the myriad of artists, actors and architects that Alexander seems to attract wherever he goes. The fourth..." Iolatos pointed as they exited the gate in the blue wall, "...belongs to the higher officials, the men who govern the empire."

The next gate, the one in the orange wall, was shut. Iolatos called out as they approached, then halted the squad. An officer emerged from a guardroom and demanded their passes. Iolatos passed over an engraved tablet for scrutiny. After a few minutes they moved on, the great cedar wood gates swinging shut behind them.

"Here are the embassies," explained Iolatos. "At the moment the citadel is full of foreigners babbling away in their own tongues. It makes security very difficult."

"Are my friends the Scythians on this level?" asked Nikometros.

"Yes. Over there somewhere, I think." Iolatos waved vaguely in the direction of some buildings nestled in trees displaying the first signs of autumn colours.

Nikometros and Timon pulled their horses up, half turning in that direction. Iolatos frowned and leaned over, catching at the bridle of Nikometros' horse. "Later maybe, lieutenant. The king awaits you."

Reluctantly, Nikometros and Timon let themselves be turned away, renewing their upward climb, now nearing their destination. They passed through the heavily guarded gate in the silver-plated wall. The weak afternoon sunlight beat about them, shimmering and flashing off the beaten metallic surfaces. Within the last two walls lay a huge flat stone-paved courtyard stretching away in a great crescent. Fountains erupted toward the sky and brightly coloured birds flew through the branches of fruit trees and flowering shrubs. The place was deserted save for several fat men in richly embroidered tunics tending the gardens.

"The old harem of the kings of Persia," said Iolatos with a grimace of distaste. "Largely deserted now as the king has little use for the women. The royal wife is here with her ladies, of course."

"The Bactrian?" asked Timon.

Iolatos stared at the old soldier before answering. "Yes, though you'd do well to guard your tongue. The lady Roxane hears much of what passes in the court and she...well, she thinks highly of herself."

"It can't be easy for her when the king is on campaign," murmured Nikometros.

"No," replied Iolatos. He dropped his voice to a confidential level, moving his horse closer. "The king is courteous and correct, of course, but she feels he spends too much time with a certain...dancer, shall we say?"

Nikometros raised his eyebrows enquiringly.

"Bagoas. A young eunuch of some beauty and in favour with the king. I would stress that, lieutenant," Iolatos added with a meaningful glance. "Ah! The final gate and our destination. Behold the royal palace of Ekbatana, second only to the great palace at Babylon."

The great golden walls of the innermost citadel beat back the autumn sun in waves of lustrous summer light, making the marble and granite buildings glow as if lit from within.

Several young men, neatly attired in short tunics, their bronzed limbs exuding health and vitality, darted out to steady the horses. They stood at the head of each beast, soothing and calming it as the riders dismounted and moved toward a great columned hall, brushing down their tunics as they walked.

Iolatos strode up to a richly uniformed officer standing talking quietly in the cool shadows beside one of the columns. He saluted and handed over his pass.

"Nikometros, son of Leonnatos and his adjutant, my lord Ptolemy," said Iolatos crisply. "They are here at the king's request."

Ptolemy broke off his conversation with the other man, dismissing him with a wave of his hand. Dark eyes set within a weather-beaten face stared out from beneath a shock of greying black hair. He looked briefly at the pass then handed it back to Iolatos.

"Thank you, Iolatos. I will take them in." He waited until the officer saluted and strode away before turning to Nikometros and Timon. Stockily built with numbers of scars visible on his limbs, Ptolemy showed the effects of a lifetime spent in the service of Alexander and his father before that, Philip of Macedon. Now in his early forties, he remained a close and trusted friend of the king. He regarded Timon briefly then turned his silent attention to Nikometros. For several minutes he scrutinised the young man in front of him, at last nodding as if he found what he saw satisfactory.

"Follow me," Ptolemy said, turning to walk down the vast colonnade. "A few things you must know about Alexander, so listen closely. He is like no other king in the world. He's a man of action and prefers to do without ceremony, though he's very correct when the occasion demands. He'll be familiar with you and will probably talk as if you're his equal." Ptolemy stopped and held up a warning hand. "Don't be misled. You must maintain a proper respect." He walked on a few more paces then stopped in front of large double doors.

"Address him as sir, or sire, never by name unless he specifically requests you do so. When you walk in, march up to him, stopping about five paces away and salute, state your name and lineage, and then wait to be addressed. Answer his questions fully and truthfully. He hates prevarication. Got that?"

Nikometros nodded. Ptolemy kept silent, questioningly raising an eyebrow. "Yes, sir," said Nikometros.

"Aye, sir," Timon replied.

Ptolemy put his hands on the doors of the chamber. "One more thing, Nikometros. If the king should offer you a reward, be modest. He detests greed. Indeed, he is generous to a fault. Though he owns great riches they don't control him."

"Why should he offer me...?" Nikometros broke off as Ptolemy threw open the double doors to the royal audience chamber, ushering his two charges inside.

# Chapter 9

The vast audience chamber stretched out on all sides from great double doors. Rows of towering carved columns marched the length of the hall, perspective drawing the eye to the raised dais and magnificently ornate throne at the far end. Huge murals of Persian kings in full regalia or in hunting chariots decimating wild beasts emblazoned the walls, while intricate mosaics covered the marble floors. Huge windows, stretching from floor to ceiling, let in shafts of sunlight, softened by gloriously coloured drapes that flapped stiffly in a chill breeze.

Appearing very small and insignificant amid the grandeur, Nikometros and Timon followed Ptolemy across the great chamber, the sound of their boots echoing off the distant walls. As they drew nearer to the throne dais, Nikometros noticed a small group of people clustered around the base of the steps. Ptolemy altered his course slightly and raised one hand in greeting.

"Here they are, Alexander. Delayed a bit by the mud in the camp."

Ptolemy stepped to one side and waved Nikometros and Timon forward. Faces turned toward them. With a feeling of warmth, Nikometros recognised some familiar faces among the strangers. Seated on comfortable looking couches sat Tomyra and Bithyia, dressed in new robes and radiant with jewellery. Behind them stood Tirses, bedecked in gold ornamentation and looking every inch a Scythian ambassador. The old Egyptian Ket sat comfortably on a cushion on the steps, fondling his black cat Bubis. Standing around in relaxed poses were several men, mostly young to middle-aged, though all showed the weather-beaten calmness of professional soldiers at rest.

A figure rose from the steps near Tomyra and lightly stepped forward. Dressed simply in a plain tunic and cloak, he stood out against the richer, more colourful clothing of the army officers. Though the top of his head came only to the shoulder of the tall men around him, his presence filled the whole chamber. His eyes, one pale, one dark, measured the men in front of him as they approached.

Nikometros advanced, came to attention and saluted. "Nikometros, son of Leonnatos of the house of Ermacyon, sir. At your service."

Timon saluted beside him. "Timon, son of Kerobates, from Messa near the Illyrian border, sir."

Alexander smiled, white teeth sparkling in a bronzed face. "Thank you," he said softly. He looked at Timon thoughtfully. "From Messa you say? I remember a Kerobates from Messa. A big man, powerfully built, with a scar on his right cheek."

Timon grinned. "Aye, sir. That was my father."

"I remember him from when I fought the Illyrians just before my accession. He fought bravely and well."

Ptolemy leaned across to the man next to him. "How does he remember men met briefly so many years ago?" he whispered.

Alexander turned quickly, a serious look replacing the smile on his face. "A good commander knows his men, Ptolemy. How else will a man fight and risk his life unless he knows you recognise him personally?"

"Yes, Alexander," Ptolemy grinned.

Alexander turned back to Timon. "From what I hear, you're your father's son. I am honoured to have you with me." He stepped forward and clasped Timon by the shoulders, kissing him on the cheek. "Now," he went on, guiding Timon toward the seated ladies, "Be seated, and greet your lady."

He gestured and a youth stepped up with a cup of wine, offering it gracefully to Timon. Timon took the cup absently, his attention focused on Bithyia.

Alexander beckoned to Nikometros. "Your lady awaits you too, I think." He smiled as Nikometros walked over to Tomyra, clasping her hands as she rose to greet him. He turned away to give them a moment's privacy, warming his hands at a glowing brazier. The king waited patiently for the first murmurs of greeting and solicitude to die away before interrupting the young couple.

"Your lady tells me you conquered the Scythian tribes almost single-handedly," Alexander stated with a smile.

Nikometros flushed and looked down. "An exaggeration, sir. Circumstances favoured me."

"An able man does not bow to circumstance, Nikometros," Alexander replied with a faint hint of disapproval in his voice. "Rather, he seizes his chances and makes the most of them. You belittle yourself."

Nikometros hesitated and glanced at Ptolemy's intent face before plunging ahead. "Perhaps, sir, yet I was favoured by the Goddess of the Scythians."

"Indeed?" Alexander leaned forward, his eyes lighting up. "How?"

Nikometros described his first encounter with the Massegetae tribesmen and how his armband saved his life, both at his capture and later in the sacrificial combat.

"You have this armband?"

"I gave it to Tirses." Nikometros gestured at the resplendent young man. "As a symbol of my authority before battle, sir."

"May I see it?" Alexander waited while Tirses slipped the armband off his arm and passed it to him. He turned the antique spiral band, noting the fine details of the figure of a woman drawn out into the body of a serpent. His eyes sparkled as his fingers traced the raw cut in the band, revealing the iron beneath, now dulled by a patina of rust.

"That must have been a fight worth seeing," mused Alexander. He looked up at Nikometros keenly. "You felt fear?"

Nikometros hesitated. "Yes sir."

Alexander nodded. "So do we all. Yet the brave man overcomes that which he fears and turns it to his advantage. Never fear death itself, only an unworthy death. Well said, Nikometros." He handed the armband to Nikometros. "Wear it again. Plainly the Goddess is with you. I will give Tirses some other token of our trust and friendship."

Tirses bowed deeply. "As it pleases you, great Alexander," he murmured.

Alexander nodded. "Good. Now come and tell us all that happened to you since you were captured. I have heard it all from these ladies but I wish to hear your insights. Also, my friends here have only heard the half of it." He grasped Nikometros firmly by the elbow and turned him toward the Macedonians standing silently in the rear.

"Ptolemy you have met already, also Hephaestion." He smiled warmly at the tall man for a moment before continuing. "Perdikkas and Peukestas you don't know but no doubt will."

Perdikkas nodded without speaking.

"I regret I must depart, Alexander," murmured Peukestas. "I have some urgent negotiations with the Arabian delegations I must attend to." He saluted casually and walked off.

"I'll tell you about it later!" Alexander called after him.

Nikometros sat on the couch by Tomyra and sipped from the cup of excellent wine thrust into his hands.

Alexander took a cushion and sat on the steps opposite him, leaning forward, elbow on knee, with his head resting on his fist. His eyes sparkled as he listened.

Nikometros launched into a description of his days among the Massegetae, roaming the windswept plains of Scythia. He spoke a long time, sipping at the wine at infrequent intervals to moisten his throat.

Alexander listened quietly for the most part, interrupting only to ask searching questions about specific customs, differences in methods of fighting between the tribes and the state of the borderlands. Nikometros answered as best he could, helped by the observations of Timon and Ket and the more detailed knowledge of Tomyra, Bithyia and Tirses. At one point, Alexander stopped the narration and sent out for a scribe to copy down the description of an obscure religious ritual. At last, the narrative reached the point of their exit from Scythia.

Alexander leaned back, oblivious of the stretching and yawns of the Macedonian generals behind him. He glanced up at Tirses, then at the two women before switching to the broad Macedonian patois of the army. "Can I trust the Massegetae and their new chief, Parasades?"

Nikometros thought for a moment before answering in the same tongue. "Yes, sir, providing they are left to govern themselves. Parasades is an able man but wants his tribe to be independent."

Alexander nodded. "We shall talk of this again." Smoothly switching back to a clear Classical Greek he rose to his feet and addressed Tomyra. "Lady, I fear we have tired you with all this talk. I will let you rest and refresh yourselves."

Tomyra rose to her feet and inclined her head graciously. "My lord Alexander," she replied. "It has been a delight to converse with you, a delight that I hope to enjoy again soon."

Tomyra bowed again briefly and withdrew, followed by Bithyia, Ket and Tirses. When Nikometros and Timon made to leave, Ptolemy put his hand out, signalling them to remain.

The great double doors closed and Alexander turned toward Nikometros with a serious expression on his face. "So, you trained a cadre of Scythian horsemen in the skills of Macedonian cavalry. Was that a considered decision?"

"They're natural horsemen, sir, lacking only discipline. I provided that."

"Have you created a weapon that will be used against us?" rasped Perdikkas.

Nikometros turned. "I believe not, sir. They are a loyal people but also fiercely independent. The men under Tirses owe loyalty to me personally but in the absence of a disciplined commander their fellow tribesmen will revert to their old ways."

"What of the Serratae?" Alexander softly asked.

"You read the report, sir?" asked Nikometros in his turn.

"I would like your account."

"The Serratae were brought in by Areipithes to murder the lawful chief of the Massegetae--a man I came to think of as my brother." Nikometros hesitated. "Their leader--Dimurthes--captured and injured Tomyra and I sought revenge, as is my right. I didn't know they had entered into a treaty with you, sir."

"She told me, Nikometros. I, too, would have had his life for that action." Alexander shook his head. "It seems the governor of the borders was too eager to sign a treaty and didn't measure the worth of the tribes beforehand." He walked over to one of the chairs and sat down. "Alcimenes will be reprimanded but not too severely, he is otherwise a competent man."

"And the charges against Niko, sir?" muttered Timon.

"They are dismissed, as are the charges against you," replied Alexander with a smile. "Alcimenes found the report from your Persian man, Mardes, and forwarded it. It just arrived."

"And Mardes, sir?" asked Nikometros eagerly.

"He was drafted into a garrison in eastern Sogdiana. I have sent for him, though he may be a while arriving."

"That's good news sir. Thank you."

Alexander smiled. "I value loyalty and friendship."

"There is the matter of Lymnos, Alexander," put in Hephaestion. "I admire initiative in my men but I also require obedience."

"Nikometros?" asked Alexander.

"The man is half-witted," explained Nikometros. "He didn't know what he said nor recognise the meaning. He only repeated what another man said."

"Men have still been tried and executed for repeating treasonous gossip," growled Ptolemy. "Why not this fellow?"

"The Massegetae have a saying, sir. 'If you kill the lark you won't find his mate.'"

Ptolemy snorted. "And this truly delightful saying means what, exactly?"

"Only that if he dies, those who said the treason in the first place will disappear. Keep him alive and he may remember the speaker."

"Yes, that was my thought too," Alexander said. "Hephaestion, I want you to remove Kerros from command of the Fourth. Give him some sinecure where he cannot cause too much trouble. Perhaps some border post. I'll let you decide on his replacement. As for the man Lymnos, he's pardoned. Caution him against listening to gossip and let him return to his duties." Alexander nodded and stood, turning to face his generals. "I think we've heard enough gentlemen. You already know my thoughts on this man. Do any of you disagree?"

"No, Alexander," said Hephaestion.

Perdikkas and Ptolemy shook their heads.

"Very well then." Alexander turned and faced Nikometros. "Nikometros, you are from this moment relieved of your rank and position within the Fourth Squadron of the Companion Cavalry." Nikometros paled but stood firmly at attention.

"Instead, you will assume a position within my personal staff under the command of General Perdikkas. You are promoted to the rank of colonel with the pay and privileges that go with it. Your duties will be specifically to help in the planning of the Caspian Expedition and more generally to assist my scribes in the compilation of a book on Scythian customs and language. I'm sure your wife Tomyra will be most helpful too."

Nikometros opened his mouth then hurriedly shut it.

Alexander cocked his head. "Yes, Nikometros?"

"Er...Thank you, sir. I'm honoured but Tomyra is...er, she isn't my wife, sir."

Perdikkas raised an eyebrow, while Ptolemy smiled. Hephaestion remained stony-faced, watching Alexander.

"All my generals, my staff officers and friends took wives from among Persian nobility when I married," Alexander said. "It's a sign that we regard them not as a conquered race but rather as one joined with us. I see our children, mixed Macedonian and Persian, ruling this great empire after us."

"A noble vision, Alexander," murmured Hephaestion.

"Will you be part of my vision, Nikometros?" Alexander asked. "Marry your lady Tomyra--tomorrow."

Nikometros gaped then blushed as he struggled for words. "Er...I would...that is, I haven't...she...I haven't asked her, sir. She might refuse."

Alexander smiled warmly. "Ask her, Nikometros. I doubt she'll refuse, so I'll make the arrangements for tomorrow." He looked across at Timon, who stood watching his friend with a great grin. "And what of you, Timon of Messa? Will you marry your lady too?"

"Aye, sir!" rumbled Timon. "It's what we've always wanted."

"Then it's settled," Alexander declared. "Tomorrow will see the union of Macedonia with another of the great peoples of this land, the Massegetae of Scythia." He turned to his generals and started pacing, counting off points on his fingers. "Ptolemy, arrange the feast, invite the guests. Not too many, no more than a hundred or so. The Scythian envoys of course, my Staff officers and their wives. The Persian nobles at court also. Hephaestion, get with Tirses and the priests. Find out the proper gods to invoke and the required prayers. Perdikkas, send for the finest tailors. We must make this an occasion to remember."

Alexander laughed, his eyes sparkling.

Hephaestion's eyes softened as he gazed at his friend and ruler striding across the throne room. The afternoon sunlight threw great yellow swathes across the mosaic floor. The king's golden hair glinted in the mellow light, masking the streaks of grey and the deep lines etched into his brow.

"Yes," Alexander said firmly. "My vision will bear fruit. One people, out of many."

# Chapter 10

The Great Hall in the King's residence blazed with the fire of a thousand torches, warm light reflecting off rich tapestry hangings and the soft wool carpets. A mass of people, intensely varied in appearance, filled the hall with a susurration that rose and fell like the tides of the world-encircling Ocean. Alexander's generals, ever mindful of their friend and king, moved through the throng, their Persian wives discretely beside them, greeting and talking to the guests. Staff officers, some married but many more devoted only to the army, stood in groups, talking quietly and disdaining the fellowship of foreigners.

Tirses and the other Scythian envoys stood off to one side, quietly eyeing the assembled people. They fidgeted, their hands creeping often to their belts, mindful of missing swords. Their behaviour declared that the mass of strangers concerned them and they longed to be out in the open air, astride their horses.

Persian nobility, distinguished by their height, beautifully coiffed beards and rich garments, stood in posed groups. They nodded politely to anyone who looked in their direction but maintained an aloof silence for the main part.

To one side of the raised dais at the far end of the hall stood a group of ladies garbed in the rich clothing of nobility. Veiled against the coarse looks of common people, the ladies whispered softly amongst themselves as they gazed around.

Several armed guards stood facing outward, their faces watchful. Tall and muscular, only a certain grace and beauty hinted at the loss of their manhood, the price they paid for the privilege of guarding the wife of Alexander. Roxane herself, short and dark, with the smouldering beauty of Bactrian women, stared haughtily about her, ignoring the deferential bows of the other guests.

Servants bustled through the crowded hall, bearing trays of finely worked silver goblets filled with iced citron and well-watered wine. Others bore huge platters of sweetmeats redolent with the aroma of pungent spices.

Tomyra gazed down on the packed hall from a small room near the rear of the hall, where a flight of marble stairs descended to the main chamber. She nervously smoothed the rich red woollen cloak about her as a flock of women busied themselves primping her hair, adjusting its raven folds beneath a golden diadem. Some touched up elaborate makeup while others fastened gold and enamelled brooches to her gown and cloak, fussing and clucking to each other in a mixture of Greek and Persian. One lifted the hem of Tomyra's flowing white silk gown; tucking and fastening the folds clear of hennaed feet within softly tooled calfskin sandals. She glanced to her right where Bithyia stood patiently undergoing the same detailed treatment.

Bithyia felt her mistress's gaze and turned with a grimace. "My lady?" she enquired, in the Scythian tongue.

"Nothing, Bithyia." Tomyra sighed and looked out over the crowded hall again.

"What is wrong, my lady? I thought this day would be joyful." Bithyia slapped a hand away from where an old woman was struggling to attach a brooch to her gown. "You are marrying your lord." She grinned. "It's unheard of for a serving priestess to marry. The Goddess must truly favour you."

"Does Niko marry because he wants to or because he must?" Tomyra looked down at her manicured hands. "Alexander commanded it. You too, Bithyia," she added.

Bithyia shrugged. "Timon and I planned to marry anyway. I know Nikomayros loves you, my lady. He would have asked you I'm sure." The tall Scythian girl smiled again. "Besides, how many chiefs or kings have a wedding like this?" She fingered her shimmering blue silk gown. "They say this gown came from Chin and was a year on the road. I shudder to think what it cost."

"And what is all this costing?" asked Tomyra. "Yet I cannot even bring a dowry to my lord."

"No more can I. Yet Niko...and Timon are rising in the world. If Alexander chooses to give us such a rich gift, can we refuse?"

Tomyra shook her head, ignoring the cries of annoyance from the women touching up her hair. "No, it would be neither polite nor politic, yet I would rather wed Niko simply in some village than with all these riches in the hall of a king."

A cascade of trumpets sounded in the Great Hall, followed by loud cheering. The mass of guests surged toward wide entrance doors, clapping and shouting. Flushed by the occasion and a liberal consumption of wine, even the tall sombre Persian lords unbent sufficiently to bow towards the entrance. The younger Macedonian officers scowled at the Persians then ignored them once more, taking fresh drinks from the servants. A few called out and made ribald remarks as the wedding procession entered the hall.

The Great King Alexander led the procession, resplendent in a pristine white tunic and a cloak of Tyrian purple. A garland of olive leaves rested on his golden hair. He walked lightly up the avenue of onlookers toward the raised dais at the far end of the chamber.

Nikometros and Timon paced behind, each arrayed in fine white linen. Nikometros' hair was freshly washed, brushed and ribboned, rivalling the king's in its lustre and hue. Timon's black beard was trimmed and curled, lending a regal air to the stolid soldier. Behind the two bridegrooms walked a small group of young army officers and lower ranks from the Fourth Squadron of the Companion Cavalry. In the absence of close kinsmen, the cavalrymen stood in for the families. They followed, laughing and singing praise songs and nuptial hymns.

Alexander led the grooms up to the dais then turned and faced the noisy throng. He lifted his arms and waited patiently, a smile on his face, for the hubbub to die away. When all was quiet, he spoke, softly, but in a voice that carried to all parts of the great chamber.

"Greetings friends, Royal Kinsmen, noble lords and ladies, men of Macedonia...we are gathered once more to join together two races in marriage. It is my desire that the peoples in whose land we now reside, scions of the race of Great Kyros..." Alexander bowed toward the Persian nobles who bowed deeply in acknowledgement. "...should evermore be one with us. I see a future in which no man is judged to be Persian or Macedonian, but rather a citizen of the world's greatest empire. But we must not forget that other races exist. To the north of us lies a great open land, rich in pastures and horses, peopled by a fierce but noble race, the Scythians. It is my desire that we forge ties of blood and kinship with these people. From Macedon comes Nikometros, son of Leonnatos of the noble house of Ermacyon, and Timon, son of Kerobates of Messa. These men have served loyally and with distinction in my Companion Cavalry. More recently, they have furthered our interests in Scythia. Here, Nikometros so distinguished himself that he earned the praise-title of Lion of Scythia.

"These valiant soldiers are to wed Tomyra, daughter of Spargises, king of the Massegetae Scyths and her warrior hand-maiden Bithyia, daughter of Allotroces." Alexander paused, letting his words fade into the silence before lifting his voice in command. "Let the brides come forth."

Heads turned toward the staircase at the rear of the chamber as Tomyra and Bithyia appeared. Tomyra took a deep breath and, quickly squeezing Bithyia's hand, started down toward the sea of upturned faces. Despite being used to the attention of crowds in her capacity of priestess, Tomyra quailed slightly. She caught a glimpse of Nikometros and steadied herself, descending calmly to the floor of the chamber. As she stepped on to the carpet an old lady thrust a burning torch into her hand and another into Bithyia's.

"From your quarters, my lady," muttered the old woman. "As if from your home hearth."

The crowd parted before Tomyra, whispering and smiling as curious eyes took in her beauty. A shower of flower petals, seeds and nuts speckled her robes and crunched underfoot as she walked slowly toward the dais. As she drew level with the group of ladies and eunuchs around Roxane, she felt her presence. Tomyra glanced at her and for an instant caught a look of intense malevolence. She shivered, despite the warmth of the chamber, and looked away.

Alexander smiled again as the two brides came to a halt in front of him. "Greetings Tomyra and Bithyia." Raising his voice he addressed the assembled crowds. "Let all things be done and be seen to be done. Let all customs be followed that this union be blessed. The gods have been invoked and the sacrifices accepted. The gods and goddesses of Macedon, Persia and Scythia look down with favour on these marriages."

Alexander smiled at the two couples standing in front of him and lowered his voice. "In the interests of all parties I altered the wedding proceedings somewhat. I know, Tomyra, that in Scythia you would invoke the Goddess for a marriage ceremony, but it wouldn't be proper for you to do so on your own behalf. However, Tirses sacrificed to your other gods for you and I myself have petitioned Apollo and Artemis. The portents were all favourable."

Alexander turned to Hephaestion who stood beside him bearing a silver tray. He picked up a loaf of wheat bread and ripped it in two, passing the halves to Tomyra and Nikometros. He repeated the action with Timon and Bithyia. Turning to Hephaestion once more he lifted a great golden cup from the tray and a Scythian arrow. He dipped the arrowhead in the wine and flicked the liquid toward the north, south, east and west before passing the cup to Nikometros. He drank and passed the cup to Tomyra. When both couples had drunk from the cup, Alexander drained it and put it back on the tray. He lifted up his arms and addressed the wedding guests.

"Behold, Macedon weds Scythia. May the gods bless their union."

The hall erupted into a cacophony of cheering. Blessings and good wishes washed over the couples in several languages and a storm of flowers, nuts and small fruit cascaded over them.

Alexander let the cheering carry on for a few minutes before raising his arms once more to call for quiet. "As Nikometros and Timon are far from their homes in Macedonia I have given them rooms in the Ambassadors Palace. Let them be escorted there and the ceremony be complete."

With a renewed burst of cheering the guests surged forward, pushing the wedded couples down the hall. Tomyra and Bithyia held their torches high as women, young and old, surrounded them, whispering suggestions and tales of the marriage bed. Nikometros and Timon, with big grins on their faces, bore the coarser jestings of the army men. The procession left the

Great Hall and passed through wide corridors where large numbers of servants and officials paused in their duties to watch or participate.

By the time the wedding party reached the road, the couples were together again and the procession became more formal, falling in behind them. A pair of chariots stood by the palace steps, tall white horses yoked to them nervously stamping at the noise. A charioteer stood by each vehicle, reins in hand, awaiting the newlyweds.

Tomyra and Nikometros climbed into one and Timon helped Bithyia into the other. The crowd raised the marriage paean, startling the horses and sending a flock of birds screeching up from the trees overhanging the roadway. The charioteers shook the reins and urged their horses on, setting off at a walk. The crowd of guests followed, singing a nuptial hymn to the music of flutes and lyres. They progressed slowly through the gates in the gold and silver walls, attracting further crowds as they went.

Tomyra squeezed Nikometros' arm, smiling up at him. "Happy, Niko?" Nikometros grinned, waving to the cheering crowds. "Oh, yes. Can you doubt it?"

He looked over at the other chariot where Timon and Bithyia stood kissing. The chariot lurched over a pothole, throwing Nikometros against his bride. He lowered his face and kissed Tomyra, eliciting a fresh burst of applause from the guests.

The chariots came to a halt outside the Ambassadors Palace and the newlyweds stepped down. Servants hurried up, ushering them into the portico of the palace where fountains splashed among citrus trees, perfume heavy on the still air. The wedding party moved on, led by the servants, through the hallways, to a pair of great double cedar doors.

The servants flung one of the doors wide, revealing a bedchamber. A huge canopied bed dominated the room, the white linen sheets and covers thrown back, pillows cascading over it and onto the carpeted floor. With a shout, the crowd urged Nikometros and Tomyra into the room and Timon and Bithyia toward the other bedchamber before pulling back to the doorways where they jostled and called out, staring avidly into the chambers.

Tomyra frowned at the ribald crowd. "Do they mean to watch us?" she muttered.

Nikometros grinned. "No, my love. But we're not fully married until you light the fire in the grate with your torch and eat the honey cake. They must see us do that."

Tomyra looked around the chamber then moved over to the fireplace. She thrust her torch into the kindling and watched as the flames shot up. She turned to find Nikometros standing behind her, a large honey cake in his hands. He broke off a piece and handed it to her, watching as she nibbled on it.

Nikometros followed suit then turned with her to face the crowd. "Forgive us, friends," he said with a grin. "I wish to be alone with my wife." A great cheer erupted, sprinkled with lewd remarks. "Please return to the Great Hall where a feast awaits you." He gestured to a young man hovering at one side of the doorway. "Dymnos, will you keep our door?"

Dymnos grinned and waved a large flask of wine above his head. "Aye, Nikometros. I came prepared." He spread his arms wide and ushered the guests away from the doors before closing them. The crowd backed away, grinning and calling out until the doors shut then turning back to the King's Palace.

Nikometros barred the door then turned to stare at Tomyra, standing by the great bed in the firelight.

Tomyra smiled uncertainly at his continued silence. "Do I please you, Niko?" she whispered.

Nikometros smiled. "Do you need to ask?"

"This marriage was forced on you, Niko. I won't hold you to it unless you wish it."

"No one forced me. The king wished us to wed, it's true. It's part of his foreign policy. However, I wouldn't have done so if I hadn't desired it also."

"Truly?"

Nikometros crossed to the bed and took Tomyra by the shoulders. He bent to her upturned face and gently brushed his lips across hers. She flushed and returned the kiss, harder.

"I love you, Tomyra," he murmured. "Never forget that." He unfastened the clasp at her shoulder and let her cloak slip to the ground.

She shivered and put her arms around him, hugging him closely. Nikometros kissed her hair then, as she looked up, kissed her full on the mouth.

After a moment, Tomyra gently disengaged herself and stepped back. She loosened her gown and let it fall, standing by the huge bed clothed only in firelight. She looked down at her swollen belly and blushed, her hands covering herself. "I'm sorry, Niko. I should come to you a virgin."

Nikometros stepped forward and gently pushed her hands aside. He ran a callused hand over her belly. "I love you my fierce Scythian, and I shall love your child," he whispered. "The next one will be mine."

Tomyra smiled and loosened his tunic. "Then my lord," she said softly, "Let us practice for that happy day." She drew him with her onto the bed and lost herself in his love.

# *Chapter 11*

"I knew I should have killed him myself on the Royal Road rather than let you arrange it." Scolices cast a bitter look at the man seated by the fire and continued pacing. "Now he's safe within the citadel of Ekbatana."

Parates looked up from his contemplation of the flames. His hands continued to roll a silver goblet between his hands, dark wine swirling within it. "I misjudged the issue, I admit," he said mildly. "However, there'll be other opportunities."

"You think so?" snarled Scolices. "He's high in the king's favour, married to the bitch and with a household and command of his own. How are we to get close to him?"

Parates smiled. "There are always ways, my friend."

"Such as?"

"Certainly not by running at him with a drawn sword, as you would like to do. Your own death would be assured."

"At least I'd die knowing I accomplished his."

"I, on the other hand, would rather live, savouring my victory." Parates drained the wine from his cup and got up, stretching as he did so. He walked to a table and poured himself some more wine. He picked up another cup, briefly inspected it, wiping the rim with his fingers before filling it. "No, my eager friend. There are ways to bring death with no man knowing it." He handed the other cup to Scolices and walked back to his chair.

Scolices grunted and sipped from the cup. "So, friend Scorpion," he grated. "Enlighten me."

"Don't call me that here," snapped Parates. "Here, I'm a respected merchant prince having no connections with that border brigand. Remember that. My life would be forfeit if the authorities knew...as would yours."

Scolices grunted again and drew up another chair to the fire. He sipped again from his wine, staring into the flames.

"The royal court is a dangerous place," Parates mused after a few minutes. "One must be careful not to make enemies, or else have powerful friends."

"The Greek has powerful friends," Scolices said. "You cannot get more powerful than Alexander."

Parates laughed. "Alexander isn't his friend. A king doesn't have friends." He chuckled and raised his cup to his lips. "Well, some maybe. There's no doubt of his love for Hephaestion but they were lovers once." He shrugged. "Maybe one or two of his generals but certainly not a young untried cavalry officer. No, Alexander recognises ability and means to use him, but they aren't friends."

"Your point being?" Scolices asked in a surly voice.

"No matter who he befriends, he'll make enemies. In a court filled with ambitious men it's almost impossible to avoid intrigue. If he makes friends with Ptolemy, Perdikkas will hate him; if he follows Perdikkas, Eumenes will plot against him; if Eumenes, then Peukestas. They all hate each other."

"And how does that work to our advantage?"

"There are many men of lesser talents in the retinue of generals. If one of these lesser men thought Nikometros a danger, he'd try to remove him. I, or rather one of my intermediaries, would be happy to assist him."

"So, we are to rely once more on someone else's sword, rather than our own? Look what happened last time you tried that."

Parates shrugged. "There are more direct ways. A dagger between the ribs while out walking in the streets of the city or a stray arrow during an army exercise would take care of him. The assailant would almost certainly be apprehended and tortured to reveal whence came his orders, of course."

"So, we can do nothing? Except plot and hope that someone else will do our work for us?"

"Maybe there'll be a war and Nikometros given a command. Accidents happen in war."

"What war?" snapped Scolices. "Alexander has conquered everyone. Who will he make war on?"

"On the other hand, perhaps he'll eat something."

"Eh? What do you mean?"

Parates sipped his wine and looked over the rim of his cup at the other man. "How is your wine, Scolices?"

Scolices grunted. "I've tasted better. I would think with your money you could afford...why?" He lowered his cup and stared suspiciously at Parates.

"Slightly bitter aftertaste, perhaps? Maybe a mild twinge of pain in your guts?" Parates smiled and lifted his own cup again. "Probably too soon for your senses to be affected."

Scolices licked his lips and dropped his gaze to the cup, swirling the dregs of the wine. He raised his eyes and stared across the fire at the merchant.

"You...you have...?" His hand shook and he put the cup down on a stool by his chair.

"Have what, Scolices? Poisoned your wine?" Parates grinned, his eyes sparkling in the firelight.

Scolices paled. He struggled to his feet, trembling hands tugging at the dagger in his belt. "You b...bastard," he stuttered. "I'll have your..."

Parates dropped his cup and sprang to his feet. His left fist cracked against the other man's jaw as his right hand locked onto Scolices' arm. He twisted hard and pushed.

Scolices gave a cry of pain and dropped the dagger, falling back into the chair, toppling over with it onto the floor. He lay whimpering and rubbing his wrist.

"I haven't poisoned you," Parates softly said. He stared down at Scolices, with a small smile on his face. "You don't believe me?" Parates stepped back and picked up Scolices' cup. He lifted it and drained the dregs before upending it and flinging it to the floor. Stifling a belch, he sat down again and stretched his legs to the fire.

Scolices slowly got up and picked up his dagger. He hesitated a moment then put it back in his belt. Righting the chair, he moved it further from Parates and sat down again. "Why...?" He cleared his throat. "Why did you say...?"

"That I poisoned you? I didn't, but you thought it likely. Now, why is that, I wonder?" Parates smiled and stared into the flames. "Perhaps because poison is easy. Easy, but hard to hide by its very nature."

"Women use poison."

Parates looked up sharply. "I hope you aren't calling me a woman," he said softly. "Women use it because little else is available to them. They aren't trained in the use of weapons." He turned back to his contemplation of the fire. "No, any fool can use poison. It's more difficult to cover one's tracks though. A slow poison is less certain but by the time it works the evidence has been cleared away. A swift one is surer but more likely to be detected. The cook, the food server, the supplier...all will be questioned. And they'll talk; you may be certain they'll be tortured."

"So, you rule out poison..."

"I rule out nothing. However, such an action must be carefully considered." Parates sat in thought, his hands steepled in front of him. "A wedding gift perhaps," he mused. "Brought as if from someone close, the bringer disposed of immediately..."

# Chapter 12

The roar of excited crowds shattered the warmth of the autumn afternoon. Tirses led his small band of Scythian horsemen into the great stadium of Ekbatana at a full gallop. A dozen horsemen, astride extravagantly caparisoned mounts, circled the arena, shouting and waving their short double-curved bows above their heads before bringing the horses to an abrupt and dust-laden halt before the royal canopy.

Tirses leapt to the ground, strode forward a few paces and dropped to one knee, holding his bow out in front of him. He shouted a few phrases in the Massegetae tongue before rising to his feet and striking a pose, hand on hip.

Alexander, sitting upright on a plain wooden stool in the shade of the royal canopy, leant over and whispered to Perdikkas who sat beside him on a cushioned chair.

The general looked around at the crowd of army officers and court officials and frowned. He beckoned to Nikometros, who stood to one side talking quietly to Iolatos, the king's equerry.

"Ah, Nikometros," exclaimed Alexander. "Just the man. What did Tirses say?"

Nikometros hesitated a moment to be sure of the translation. "He offers his bow to you as a token of loyal service, sir."

"Truly?" Alexander swivelled round and stared at the young Scythian. "I'm surprised. I thought these northern tribes to be fiercely independent."

"As indeed they are, sir," replied Nikometros. "However, the way he said it and his posture adds a...how shall I put it...a flavour, a distinction in meaning."

Alexander cocked his head on one side, his eyes sparkling. "How so?"

"There are levels of loyalty, sir." Nikometros paused, searching for suitably diplomatic phrases. "He pledges to fight your enemies but only to obey lawful commands. He offered this on one knee only, signifying homage to a friendly chief or king, not on both knees as he would to his own chief."

"Well said." Alexander nodded. "All men should behave with honour, even kings." He smiled. "Especially kings. One must always obey the laws of the gods, leading the people by example." He turned back to Tirses and rose to his feet. Raising one arm, hand outstretched, he thanked the Scythian then half turned his head toward Nikometros. "Translate for me, Niko," he said. "Thank him and tell him I am honoured by his service."

Nikometros stepped to the edge of the raised platform and called out to Tirses in a series of Massegetae phrases. Tirses frowned for a moment then abruptly smiled and nodded. He leapt up onto his horse and raised a fist in salute. At a shouted command, the Scythian horsemen wheeled and galloped off around the arena again. As they reached one end of the long, oval space, half of the riders stopped, letting the others continue on to the far end.

The far group paused and fitted small circular wooden shields to their left forearms. They dug their heels into their horse's sides and raced down the centre of the arena. The near group whipped out their bows and, their mounts already in motion, fitted long arrows as they rapidly closed the gap. Crouching low over the necks of their horses, they loosed a volley of arrows and then another before the first ones found their targets.

The horsemen with shields raised them in a swift motion, the arrows thudding into the wood. The shields-men brought their mounts to a halt in the centre of the arena. The archers turned and galloped past them, then around in a large circle, releasing further volleys of arrows as they did so. The arrows, with one exception, buried themselves in the round shields. One, however, glanced off the rim of a shield and struck one of the Scythians in the arm. The man yelled and fell off his horse.

The crowd of watching soldiers laughed and jeered at the unfortunate man. The wounded man clambered to his feet with a shrug. He gripped the shaft of the arrow with his free hand and snapped it, binding the jagged end with a scrap of cloth before vaulting up onto his gelding again. The jeers and catcalls of the watching army turned to cheering.

Under the royal canopy Alexander clapped his hands in appreciation as he leaned over to Perdikkas. "A pity Hephaestion cannot be here," Alexander murmured. "He would love this." To Nikometros he added, "Formidable accuracy for horseback archers."

"How is he today, Alexander?" Perdikkas asked.

"A little better, I think." Alexander smiled and signalled for the Scythians to depart the arena. "I've told him often enough not to drink the local water. It's his own fault if he now starves on the slops the doctor feeds him."

Perdikkas nodded and looked around, searching the knot of familiar faces around the king. He found who he was looking for and beckoned. "Alexander," he said, "I didn't want to bother you with this earlier but the Persian governor of Celicia has been embezzling the taxes." He stared up at the man who approached, his lips drawing back in a grimace of distaste. "Eumenes, tell him."

Eumenes sauntered up to the royal canopy. Slight in figure, with dark hair drawn back and elegantly coiffed, his clothing reflected a man meticulous in his grooming. When he spoke, it was with a clear Greek accent, unmarred by the almost ubiquitous Macedonian slur.

"Alexander." Eumenes gave a slight bow then glared at Perdikkas before averting his eyes. "It's true. The satrap Merabarses fled with this year's taxes."

Alexander maintained a neutral expression. "Thank you, Eumenes," he replied. "Have Peukestas deal with it. Replace the governor with a Macedonian."

Perdikkas smiled at Eumenes, baring his teeth. "I believe Hephaestion knows of a loyal man, Alexander. I'm sure Eumenes would be happy to discuss the selection with him as soon as he's recovered."

Eumenes scowled, flashing Perdikkas a look of pure hatred. With an effort, he smoothed his taut features as he bowed to the king. "I'll be happy to do so, Alexander," he agreed. "May I enquire after his health?"

"He's better. Thank you Eumenes," replied the king. "The doctor's regime is having an effect."

"I'm pleased to hear it," responded Eumenes. "I'll call on him this evening." He bowed again and withdrew.

Nikometros edged out earshot of Alexander and murmured to Iolatos. "Am I missing something here?"

Iolatos shot Nikometros a hard look then nodded. "I forgot you've been absent from court." He looked around carefully before continuing. "Eumenes is Alexander's private secretary. Quite a competent field officer too, for all he's an effete southern Greek. Well, Eumenes and Hephaestion quarrelled. Alexander had to step in to keep the peace."

Nikometros frowned. "It seemed more."

Iolatos nodded. "After the Gedrosian crossing...you know about Gedrosia?"

"The march through the desert?" Nikometros asked. "Yes, I heard."

"The money supply ran out and Alexander needed to pay the army. He asked all his friends for a loan. Eumenes pretended poverty...stupid of him." Iolatos shook his head. "Alexander is a generous man and it annoyed him that Eumenes was mean-spirited. So he set fire to his tent."

Nikometros gaped. "The king?"

Iolatos grinned. "Well, he arranged for it to be done. He wanted to see what Eumenes saved from the fire. Over a thousand talents of silver, an enormous fortune." He looked around again then, reassured that everyone was watching a display of javelin throwing, he resumed his explanation.

"Eumenes was sure the fire was Hephaestion's doing. Later, at Susa, during a festival, Hephaestion ordered a visiting musician billeted at Eumenion's house, without asking him. They quarrelled openly."

"What did Alexander do?"

"Then, nothing," replied Iolatos. "But by the time the army reached Opis it was too late. Both parties felt slighted and factions grew up around them. The quarrel may even have contributed to the army's mutiny."

The javelin display ended to a burst of applause from the army and a more restrained scattering of clapping from the watching officers and nobles. The squad trooped from the arena as a body of athletes entered. They immediately started their warm up exercises.

"After the mutiny it nearly flared into a brawl," Iolatos continued. "Weapons were drawn and it was only the timely arrival of the king that prevented blood being spilt."

"What happened?"

"Alexander was really angry. He reminded both Hephaestion and Eumenes that they were nothing without him and that whoever resumed the feud would be condemned to death. The king meant it too, though you could see it cost him dearly to be so harsh with Hephaestion. He ordered them to resolve their dispute and make up. Eumenes was willing enough to do so but Hephaestion was reluctant. Still, for love of Alexander they both did it."

"But the tension remains?"

"Just so. Oh, they're both polite and formal when they meet but the dispute hasn't gone away. It's just hidden well."

The athletes in the stadium lined up for a foot race, naked, oiled and bronzed. With a shout, they leapt from the line and sped off down the arena, followed by the cheers of the crowd.

"Eumenes did it for fear of Alexander, of course," Iolatos said matter-of-factly before turning his attention to the ring. "Oh, yes, see Nikometros, Hippias is sure to win!"

In the stadium, the runners rounded the mark at the far end and raced for the finish, a spare fair-haired youth drawing away from the others.

"And Hephaestion?" asked Nikometros.

"He did it because Alexander asked him to but you could see it hurt him that the king didn't take his side." Iolatos nodded his head when the youth arrived at the finish line. "There, I knew he would win. I should have put money on him."

The youth Hippias waved to the crowd, a big grin on his face. Then he ran lightly up to the royal box and saluted his king, still naked and covered in dust. To the roars of the crowd, Alexander advanced to meet the youth then embraced him, kissing him lightly.

"Hephaestion thinks the king should value his friendship above mere statesmanship...well, sometimes Hephaestion can be a fool," growled Iolatos. "Anyone could see it hurt Alexander to hold his friend accountable but he had to do it."

"What about Perdikkas? It seems to me the general dislikes Eumenes too."

Iolatos shrugged. "Just court politics. Everyone is trying to win favour with the king. Perdikkas envies Hephaestion but hates Eumenes who has risen fast at court." He turned and stared at Nikometros. "You would do well to stay out of it."

Nikometros stood and watched as Hippias rejoined the other competitors. The men paired off and prepared for the wrestling contest. Hippias found himself pitted against a heavyset soldier who overtopped him by a head and shoulders. "How do you think he'll do?" Nikometros asked.

"Outclassed. He's a runner, not a wrestler."

"I meant Perdikkas."

"He's ambitious but he's risen as far as he can. As long as Hephaestion is Chiliarch, the most powerful man in the empire under Alexander, Perdikkas will never be more than a general." Iolatos pursed his lips and looked at Nikometros. "Be careful who you follow, my friend."

Nikometros met the other man's eye. "I serve the king," he said quietly.

In the dust, Hippias feinted then reached out and caught his opponent off balance. He twisted and threw the heavier man to the ground, dancing lightly out of the way of his opponent's flailing limbs.

"Good man." Iolatos murmured.

# *Chapter 13*

Tomyra groaned and shifted uncomfortably on the huge padded couch in her private rooms. She wrapped her arms around her swollen belly and grimaced as Bithyia padded across the chamber with a look of concern on her face.

"How do women get through this torture, Bithyia?" she muttered.

"It's very natural, my lady," Bithyia calmly replied. "Draw on the strength of the Mother Goddess. It will pass soon enough."

"I cannot wait to rid myself of this burden."

Bithyia frowned. "It's still your child, my lady, even though it was put there by ..."

"Don't speak his name," hissed Tomyra. "It's bad enough I must carry that man's child to term. Don't bring ill luck by speaking his name. I cannot think why the Goddess put me through this."

"No doubt She has a purpose, my lady." Bithyia paused, a contented look on her face. "I, too, am with child."

Tomyra's eyes widened. "Does Timon know?"

"Not yet. I missed my moon but I'll wait until I'm sure."

"Do you...are you happy, Bithyia?"

Bithyia smiled. "Oh yes. Timon wants sons and I hope to present him with many."

"Then I'm happy for you." Tomyra shifted her weight and looked out at the grey autumn skies. "I cannot stand being confined, Bithyia. I want to be out riding, racing across the broad steppes without a care in the world. Instead, I sit in this dreary building..." Tomyra looked up and caught the other woman's eye. "All right, in this sumptuous palace, being waited on hand and foot." She laughed, Bithyia joining in.

"Are you hungry, my lady? Wedding presents pour in and many of them are food. I can offer you some delicious looking fruit from the trader's guild." Bithyia walked to a large trestle table along one wall and ran her hand over the many gifts and packages arrayed there. She lifted covers and peered at handwritten notes. "Or perhaps you would rather have some wine from the cellars of Eumenes, no less; or dried meat from Thracian ambassador; or sweetmeats from Ptolemy?"

"No wine," Tomyra groaned with a shudder. "It's been giving me awful indigestion lately. Perhaps something sweet or some nuts."

Bithyia ran her gaze over the table. "No nuts, my lady, unless you want me to go out and get some. There are sweet things though. Perhaps these from Ptolemy?" She picked up a small silver platter and walked to Tomyra. "A little fair-haired boy brought them an hour ago, despite the lord Ptolemy having brought that magnificent set of gold dishes himself." She shrugged. "Probably just an afterthought. Something from his table."

"What's in them? No apricots I hope. My bowels are disturbed enough without that. You know how they affect me."

Bithyia grinned. "Too early for apricots, my lady." She sniffed and poked at one of them with her finger. "Apple I think, with almonds." She dipped the tip of her finger into a small puddle of liquid on the tray then licked it. "Yes, definitely apple, with cinnamon." Bithyia offered the tray.

Tomyra took one of the rounded sweets and bit into it. She chewed and swallowed then put the rest onto the couch beside her, licking her fingers. "Flavoursome, but too sweet for me," she said. "Get me some water, will you please, Bithyia? It's left a strange taste in my mouth."

Bithyia put down the tray of sweetmeats and walked to the pitcher by the door. She hefted it and filled a cup with the clear liquid. Putting down the pitcher she started back toward Tomyra then stopped with a puzzled look on her face. "Forgive me, lady," she murmured, and sipped from the cup. She held the water in her mouth and looked around before darting to the gift table and spitting into a beautiful golden bowl. "My tongue is tingling," she muttered.

Tomyra looked up with an expression of concern. "Are you all right, Bithyia?" She pushed herself to her feet then stopped, one hand flying to her throat. She gagged and reeled for a moment before dropping back onto the couch. "I feel sick, Bithyia. My throat is burning." Tomyra looked around, her eyes wide. Then she retched violently, a thin rope of milky spittle drooling from her mouth as she doubled over.

"Poison," whispered Bithyia, letting the cup fall. "Poison!" she screamed, throwing herself at the couch. She grasped Tomyra's shoulders and threw her back on the couch, gasping as she saw her friend's pale face, with eyes rolling up in their sockets. She scrabbled at Tomyra's mouth, pulling her head to one side and stuck her finger down the other woman's throat.

Tomyra gagged and tried to knock Bithyia's hand aside. She gagged again then threw up, vomit cascading over them both. Amber flecks of the sweetmeat swam in a milky fluid, stained with fresh blood.

"Great Mother, help her," gasped Bithyia. She leapt to her feet, leaving Tomyra sprawled on the couch and raced back to the pitcher of water. She dashed handfuls of water in Tomyra's face then held her head up, forcing water into her mouth. "Drink, my lady," she urged. "You must drink."

Tomyra spluttered and choked, swallowing and coughing. "It hurts," she rasped, pushing Bithyia away.

Bithyia held her head, forcing more water into her. She put the pitcher down and pushed her finger down Tomyra's throat once more. The vomit came up almost clear but still bloody. She made her drink again.

Twice more Bithyia forced Tomyra to vomit, until all that came up was water with curdles of blood. She eased her friend's head back onto the couch and strode to the door, flinging it wide. "Sisyphis!" she yelled. "Sisyphis, send for a doctor then come at once. Sisyphis!" Bithyia hurried back to the couch.

A few moments later a patter of footsteps sounded in the corridor and an old woman peered around the jamb. "Did you call, young mistress?" the old woman enquired. She stared at the mess puddled by the couch and clucked her tongue. "Upset stomach, eh? No need for a doctor, no need at all. I can deal with that." Sisyphis tottered into the room.

"Get a doctor," yelled Bithyia. "She was poisoned, you old fool."

Sisyphis stared down at Bithyia then at the bloody mess on the floor. She nodded sharply and turned, lifting the hem of her skirts as she tottered with surprising speed for the door. She disappeared down the corridor, screeching in Persian.

Minutes passed. Bithyia wet her sleeve from the pitcher and bathed Tomyra's face, peering anxiously at her pale features. Tomyra's eyelids fluttered and opened, her dark eyes staring unfocussed. Shouts rose from outside and footsteps echoed. Sisyphis returned with two young girls and a wan young man in tow.

The young man hurried to the couch, neatly lifting his robe over the puddle of vomit. He sat on the edge of the couch and peered at Tomyra. Bending over her face, he sniffed delicately then touched a forefinger to the reddened marks on her lips. He picked up a limp wrist and turned her hand over to examine the palm. "How long since the poison was administered?" he asked.

Bithyia shook her head. "I'm not sure. Not long."

"Give me some idea," snapped the doctor. "A day? An hour?"

"A few minutes only. The sweetmeats were poisoned." Bithyia pointed at the silver tray. "She ate a piece, asked for water, then collapsed."

"And this?" asked the doctor, indicating the pool of vomit.

"I made her vomit then gave her water and made her vomit again."

The doctor looked up at Bithyia and nodded. "A reasonable action...unless the substance is caustic." He bent over and prodded at the flecks of sweetmeat in the vomit then picked up one of the pieces still on the silver tray. "She ate one of these?"

Bithyia nodded and looked around, picking up the remnant of bitten sweetmeat from where it had fallen. "This was the piece she actually bit."

The doctor placed the piece he held back onto the tray and took the half-eaten piece from Bithyia. He peered at it then sniffed it. He lifted it to his mouth and touched the tip of his tongue to the morsel. Pursing his lips, the young doctor surveyed the ceiling intently for a few moments then spat on the floor.

"As I suspected," he said. "The poisoner opted for speed rather than subtlety. Arabian death weed I would say. A few moments more and the poison would have corroded her stomach, killing her within hours. As it is, the action of the death weed, both in the original swallowing and in the subsequent vomit may have caused a rupture of the throat. A better action would have been to neutralise the death weed within the stomach." The young doctor looked up at Bithyia's anxious face. "However, you could not know the agent, or the proper remedy."

"She will be all right?"

The doctor shrugged. "Perhaps. I shall prescribe a tonic to strengthen the blood and the digestive humours. I'll add some of the antidote. My servant will bring it round within the hour. See that she drinks it and that the appropriate sacrifices are made to the gods. It's in their hands now."

"What happened?" The words cut like a lash in the still air.

Bithyia turned to see Nikometros in the doorway, staring at the scene. His face paled as the doctor rose to his feet, revealing the supine form of Tomyra sprawled on the couch. His eyes widened and he stepped forward, a hand rising in supplication. "Tomyra...she is..."

"Recovering," said the doctor. "It appears she was poisoned."

Nikometros dragged his eyes away from Tomyra and stared at the doctor. "Poisoned?" he whispered. "Who...?" He looked at Bithyia.

Bithyia nodded. "Someone sent us poisoned sweetmeats, Niko. If she had taken more than a bite..." She shuddered.

"But she's all right?"

"Oh, yes, very probably," said the doctor, wiping his hands on his robe. "With the proper care she will recover fully, though her voice and her digestion will be sensitive for a few days. The poison no doubt put a strain on her body but a fit young woman should have no after effects. Now," he continued briskly. "There's the matter of my payment. I'll send my servant to present my bill tomorrow. I would be grateful..."

"And the baby?" interrupted Nikometros.

"Baby?" said the doctor blankly.

"My wife is nearly full term. Is the baby at risk from the poison?"

"She's pregnant?" The doctor gulped and spun round. He took a step toward Tomyra, his hand outstretched then pulled back quickly. "Er...a baby...yes, this is another matter," he muttered.

On the couch, Tomyra groaned and shifted her body.

"What is it, doctor?" asked Bithyia. "Is there a problem?"

The doctor tugged at his short black beard, his eyes worried. "Er, maybe. This isn't good. Arabian death weed can cause a miscarriage if it doesn't kill the woman outright."

"Then examine her, doctor," snapped Nikometros. "Make sure the baby's safe."

The doctor stared at Nikometros. "Sir, I'm a doctor, not a common..." He paused and drew himself upright, his face disdainful. "No doctor worthy of the name will examine a woman's...er, parts. You must bring in a midwife." He gathered his robes about him. "Now, I will depart and leave you to minister to your patient." He walked slowly to the door before turning. "I really would advise you to bring in a midwife."

Tomyra groaned again and opened her eyes. She moved her hands over her robes, holding her belly. "It hurts, Bithyia," she rasped. Her eyes widened and she attempted a weak smile. "Niko? What are you...doing here?"

Nikometros dropped to his knees beside the couch. "My love, the hurt is past. The doctor says you'll recover."

"Poison. In the sweets," whispered Tomyra.

"I'll find who sent them," Nikometros growled. "They'll die for this."

Tomyra shook her head. "The note says 'Ptolemy' but...aah!" She clenched a fist, her back arching. "It hurts, Niko." A small whimper escaped her clenched jaws and a hand plucked at her robe.

Nikometros looked up at Bithyia, a bleak look on his face. "Send for a midwife. Quickly Bithyia!"

Bithyia nodded and turned to the old woman, Sisyphis, who watched from the fireside with one of the young girls.

Sisyphis grinned, gap-toothed. "I already sent for Molossa. She's on her way."

Footsteps echoed in the corridor outside and another old woman hurried in, the other young girl close behind her. The girls busied themselves around the fire, steam already rising from a large pan of water.

The old woman, her grey hair bound and drawn back away from her face, bent over Tomyra. She ran her eyes over the girl without touching her before turning to Sisyphis. "Have you called me here without cause, Sisyphis? Her labour pains have not started."

"The servant girl didn't tell you, Molossa? She was poisoned. Arabian death weed."

Molossa frowned then bent over her patient again. She smiled encouragingly at Tomyra. "You are lucid, child? Yes, I see you are. Tell me exactly where the pain strikes."

"In the small of my back," whispered Tomyra. "A constant ache...but there are also stabbing pains in my...my womb."

"I must examine you, child." Molossa gently drew up Tomyra's robes then glanced up at Nikometros. "Who is this man?" she asked, her voice rising. "Why is he here?"

Bithyia hurried forward. "This is the lord Nikometros. Husband of Tomyra."

Molossa snorted and turned back to Tomyra. "This is no place for a man. Please leave."

"I will not leave," growled Nikometros. "Not until I am certain my wife and baby are safe."

"Then stand over there out of the way." Molossa waved in the general direction of the fireplace. "This is women's business now." She ignored Nikometros and leaned over Tomyra's swollen belly, gently feeling and prodding with her bony fingers. "Yes," she muttered. "There is blood. I think she will miscarry."

Turning to Sisyphis, she called for hot water and cloths. When they arrived, she used them to clean the blood from Tomyra's thighs. "She's close to eight months?" she muttered as she worked. "As I thought. Well, that's worse for her but perhaps there's a chance for the child. If she expels the infant quickly it may yet live. If not..." Molossa glanced up at Tomyra's wide eyes and lapsed into Persian. "If not, we'll lose both her and the child." She ran her hands over Tomyra's thighs and lower abdomen, feeling the muscles. "She's tight, her hips are small. Not good."

Sisyphis nodded. "She's a Scythian. Like all barbarians she was born astride a horse and has the body of warrior, not of a woman." The old woman grinned and glanced sideways at Nikometros. "He must be strong to have planted his seed in such a one."

"Well, she'll need her strength." Molossa glanced at Tomyra again and smiled reassuringly. "Nothing to worry about, my pet," she murmured in broken Greek. "Lie back and try to relax. I'll mix you up an herbal that will dilate you."

Nikometros stood awkwardly by the fireplace, his attention riveted on his wife. He strained to hear the old women's conversation and make sense of their whisperings. He knew enough Persian to be worried. He moved forward when the midwife got to her feet and took Sisyphis roughly by her arm. "I think we should find another midwife or call the doctor back. Does this woman even know what she is doing?"

Sisyphis winced and looked up at the tall Macedonian. "No doctor of any note will aid in a birth." She shrugged. "You may find a horse doctor or some barbarian potion-maker if you search. As for Molossa, you won't find a better midwife." She tried to pry Nikometros' fingers from her arm. "Now, my lord, if you'll release me I'll prepare your wife for her ordeal."

As she spoke, Tomyra drew a shuddering breath and her back arched again as a new wave of pain struck her.

112

Bithyia grabbed hold of Nikometros and drew him away from the old woman. "My lord, please," Bithyia said, her voice shaking with emotion. "You must let them do their work." She guided him to a chair against the far wall and knelt before him. "Niko, I'll remain with her and help her through this. It isn't seemly that you should be here though. This is a thing for women. We're trained to the mysteries of life, birth and ..." Bithyia's voice trailed away awkwardly.

Nikometros looked past her to the couch and his wife, racked with pain. "I'm staying," he growled.

"Then stay here and let me go to her."

She got to her feet and returned to the couch. Taking the cup of steaming liquid from Molossa, she knelt beside the couch, supporting Tomyra's head as she held the cup to her mistress' sweat-soaked face. She waited patiently as Tomyra sipped the pungent brew.

The two young girls, aided by Bithyia, got Tomyra to her feet and eased her across to the bed. Deftly they stripped away her crumpled and soiled robes and eased a clean white shift onto her before laying her on the bed. One girl bundled up the robes and removed them while the other started stroking Tomyra's face and arms with damp cloths.

Tomyra groaned again and tried to roll over onto her side. She drew her knees up, cradling her belly with her hands. "Niko!" she whispered.

"I'm here, my love," called Nikometros, getting to his feet and starting across the room. "Tell me how I can help."

Tomyra gazed across at him, her eyes wide as pain washed across her face. "Niko, my...love," she panted. "You must leave. It isn't right that...that you stay."

Nikometros shook his head. "I'm staying with you, Tomyra. I love you, I cannot leave you now."

"You must, Niko." Tomyra paused as a fresh pain stabbed her. "Every woman...whether Scythian, Greek...or Persian...gives birth with her women present." She paused again, panting. "Never with men, Niko. I'm in the hands of the Great Mother. She will help me. Leave me, please."

Bithyia came across and led him by the arm toward the doorway. "Listen to her, Niko. The Goddess brought her to this. Do you think She will desert her now?" She left him by the doorway and hurried back to the bed.

Molossa glanced across at Nikometros then dismissed him, turning her back and busying herself with the preparations. Sisyphis worked beside her, pulling back Tomyra's shift and applying warm herbal compresses to her belly. Across the bed, the two girls ran back and forth from the fire to the bed, renewing the cloths, bringing bowls of hot, clean water. One of the girls, returning from the pan of hot water on the fire, stopped abruptly, staring.

From the doorway came a strong clear voice. "I came as soon as I heard. How is she?"

Nikometros swung round and saw the tousled head of Alexander by his shoulder. The king glanced up at Nikometros and smiled, his eyes, one dark, one light, reflecting the depths of his worry. He put a hand on Nikometros' arm.

Molossa stiffened at the male voice and, without turning, raised her head. "How many more foolish men must I put up with? Go away," she snapped. "And when you go, at least make yourself useful by sending in more water."

Sisyphis looked up at the awestruck faces of the young girls then turned to the doorway. Her mouth fell open and she scrabbled with one hand to attract the midwife's attention.

Molossa glanced up at Sisyphis. "What?" she asked irritably. Turning, she caught sight of the king standing in the doorway beside Nikometros. With a gasp, she dropped to her knees on the floor and prostrated herself on the carpet, her action sending the other Persian women scrambling to follow suit.

Bithyia took Tomyra's hand firmly and remained standing, though she lowered her eyes.

Alexander grinned and stepped into the room. He walked over to the old midwife and stooping, lifted her gently to her feet. "Get up, old woman," he said softly. He looked into her eyes and smiled again. "Molossa, isn't it?" He turned to Nikometros. "She's delivered more babies than I have killed men." He laughed. "You could ask for no better midwife."

The king turned back to Molossa as she regained her feet. "Care for this woman well, Molossa." He turned back to the door and grinned again. "I'll send for more water too," he added.

In the doorway, Alexander looked back as the women hurried back to their business, once more unmindful of affairs outside the immediate task of birthing the woman before them. Alexander took Nikometros by the arm and ushered him into the corridor. "Come, Nikometros," he said. "Leave them to their mysteries. You cannot aid her in this."

"I know sir," replied Nikometros. "Yet I feel as if I'm abandoning her."

"They'll bring word to us if there's any development. Babies are born every day."

"Not every baby is induced by poison though," Nikometros grimly replied.

Alexander stopped and looked sharply up at the other man. "Poison?"

"Tomyra ate a sweetmeat poisoned by Arabian death weed. She was saved but the poison caused her to birth prematurely. The baby may die."

"Whence came the sweet? Do you know?"

"The note with it said Ptolemy, but I cannot believe it of him. There is no reason."

Alexander shook his head, his eyes blazing in the torchlight in the dim corridor. "Never Ptolemy. Few men are truer of heart." He stared off down the corridor for several moments. "I shall find out," he said slowly. He looked up at Nikometros. "I will find out, believe it of me. Poison is a dirty business, a coward's way, and I shall have their lives. No matter whom they are."

Nikometros grimly stared into Alexander's eyes and nodded.

Alexander smiled and took Nikometros by the arm. "Put it from your mind if you can. All that can be done will be done. Believe me. Now come, I would welcome your presence this morning."

Alexander led the way out into the courtyard where a squad of cavalry stood at attention. A servant brought a fine wool robe of white and purple, helping Alexander fasten it. A groom brought up a fine-looking white stallion to the king, while another led a bay stallion to Nikometros.

"There's an athletic contest for boys this morning," remarked Alexander while he led the squad clattering down the hill road through Ekbatana. "There are some promising young men among them. I told Hephaestion I would tell him all about it later."

"How is he sir?" enquired Nikometros.

"A lot better," replied Alexander with a laugh. "In fact, last night he wanted to get up and join me for supper. I told him to keep to the doctor's regime and we'd see how he felt today. It'll be good to have him out and about again." The king lifted his face to the warm sunshine and breathed in the cool morning air. "What a glorious day! I can tell this will be a day to remember."

# Chapter 14

Cheering erupted from the packed stadium as Alexander ran lithely up the wide marble steps to the Royal enclosure, his white and purple robe billowing behind him. He waved to the crowds, a broad smile on his face then turned to greet his friends and other high-ranking officials who stood expectantly near the raised dais.

Nikometros followed slowly, his mind preoccupied with worry. He nodded perfunctorily to the generals and other court officers before finding a seat near the parapet overlooking the arena. The sand of the stadium floor gleamed in the sunlight, swept and cleaned from the previous day's events. At either end of the stadium, huge doors stood open, ready to disgorge the current day's crop of competitors. Nikometros' eyes slipped upward, over the crowds rising in great serried ranks around the arena, to the distant spires and gilded roofs of the King's palace.

*What am I doing here?* he thought. *I should be with Tomyra.*

The king stepped forward to the edge of the enclosure and raised his arms. Rapidly the noise and chatter of the crowd died away, the stadium lapsing into an expectant hush. Alexander smiled and pitched his voice into the silence like a trumpet call on a still day. "Friends," he called, the acoustics of the stadium carrying his words to the farthest seats. "Today we see the future. Before us, the youth of our great empire, of Macedonia and Persia and the most distant lands compete for the crown of victory. Join with me in this celebration of youth." Alexander signalled and a trumpet note rang out, releasing a torrent of young boys and youths from either end of the arena.

The crowd surged to its feet, clapping and cheering. Alexander grinned broadly and sat down, his eyes gleaming as the boys formed up into precise ranks in front of him and raised a treble paean of praise. He acknowledged the tribute with a nod and a wave. The boys broke formation and hurried to different parts of the arena to start several varied competitions.

Alexander accepted a cup of wine and beckoned his friends to pull their chairs closer to his.

Nikometros noticed the Macedonian officers readily accepted the invitation, casually pressing in around the king, even walking in front of him. The Persian nobles seemed perturbed at this familiarity and bowed deeply, carefully walking round behind Alexander, keeping their heads lowered as they approached.

"Nikometros!" called Alexander. "Join me." He indicated a seat beside him, occupied by Peukestas.

The general got up and nodded to Nikometros as he approached, moving back to evict a lesser officer a few rows back. Nikometros pushed through the throng, excusing himself as he went, then stopped as someone stood up in front of him. He looked up to see Ptolemy's smiling face.

"Good day to you, Nikometros," Ptolemy said.

Nikometros stared at him, his suspicions raging up inside. He opened his mouth to accuse him, thought better of it and pushed past to the recently vacated seat.

Ptolemy looked after him with a frown on his face.

Alexander pointed at the activity in the arena as Nikometros sat down. "See, the footrace is about to begin. Perdikkas, who do you pick to win?"

Perdikkas leaned forward, examining the runners warming up on the starting line. "A short race, Alexander. No stamina required. I think the tall dark one."

Ptolemy snorted. "You obviously have not seen Kepher run. The Egyptian. A head shorter but well built." He smiled again, hesitantly, at Nikometros. "You agree, Nikometros?"

Nikometros shook his head. "No. The dark one," he muttered.

Perdikkas leaned across and clapped Nikometros on the shoulder. "Good man. You choose well."

Ptolemy frowned again and turned back to the arena.

Alexander grinned. "What about the tall fair one? He has the look of a runner. What do you think Eumenes?"

Eumenes smiled ingratiatingly and dropped his gaze. "Oh, yes, Alexander. An excellent choice. Without a doubt, the tall fair one."

Alexander raised an eyebrow while Perdikkas openly sneered.

"Care to put a wager on that, Eumenes?" asked Perdikkas. "I have a thousand gold darics that say the dark boy beats your fair one."

Eumenes glowered and shook his head.

Perdikkas laughed loudly. "No balls, eh, Eumenes? The gods know you have wealth enough."

Eumenes flushed and glared at the general. "Very well then, if you insist," he ground out.

Alexander leaned over and tapped Perdikkas on the knee. "I'll take half that wager myself."

Ptolemy grunted and nodded. "A thousand on the Egyptian then. Any takers?"

Perdikkas smiled. "I think Nikometros and I have enough confidence in our boy to cover that, Ptolemy."

Nikometros opened his mouth to comment when a shout went up from the crowd as the runners leapt into action.

The Egyptian boy, Kepher, raced into the lead, closely followed by the tall fair-haired boy and a tall Persian youth. The rest of the runners followed in the dust, the tall dark boy trailing the pack.

Perdikkas groaned. "What in Hades is wrong with the boy? Come on!" he yelled, rising to his feet.

The boys ran on down the stadium to the far marker. Rounding the stone pillar, the boys jostled for position and Kepher lost his balance, sprawling in the dust. Two boys fell with him but the fair-haired youth leapt over the tangle of limbs and set off for the finish. The main body of youths rounded the mark, the dark boy swinging wide and bypassing the confusion. He raced off after the leader, his dark limbs pumping.

Alexander rose to his feet in excitement as the boys neared the finish. "Oh, bravely run!" he cried. "I think your boy will catch him Perdikkas."

The other generals and lesser officers surged up as the dark boy passed the marker half a step ahead of his fair rival. A colonel of infantry threw up his arms with a curse and caught Alexander a glancing blow. The officer, unaware, muttered an apology through the side of his mouth, his attention riveted on the finish. The Persian nobles gasped at the insult, waiting for the man to be hauled off to his death.

Alexander just smiled and leaned toward Eumenes. "It seems we're not the only ones to lose money on this race." He turned back to his other friends as they resumed their seats. "A good race. Call at the treasury, Perdikkas. I'll see the money awaits you...and Nikometros. Ptolemy, Eumenes...I'll leave you to make your own arrangements." He looked into the arena again. "What's next? Archery?"

The archery competition progressed slowly, the boys firing at a straw figure. Gradually the number of contestants fell away until only two were left. Attendants carried the arrow-riddled target from the arena and another attached a live pigeon by a cord on one foot to a tall pole that he raised aloft. The bird fluttered wildly, pulling at the cord.

A small Cretan boy stepped up to the mark and loosed an arrow. The shaft flashed by the moving pigeon, dislodging a small feather that spiralled downward in the gentle breeze. The crowd applauded, the noise dying away when the second archer approached.

The youth, a tall Hindu from the eastern empire, took a long time selecting an arrow. Having done so, he turned toward the Royal dais and bowed then turned his attention toward the fluttering bird. He drew back the bow and stood motionless as the bird flapped and tugged at its restraint. He released the arrow as the bird fell back, dangling from the cord.

A gasp went up from the crowd when the arrow sliced through the cord a finger-width from the bird. The pigeon fell, recovered itself and flapped frantically, soaring up into the sky.

Alexander led the applause. "A difficult choice for the judges," he remarked. "Though I think on balance the second..."

Almost every eye in the stadium watched the swiftly shrinking dot of the pigeon as it flew up over the stands. Few saw the Cretan boy snatch an arrow from the ground, fit it as he whirled about and loosed into the void. Far above, the soaring bird abruptly slumped and plummeted to the ground, transfixed. It landed with a thump not far from the Royal enclosure, bright blood staining its white plumage. For several moments the crowd sat in stunned silence then erupted into a cacophony of shouts and clapping.

"By the gods," breathed Alexander. "My best archers couldn't do that." He beckoned to the attendants. "Fetch that boy up here!"

The boy arrived, breathless but grinning. His eyes widened when he recognised the fair-haired man standing smiling on the steps in front of him. Dropping clumsily to one knee, he looked down at the ground.

Alexander's smile widened and he stepped forward, grasping the boy by his shoulders and raising him to his feet. He stooped and kissed the boy lightly on the forehead. "What is your name?" he asked.

"A...Aristes, sir," stammered the boy.

"Well, Aristes, that shot will be talked about for years. What god did you pray to this morning?"

"A...Apollo, sir. Far...far-seeing Apollo," stuttered Aristes. "It seemed only right to pray to the Archer."

"Indeed," replied Alexander. "And he heard your prayer. You must remember to sacrifice to him tonight." He smiled. "A pigeon perhaps." Alexander dug into the small calfskin purse at his belt and took out a gold coin. He handed it to the boy.

Aristes stared at the coin for several moments before muttering breathless thanks. He backed away, his hand knuckling his forehead.

Alexander sat down again amid a smattering of applause from his friends. He grinned and called for another cup of wine, sipping it as the attendants in the arena organised the next event.

"Javelins," commented Ptolemy. "This should be interesting, Alexander. I was watching some of them practicing the other day and one or two of them..." He broke off as heads turned toward the stadium seating. "Now what?" he asked, with a trace of annoyance in his voice as he rose to his feet.

A court official ran up the stairs from the stadium entrance, pushing aside anyone who got in his way. An attendant stopped the official at the entrance to the Royal enclosure. The official tried to push past, his voice rising in agitation. Alexander looked over at the disturbance and frowned, signalling the man over.

"My lord," quavered the official as he bowed to the king. "You must come...er, that is...lord Hephaestion, he..." The man's voice ran down and he stood staring at the ground, his fingers gripping and pulling at his tunic.

"Speak plainly, man," Alexander said softly. "What is it you are trying to say?"

The man took a deep breath and raised his eyes hesitantly to the king's. "Lord Hephaestion, sir. He...he has collapsed. I think he may..."

Alexander blanched beneath his bronzed tan. He raised his eyes briefly to the distant citadel of Ekbatana then pushing through the throng of his friends and officers and raced down the broad stadium stairs toward the entrance.

A heartbeat passed as Ptolemy and Perdikkas stared at each other then they too ran for the stairs.

Nikometros hesitated a moment longer before signalling to the other adjutants. "Follow," Nikometros snapped. "Go with the king. We must guard him."

By the time Nikometros and the others emerged from the stadium, the king was nowhere to be seen. Men stood and stared up the road that led to the palace, muttering and pointing. The army officers at once commandeered horses and set off at a gallop toward the city, flogging their mounts hard in an effort to catch up.

As they rode into the palace courtyard, the horses blowing hard in a lather of sweat, Nikometros caught sight of Ptolemy and Perdikkas disappearing between the columns into the cool darkness of the palace.

Seleukos, one of the adjutants, pointed off to the left. "Hephaestion's quarters. Hurry!" He leapt from his horse.

Their footsteps echoed and clattered along the corridors, servants clustering in the doorways, whispering. They were on the main stairway when a great cry of anguish arose from the darkness in front of them.

Nikometros felt the hair on his neck prickle and he paused for an instant before hurrying on, a feeling of dread rising in him.

Hephaestion's room was richly furnished in crimson wall hangings and ornately inlaid wood. A smell of sickness hung in the still air. On the bed lay Hephaestion, his pale face turned up, his mouth and eyes open wide.

Alexander lay across the body, gripping it fiercely, his face buried in the long golden hair. He raised his head, his eyes blank and staring and uttered another anguished cry.

Perdikkas stepped forward. "Alexander," he said hesitantly.

Alexander looked up and through the throng of people at the door to the room. With a struggle, his eyes focused and he leapt off the bed, pacing toward the door. "Where is he?" groaned the king. "Where is the doctor?"

Ptolemy looked around then shrugged. "I don't know, Alexander. At the games, maybe?"

A noise erupted from the corridor behind Nikometros and he turned to see the doctor pushing through the crowd, a worried look on his face.

Alexander strode across and, gripping the man by his tunic, threw him across the room. Leaping after him, he dragged him to his feet and shook him like a dog shakes a rat, screaming at him. "Murderer!" yelled Alexander. "Why did you leave him?" He thrust the doctor's face toward the dishes beside the bed, where the remains of a chicken still sat in congealed grease. "Why did you let him eat?"

The doctor stammered, his eyes rolling in his head. "He...he seemed better, sir. But I ordered only broth, not chicken."

Alexander threw the doctor to the floor. "Hang him," he said coldly. "Now."

Perdikkas looked across at Ptolemy then nodded. He beckoned Seleukos and Nikometros. "Take him away," he ordered.

Nikometros hauled the trembling doctor to his feet and walked him to the door, Seleukos picking out a dozen soldiers as an escort. Nikometros glanced back as he left the room. Alexander laid on the body of his friend once more, sobs wracking his frame. The purple and white state robe he wore covered them both like a shroud. Generals and adjutants stood off to one side, silently, looking at their king and each other.

Nikometros and Seleukos marched the doctor down the corridors and out of the palace. The only sound, apart from the measured tread of the soldiers, was the snuffling sobs of the prisoner.

"Do we really hang him?" whispered Nikometros.

Seleukos frowned. "Ordinarily, I wouldn't hesitate. One doesn't question the king's orders. However, the king is..." he hesitated. "...distracted."

"So, what do we do?"

Seleukos shrugged. "What do you suggest?"

Nikometros thought hard. "The king is, as you put it, distracted at the moment. When he comes to his senses he may want to question the doctor. It'd be a pity if we were too zealous."

Seleukos looked at him sidelong. "Dangerous," he muttered. "If he thought we disobeyed him..."

"Lock him up," urged Nikometros. "If after a few days the king shows signs of wanting to find out what happened, we can produce him. If not," he shrugged. "Then we follow our orders."

Seleukos led the soldiers down through the city to the main barracks and the prison cells. He hesitated at the entrance to the execution courtyard then turned aside toward the cells. "Very well, Nikometros," he said as the soldiers locked the doctor into one of the dirty stone chambers. "We'll wait until the king is himself again."

# Chapter 15

Nikometros struggled out of a fitful sleep before daybreak. He rubbed itching eyes and looked across to where Timon sat by the window, staring out at the paling eastern sky. "What news?" he croaked.

Timon turned with an expression of concern. "None yet, Niko. Bithyia was here a few moments ago. The night passed quietly enough but the midwife thinks the birth will come soon."

"Gods," muttered Nikometros, running fingers through his tousled hair. He yawned and stretched, getting up and walking to the far corner. He passed water into a large urn, leaning against the wall as he did so. "How is Tomyra holding up?"

"Well enough, considering." Timon poured two cups of wine and passed one to his friend. "She's sleeping for now. Don't concern yourself, Niko. She's in good hands."

Nikometros walked to the window. Below him, Ekbatana slowly awoke to the new day. "What of the king?"

Timon frowned. "No change. His friends--Perdikkas, Peukestas and Ptolemy--persuaded him to move to his own room. He's there now."

Nikometros sipped wine for several minutes as the sky lightened. He rubbed a hand over the stubble on his chin and yawned again. "I must attend to the king," he murmured. "But first I must make myself presentable and see Tomyra."

The sun shone warmly on the walls of the chamber by the time Nikometros stood washed and shaved and clad in a clean tunic of Timon's. He donned his crumpled robe from the day before and refastened his sandals. Leaving the room, he and Timon marched down the hallway to his quarters where they were forced to wait while the main doors were unbarred. A young serving girl poked her head round the door. She squeaked and ducked back inside, trying vainly to close the door against the determined efforts of the men.

Nikometros pushed into the room and stared across at the great bed. Tomyra lay still under the rumpled sheets, her black hair lying matted and untidy on the pillows. Beside her sat Bithyia, a rag in her hand as she wiped the unconscious woman's face. The coppery stink of blood mingled with the heavy odours of herbs and wood smoke.

The midwife hurried to intercept Nikometros. "You cannot stay, sir."

"I will see my wife."

Molossa hesitated then nodded. "She's sleeping, sir. Go to her but don't wake her. She'll need her strength."

Nikometros crossed to the bed and gently sat across from Bithyia. "How is she?"

Bithyia smiled wanly, exhaustion showing in every line on her face. "She's strong, Niko. She throws off the effect of the death weed, but the baby...well, it comes too soon."

Nikometros took one of Tomyra's hands in his, feeling a fluttery pulse through his fingertips. He leaned forward and kissed Tomyra's cheek then her hand. "Look after her, Bithyia," he murmured.

"You must go, sir," Molossa said while plucking at his sleeve. "I must prepare her for the birth."

"Don't let her die, old woman."

Molossa shrugged. "She's strong and the Mother sustains her. As for the child...that's in the hands of the gods. I'll do my best. Now go."

Nikometros and Timon walked out into the courtyard then under the colonnades toward the palace. The buildings hummed with unease, groups of servants and officials, high-ranking officers and common soldiers milling around talking in low voices. Slaves busied themselves as they took down festive banners and replaced them with mourning wreaths.

"Where to, Niko?" asked Timon.

Nikometros shrugged. "To see Perdikkas, I suppose. He's my immediate superior."

However, none of the office clerks knew the whereabouts of the general. They intimated that he had not sent word and for all they knew was still in the west wing of the palace. 'Was it true,' the secretaries asked, 'that lord Hephaestion was poisoned and the king maddened with grief?'

With some difficulty, Nikometros and Timon extricated themselves from the offices, fending off searching questions with noncommittal answers.

On the way to Hephaestion's chambers, they ran into Seleukos. The adjutant was hurrying through the corridors with a harried look on his face. "Nikometros, thank the gods I ran into you," he babbled. "Look, I'm worried we acted out of turn yesterday. The doctor, Glaukios, I think we should hang him after all."

"I thought we decided to keep him alive until the king had the opportunity to question him? He wasn't thinking clearly when he ordered his death." Nikometros took Seleukos by the arm and drew him aside. "People are saying he was poisoned."

Seleukos licked his lips nervously. "All the more reason then."

"What do you mean?"

"If Glaukios did...you know..." Seleukos glanced around the halls and dropped his voice to a whisper. "Who had reason to hate Hephaestion? Who stands to gain by his death? One of the top generals. And what happens when they find out we're keeping him alive?" He shivered. "No, we must kill him."

"He's right, Niko," murmured Timon. "Not only that but you say the king ordered it? You cannot disobey a direct order from the king."

Nikometros frowned. "I don't like it. If there's a poisoner at work...Ptolemy?"

Seleukos stared at him. "What about Ptolemy? What have you heard?"

"My wife was poisoned yesterday. She lives but the poison came from Ptolemy, or so says the note."

"You have this note? Let me see it."

Nikometros fumbled in his purse and handed over the crumpled piece of paper.

Seleukos read it, turned it over, held it up to the light then reread it. "It isn't in his hand, but then I wouldn't expect it. The paper is coarse too, not palace paper." Seleukos sighed and handed the note back. "I wouldn't expect it of Ptolemy."

"Nor I." Nikometros jerked his head toward Hephaestion's chambers. "What's happening up there?"

"Not much. The embalmers are seeing to him, thank the gods. Much longer in this heat and he would stink."

"And the king?"

"In his own rooms still and his friends attend him."

"Embalmers?" asked Timon. "Isn't he going to be cremated then?"

Seleukos shrugged. "No doubt, but Alexander will want to see to the funeral arrangements himself. If there is to be a delay then the body must be preserved. There are plenty of Egyptians in the city...why, even your old priest volunteered."

"Ket?" asked Nikometros. "He's in there?"

"Yes, well, I must be going," said Seleukos. "Think hard about the doctor, Nikometros. If I hear nothing to the contrary from the king by midday, I intend to hang him." He nodded and hurried off down the corridor.

Nikometros grimaced and resumed walking toward Hephaestion's apartments. Guards nodded to him at the door, letting them into the chamber. The body of the Chiliarch lay on a stretcher beside the bed, washed and anointed with pungent ointments to hold back the odours of decay. Several men busied themselves around the corpse, their bald heads and crisp white linen kilts marking them out as Egyptian. To one side stood the priest Ket, clad in a long white robe with a broad gold necklace hanging over his chest. He looked up with rheumy eyes as Nikometros entered.

"My lord Nikometros," Ket said, bowing. "And Timon. We have nearly finished here. In a few moments we will transport lord Hephaestion to the mortuary and prepare his body."

"Greetings, Ket," replied Nikometros with a smile. "I didn't look to see you here." He glanced around the chamber. "You're in charge of the embalming?"

"Indeed. I am a priest of Ammon-Ra. I am familiar with the procedures."

One of the embalmers approached and bowed low to Ket. "He is ready, high one."

Ket nodded. "Take him then, but with dignity. Remember he was a lord in life and beloved of the king."

The embalmers covered the corpse with a clean linen sheet, picked up the stretcher and walked sedately from the room. Ket followed.

Nikometros followed the procession. He watched as it set off down the road toward the lower levels of the citadel and the city mortuary. He turned and looked back toward the palace before gesturing to Timon. Then he set out for the Royal apartments.

The halls leading to the king's quarters bristled with people, subdued but eager for any word of the king's health and frame of mind. Nikometros pushed through, his rank giving him access to the less crowded antechambers. He saw Perdikkas and Ptolemy in earnest discussion, with a steady stream of junior officers bringing in reports and hurrying away with orders.

Perdikkas looked up as Nikometros approached. "Ah, there you are!" he exclaimed. "I wondered where you'd got to. We have a busy day ahead of us."

Nikometros glanced toward Alexander's chamber. "The king is recovered then?"

"No. However, the business of the empire must go on regardless. He won't thank us if the place is in chaos."

"Where is the doctor hanging?" asked Ptolemy. "He's sure to ask."

Nikometros hesitated. "He's still alive, sir."

"Alive?" Ptolemy glanced around and lowered his voice. "What in Hades do you think you're doing? The king gave you a direct order."

"Sir...there's talk that he...that Hephaestion was poisoned. If the doctor is killed we may never find out who gave him his orders."

"Are you mad?" hissed Ptolemy. "Let people think he was murdered and we'll have a civil war on our hands."

"He died of a flux, Nikometros," interposed Perdikkas quietly. "The doctor erred only by leaving him untended. Solid food too soon after a weakness of the stomach can kill." He held his junior officer's eye. "That is all that happened. Unfortunate, but life goes on for the rest of us."

Nikometros looked from one general to the other. "Yes sir," he said at length. "Yet there is a poisoner in our midst."

"I thought I just told you..."

"An attempt was made on my wife with poison yesterday, sir."

Perdikkas stared at him. "Your wife?"

"She lives?" asked Ptolemy. "Are you sure it was poison and not some illness?"

Nikometros opened his purse and drew out the note. He passed it to Perdikkas who read it then held it out to Ptolemy.

Ptolemy stared at Nikometros with a stiff look of insult. "You think I did it?"

"Come," said Perdikkas with a glint in his eyes. "I'm sure he means no such thing. Anyone can see it isn't in your hand."

"Do you think I would be fool enough to sign my name to such a thing?" Screwing up the piece of paper and flinging it to the floor, Ptolemy spun away and started for the door. Abruptly he turned back and pushed his angry face close to Nikometros. "I thought better of you. For your mother's sake I was...ah, to Hades with you." He stormed off, pushing past Timon.

Perdikkas raised an eyebrow. "For your mother's sake, Nikometros? What's the significance here?"

Nikometros cleared his throat and looked toward the doorway. "He is...my mother and he..."

Perdikkas snorted. "By the paps of Aphrodite! Born on the other side of the blanket, eh? Well, no great shame there. A man is what he makes of himself." He clapped Nikometros on the shoulder. "I can recognise your talents, young Nikometros. Stick with me and you'll go far."

Timon stooped and retrieved the crumpled note. He carefully smoothed it out and put it into his purse.

Perdikkas drew Nikometros aside and put his arm around his shoulder, talking quietly. "Now, we've cancelled the games and ordered the city into mourning. Peukestas is handling the foreign visitors and Eumenes concerns himself as usual with such correspondence as cannot wait. Ptolemy is keeping a firm hand on the army and I control the court. There is not much else we can do until we know Alexander's mind. What you must do, immediately, is hang the doctor."

"Seleukos is to do it at midday if there's no word from the king."

Perdikkas shook his head. "Don't wait; do it now." He glanced at Timon. "Send your man. There are important things we must discuss."

Nikometros nodded to Timon. "You heard? Then do it, Timon. I'll meet you back at our quarters."

# Chapter Sixteen

Timon sat in a seedy-looking tavern in the Street of Horses, nursing a large mug of watered wine. He grimaced, remembering the screams of the doctor Glaukios when they dragged him away to his death. He lifted the mug and swallowed half the contents in a series of great gulps.

Across from him, similarly engrossed, sat Tirses and Berinax. The two Scythian warriors looked out of place in the city, their dark brown eyes dreamy and fixed on a place only they could find, seeing in their minds the vast rolling plains of grass of their native land. Increasingly of late, as the full extent of their self-imposed exile sank in, the Massegetae followers of Nikometros sought solace in drink. Warriors of the horse, they gravitated to familiar surroundings and were often seen in the horse lines, along the streets bordering the stockyards, and in the shops and stalls selling horse tack and feed.

Timon pulled the crumpled scrap of paper from his purse and smoothed it out on the table. He read the elegant script slowly, his mouth forming the words silently then read them again.

Berinax leaned over the table and tapped the paper with his forefinger. "What's that then?"

"A note," replied Timon shortly. "It came with a gift to Tomyra."

Tirses belched and peered down at the piece of paper. "A gift." He attempted a smile but only achieved a drunken leer. "Nice to have gifts."

"Not this sort," muttered Timon. "Someone tried to poison her."

Tirses stared at Timon and carefully placed his cup on the table. "Poison? Our priestess? When did this happen?"

"If you attended upon your lady and your commander instead of carousing in the brothels and taverns, you would know these things."

"Answer me, Timon," grated Tirses. "When did this happen and who did it?"

"Yesterday morning." Timon shrugged. "It wasn't successful but it brought on the birth early. She may miscarry."

Tirses staggered to his feet and stood swaying over the table, staring down at Timon. "I will have his blood for this," he shouted. "I will cut off his genitals and feed them to the dogs, I will..."

"Sit down," snapped Timon, grasping Tirses' arm. "And keep silent if you wish to help your lady. You too, Berinax," he added as the other Scythian opened his mouth. Timon waited until the conversation around them at the other tables started up again. He looked round the room then turned back to his companions. "We don't know who sent the poison," he whispered. "Only that this note came with it." He shoved the note across the table.

Tirses scanned the note then turned it over and examined the blank back. "What does it say? I cannot read Greek."

"It's in Macedonian. It says 'A Gift from Ptolemy'."

"Then let us find this Tol...person and kill him," Berinax declared.

"Why haven't you done so already?" asked Tirses. "Who is this Tol-me?"

"Lord Ptolemy. General of the Armies, half-brother to Alexander and father of Nikometros." A wry smile twisted Timon's mouth. "You see why we cannot just kill him."

Tirses became subdued. "Even so, this is a land of law. Surely even such as he must answer to the king."

"Or is the king guilty too?" muttered Berinax.

"Hsst!" Timon grabbed Berinax's arm. "Don't even think that," he whispered. "Men who accuse kings, die. Even one like Alexander who binds himself by law." He shook his head. "No, the king isn't involved. Nor do I really believe Ptolemy is responsible. The only evidence is the note."

"It names him," Tirses hissed.

"Would you put your name to such a gift? No, someone used the general's name to cover himself. Maybe to get past the guards too."

"So what do we do?" asked Tirses.

"We must ask among the servants of the court. Servants and slaves see many things. Someone must have seen who delivered the poison."

"The Lions can ask in the city," added Tirses. "We can go places gentlemen such as yourself couldn't go."

Timon nodded. "Berinax. Can you be trusted to deal with this? You cannot tell anyone who is suspect but you must get your friends searching immediately. Look for anything suspicious, anyone who might bear Nikometros or Tomyra a grudge. Be discreet and report back if you find anything."

Berinax rubbed his eyes and belched again. He nodded and pushed his stool back. "Aye, Timon. You can rely on us. If there's anything to find in the city, we'll find it." He straightened and staggered toward the door, pushing his way past the other customers of the tavern.

"Don't worry," Tirses said with a slight smile. "He may be drunk now but he'll sober up fast enough. He's a good man." He ran his fingers through dark hair and shook his long locks out. "What do we do, Timon?"

"Back to the court. Someone must have seen the person who brought the gift. I have an idea where to start."

Together, the two men left the tavern on the Street of Horses and turned toward the main thoroughfare that ran up through the seven levels of the citadel. The crowded city streets bustled with a hundred businesses, every man shouting his wares, pointing to a shop or craftsman, gossiping, arguing, touting or pimping for customers. Children, from ragged clothed urchins to finely dressed scions of merchant houses, ran and played, ducking and weaving through the crowds. Whores plied their trade from street corners or in darkened doorways. A dozen languages assailed their ears and many more odours assaulted their nostrils. Exotic perfumes, cooking foods, spices and ordure, animal and human, filled the air. People from the far reaches of the empire, drawn by the glittering promise of Alexander's court, surged through narrow streets, seeking the riches that followed a conquering army.

Pushing up to the gates of the first tier, Timon and Tirses were challenged by the guard.

Timon grinned and nodded in recognition. "Ho, Stenos," called Timon. "I thought you weren't on duty today."

The guard looked at Timon and spat to one side. "I wasn't until my rotting commander put me on extra detail."

"I have no doubt it was completely undeserved."

"Aah, it was nothing," grumbled Stenos. "Pissing in the guardroom instead of going all the way out to the privy. It was a dark night and I wasn't feeling well. What's the harm?"

"Indeed," commented Timon. "Well, will you sign us through, Stenos?"

Stenos nodded and signed to a clerk who sat at a rough table in the shade of the citadel walls. "Timon, inner court and...yes, Tirses, Scythian envoy."

The clerk rifled through a few pages of parchment and found their names. He made a mark by each and nodded.

Stenos turned back to Timon with a lascivious grin on his face. "Perhaps I can interest you gentlemen in a rather extraordinary pleasure?" He rubbed his hands together.

"Another time," Timon replied as he stepped through the gate.

"What pleasure?" asked Tirses.

Stenos furtively scanned the area and pulled Timon and Tirses to one side. "Odda," he said. "Odda the Galician. She's a whore, but no common one. Newly arrived from Babylon and well versed in all the tricks of the trade. If you tell her I sent you, she'll..."

"I think not," interrupted Timon.

Stenos scowled and shrugged. "Well, next time maybe. But don't delay too long. She's in great demand."

Leaving Stenos in the gateway, Timon and Tirses hurried on up the main street. The guards at the other gates leading to the higher levels also knew Timon but their rank was higher and their manners more refined. They passed the two men through while exchanging only pleasantries. When they reached the level where the minor court officials and servants resided, Timon turned aside into a small, winding street. He pointed toward a solid but unassuming house surrounded by a small courtyard. He knocked on the outer door and, after exchanging a few words with the gatekeeper, entered a shaded courtyard.

A few moments later, a portly man in rich silks appeared in the portico of the house and hurried across to them, his arms open wide and a broad smile on his face. He embraced Timon exuberantly then stepped back. "Timon," he exclaimed in a high-pitched voice. "Why have you taken so long to come and see me?" He turned to Tirses and cocked his head to one side expectantly.

"Chrysoas, may I present the leader of the Massegetae delegation, Tirses, son of Pragmyges. Tirses, this is Chrysoas, Entertainment Master to the high court."

"Er...yes, greetings," stammered Tirses. He bowed low to cover his confusion.

Chrysoas smiled and bowed low himself. "I am delighted to meet you at long last," he enthused. "I'm eager to hear what you think of Persia. It must be very different from your empty plains." He turned toward the house and sharply clapped his hands. "Where is that boy? Excuse me, my friends, pray be seated and I'll find us some refreshment." He gestured at some cushioned benches in the shade of a large peach tree before hurrying off toward the house.

"Timon," hissed Tirses as soon as Chrysoas disappeared. "He...is he...you know, a 'cut' man?"

"Chrysoas is a court eunuch, if that's what you mean. He's a good man, unambitious and unassuming. He has access to many parts of the court we could never get to."

"But a eunuch..." Tirses shook his head. "I've heard stories of them. Is he cut down to...to a woman's parts? Who would want to be such a thing?"

"He didn't choose his life," Timon snapped. "He was sold into it as a young boy. Chrysoas made the best of what the gods threw at him." He glanced toward the house. "Now be polite, Tirses. We're his guests, in his house. Treat him as you would any other gentleman."

Chrysoas bustled up with a young boy who bore a large silver tray. The boy clumsily set the tray down on a small table, bowed to his master and scampered off. Chrysoas sighed and shook his head. "It's so hard to find good servants these days." He turned back to his guests with a smile. "May

I offer you refreshment? I have a delightful citron drink in crushed ice. I bring the ice from the mountains to the north, five days travel. Dreadfully expensive, but citron is really not worth drinking unless it's cold." He poured the drink into tall silver cups and passed them to Timon and Tirses.

Timon sipped and smiled. "Delicious, Chrysoas. Your hospitality truly overwhelms us."

Tirses also drank then muttered his appreciation.

"I find citron so much more refreshing than wine," Chrysoas said. "Also, one can keep a clear head. I feel this is important when discussing delicate matters."

"Indeed," Timon agreed. "Misunderstandings often stem from over-indulgence."

"And what of Scythia, Tirses son of Pragmyges? Do Scythians drink wine?"

"Er...no. That is...yes, sometimes," Tirses stammered. "It is expensive as grapes don't grow in our land."

"Interesting. What is it you drink then?"

"Koumiss. We make it from the milk of mares, fermented in leather flasks."

Chrysoas averted his eyes, lifting a delicately embroidered napkin to his mouth as he gave a small shudder. "Fascinating," he whispered.

An awkward silence fell. Chrysoas poured more iced citron and the three men sat in the dappled shade sipping at their drinks.

At last Chrysoas put down his cup and cleared his throat. "We waste time with trivialities. I regret you didn't come to see me out of friendship, did you Timon?"

"I value your friendship, Chrysoas, but...no."

"The whole court is in an uproar over the death of lord Hephaestion," stated the eunuch. "Many fear for the sanity of the king. Perhaps this concerns you?" He watched Timon closely then shook his head. "No, not this. Then it must be the attempt on the life of your lord Nikometros and his wife."

"You know of this?"

Chrysoas smiled. "Little goes on at court that doesn't reach my ears sooner or later."

"Have you heard anything about who is responsible?"

Chrysoas pursed his lips and thought for a few moments. "You have the note that came with the gift?"

Timon raised his eyebrows then dug into his purse before passing over the soiled paper.

Chrysoas examined it for a moment, rubbing the paper between delicate fingers and lifting it to his nostrils before passing it back. "Who do you suspect?"

"This Tol-me person," blurted Tirses. "But Timon explained..."

"It was not lord Ptolemy," interrupted Chrysoas.

"You know this for a certainty?" asked Timon, leaning forward. "How?"

Chrysoas reached over and tapped the note with a manicured fingertip. "The language is Macedonian but the writer was not Macedonian."

"Eh?" Timon looked down at the scrap of paper. "How can you tell?"

Chrysoas leaned back and steepled his hands on his large belly. He gazed up at the leafy branches above him. "Timon, my friend," he quietly replied. "Forgive me, but your family in Macedonia...were not at the royal court very often, were they?"

Timon flushed and looked down at his boots. "No. My father was a hill chief. He never went to the court. Neither did I until I enlisted and then it was just to pass through Pella on the way to war."

"I didn't mean to cause you offence, my friend. I merely wished to make the point that you are relatively unfamiliar with court etiquette and the forms of nobility."

Tirses frowned. "You talk in riddles."

Chrysoas smiled. "A note that came from the office of Lord Ptolemy would use an honorific and almost certainly would use the full form of his name rather than his familiar army abbreviation."

"More riddles!" snorted Tirses.

"His full name?" Timon frowned.

"Ptolemaios. If the note derived from his offices, it would probably read 'A gift from Lord Ptolemaios'."

"So, where did it come from?" asked Tirses.

"Ah, that is harder," replied Chrysoas with a smile. "However, I would hazard it came from the pen of a scribe in the Street of Artists, near the Amphitheatre. Probably one that is situated near a shop selling kohl and henna."

Timon frowned. "This isn't a subject for jest, my friend."

"Nor would I. The paper is coarse, not at all the quality one might expect from the court. The hand is neat, as from the hand of a scribe or artist, not scrawled, and there are faint smudges of makeup powders on the back of it." Chrysoas' smile grew broader. "Unless you have taken to making yourself more beautiful, my friend."

"Makeup?" Timon queried.

"Also cinnamon, but that came from a small stain that might have come later."

Tirses muttered a string of expletives under his breath. Then, "You got all that from that scrap of paper?"

"When you live long in a place where every man seeks betterment at the cost of your own, you learn to be observant."

Timon nodded and got to his feet. "Chrysoas, my friend, I thank you," he rumbled. "I don't wish to seem rude or hasty..."

"But you must take your leave," finished Chrysoas. "I quite understand. Perhaps you would be so kind as to send word if your search is successful?" He ushered the two men to the courtyard gates and bid them farewell.

Tirses turned to Timon as they hurried back onto the main citadel road. "You believe him? All that nonsense about scribes and makeup?"

Timon shrugged, turning down through the walled fortress toward the city once more. "Possibly. He knows many things. Anyway, we shall see presently."

The Street of Scribes wound haphazardly along the contour of the hill, close to the vast bowl of the amphitheatre. Timon and Tirses walked slowly along the length of the street, pausing at each scribe's place of business and scanning the surrounding shops and stalls for cosmetic supplies. The afternoon wore on as they continued, eventually stopping at a stall to buy a cup of thin wine apiece.

"This is pointless," grumbled Tirses. "There are dozens of scribes and such stalls as sell kohl and henna wander from place to place on different days. We could already have passed the place."

Timon drained his cup of wine and stifled a belch. "What else do you suggest we do?" Turning to the wine seller he held out a small silver piece. "We are looking for a shop that sells cosmetics. Not a stall, you understand, but a reputable shop. Our mistress wants good quality."

The wine seller took the coin and examined it closely before slipping it into his tunic. "Up the street." He jerked his thumb in the general direction of the amphitheatre. "Can't miss it. Has a red awning." He turned away to serve another customer.

"Why a shop?" muttered Tirses as they set off up the street. "It could just as well be one of these itinerant stalls."

"If it was a stall then we have to question every scribe in the street. If it was a shop then chances are there will be only one or two scribes nearby."

In fact, there were two. The cosmetic shop with the red awning dominated a street corner. Opposite, across the narrow street, a single clerk sat in a small room open to the public, scribbling on a roll of parchment. He looked up when Timon stepped across the threshold.

"Whatever it is," the clerk said in a peevish voice. "I cannot possibly attend to you until tomorrow."

"It's nothing much," said Timon. "I was merely interested in finding the author of this note." He waved the piece of paper in front of the man. "I admire the penmanship. If I find the author there will be more work for him."

"Let me see," snapped the clerk, grabbing at the note. He perused the paper for a moment before his lip curled in a sneer of contempt. "This? You admire this? This is amateurish and clumsy."

"Yes," agreed Timon straight-faced. "Perhaps you are right. However, the person who gave me the note was certain it came from here."

"Not from here," the clerk grated. "Maybe the Jew, over there." He waved a hand toward the street. "Now get out, I have work to do."

Timon backed out of the shop with a mutter of thanks.

Tirses shot his companion a disgusted look. "You're too polite for your own good, Timon. I would thrash the man to teach him some manners."

"Leave him, Tirses." Timon strode over to the cosmetic shop and ducked inside. Emerging a few minutes later, he nodded in satisfaction. "Around the corner. Josiah the Jew."

Josiah proved to be a tall, powerfully built man. He rose from behind a table when Timon and Tirses entered the premises.

"How may I be of service, good sirs?"

Timon glanced quickly around the interior of the shop before passing the note to the tall Jew. "I'm seeking the writer of this note. I was told you might have written it."

Josiah examined it carefully then handed it back with a shake of his head. "I'm sorry," he said with a faint smile. "I didn't write that. In all modesty, I produce better work."

Timon nodded glumly. "It was worth a try. My friend said it came from a scribe who lived very close to a cosmetic shop but could not remember which one. Perhaps you know of another cosmetic shop near here?"

Josiah thought for a moment then shook his head again. "Not around here." He bowed slightly and held back the curtain over the doorway for his customers. "May you find what you seek."

As Timon stepped out onto the street, Josiah hesitated. "Wait a moment, sir. When was this note written? Only a day or two? I have been away on business and may not be aware of who was here that day." Josiah turned and called into the shadowy recesses of the room. "Benjamin? Where are you boy?"

A tall gangling boy emerged from the back of the shop, walked slowly into a shaft of sunlight and stood staring at the floor. "Yes, father?"

Josiah gently took the note from Timon and held it out. "Did you write this, Benjamin?"

The boy glanced at the note and flushed. "Yes, father," he whispered.

Josiah looked closely at his son. "Benjamin, I'm not angry with you, though I am somewhat disappointed with the quality. These gentlemen are looking for the author of this note. Are you certain you wrote this?"

Benjamin glanced from his father to Timon and Tirses, then back at his father. "It was such a small thing, father. I didn't think you would mind."

"Who asked you to write it?" asked Timon.

Benjamin hesitated and looked to his father again. When Josiah nodded, the boy shrugged. "I don't know his name."

Tirses swore softly.

Timon grimaced. "It was worth a try I suppose."

"But, I have seen him before," said Benjamin. "He often accompanies the food buyers of his household. It was the first time I saw him alone though."

"Oh? And do you know which household?"

"Of course. He's a servant in the house of Lord Ptolemy."

Tirses turned away with a hiss, his fists clenching.

Timon frowned. "You're sure of this?"

"Yes, sir," Benjamin replied. "One of the men came in here once to buy paper. We sell good quality paper and many lords buy from us. I thought it strange that the boy brought his own scrap with him."

"And you wrote the words," said Timon. "You can write Macedonian?"

Benjamin grinned. "A little. Enough for this anyway."

"You didn't wonder why Lord Ptolemy would ask a servant boy to bring a scrap of paper into the city when he must have scribes of his own?"

The boy shrugged. "I assumed the boy was given a gift by his lord and wanted a note to go with it as a remembrance."

Timon grunted. "You have no idea of his name?"

Benjamin shook his head. "You cannot mistake him though. He is a Kelt, from the north. His hair is yellow and his eyes are blue."

# Chapter 17

Nikometros sat on a hard stone bench in the afternoon sunshine. Banished from his apartments by a bevy of women attending to his wife, he alternately paced the width of the small courtyard or sat fidgeting on one of the benches. At every noise or movement in the dim shaded colonnades of the palace, he started, often rising to his feet in anxious anticipation. The day wore on and the lack of news steadily increased his agitation.

He cast his mind back over the months, clinging to memories of Tomyra. Once more, in his mind, he rode the vast rolling grass seas of the high plains of Scythia, hunted in the forests by the broad stony rivers, or made love to his woman beneath the black night, awash with stars. He smiled, remembering the dangers they faced together--at first because of her inviolability as a sacred priestess, later as they fought side by side against the armies of her half-brother Areipithes.

Gone now was her lithe athletic body, though her fierce will and determination still flared despite the confines of her pregnancy. A pregnancy brought about by rape. Nikometros ground his teeth at the thought of the

Serratae chieftain Dimurthes. He would dearly love to have been the one to bring about the man's death. Yet, for a reason that still escaped him, Dimurthes killed himself in Tomyra's presence.

His thoughts switched abruptly to their bedchamber, where Tomyra fought against the Arabian death weed and her imminent parturition.

*What if she dies? No, she's in good hands.* Everyone he talked to had only good things to say about the court midwife, Molossa. *She wouldn't allow anything to happen to her charges. Yet women do die in childbirth--even without the effects of poison.* Nikometros leapt to his feet and paced once more.

The sun dipped below the palace roof, throwing the courtyard into cool shadow. Movement within the shaded colonnade caught Nikometros' eye and he swung round. Bithyia came toward him across the paving, her face pale, and her body rigid. She halted in front of him and essayed a hesitant smile. "A girl, Niko. You have a baby daughter."

Nikometros caught his breath, a grin surging over his face, even as he noted the pain in the young woman's eyes.

"Tomyra?" he whispered.

"She lives, Niko, but she...she lies as though asleep. Yet she cannot be wakened."

Nikometros pushed past Bithyia. "I must go to her." He broke into a run, rapidly crossing the courtyard and entering the passageway that led to his apartments. Servants and passers-by stepped aside as he raced by.

He burst into his apartment and stopped dead, his gaze taking in the disarray of the room. A bundle of bloodied sheets lay in one corner where a young girl knelt, pushing them into a wicker basket. Another girl sat by the fire, holding a squalling infant, cleaning it with a wet cloth. His eyes turned reluctantly to the bed.

Tomyra lay motionless, a red woollen blanket drawn up around her, her arms lying free. Nikometros walked slowly to the bed and sat down on the edge. Taking Tomyra's hand he raised it to his lips. She lay still, unaware.

"What happened?" asked Nikometros, without turning. "Why is she like this?" He raised his gaze to the midwife.

Molossa shook her head. "I don't know. It sometimes happens that the woman's spirit is expelled with the infant, yet she lives still."

Nikometros leaned forward and gently stroked Tomyra's forehead, brushing several strands of damp hair from her face. "When will she wake?"

Molossa stood silently as Nikometros stared up at her questioningly. "That is with the gods," she said. "I'll look after her for as long as life remains, but without food..." She glanced across to the girl by the fire. "See, my lord. You have a daughter."

Nikometros looked across at the infant, now sucking enthusiastically at the girl's breast, then back to his wife's pale face. He leaned over and kissed her lips lightly before getting to his feet and moving across the room.

"Let me see her." Nikometros squatted beside the girl, who smiled and disengaged the baby's mouth from her nipple. A drop of milk ran down over her breast.

The baby, her eyes tight shut, waved tiny fists and took a small breath before expelling it in a loud wail of complaint.

Nikometros smiled and touched her hand with a callused finger. "So small," he breathed.

The old servant, Sisyphis, stood over the girl. "What name do you give her, lord?"

Nikometros hesitated. "Her mother should name her."

"She cannot," replied Sisyphis. "The baby must have a name. How else can we petition the Goddess for her protection?"

Nikometros thought. "Starissa then. It was her grandmother's name. She was a Sauromantian priestess from the shores of the Euxine Sea. Both she and her daughter..." Nikometros' eyes flicked toward Tomyra, "...were priestesses of the Mother Goddess. She will look after Her own."

Sisyphis nodded. "A good name." She signed to the young girl to resume feeding the infant. "This is my granddaughter Petis, my lord," she continued. "Her baby died but two days ago," she added matter-of-factly. "She'll be happy to wet nurse your daughter until your wife awakes."

The girl looked up at Nikometros with joy and tears in her eyes before bending over the infant girl once more.

Nikometros moved back to the bed where Bithyia now sat, holding Tomyra's hand fiercely. "What of my wife? How do you plan to care for her?"

"There is little we can do, my lord," the midwife replied. "Beyond keeping her clean and comfortable. We must pray she wakes before she starves."

"Surely we can feed her?"

"Fluids only, and little of that, else she chokes."

"Oh gods," muttered Nikometros. He sat down on the bed, staring hopelessly at his unconscious wife.

"Don't worry, Niko," said Bithyia, squeezing his arm. "I'll be with her. I'll take care of her."

"No." Nikometros shook his head. "Or rather, yes. I thank you, Bithyia, but I'll stay by her. Seek out your husband and tend to his needs. I'll tend to my wife's." He reached out and took a cup of water from a small table by the bed. Carefully propping up Tomyra's head he gently let water trickle between her lips, wiping it away as it spilled over her chin. "Go, Bithyia," he whispered. "Leave me with her."

Bithyia slowly rose then crossed to the door. She looked back and smiled gently before slipping out of the room. She emerged from the palace into late afternoon sunlight. Drawing the fresh clean air deeply into her lungs, she leaned against the rough bark of an old fruit tree and closed her eyes, feeling the staleness of the birthing room wash away in the soft scented breeze.

"Love?"

Without opening her eyes, Bithyia stretched a hand out behind her and took hold of Timon's. "Not good, Timon." She clenched her hand and turned, opening her eyes to stare into her husband's concerned face. "She has given birth...a daughter, but she doesn't awaken."

Timon frowned. "She lives though? What of Niko? How does he take it?"

Bithyia's eyes flashed. "Hard. How else?" Her expression softened and she moved closer, into his arms. "I'm sorry, husband," she murmured. "They've suffered enough. I thought that now they could find happiness."

Timon gently kissed his wife's brow. "She'll recover, my love. The Goddess brought her here for a reason."

Bithyia turned away and stared at the palace, brooding in the gathering shadows. "Curse the man who poisoned her," she whispered. Then in a strengthening voice, "Goddess, hear me. Avenge my mistress. Let the man who did this die a cold death, far from his lands and family." She paused, listening to the wind and the distant susurration of city sounds. "Was it Ptolemy?"

"It appears so. We traced the note to the scribe who wrote it."

"Then let us confront him. Bring it before the king."

"We would not see him. He grieves for his friend, Hephaestion." Timon moved forward, coming up behind Bithyia. He placed his hands on her shoulders. "Besides, we couldn't prove it. We only know a servant boy in his household, a Kelt from the north, had the note written."

Bithyia turned to face her husband again. "A Kelt? Fair-haired? A boy like that brought the gift." Her lips curled into a snarl. "Then let us find him and make him tell us."

Timon nodded then hesitated. "Is it possible...are you sure the note came with the gift? Could it be we are led astray by it? Lord Ptolemy did send other gifts."

"Let me see it." Bithyia held out her hand. She examined the crumpled paper and sniffed it. "There, that small stain. It smells of cinnamon. It came with the poisoned sweetmeats."

Timon grunted. "Then let us find the boy. At least he can tell us who gave him instructions."

Smells of cooking filled the corridors of the lower palace as Timon and Bithyia made their way toward the kitchens and servant quarters. The huge kitchens that serviced the palace bustled with a warm and pleasant confusion, in stark contrast to the nervous anticipation surrounding the king's apartments. In response to their inquiries, Timon and Bithyia found themselves directed away from the kitchens toward the palace library.

Housed in an older and somewhat dilapidated wing of the palace, the library nonetheless showed signs of recent and constant use. Oil lamps burned on broad tables down the centre of the hall, where shelves containing scrolls and bundles of papers climbed the walls on all sides. Several men looked up from the tables as they entered.

One rose and approached them. "May I help you?" the man inquired pleasantly.

Timon glanced around the room. "We're looking for someone."

The man waited, his head cocked slightly to one side.

"A young boy," went on Timon. "A Kelt...with fair hair and blue eyes."

"Indeed. And what do you want with him?"

"We just want to ask him a few questions."

The man stood silently once more.

Timon fidgeted and opened his mouth to speak again.

"We mean him no harm," Bithyia interrupted. "He brought a gift to our friend's wedding but we lost the accompanying note. We wanted to ask him who sent it."

The man frowned. "You must mean Madoc. You haven't heard?"

"Heard what?" rasped Timon.

The man nodded and turned away. "Follow me. I'll take you to him." He walked across the library, skirting the broad tables and the other men. As he passed, he picked up one of the oil lamps then stepped through a side door into a gloomy corridor.

Timon and Bithyia followed, hurrying to catch up. They moved through the dark corridors, the tiny pool of light thrown by the lamp accentuating shifting shadows. The man led them down past storerooms and dusty rooms filled with disused furniture.

"Where is he taking us?" muttered Bithyia. "This doesn't feel right."

Timon grunted and hurried on, but he loosed his sword in its sheath, keeping his hand near the hilt.

At last, the man reached a large door and, pushing it open, gestured Timon and Bithyia to pass through. The room glowed with soft dappled light and splashing water sounded incongruously in their ears. A cool draft blew in their faces.

Timon stepped cautiously across the threshold, followed by Bithyia. The man closed the door behind them and pointed across the large room.

The room was lit by the last rays of the setting sun, filtering through dappled leaves beyond huge open bays in the western wall. A sheet of water fell at the far end of the room, collecting in a large shallow pool before gurgling into a conduit that passed through the eastern wall. The air felt moist and cold after the warmth of the corridors. At the far end lay a series of low stone slabs, a number of them occupied by naked bodies.

"Over here," said the man, walking toward the slabs. "Though I fear he's a bit past questioning."

On the slab in front of them lay the body of a young boy. His pale corpse lay naked and defenceless, his straw-coloured hair tousled and untidy. Pale blue eyes, milky with death, bulged in an open-eyed stare at the ceiling, while his mouth gaped as if in an agonised shout.

"Madoc," said the man quietly. "He is...was, the only Kelt in the palace. A member of Lord Ptolemy's household."

Timon stared at the young body in dismay. "When did this happen?"

The man shrugged. "They found him just after the noon meal. In the shrubbery near the servant's quarters."

Bithyia's eyes glistened. "Poor child," she murmured. She stepped closer and attempted to close the boy's staring eyes. The lids resisted and she gave up with a sigh. "How did he die?"

"Choked," answered the man. "See?" He stepped up to the body and, firmly holding the head, pulled the jaw down, forcing the tongue to one side. "See down there? A plum. He must have swallowed it whole." The man moved away and rinsed his hands in the pool before drying them on his tunic. "Madoc loved plums."

Timon moved closer, his mouth turned down in an expression of distaste. He peered at the boy's body for a few moments then pointed. "What is that?" he asked. "There, on his shoulder."

Bithyia and the man leaned over. "That?" said the man. "Just a bruise."

Timon touched the bruise gently with a finger. "Here is another...and another." He spread his fingers to cover the bruises. "As if a hand made them," he mused.

The man smiled. "Madoc was a boy...and a slave. Sometimes he needed discipline."

"And this," said Bithyia. She delicately peeled back the boy's lips and pushed the tongue to one side. "There is blood on his teeth, yet he didn't appear to bite himself." She looked up at Timon. "Restrained, and then he bit...hard, before swallowing the plum."

Timon stared back at Bithyia then nodded slowly. "This was no accident," he growled. "This boy was murdered because of what he knew."

# Chapter 18

Iolatos, the king's equerry, stuck his head round the door and called to the man dozing on a couch by the large bed.

"Nikometros! By the gods, wake up! The king is out and calling for you."

Nikometros started up then groaned. He knuckled the sleep out of his eyes and stared blearily across the room. "For me? He calls for me?"

"Don't be a fool. Not just for you. He calls for all his staff. Perdikkas sent me to find you. Now hurry!"

Nikometros staggered to the bed and bent over the still figure of Tomyra. He leaned across and stroked her cool forehead. "I cannot leave her."

Iolatos ground his teeth and strode across the room then grabbed Nikometros by the arm. "Didn't you hear me? The king sends for you." He glanced around the room and pointed at an old woman curled up asleep by the embers of the fire. "She'll do." He stepped across and nudged the old woman awake with his boot. "Get up, old woman," he snarled. Without waiting for her reaction, Iolatos turned back to Nikometros and hustled him across to the door. "The old woman will see to her needs. Now hurry!"

Nikometros looked back at his wife as he was dragged out into the corridor. He shook off Iolatos' hand and ran with the equerry toward the king's apartments. As they passed through a small courtyard, Nikometros turned aside and doused himself with cold water from a fountain. He dried himself on a nearby wall hanging then ran on.

Outside the council chamber, the two men halted and caught their breath before pushing the doors open. A large table dominated the room, with chairs pushed back to the walls. A dozen men stood around the table, their backs to the door.

At the head of the table stood Alexander, talking quietly but firmly. He looked up when Nikometros and Iolatos entered the room, breaking off in mid-sentence. The king stared at the two newcomers, his eyes wide and unfocused. His blond hair, streaked with grey, stood in an untidy tangle, shorn near to the scalp in places, hanging long in others.

The silence dragged on as Nikometros and Iolattos saluted and joined the other officers.

"As I was saying," Alexander murmured, dropping his gaze to the table. "It isn't enough that the city mourns. Send riders to every part of the empire. Let every man mourn his passing. When was there ever such a man as he?" Alexander's voice trailed away and he looked around at the serious faces of his friends and officers. "I see you mourn him too," he went on. "Ptolemy, Peukestas, Perdikkas...you offered up a lock of your hair. That is proper." His eyes wandered over Eumenes. The king's face changed. "You hated him, Eumenes."

Eumenes paled. "No, sire. I...I was reconciled and counted him a friend. I mourn him too. See?" He snatched a dagger from his belt and, grabbing a handful of his hair, sawed at it with the blade. He threw the handful of dark hair on the table in front of Alexander.

"Liar," mouthed Perdikkas behind his hand.

The other officers who had not cut a lock of hair hurried to follow suit, Nikometros among them.

The king nodded, his expression once more distant as he wandered away from the table. "Crop the horses' manes, Peukestas. Let even the animals mourn him." Alexander stopped by the open window and listened. Far below in the city the faint sounds of music wafted up to them. The king's face darkened. "No music!" he shouted. He breathed hard, his hands clenching. Then he turned, forcing calm into his expression. "There will be no public music until the funeral."

Peukestas cleared his throat. "All your commands will be carried out, Alexander." He paused and flashed a quick entreaty at his fellow officers. "When will the funeral be?"

"He lies with the embalmers," whispered Alexander. "Yet he too was Alexander." He looked around the room and continued in a firmer voice. "Gather together the riches of the empire--incense, cedar logs, gold, fine cloth. I shall build him such a pyre that the world has not seen. Even the gods will look down in wonder...even the gods..."

"Alexander?" Ptolemy moved closer with an anxious expression.

"I am a god, am I not?" Alexander demanded, staring wild-eyed at his half-brother. "The oracle at Siwah said I am. Son of Ammon-Ra."

"Yes, Alexander." Ptolemy nodded. "Of course you are. Anyone can see the godhead within you."

"But mortals don't go to the gods. Only the immortals live with them." A tear trickled slowly from his grey eye. "I shall be separated even in death from my beloved Hephaestion."

Ptolemy opened his mouth then shut it. He looked round at the others, his hands moving in a silent plea for help. Everyone looked away except Eumenes, who smiled, his eyes glittering. "The gods can do anything," he said softly.

Ptolemy stared at him. "What?"

"Petition the gods, sire," Eumenes replied. "Ask your...father...Ammon-Ra to allow lord Hephaestion to be with you."

Alexander wrinkled his brow for a few moments then his eyes cleared. "Yes. Hephaestion was the best of men. I shall send to Siwah to ask that he be made a god. After my death we shall be gods together." He smiled at Ptolemy. "You know Egypt, my friend. Organise an embassy to the oracle immediately."

Ptolemy nodded. "At once, Alexander."

"I shall have to get an architect, you know," said Alexander. "The pyre shall be royal, for a king...and games; we must have proper funeral games. Nothing shall be withheld. I have drawn up plans." He riffled through a pile of papers on the table. "Where is the doctor?"

"Eh? Er...you ordered him...er, hanged, Alexander," stuttered Peukestas.

Alexander turned and stared at the man. "I know," he said softly. "I didn't ask whether you killed him, only where he was hanging."

Peukestas flinched and turned to Seleukos. "Where is he hanging?"

"Outside the city gates, sire. The crows feast on him already. Shall I cut him down?"

"Yes, then crucify his body by the city midden until it falls apart." Alexander turned back to Ptolemy. "Let no man bury him. His shade shall wander unshriven for this crime." He paused before resuming in a calm voice again. "The funeral will be in Babylon. It is only right that it should take place in the empire's capital. Next spring, I think. That will give ample time for the arrangements to be made." He looked round at the assembled officers and frowned. "Well, what are you waiting for? You have your orders. Carry them out." He turned on his heel and stalked from the room, disappearing through a small door at the rear of the chamber.

Perdikkas watched as the officers filed from the room. He beckoned Seleukos and Nikometros to him. "What do you think?"

"Has he lost his wits?" muttered Nikometros. "Asking for this companion to be made a god?"

Perdikkas kept a bland expression on his face. "I would be extremely careful who I said that to, Colonel. You may find yourself hanging alongside the good doctor."

Nikometros flushed. "Yes sir. I'm sorry, sir. I meant only that the king isn't his usual incisive self. And really, a god? Isn't that blasphemy?"

"As that little toad Eumenes pointed out, a god can do anything he wants. You were there at Siwah, Nikometros. You saw the king afterward. Didn't he appear to be a god? Do his exploits since then not reek of divinity?" Perdikkas turned to the other man. "And what do you think Seleukos?"

Seleukos smiled coldly. "I think there is great opportunity here, sir."

"Indeed, there is," agreed Perdikkas. "Hephaestion was Chiliarch-- Vizier--the most powerful man in the empire after the king. That position is vacant, but not for long, I think."

"You're the obvious choice, sir," said Seleukos.

"Yes, I rather think I am. And when I'm Chiliarch I'll remember those loyal to me." Perdikkas nodded. "However, there are those who bear watching. Seleukos, keep an eye on Peukestas for me. Your efforts won't go unrewarded."

Seleukos saluted and left the room.

Perdikkas watched him go then turned to Nikometros. "You're an able soldier but you're naïve when it comes to the court. Learn from Seleukos if you want to get ahead, Nikometros. Events are moving fast and I have need of loyal men."

# Chapter 19

"I tell you, Berinax, it was him, that slimy spy who betrayed us. Sco...something."

Berinax frowned and glanced around at the busy street. "Scolices. Here? In Ekbatana? How likely is that? I thought he died in that last battle back on the high plains."

"By the balls of Papaeus, I wouldn't forget that traitor. Ask Gerrades when he gets back. He'll tell you."

Berinax glanced nervously at the sky. "Don't blaspheme against our gods, Menares, even this far from Scythia. And just where is Gerrades anyway?"

"Following the traitor. I came back to find you as soon as we saw him."

Berinax grabbed Menares by the shoulders. "Where did you leave him? Take me there."

Menares led Berinax through the bustling streets of Ekbatana, outside the walls. Pushing through jostling crowds, they left the well-to-do areas and entered a district where the shops and stalls were dirty and full of shoddy goods. The streets swarmed with beggars, prostitutes and hard-faced men who stopped and stared at the Scythians as they passed. At length they came to a run-down tavern above which flapped an incongruously cheerful banner of a rayed sun.

"This is the place," said Menares. "We're to meet here after he knows where he's going."

Berinax grunted. "Well, we might as well have a drink while we wait."

They pushed their way into the dim tavern and found seats at one of the grimy tables. The other patrons at the table gave them a sour look and reluctantly shifted along the benches. The tavern keeper put two wooden mugs in front of them and sloshed raw red wine from a jug. He pocketed the copper coins Berinax threw on the table and disappeared into the gloom.

Berinax sipped his wine and grimaced. "Gods, what foul stuff."

Menares grinned and raised his voice above the clatter and conversation around them. "You've grown too fond of court wine, Berinax. You need to come drinking with us poor common men more often." He lifted his cup, drank deeply then swallowed. Then he froze and nodded toward the doorway. "Here he is. Ho, Gerrades! Over here!"

A short, stocky young man with a straggly, unkempt beard and moustache made his way to them, his face bursting with excitement. "It's him, Berinax. And I know where he lives."

The men slammed their cups on the table and hurriedly left the tavern. Gerrades led them out into the street and set off down a winding alley. "He didn't suspect a thing," he chattered. "Strolling around as if he owned the place. And just wait till you see where he led me."

Gradually they left the poorer area of the city and moved once more through cleaner streets, among richly dressed men and women. Gerrades slowed by a busy shop and pulled his companions to the side. "In there." Gerrades nodded at the doorway and grinned.

Berinax grunted. "So, you followed him here. What makes you think he lives here?"

"Went around the back, didn't I? Found a room where he and this other man were drinking and talking."

"Oh? What were they saying?"

Gerrades shrugged. "Couldn't get close enough to hear, could I? But guess who the other man is?"

Berinax shook his head. "Who?"

"Parates." He stared at the blank expressions on the faces of his companions with dismay. "You don't know of Parates?"

"Never heard of him," said Menares. "Who is he?"

"A brigand and a trader. I was on guard detail once, with Tirses, a couple of years back, when this Parates arrived. Seemed he knew our chief's son, Areipithes, well. He wasn't there so he spoke with Scolices, didn't he?"

Berinax scratched his armpit. "So Scolices is here in Ekbatana talking with a friend of Areipithes..."

"And an attempt is made to poison our lady!" interrupted Menares.

"Where is the connection to this Tol-me person that Timon talked about?" asked Berinax.

Gerrades shrugged. "Who knows? Do we march in and grab them both, or wait for Timon?"

Berinax thought for a few minutes. "Wait for Timon. We need more people. Menares, get up to the palace as quick as you can and find Timon. Tell him the situation and suggest he brings some soldiers with him."

Menares disappeared into the crowd and the other two men settled down to wait. They wandered over to a nearby tavern with outside trestle tables sheltered from the elements by a gaily-coloured awning. Settling down with cheese, bread and wine, Berinax and Gerrades sat and watched the shop front.

The sun rose in the morning sky then passed the zenith before Timon arrived. He arrived quietly, slipping into the tavern courtyard and sitting down next to Berinax. Tirses, Menares and five other Scythian Lions seated themselves at a nearby table, watching Timon with fierce anticipation.

"You're certain it's Scolices?" asked Timon. "And this Parates, who exactly is he?"

"A man without a tribe," growled Gerrades. "A brigand who trades with all the southern tribes of Scythia."

"I met him," interposed Tirses as he slipped across from the other table. "A cultured man but a thief and a murderer when it suited him."

"How do we take them, sir?" asked Berinax.

"Carefully." Timon considered the problem. "Berinax, you'll take five men and try to secure any exits there might be at the rear and sides of the building. Tirses, you'll accompany me. Look at him carefully, make sure it is the man you remember then challenge him. Watch his eyes. If he's guilty he'll betray himself."

"What of Menares and myself?" asked Gerrades.

"Wait by the door and be ready to come to our assistance. Berinax, if you hear my shout, come running. But remember, it's vital we take them alive."

Timon rose from the table and waited in the street with Tirses as Berinax and his companions sauntered into the narrow alleys alongside the shop. After a few minutes he nodded and, crossing the street, pushed open the door of the shop.

The interior, lit only by numerous smoky oil lamps, swam in a tenuous blue haze. Odours, of which smoke and spices dominated, battered at their nostrils. Grain crunched beneath their feet, their passage disturbing large fat cockroaches that fled to the shelter of some food crates. The place was deserted except for two men examining bolts of cloth along one wall and a sour-faced youth picking his nose behind a wooden counter in the shadows at the rear.

Tirses, with a glance at his companion, drifted across to some barrels and began lifting the lids to examine the contents.

Timon weaved a path through the scattered merchandise toward the youth.

The youth turned to Timon as he approached and roused himself from some internal contemplation, wiping a finger on his grubby tunic. "Yes?" he asked in a bored voice.

"I wish to speak with your master," said Timon. "Please be so good as to fetch him."

The youth shrugged. "He's busy. What do you want to see him for?"

"My own business. Fetch him here now."

"I told you, he's busy." The youth yawned, not bothering to cover his mouth. "Come back tomorrow."

Timon slipped a dagger from his belt and slammed it into the wooden counter.

The youth jumped back, his eyes widening. The two men examining cloth turned and stared for a few moments before resuming their quiet discussions.

Timon leant on the counter and glared at the youth. "Now, I'm a reasonable man, so I'm willing to overlook your insolence. Are you going to fetch your master or do I have to explain to him why he lacks an assistant in his shop?" He glanced significantly at the dagger.

The youth gulped, his throat working convulsively. "I'll get him," he squeaked before diving for the curtain at the rear of the shop.

"Good," Timon muttered to himself and pulled the dagger out of the counter and slipping it into his belt. He turned and surveyed the smoke-filled room, nodding at Tirses.

"How may I be of service?" The curtains parted and a tall, dark man emerged, his glossy shoulder length hair swinging as he walked. His handsome face showed only a polite curiosity as his dark eyes swept the room. He hesitated briefly at the sight of Tirses bent over an open barrel before turning to Timon.

"I wish to buy weapons," Timon said. "Short swords, daggers. Some decent bows if you have them."

"I don't sell weapons," the man replied. "Only a selection of knives for eating." He waved a manicured hand toward the curtain. "My servant could have shown you these if you had asked, instead of threatening violence."

"I was told you sold weapons."

"You were misinformed. Now if there is nothing else?" The man bowed slightly and stepped back. A movement caught his eye and he turned toward the small Scythian approaching him. His brow furrowed though his eyes remained guarded.

"I know you," said Tirses. "Parates, is it not?"

"Have we met?" asked the man coolly.

"Once," replied Tirses. "At Urul. You came to see the chief's son Areipithes."

"Ah, yes. I thought you had the look of a Massegetae. How fares Areipithes these days?"

"Dead. As I'm sure you know."

"Do you know a man called Scolices?" interposed Timon, leaning forward.

Parates' eyes flickered before settling back into calm. "Scolices?" He shook his head. "I cannot say I know the name."

"Strange," said Tirses. "He was a confidante of Areipithes. And stranger still, you talked with him last time you were in Urul."

167

"Really? I cannot be expected to remember the name of every servant or common man I meet." Parates shook his head as he casually straightened his cloak, flicking a piece of grime from the cloth. "It was three years ago at least."

"Two," said Tirses. "You haven't seen him since?"

"Didn't I just say so?" Parates moved slowly back behind the counter. "Now, I have other business to attend to, gentlemen."

"You lie," yelled Tirses. "We followed Scolices here. Even now he sits in your rooms." He dragged his sword from its sheath and lunged across the counter at Parates.

Parates stepped to one side and smoothly slipped his own blade out. He slammed his sword down, trapping Tirses' sword against the counter. At the same moment he leaned across and snapped his fist out, sending Tirses reeling back against Timon. Turning, he leapt for the curtain at the back of the room and disappeared beyond it.

Timon pushed Tirses off him with a bellow of anger. "Gerrades, Menares! Take him!" He wrenched his sword out and flung himself around the counter.

The Scythians scrambled after him, yelling for Berinax to beware.

They plunged into a dark warren of passages, full of shifting shadows. Timon cursed, holding his sword out, ready for a sudden attack. Shouts from deeper within the building, followed by the sharp clash of metal, drew them forward once more at a run. Bursting through a doorway, they emerged into a courtyard open to the street.

Parates stood with his back to the wall of the building, defending himself against the concerted attacks of Berinax and two other Scythians. To one side, sprawled on the ground, lay the other three Massegetae Lions, nursing wounds.

Timon strode into the middle of the courtyard and shouted for Berinax to pull back. Reluctantly, the Scythian obeyed, falling back but keeping his weapon at the ready. "Where is Scolices?" grated Timon.

One of the wounded men cursed and spat. "Fled. The bastard ran as soon as he saw us."

Timon cursed in turn then swept his gaze around the courtyard. Aware of the rapidly increasing crowd of onlookers pushing into the courtyard from the street, he called to them to stand back, then to Parates to surrender.

Parates lowered his curved sword and stood staring at his attackers, breathing heavily. He raised his other hand and beckoned toward the crowd. "Good citizens!" he called. "Send for the Guard. I am attacked in my own place of business."

"Surrender!" yelled Timon, trying to hold back Tirses who struggled to get to grips with his enemy. "No harm will come to you."

Parates remained silent, his eyes flickering over his assailants and the swelling crowd. The crowd parted and a dozen fully armed infantrymen ran up, their swords drawn and armour jangling.

The leader of the guard detachment inspected the group in the courtyard then addressed Timon. "Identify yourself and your purpose."

"Timon, adjutant to Nikometros, staff officer of Perdikkas."

The guard commander grunted and turned to Parates. "And you?"

Parates inclined his head politely. "My name is Parates. I'm a respected trader in this city. These men assaulted me in my own shop."

The guard turned back to Timon. "Why did you assault him?"

"He's wanted in connection with the attempt on the life of the wife of my commander."

"Put down your sword, sir," said the guard.

"I will not," replied Timon. "This man is coming with me."

"No he isn't, sir," stated the guard commander firmly. "I'll take you all into custody, pending an investigation." He waited for a response from Timon. "Believe me, sir. There'll be bloodshed unless you obey me."

Timon forced down a feeling of anger and frustration. "Your name?" he ground out.

"Aristobolous."

"Very well then, Aristobolous. We'll put up our weapons." Timon signalled to Tirses and Berinax. "However, I'll hold you personally responsible if this man escapes." He sheathed his sword.

Aristobolous signalled to his men and they rapidly disarmed the angry Scythians and bound their wrists. The wounded men were assisted to their feet and bound also. Allowing Timon and Parates to retain their swords, Aristobolous led the detachment off toward the prison at the bottom of the citadel where Glaukios the doctor had so recently spent his last hours.

# Chapter 20

Peukestas sighed and pushed back from the table, papers spilling to the floor as he did so. He looked around the small guardroom at the men in front of him. Nikometros and Timon stood at attention while the Scythian, Tirses, almost trembled in his desire to fly at the Persian trader, Parates. The trader stood as if relaxed and at ease, only his watchful eyes betraying any hint of uncertainty. Aristobolous, the captain of the city guard, watched the proceedings with sword drawn.

"Let me see if I have this straight," Peukestas said. "You're accusing this man Parates of complicity in the poisoning of your wife, Nikometros, because he has a man living with him who once worked for your wife's brother?"

"That's not how it is at all, you addle-pated..."

Nikometros put out a hand to restrain Tirses' outburst. "I'm sorry, sir, you must excuse this outburst. Scythians are unused to formal authorities and tend to speak their minds. However, your summing up is an oversimplification. If I might explain?"

Peukestas nodded, the colour rising in his cheeks. "Please do."

Nikometros thought for a moment, marshalling his thoughts. "My wife's brother was Areipithes, the previous chief of his tribe. He hated his sister and myself and tried to kill us many times. Though he is now dead, one of his close associates, the man called Scolices, still hates us and seeks our deaths. He was seen in the city and followed to this man's shop." He pointed at Parates. "Parates is known to have been an associate of the dead chief. It is very possible the attempt on my wife's life was instigated by Scolices and it is possible that Parates is involved. I ask that he be put to the question."

"These are serious charges," mused Peukestas. "Parates, what have you to say?"

Parates drew himself up and smoothed down his cloak before looking directly at the general. "My lord Peukestas," he said quietly. "It grieves me that I should be accused of such a thing. You must surely know that I have been a good friend of our Macedonian...ah...liberators, even to the extent of supplying your army with food and other supplies."

Peukestas nodded. "Yes, yes, of course I'm aware of this, but it doesn't answer the charge. Do you know this Scolices?"

Parates shrugged. "Can any man really know another? However, to answer your question, yes, I've met him on several occasions and talked with him."

Tirses hissed and scowled. Timon nodded. "He admits it."

"Why didn't you admit this when Timon questioned you?" asked Peukestas.

"In my business, I deal with many important people. Who would trust me if I revealed their confidences to any who asked?"

"So Scolices confided in you?" asked Nikometros.

"Sometimes even the presence of a person can be regarded as a confidence." Parates smiled. "I wasn't about to reveal the whereabouts of one of my business associates to a stranger."

172

"What did you talk about with Scolices then?" growled Timon. "The weather?"

Parates stood silently, a slight smile on his face.

Peukestas coughed. "Come Parates, this is a serious matter. Tell us the nature of your conversation. These men aren't traders. You won't be giving away any economic advantage."

"As my lord wishes." Parates bowed to Peukestas then turned toward Nikometros. "I have traded with the tribes along the northern borders of Persia for many years. I knew Areipithes no more than I knew half a dozen other chiefs or chief's sons. In the course of my visits, I met other men like this Scolices." He paused, a quick smile quirking his lips. "Truth be told, I don't like the man, but when he came to my shop, I offered him hospitality, as custom demands. I asked him for news of the borderlands and he asked about affairs within the empire. Nothing was said of poison, or of any man here present."

"You swear by your gods that you had nothing to do with the attempted poisoning?" asked Peukestas.

"I am a follower of the Light, my lord," replied Parates with dignity. "I believe in Truth."

"You have Arabian death weed in your shop, don't you?" grated Tirses. "I saw it there."

"People use it to kill rats, I'm told," replied Parates. "It's supposed to be very efficacious."

"Why did you wound three of my men instead of explaining all this?" asked Nikometros.

Parates raised an eyebrow. "I was attacked in my place of business by strangers. I could easily have killed them but I refrained."

"Where is Scolices now?"

"I don't know. If, as you say, he bears you malice, then I suspect he's far away. If you are forewarned then he won't succeed in harming you."

Peukestas nodded and stood up. "Well, gentlemen," he said. "I've heard enough. I find that there's no evidence to link this man to the attempted murder. The presence of Scolices within the city may be innocent enough; we have no information on that. However, even if he is guilty, nothing beyond mere acquaintanceship links him to this respected merchant."

Peukestas paused and turned to address Nikometros. "Nikometros, you're responsible for the actions of your men. I'm dismayed that they should launch an unprovoked attack on a respectable citizen instead of bringing this matter to the proper authorities. I therefore fine you twenty mina of silver, this sum to be paid to Parates as recompense for the damages caused. You will also apologise to him."

"By the fornicating shades of Hades," muttered Timon. "That's a small fortune, Niko."

Nikometros gritted his teeth, his nostrils flaring. He stared above his superior's head and forced himself to reply. "If you command me sir, I will obey." He turned to Parates and gave a stiff bow. "My apologies," he grated. "I regret that you have been inconvenienced."

Parates smiled and returned the bow, gracefully. "Your gracious apology is accepted, my lord. My thoughts are with you in your troubles and I would like to call on your lady to ask after her health."

"That is not possible. She hasn't recovered from the effects of the poison."

"Then permit me to call when she is recovered. I have many fine pieces of Scythian gold and jewellery. It would please me to present your wife with a gift in remembrance of the hospitality I enjoyed among her people."

Peukestas rubbed his hands together, his smile broadening. "Come then, Nikometros. That's a generous gesture. Will you not clasp hands in friendship?"

Nikometros glanced around the room, holding eye contact with Timon and Tirses for a few seconds. "As my general commands," he said. Stepping forward he held out his hand to Parates. The two men clasped hands, their eyes locking.

With another low bow to Peukestas, Parates withdrew from the room. A few moments later, Peukestas and Aristobolous followed.

As the door closed behind them, Timon let out a string of extremely coarse and colourful expletives. "How is this possible, lord?" hissed Tirses. "Does this general of yours mean to let the bastard go with not even a reprimand? And reward him too?"

"Yes, Niko," added Timon, his face screwed up with worry. "How in Hades will you be able to pay the fine? I have a bit put aside from my pay you can have but nowhere near that amount."

Nikometros snorted. "Have you forgotten the wedding gifts settled on us by Alexander? By my reckoning I could pay the fine forty times over from that gift." He shook his head. "No, that doesn't worry me, though the apology rankles somewhat. I know he's involved, Timon. I know it but I cannot prove it."

"Then let me take care of it, lord," urged Tirses. "A dark night, a knife between the ribs."

Nikometros rounded on the Scythian. "No. I forbid it, Tirses."

Tirses shrugged. "As you will lord, I won't kill him."

"Nor any of your men, Tirses. On your honour."

Tirses looked away and exhaled loudly. "I obey." Suddenly he grinned, his teeth white against swarthy skin. "It would be the answer to our problems though."

175

Timon looked thoughtful. "I don't see any connection between Lord Ptolemy and Parates though. Nor with Scolices. I cannot see a Macedonian general stooping to such depths."

"Neither can I," agreed Nikometros. "Perhaps it's only coincidence that your dead Kelt was in the employ of Ptolemy. We know he frequented the city. It would be only too easy to bribe him to carry a gift to someone in the palace. I doubt he even knew the nature of the gift."

"And he was murdered for it. A child, Niko," hissed Timon. "Who murders a child?"

"A man who doesn't fear the gods," replied Nikometros. "Areipithes was such a one and I think his man Scolices is another. Remember the Jartai village."

"And Parates?"

Nikometros shrugged. "He may be innocent. Perhaps Scolices called on him merely as a contact in a foreign land. However, I think..."

A loud knocking peremptorily interrupted Nikometros. The door swung wide and Bithyia stumbled in, hair awry and breathing hard. "Niko! Come quickly," she blurted. "Tomyra has woken."

# Chapter 21

A cold wind blew out of the north, rattling the bare twigs of the trees and raising tiny flurries of fine flakes from the sparse drifts of snow huddling in the lee of boulders and thickets. The nearby river, gripped by a rime of ice along its stony banks, flowed sluggishly, the colour of slate beneath a leaden sky. Two horses stood on a small hillock overlooking the river, their riders hooded and cloaked against the cutting wind. A hundred paces away, five other horsemen waited patiently in the shelter of a stone outcrop, watching the pair on the hillock.

Nikometros, wrapped tightly in a woollen cloak, edged his horse closer to the rider beside him. He looked over at the pale face showing beneath the rider's hooded cloak. "You shouldn't be out in this weather, my love," he said in a voice edged with concern. He glanced up at the overcast sky, feeling the first thin drops of rain on his upturned face.

"I am not a soft Persian woman to be locked away, nor am I a Greek woman expected to sit at home spinning wool," replied Tomyra impatiently. "I am a Scythian warrior woman, daughter of warriors. I need the open spaces."

"I know Tomyra, but it's only a month since you...since Starissa was born."

Tomyra's eyes flashed. "Why did you have to give it my mother's name? Now, every time I think of her I'll be reminded of Dimurth...of that bastard, and what he did to me."

Nikometros frowned. "Starissa is your daughter too. Anyone can see the resemblance."

"Conceived in hatred, carried unwillingly and born in pain. She isn't mine," rasped Tomyra. "I disown her."

"Tomyra, you don't mean that. If you'd spend more time with her, feed her, you'd come to love her, even as I do."

"My milk has dried, thanks be to the Goddess, and I have nothing to give her. Anyway, that stupid cow Petis gives her all the milk she needs. Love too, no doubt."

Tomyra's agitation spread to her mount and the mare stamped, edging away from the other horse. She pulled its head round and dug in her heels, sending it slipping down the icy incline. When Tomyra reached level ground she urged it forward, bending low over its neck.

Nikometros hesitated for a moment then followed, his stallion picking its way carefully down the slope. Behind him he could hear the startled cries of the other horsemen as they whipped their mounts into a belated pursuit.

Nikometros gave his stallion its head and its stride lengthened, setting out after the already distant mare. Blinking in the fine drizzle, he saw Tomyra's horse galloping toward the thick leafless woods along the riverbank. As he watched, a gust of cold wind ripped the cloak away from her and sent it flapping out over the river. A moment later she disappeared into the trees. With a curse, Nikometros urged his stallion onward.

Forced to slow his pace through the dense thickets and winding paths of the wood, Nikometros fretted, allowing his horse to pick its way over exposed roots and slippery drifts of wet leaves. Behind him he could hear the cries of his bodyguard as they urged their mounts directly through the forest, trampling the undergrowth.

The land rose steeply as the woodland thinned, slowing his pace to a walk. When Nikometros finally emerged from the undergrowth, he found himself on a rocky bluff overlooking the river. A few paces away sat Tomyra, her mare's head turned to the north, staring out over the river and rolling countryside.

Tomyra turned her head as Nikometros guided his stallion alongside her. She smiled wanly and shivered as the wind tugged at her robes. "It smells of home, Niko," she said, waving a hand toward the north. "I can smell my home on the wind."

Nikometros nodded and unclasped his military cloak. He leaned over and wrapped it around Tomyra, refastening the pin. "You miss the great Scythian plains, don't you, my love?"

Tomyra stared northward. Scuds of ragged grey cloud ran before the wind, trailing mists of rain. She nodded. "My people will be in Urul now for the winter. There will be feasting and drinking of koumiss, young men boasting of their exploits, old men telling stories of heroes and gods." Tomyra turned her solemn face to her husband. "Yes, I miss it, Niko. Life here is very different."

Nikometros stared out over the river, refusing to look into his wife's eyes. "Do you want to go back?"

"Would you come with me?"

"I cannot. My duty lies with my king. But if you need to go..." Nikometros' voice caught, "...then you should go."

Tomyra leaned closer and touched her husband's arm. "Then we stay together." She sighed and brushed the rain away from her face, shaking her wet hair. "Niko, my place is with you. The Goddess sent me away from my people for a purpose. I will stay and await Her instruction."

Nikometros nodded. For several minutes they watched the interplay of clouds and rain over the sodden landscape.

At length, Tomyra turned toward Nikometros and stared up into his face. "I love you, Niko. I haven't been all that a wife should be of late. I'll make it up to you."

Nikometros smiled. "And Starissa?"

Tomyra shook her head. "She's blameless, I know. Yet I cannot find it in me to love her as a mother should love her child. She should be your child, Niko. I've failed you, and every time I see her, I'm reminded of that failure."

"I seem to remember you lecturing me about not feeling shame for something you had no control over."

"No shame, Niko, but I failed you all the same."

"You didn't fail me, Tomyra. You were forced and no blame lies with you. Besides, I...I love the child." Nikometros grinned. "She screams louder than I thought possible. She stinks and pukes every time I see her...yet she reminds me of you, and so I love her."

Tomyra gaped and swung her fist, catching Nikometros painfully in the ribs. "You pig," she laughed. "Are you saying I scream and stink?"

Nikometros fended her off with one hand while he rubbed his side. "Well, now that you mention it..." He dodged another blow. "No, my love. Your voice is as soft as a summer breeze and you're as fragrant as blossoms."

Tomyra poked her tongue out. "Liar," she said with a smile. "But a nice liar. I think I'll keep you." She leaned over and kissed Nikometros firmly on the lips.

A discreet cough interrupted their play. Tirses edged his horse up alongside and nodded deferentially. "My lord...lady," he said. "We should be getting back."

Nikometros looked toward the woods and saw the rest of the bodyguard waiting. He nodded and turned his horse's head to follow the bluff along the river. Tomyra followed, with Tirses and the bodyguards close behind. They skirted the trees and picked their way carefully down the sodden slopes to the river plain once more, before turning to where Ekbatana lay hidden in the mist.

Tomyra pulled a golden figurine from within her robes and turned it in her hand, admiring the workmanship. "I don't need to see Urul again, Niko, when I have such beautiful things to remind me. Thank you for finding it for me."

"I'm glad it pleases you." Nikometros frowned. "Yet I wish I could have obtained it elsewhere."

"Parates has been very kind. He cannot be held to blame for the actions of others. Besides, he's good company. You've been so busy of late."

"I'm sorry for that. Although the king hasn't recovered from the death of Hephaestion, the business of the empire goes on. Perdikkas keeps me very busy."

"I understand...really." Tomyra rode in silence for a few moments. "You must come and hear the stories Parates tells. He's travelled widely and met so many important people."

"Including your brother. They were good friends I believe."

Tomyra laughed. "Not really. He met him once or twice but only to trade. He hasn't said so, but I don't think he liked my brother."

"I don't trust him, Tomyra. Be careful. Never see him alone."

Tomyra shook her head. "I wouldn't, my love." She frowned. "More like, I couldn't. Bithyia keeps such a close eye on me I find it hard to be alone."

"She's concerned."

"I know." Tomyra cocked her head on one side. "How long since you drank koumiss, love?" She laughed at Niko's sour expression.

"Not since we left Urul. Months."

"Parates says he can get me some. Now that the cooler weather has arrived he can bring it south. He promised me a jar."

A look of alarm wafted across Nikometros face. "You cannot accept it." He frowned. "He hasn't offered you food or drink, has he?"

"Only a flask of wine. It was very pleasant." Tomyra smiled. "Don't concern yourself, my love, I'm not a fool. I made sure he drank some first."

Nikometros grunted. "Just be careful. There's something not quite right about the man."

"I wish Ket was here. He's such a good judge of character. You'd believe him. When will he be back?"

"Not for some time. It's a long way to Siwah in Egypt. By now they won't be much further than Babylon."

"I hope he hurries."

Slowly, the rain tapered off to a few scattered showers by the time they reached the Royal Road again. The clouds started to thin and a weak sun lit their faces. Pools of water lay everywhere and the horse's hooves squelched and sucked in the deep mud. The Road lay almost deserted until they neared the city. As they passed the army camp lying sullen in the sodden fields, they heard the sounds of a body of horsemen approaching fast from the southwest.

Nikometros guided the party off the road and watched as the riders approached. Tirses and his men moved up around their charges, their hands fingering the handles of their swords.

The riders came fast, a tight body of horsemen some twenty strong and fully armed. As they swept past Nikometros toward the city, one of the riders turned and stared. Cold, cruel eyes set in a craggy, weathered face took the measure of the little group, weighed their potential and dismissed them as inconsequential. The horsemen topped the rise and disappeared from view, the sound of their passage fading with them.

"Who are they?" muttered Tirses.

Nikometros took his hand from his sword and rubbed it. His knuckles ached from the grip and he grimaced when he realised the tension he had been under. He urged his horse back onto the road and set out for the city. "I don't know but I'll find out."

People milled everywhere in the lower city, gossiping and chattering. Nikometros pushed his way through the crowd toward the first of the citadel gates and called out to the guard.

"Drimon, who are those horsemen, the ones who just passed?"

The guard scowled and jerked his head in disgust. "Ill-mannered louts are who they are. Kossaians by all accounts. Said they was here for their money, they did." Drimon spat in the mud. "Still, theys had the Royal Pass so I couldn't refuse them entry."

# Chapter 22

"He said what?" Alexander raised his eyes from a report by the architect, Dolochos, on the design of Hephaestion's funeral pyre. He stared at the chamberlain in disbelief, eyebrows raised.

"Er...the er...Kossaian ambassador, sire. He says he's here to collect the annual tribute." The chamberlain shuffled his feet and looked down, unwilling to meet his king's pale eyes.

"Tribute?" Puzzlement replaced disbelief. "He thinks I should pay him tribute? Why?"

"It...it's the...the custom, sire," stammered the chamberlain. "Every winter they come to be paid." The man started to wring his hands. "It's a fee, sire; a payment for services. King Darius always paid it promptly..."

"I'm not King Darius," said Alexander coldly.

The Persian chamberlain gave a squeak of fear and dropped into a full prostration on the cold marble floor. "No sire, of course not, sire. Your power and majesty have been exalted to the heavens, your benevolence and gracious mercy..." babbled the terrified man.

Alexander glanced down at the prostrate official and got lightly to his feet. He nudged the man with the toe of a sandaled foot. "Be quiet." Striding over to the door of his chamber he threw it wide.

The guards at the door, young squires hardly old enough to shave, fumbled their spears as they turned in surprise.

"Send for my council, now!"

One of the young men snapped off a salute and raced off down the corridor. The other remained at attention, his eyes fixed at a point on the wall above his king's head. The youth trembled, his spear shaft clattering softly against his armour.

"At ease, soldier," said Alexander with a faint smile. "Hippolytos isn't it?"

"Yes, sire," breathed the young man.

Alexander nodded and turned away. "Show the council in as soon as they arrive, Hippolytos. You have my thanks." He re-entered the room and shut the door.

The young guard grinned and took up his position again, pride swelling his chest.

Ptolemy arrived first. He knocked and entered the king's chambers. He looked at Alexander quizzically, then at the Persian chamberlain still muttering on the floor. "What is it, Alexander?" he asked.

"Wait until the others get here." Alexander flashed a look of annoyance at the terrified official. "Get him out of here."

Ptolemy lifted the chamberlain to his feet and ushered him from the room, still babbling a string of honorifics and pleas for mercy. He turned back to face his king, who stood by the window, scowling at the dissipating storm clouds. He moved to one side and assumed a position of parade rest, content to await his brother's pleasure.

185

Hippolytos opened the door wide to allow several men to troop into the room.

Alexander turned from his contemplation of the weather and waved his council to the seats around a large table. He waited until all were seated then stood at the head of the table, leaning forward, resting on his knuckles. Alexander stared around at the faces of his generals and staff officers-- Ptolemy, Perdikkas, Peukestas, Eumenes, Seleukos, Amyntas and Nikometros.

"Well, gentlemen. It appears I'm not yet king in Persia." Alexander looked coldly at the startled expressions his statement elicited and his brow furrowed. "A delegation arrived from Kossaia...with a demand for tribute." He paused. "Tribute!" he shouted, his fist crashing down on the table. "They demand tribute of me. Who in Hades do they think they are?"

The generals looked from one to another in silence. Seleukos coughed and half raised a hand. "Er...where is Kossaia?"

"I can answer that," Eumenes replied smoothly. He looked across the table at Alexander's ferocious stare and his smile slipped. "Kossaia is a mountain province between Ekbatana and the plains of Babylon. The Royal Road runs right through the middle of it."

Peukestas leaned forward. "But Kossaia is then part of Persia, isn't it? Why this demand for payment?"

Eumenes shrugged eloquently. "The area is bristling with hill forts and mountain fastnesses. The tribes prey on travellers who use the roads. The kings of Persia thought it more economical to pay the tribes off rather than mount a costly expedition against them."

"Very true," added Amyntas. "There are few tracks and fewer roads."

"Why are we only hearing of it now?" asked Nikometros. "We haven't paid them off, yet they didn't attack us as we approached Ekbatana six years ago, nor yet this last year."

"We came from Persepolis," growled Ptolemy. "From the south, more recently from the east. We skirted the mountains rather than crossing them."

Perdikkas nodded. "They heard the king is in residence and no doubt decided to demand payment before winter closes the passes."

Alexander scanned his council again then sighed and sat down, leaning back in his chair. "What are your recommendations, gentlemen?"

"You cannot pay them, Alexander," protested Perdikkas. "It would set a terrible precedent."

"It may be more expensive not to pay them," observed Peukestas. "If we refuse they'll terrorise all travellers on the Royal Road to Babylon. Trade could be thrown into chaos."

"So what?" snorted Seleukos. "We're soldiers of the greatest army on earth. Let them surrender or die."

"Easier said than done," retorted Eumenes. "The Kossaians have never been subdued. Their mountain strongholds are almost impossible to approach."

"So, you're saying we should take the coward's way out?" snarled Perdikkas. "I might have known you'd suggest that."

Eumenes flushed and rose to his feet. He hissed. "I suggested no such thing. I merely said that we should exercise caution rather than rush in like bulls whose balls are bigger than their brains."

Perdikkas leapt to his feet in turn. "Coward!" he yelled.

Chairs scraped back as the table erupted into factions. Peukestas pulled at Perdikkas' sleeve while Amyntas urged Eumenes to sit down again. Seleukos and Nikometros turned from one side to the other in agitation, their eyes shiny with excitement.

"Gentlemen!" Alexander's voice whip lashed across the table. "This serves no purpose." He watched as his officers settled back, breathing hard but under control again. "Of course we won't pay them. Peukestas, contact their ambassador and decline their invitation. Tell them I shall call on them in the spring to demand their fealty. If they swear allegiance I shall forgive them."

"Yes, Alexander."

"Perdikkas, start planning an expedition to subdue them. Sometime after the spring equinox, I think. Cavalry will be useless in the mountains, perhaps..."

Ptolemy looked around the table then back to his king, noting the abstracted way he planned the war. He leaned forward and deliberately interrupted Alexander's instructions. "I think you're wise to wait, Alexander. Some things, like attacking the Kossaians in winter, are clearly beyond the capabilities of men."

Alexander stopped talking, his hand raised, and turned to glare at Ptolemy. The other officers stared open-mouthed.

"What are you doing?" hissed Peukestas. "Sit down."

"Yes," continued Ptolemy with a sneering smile. "I doubt Heracles himself could deal with these common brigands. Certainly, none of the Persian kings were up to the task."

Peukestas rose to his feet in agitation. "Pay no attention, Alexander. Of course it is best to wait until spring. Your commands will be carried out..."

Alexander stopped him with a peremptory gesture. "Go on, Ptolemy," he said coldly.

"Wait until spring then Alexander." Ptolemy shrugged. "No one will think less of you I'm sure. No matter that the Kossaians will be snugged up in their forts, eating and drinking, enjoying their plunder and laughing at us."

"By all the gods of Olympus," roared Alexander. "No one laughs at Alexander." His lips tightened to a thin line as his pale eyes flashed angrily. Abruptly he grinned. "No one but you would dare to speak like that Ptolemy, except..." Alexander's voice trailed away, a shadow descending on his face for a moment. He shook his head, his hair grown out but ragged. "Winter it is, you fox. I'll show these Kossaians what it means to hold Alexander in contempt." Alexander stared around at the council. "Start preparations. War council tomorrow. We march within the week." He turned and strode across the room then disappeared into his private chambers.

As the meeting dispersed, Nikometros turned to Perdikkas. "What was that all about? Ptolemy risked almost certain displeasure, even death--for what?"

Perdikkas' face reflected a grudging admiration. "Alexander lost in his grief is no use to anyone. Ptolemy brought out a flash of the old Alexander. He'll find it harder to return to his grief. I think we'll see great things this winter."

# *Chapter 23*

Rocks clattered dully in the intense cold, dislodged from the narrow track by the feet of a trudging army. Macedonian soldiers, Persian auxiliaries, faces from every far-flung corner of the empire, dully watched the back of the man in front as they struggled up into the bleak mountains of Kossaia. Cloaked and muffled against the biting cold, weighed down by equipment and weapons, the army advanced up the narrow river valley toward the towering crags and walls of the bandit stronghold. Behind them, far down the valley, in the first swelling rise of foothills, lay their first encounter with the enemy. A dirty smudge of smoke clung to the land, unable to rise in the frigid air, hiding the destruction and death meted out to the homes and families of the tribes opposing the king.

Nikometros shivered despite his heavy woollen cloak as he looked out over the valley, watching columns of men moving slowly up the trails. The slow pace of their advance made them more menacing, inexorable, as they moved into the shadow of the Kossaian hill fort. He looked up at the battlements above him, seeing tiny figures of men moving, staring back down at approaching death. He shivered again and turned, picking his way down the rocky slope toward the nearest column of men.

A hundred paces or so up the track stood General Ptolemy, hunched over a map spread on a boulder in the shelter of a rocky outcrop. Around him clustered a dozen officers and adjutants, listening as he talked, his finger stabbing down at the map. Every few minutes one or more would break away and hurry off, carrying commands to various units of the army.

Ptolemy looked up when Nikometros approached, and then back down at the map. He snapped off a series of commands to the remaining officers, accepting their salutes, before turning back.

"So, Nikometros, you came after all. Hoping to see some action or just to keep an eye on me for your new master?"

"General Perdikkas hoped I might be of some service to you, sir."

Ptolemy snorted, his breath white in the still air. "Perdikkas always has an ulterior motive, boy, though he may not have told you of it. Expects you to report back regularly, I warrant."

"Yes, sir."

Ptolemy turned away and began folding up the map. "Well, I won't hold you up, Colonel. No doubt you'll want to join your unit or find your staff tent." He waved a hand dismissively.

Nikometros saluted the general's back, started to turn away and hesitated. "Sir...sir, I owe you an apology."

Ptolemy straightened but kept his back turned. "Yes?"

"Yes, sir. I was wrong to think you had a hand in trying to poison my wife. I ask your pardon."

Ptolemy turned and stared coldly at Nikometros. "You were a by-blow of my youth. By the time I even knew of your existence, your mother was in the care of a man prepared to raise you as his own." He looked away over the valley and his expression softened. "Yet I didn't forget her...or you. I gave gifts and provided what I could. I have no legitimate son, Nikometros, yet I..." Ptolemy made an abrupt chopping motion with his right hand and swung back toward his son, his face tight. "I'm keeping you from your duties, Colonel. You'll find the king up there somewhere." He gestured toward the fort. "Dismissed."

Nikometros gave a shaky salute and turned away, his face flushed. Leaving General Ptolemy, he picked his way slowly up the valley to where the army gathered in an open area just out of range of the arrows and other missiles that flew haphazardly from the fortifications. Officers pointed out where Alexander stood, in complete disregard of a shower of arrows aimed at him, close to the walled fort.

Nikometros hurried up, alert for missiles, and saluted. Alexander flicked him a glance and nodded before returning to his study of the fortifications and a disjointed discussion with the cluster of officers and engineers around him.

"Sir, catapults would reduce that wall quickly, it's only loose rock," said an engineer.

"It would take a week to bring them up. I won't wait."

"It would be safer, sir," said a young officer.

Alexander turned and looked at the officer coldly. "War is never safe. You have leave to go. Return to the city." He turned away as the young man retreated, a blush of shame colouring his face.

After a few moments of silence, a senior officer raised the same point. "Nevertheless, sir, a frontal assault will be costly unless we reduce the walls first."

Alexander nodded, the white plumes on his helmet tossing. The movement attracted another shower of arrows. One bounced off a boulder and clanged against the king's breastplate. He ignored it, staring up at the fort. "The cost must be borne. I won't wait; they have defied me and that is far more dangerous to let pass."

"The ground is too rocky to tunnel under the walls," observed an engineer.

"Perhaps we could burn the gates?" asked an officer.

"Scaling ladders?" queried another.

"No timber," replied the first engineer. "If we had it we could build catapults."

"Could we climb above them?" asked an older officer. "Like we did against Oxyartes, at the Sogdian Rock."

Alexander pointed to the crags above them. "A good idea, Eupomenes, except it would give us no advantage. There's no clear field of fire down into the fort." He shook his head. "No, we'll attack the gate directly. I'm confident we can take the place."

The engineers saluted and drew back, leaving a handful of staff officers around their king.

Alexander beckoned to Nikometros. "Your opinion, Nikometros?"

"There doesn't appear to be an alternative, sir."

"You don't approve?"

Nikometros shrugged. "I'm a soldier, sir. I'll do my duty."

Alexander said nothing, staring at the young Colonel with an appraising look.

"Perhaps a diversion?" suggested Nikometros. "Something to draw their attention. Give our men more time to breach the gates."

"Good. Take a hundred men and work your way around that hill on the right. Let them see you. When you attack the wall, I'll attack the gates."

"Yes sir."

Nikometros withdrew and hurried back to where the main body of men stood or sat around, huddled against the cold. Men looked up as he neared, apprehension showing in their faces.

"You there. Alcimon, Philos, Dymnotes...pick a hundred men. Fully armed, shields. Bows if you have them. Then follow me." Nikometros waved in the general direction of the low hill abutting the fortifications on the far end of the fort and moved away, leaving the officers to select the men.

In the lee of the hill, Nikometros explained the plan to his officers. "We must be visible. Don't hide; don't seek the cover of rocks. The enemy must see us coming and attack us. Our duty is to draw their attention from the main thrust at the gates."

Philos looked nervous and glanced at his fellow officers. "Er...they have the advantage, sir. They can fire down on us and we cannot strike back."

"Very observant, Philos. Use your shield. If the archers can cover us we may get inside the fort. Then you can strike back. If we fail in that, then let us at least buy time for the main attack. Now, disperse the men. We'll attack there," Nikometros pointed at a spur of rock jutting from the wall of stone, "And there, where the scree slope abuts the wall."

The junior officers formed the men into two groups and led them off at a run toward the designated areas. As they rounded the small hillock, heading toward the wall, cries arose from the defenders and a barrage of arrows and rocks fell about the Macedonians. Several men fell, some almost silently, with a breathless sigh and a muted clatter on the scree slope, others with a curse or a scream.

"Raise your shields, you fools!" yelled Nikometros. He pointed with his sword at the scree slope and ran toward it, his shield over his head. A large rock crashed down on him and he staggered, ignoring the sudden pain in his shield arm.

Reaching the slope, he looked around at his men. "Group together," he said. "Give the archers some protection." A dozen bowmen raised their weapons and, protected by the upraised shields of their companions, sent a ragged volley at the battlements. Another volley followed a few moments later, then a greater one as the group by the rock spur joined in. The rain of missiles from the battlements eased and Nikometros urged his men up the slope, climbing into the gully that ascended between the natural slope and the rough, loose wall of the Kossaian fort.

Nikometros climbed slowly, keeping his shield raised, his feet slipping in the loose rock. Behind him, his men stumbled and staggered, a rain of stones and small boulders showering down on them from the defenders. The missiles clanged and clattered on their shields or penetrated to strike the bodies beneath. A steady stream of curses and cries punctuated their heavy breathing. At last, the slope increased to the point where they could no longer ascend and they huddled beneath their shields some three or four body lengths below the crest of the wall. The stream of missiles increased as they crouched there, slowly battering them.

"We cannot stay here, sir," gasped Dymnotes, bleeding from a gash on his head.

A boulder crashed down, throwing a man bleeding and broken down the rocky slope. The other men grimly closed ranks, huddling closer.

"Sir," repeated Dymnotes. "We can go no further, we must retreat."

Nikometros wiped a free hand over his face, the rock dust smearing his features. He shook his head and gestured at the rock wall above them. "Climb," he said. "We must go on." He scrambled to his feet and sprang at the steep rock wall, his hands and feet scrabbling for purchase. There was a pause that lasted for two or three breaths then Dymnotes gave a yell of encouragement and followed, waving the men onward.

Spread-eagled against the wall, the rain of missiles slackened as the defenders found themselves having to lean out over the fortifications to throw stones. A shower of arrows from the Macedonian archers at the bottom of the slope sent them reeling back for cover.

Nikometros climbed on, blindly feeling for the next handhold. Stones clanged on his helmet, making his ears ring and stung his arms and back, bruising him through his armour. Dimly, he heard a distant roaring of many voices over his rasping breath. Abruptly, the rain of stones ceased and the only sound was the wind and the crunch of stones beneath his feet.

His hand met open air and he risked a glance upward. The top of the battlements met his gaze and, with a groan, he hauled himself over, struggling to bring his shield up to protect himself against the inevitable attack. No blows fell and Nikometros scrambled to his feet, staring wildly about as Dymnotes and the first of his men hauled themselves onto the top of the wall.

Nikometros stared down into the Kossaian fortress. Hundreds of men struggled and fought in the narrow spaces between stone and timber huts. The gates of the fort lay shattered and broken on the ground, a wave of soldiers pouring in over them, yelling and brandishing their weapons. At the front ran Alexander, his white-plumed helmet bobbing as he cut and stabbed.

Further along the wall, Nikometros saw his other officers, Philos and Alcimon climbing over the top, together with a dozen or so men. He yelled to get their attention and pointed down into the town before drawing his sword and leaping down behind the defenders.

A burly man in leather armour pushed a spear at Nikometros. He blocked the blow with his shield and, ducking, stabbed upward, feeling his blade slice home. The man groaned and fell back, his spear clattering to the ground. Nikometros stepped over the still quivering body and slashed at the backs of two men shooting arrows at the advancing soldiers. One fell with a howl of agony while the other dropped his bow and ran for the cover of the buildings. Alcimon snatched the spear from the ground, balanced himself and cast, impaling the fleeing archer.

Defenders in the rear ranks turned to face this new threat but died quickly, caught between the two forces of disciplined soldiers. The fighting broke up into scattered groups as the Macedonian army surged through the now-burning fort. Kossaian tribesmen fled, seeking shelter in stone huts or scrambling to climb over the walls.

Nikometros and his men hunted through the huts, stabbing and killing the snarling tribesmen. Blood ran down his blade and stuck his fingers to the hilt. A young girl, her small breasts showing through a ripped shift, flung herself from behind a door at him, her dagger thrusting wildly toward his chest. Nikometros staggered back, weaving to avoid the blade, trying to block her attack without killing her. One of his men pushed past him, knocked the girl to the ground with the edge of his shield and slashed her stomach open as she lay stunned. Blood spurted up over Nikometros' legs. The man grinned at Nikometros then left the hut, searching for other victims. Nikometros looked down at the young body at his feet and shook his head. He wiped his sword on a scrap of cloth then sheathed it before walking outside.

Soldiers milled everywhere, looting and burning, the bodies of the Kossaians lying strewn through the shattered fort.

Nikometros called his men to him and when, after a long interval, the majority arrived, started to pick his way through the rubble and carnage toward the fallen gates. He saw Alexander standing with Ptolemy and a small group of officers by the walls and approached them.

Ptolemy grinned at the bloodied and dust-streaked face of Nikometros then glanced down at the fresh blood on his tunic and legs, frowning. "You're hurt?"

Nikometros shook his head. "A few bruises, nothing more."

Alexander reached over and gripped the young man's arm briefly. "Well done," he murmured. "You drew their attention nicely." He turned and looked around the burning fort, the dense smoke clinging low in frigid air, obscuring the death around him. Screams of women and children rose in a despairing ululation. "May their blood warm your ghost, Hephaestion," he whispered. He grimaced and beckoned to General Ptolemy. "Destroy the fort and tear down the walls. Let this destruction be a salutary lesson for the rebels." Alexander looked down at the blood and grime on his body, his lips curling in distaste. "Kill them all, I take no prisoners today." He turned on his heel and stalked away, out of the fort, his junior officers running to keep up.

Nikometros turned to Ptolemy with a look of disgust. "He cannot mean it, sir," he exclaimed. "Listen. There are only women and children left alive."

"He's the king, Nikometros. The glory is his...and the pain. His soul is hurting but he will heal. This savagery will pass in time but for now his orders stand." Ptolemy nodded to his staff officers. "You have your orders," he said.

# *Chapter 24*

S now fell, blanketing stony ground and softening the harsh edges of war. The Macedonian army continued its relentless passage through the mountains of Kossaia, hunting down fugitive tribes, laying siege to walled forts and bringing death to the rebel populace. One of the sub-chiefs, Beremos, sued for peace, offering to come down from his mountain fortress and talk with the king if he was guaranteed safe passage.

Alexander sent a herald with tokens and the man came, at the head of a small retinue.

Alexander's tent sat in the shelter of a great rock, straddling the main road through the mountains to Babylon. Alexander himself sat on a plain wooden stool, poring over a map of the region. His breath smoked in the icy air and his staff officers shivered despite their thick woollen cloaks. The king disdained any show of weakness and ignored the rich cloak draped over the table. A brazier burned sullenly in one corner of the tent, giving off only fitful heat.

A squire poked his head through the tent entrance, reporting the arrival of Beremos. Alexander rolled up the map and handed it to an aide before pushing back the stool and getting to his feet. "Bring them to the great tent," he said. "And send for spiced wine." He ducked under the tent flap and strode off through the growing dusk, followed by Nikometros and the other staff officers.

Soldiers camped along the road and over the lower slopes of the valley floor. Huddling in groups of five or ten, they sat crouched by small campfires against the bitter cold, or asleep in small tents. Sentries paced and called out the challenge, scrambling to salute when the king approached.

With a nod and a half-wave, Alexander acknowledged their presence before entering the great audience tent. Several men sat around a blazing fire in the middle of the tent, an opening in the canvas roof dispersing a plume of dense smoke. The vent flapped in the wind, sending eddies of smoke curling through the interior.

The Kossaian tribesmen sat on stools around the fire, glaring suspiciously at the ring of guards along the walls. They fingered their weapons, ready for the slightest sign of treachery. Ptolemy sat on a stool opposite the Kossaians.

The tribesmen turned when Alexander entered and one of them rose ponderously to his feet, followed by his companions. The man stood head and shoulders over the Macedonians, thick set and bear-like beneath his bulky clothing. Ragged greasy locks hung down over his shoulders and his eyes glimmered in a face overgrown with hair. He stared at the clean-shaven Macedonians and rumbled a question in a broad dialect.

Alexander, his face impassive, gestured to the seats. He waited while the Kossaians reseated themselves before taking his seat by Ptolemy. Beckoning to the young Persian interpreter, he leaned over and, keeping his eyes locked on Beremos, asked for a translation of the chieftain's question.

The interpreter looked uncomfortable. "He asks whether er...eunuchs attend on him, sire. He means no insult, I think, only a comment on the lack of beards."

Alexander nodded. "Does he know who I am?"

The interpreter addressed the delegation and listened to the terse response. "Yes sire. He says your fame precedes you, though you're...you're smaller than he thought." The interpreter flushed. "I'm sorry, sire. I'll try to be more circumspect in my translation."

Alexander turned his eyes briefly to the young man. "You will translate exactly. There must be no misunderstanding." He leaned forward, looking at Beremos. "Offer him spiced wine."

The chief snuffed at the great cup of heated spiced wine handed to him by a servant but did not drink. He watched as Alexander accepted a cup poured from the same pitcher, raising the wine to his lips and sipping at the hot sweet drink. After a moment Beremos tasted it, nodded in appreciation, and drank deeply. He belched loudly and put his cup down on the hard ground.

"Why do you want to talk with me?" asked Alexander, through the interpreter.

"I want your help," replied Beremos simply.

"My help?"

"Your quarrel is with Moltossos. He's paramount chief of all our peoples. I, myself..." Beremos shrugged. "I don't wish to fight you, yet if my chief orders me..."

Alexander sat and waited.

After a few minutes, Beremos shifted on his stool and drew his cloak tighter around him. "Moltossos is in the next valley with over a thousand men. He sits behind walls that dwarf those you razed and has food and drink to last all winter. You won't pry him out."

Nikometros flushed and stepped forward. "We'll take him as we've taken every fort so far."

Beremos grinned, showing a mouth full of rotten teeth. "Your puppy barks loudly but I think he's toothless."

Alexander raised his hand as a warning for his staff officer without taking his eyes from the Kossaian. "Why do you tell me this?" he asked.

"I can guide you into his city through mountain paths. You can fall on him before he becomes aware of your presence."

"You would betray your lord?"

Beremos shrugged. "Moltossos is old and set in his ways. He cannot see that the old Persian kings have passed and there's a new force in the land." He picked up his wine cup and peered into it. He held it out to the servant who immediately stepped forward to refill it.

"And what reward do you seek for this service?"

Beremos drank again from the hot, spiced wine before replying. "Nothing of any great import. Make me your satrap and I will govern Kossaia with an iron fist. None shall rise against you and your taxes will be collected each year."

"And no doubt skimming a healthy profit off the top," muttered a young staff officer.

Beremos glanced at the officer with disdain. "You fight for your king without pay?"

Alexander frowned. "Your services will not go unrewarded. However, if Moltossos submits I will measure the man before I decide."

The Kossaian chieftain scowled and leaned toward his companions. They muttered inaudibly for a few minutes before Beremos turned back to Alexander with a smile. "Agreed. I will guide you."

Alexander smiled back, though his eyes remained hooded and watchful. He pushed the map forward. "Show me."

Beremos stared down at the piece of parchment and took it in his large dirty hands, turning it and peering at the lines and notations. He scowled again and thrust it back. "I have no use for such things. I'll show you the paths myself."

Alexander rolled the map and handed it to an officer. "Very well. Go with this man and describe to him the nature of the land we'll be crossing. I want to know details, like the width of the track, the steepness, how close it brings us to the enemy, how long it will take us to arrive. My officers know what to ask."

Beremos rose to his feet with a grunt and followed the officer from the tent. When the last of the tribesmen left the audience tent. Ptolemy turned to Alexander with a troubled look. "You would trust such a man, Alexander?"

Alexander shook his head. "Never, but I'll use him and reward him. As for Moltossos..." He shrugged. "We shall see."

# Chapter 25

Bithyia leaned back on the great bed, sinking into the soft cushions with a sigh. She fanned her flushed face and shoulders, while idly glancing at the small black fan in her hand. It was emblazoned with an impossibly contorted scarlet and gold dragon and had been a year or more on the road from fabled Chin to a small Persian hamlet on the northern road from Ekbatana to Babylon. Looking down over her sweat-sheened breasts and swollen belly, she could just make out a hairy leg poking from beneath the rumpled bed covers. She grinned and kicked out at the estimated position of a familiarly hirsute posterior. "Come on, lover," she purred. "Don't think to spend your time asleep."

The muffled snoring beneath the covers ended with a snort and a bearded face peered out blearily. A callused hand knuckled bloodshot eyes and sought to bring a semblance of order to his tousled hair. "Insatiable bitch. What do you do when I'm not here?"

Bithyia grinned and rolled over, squirming her naked body down the bed to him. "Wait patiently for my husband, what else?" She took the man's face in her hands and kissed him firmly.

After a moment, the man responded. He broke free and grinned before pushing Bithyia onto her back. He stared down at her naked body, a hand caressing her belly. "We shouldn't, my love. I don't want to harm our child."

Bithyia pouted and pulled him down on her. "Once more, my beloved Timon. Once more won't hurt."

The late afternoon sunlight crept slowly over the moving bodies and up the far wall of the bedchamber. Sated at last, Bithyia rested her head on Timon's chest and her hands complacently on her belly. They lay together in silence as twilight fell. When the last rays vanished, she stirred.

"I wish you didn't have to return tomorrow," Bithyia whispered.

"Aye, lass," grunted Timon. "As do I. But at least we had this time together. Niko was decent enough to let me carry dispatches back to Perdikkas, rather than the usual courier, so we shouldn't complain."

"Is Niko well? Tomyra is certain to ask."

"Well enough."

The silence that followed his statement was so long that Bithyia turned her head up to look at him quizzically. "Meaning?" she queried.

Timon sighed. "The king has changed since Hephaestion died. Once he killed only where necessary, sparing the lives of his enemies if they surrendered, certainly the women and children. Now whole villages are burned, everyone put to the sword. Niko hates the slaughter."

Bithyia turned on her side and stroked Timon's matted chest hairs. "You do too, my great Greek bear."

"A fine pair of soldiers, aren't we?"

"I wouldn't love you if you enjoyed killing."

Timon smiled and put a huge hand on Bithyia's head. "A little less loving might leave me with the strength to do other things...oof!" Timon gasped after a small fist caught him in the stomach. He grabbed for Bithyia's wrist and wrestled her back, pinning her with a leg. He leaned down and kissed her gently. "On the other hand, dear wife, your love is all that sustains me at war."

They kissed and Bithyia's hands moved down Timon's muscular body. He broke free with a laugh. "Enough, lass. Give me time to recover."

Bithyia smiled, her fingers tracing patterns on her husband's skin. "How much longer will these wars last? Does Alexander mean to kill all the Kossaians?"

"Not much longer, I think. Two weeks ago, we surprised the chief Moltossos in his stronghold. One of his sub-chiefs saw the way the wind blew and offered to betray him...for a reward of course. He wanted to be chief in his place."

"And Alexander dealt with a traitor?" Bithyia exclaimed. "I thought more of him."

Timon nodded. "He promised him a reward if he showed us the way over the mountains, but it turned out that Alexander's blood lust was spent. Moltossos saw he was caught in a trap and surrendered, asking only that his people be allowed to live."

"What happened?"

"The old man came into our camp with his family around him. Wives, sons, daughters, grandchildren...even great-grandchildren. He stood there proudly in front of Alexander and asked for mercy."

"But he was a bandit chief. How could he expect mercy?"

Timon shook his head. "Expect it? No. But he got it. I think all the killing and burning finally exhausted the king and he was only too willing to have an excuse to stop. He allowed the old man to go into exile with his family."

"So, he gave the traitor his reward? He made him chief?"

Timon laughed. "No. Once a traitor, always a traitor. He gave him gold and suggested quite strongly that he find another part of the country to live in."

"I would have killed him."

Timon stroked his wife's hair and smiled. "My fierce Scythian warrior."

"What happened to the tribe? Did they go into exile too?"

"No. Alexander did as he so often has in the past. He installed one of Moltossos' sons as chief, left him a Macedonian officer and squad to keep order and marched away." Timon grimaced. "He always believed in letting his defeated enemies govern themselves, though heaven help them if they betrayed his trust."

"The war is over then," exclaimed Bithyia. "You'll be home again soon."

"With luck, lass, though there's still some things left to do. Not all the Kossaian tribes followed Moltossos." Timon stretched and swung his legs over the side of the bed. He walked across to the pot in the far corner of the room and relieved himself. Turning away, he picked up his clothing and began to dress.

"I'd better pay my respects to Tomyra. See if she has a letter for Niko." Timon walked back to the bed and sat down, stooping to fasten his sandals. "How is she? Getting on better with her daughter?"

Bithyia sat up on the edge of the bed and wrapped a blanket around her shoulders. "She still refuses to acknowledge the child. She won't even feed her and is content to let her nurse look after the child."

Timon sighed. "I suppose she has the right but since Niko accepted the child's parentage you would think her own mother could come to terms."

"That isn't my greatest concern." Bithyia hesitated, putting a restraining hand on her husband's arm. "She spends a lot of time with the merchant Parates."

Timon jumped to his feet with an oath. "Parates? He's here?" His hand slid to his sword and he turned toward the door.

Bithyia caught at him, pulling him back. "Timon. Be careful, please. He offers her no harm."

Timon swung round and stared at his wife. "Then why are you concerned?"

"He...I don't trust him. He's polite and generous and obeys all the proper forms in calling on a married woman, but...there's something not quite right."

"Then I'd better call on him before I leave."

"Please, my husband, don't let him provoke you. I know your temper..."

"I won't lose control," growled Timon. "I'll call on Tomyra first then see Parates before I leave in the morning." He looked at Bithyia for a moment before flashing her a quick smile. "I won't go alone. If others are with me I'll be polite. But I will find out his intentions." He kissed his wife and strode from the room.

Timon clattered down the rickety stairs of the inn and out through the tavern. The building was packed with troops and minor officials of the court. In the street the crush of humanity seemed almost as great. He walked up the street toward the centre of town, keeping to the edges of the road and stepping aside when a mule train or squadron of wagons groaned past, laden with the trappings of a minor city on the move.

Coming at last to the door of the other inn, Timon peered up through the night at the lit windows on the upper floor. Around him, torches flickered, their shifting light and shadow made the moving crowds sway and stutter. Timon pushed through the door and up to the crowded bar where he tried to attract the attention of the innkeeper.

"Who?" yelled the harried man after several minutes. The innkeeper broke off to push a jug of wine at a customer and scoop up a few copper coins.

"The lady Tomyra," said Timon as the man passed by on his way to attend to another customer. "Which room is she in?"

"Up the stairs." The innkeeper jerked a hand toward the doorway at the back of the large room. "Ask the porter. He'll tell you."

Timon nodded and pushed away from the bar, threading his way through the jostling crowd. He peered up the darkened stairs at the faint glow of torchlight on the upper floor. He grunted and gripped the hilt of his dagger firmly as he climbed slowly.

On the upper floor, a torch burned in a wall sconce, casting an unsteady glow down a narrow hallway. Timon walked up to the first of several doors leading off the hallway and raised his hand before hesitating.

"What you want then?" snarled a thin voice from behind him.

Timon turned toward the voice, the owner detaching himself from the deep shadows of a doorway on the other side of the stairs.

"I seek the lady Tomyra. Please be so good as to tell me which room she is in."

The man, a gangling youth with a wispy beard, stared at Timon, his hand scratching idly at an armpit. "Down there." He nodded toward the hall. "On the right, second door." The youth turned away with a yawn.

Timon moved down to the indicated door and rapped on the wood. A dull murmur of voices within the room ceased and footsteps approached across creaking floorboards.

"Who is there?" enquired a woman's voice.

"Timon. I wish to see your lady."

"One moment, sir."

Footsteps creaked across the floorboards once more before fading into silence. A minute passed then Timon heard the woman returning. The latch clacked upward and the door swung open.

"Come in, sir." A young Persian woman held the door open for Timon. "My lady will see you in her chamber." She closed and latched the door before walking ahead of Timon to a door at the far end of the room. She swung her hips provocatively, glancing back over her shoulder at the bearded warrior.

On reaching the bedchamber, Timon eased past the woman with gruff thanks and pushed open the door. A bed dominated the room, covered with woven rugs, pelts and cushions. Beside it, a glowing brazier banished the early spring chill from the air and a pair of oil lamps cast a buttery glow over the room. In the far corner of the room, by the darkened window admitting the glow of the town lights sat Tomyra, curled up in a huge high-backed chair. At her feet sat a serving woman, her hands busy with some embroidery. Both women glanced up as Timon entered the room.

"My lady," said Timon. "It's good to see you."

Tomyra uncurled her feet and sat up straight, a smile lighting up her pale face. "Timon!" she cried. "You are welcome indeed. What news?"

"Niko sends his love, my lady. As for news, I have a letter." Timon reached for his pouch and extracted a folded paper that he held out to Tomyra.

Tomyra reached out a hand for the letter then drew back. Her smile faded and she turned toward another chair drawn back into the shadows. "Forgive me," she said. "I'm forgetting my manners. Parates, have you had the pleasure of meeting Timon of Messa, one of my husband's oldest and most trusted friends?"

Timon whirled, his hand dropping the letter and grabbing for his dagger. He moved to place himself between Tomyra and the figure of a man rising to his feet in the shadows.

"Yes indeed, my lady," replied Parates smoothly. "I have met him, though I regret we were never properly introduced."

"Well then, Timon, this is...Timon, what is the matter?"

"Stay back, my lady," growled Timon, drawing his dagger. "Has this man offered you any harm?"

"Of course not, Timon. Why should he?"

Parates bowed slightly, a small smile on his shadowed face. "Indeed, worthy Timon of Messa. Why would I offer any harm to such a noble lady?"

"This is the man who harboured your brother's creature, Scolices. He probably had a hand in the attempt on your life."

"Oh, Timon, Parates has explained all that," cried Tomyra. She stepped up beside Timon and put out her hand, pulling his arm down. "Now put up your dagger and sit down."

Timon grimaced but allowed his arm to fall. He slid the dagger back into its sheath, all the while glaring at the other man. Tomyra picked up the fallen letter then sat down and gestured for Parates to take his seat also.

"There, that's better," said Tomyra. "Timon, please sit down. No harm will come to us through Parates. He has shown himself this last month to be an old friend of the Massegetae people and a courteous and generous visitor." She reached down beside her and picked up a pottery flagon. With a pop she uncorked it, releasing the odour of soured milk. "See, Timon. He found me some real koumiss."

"You haven't drunk it?" exclaimed Timon. He strode to her side and knocked the flagon to the floor, the thin pale brown liquid gushing out onto the rug. The maidservant leapt to her feet and righted the flagon, mopping at the puddle with her embroidery, a look of disgust on her face.

Tomyra stared up at Timon with horror. "Timon, you forget yourself," she cried. "Parates, please forgive him. I'm sure he meant no disrespect."

"My lady," growled Timon. "Have you forgotten so soon the attempt on your life? I don't trust any gift from this man, least of all a gift of food or drink."

Parates' face darkened and he glared at the other man. "Your distrust offends me." He held out his hand to the maidservant. "Give me the flagon." He grasped it, looked around for a cup, found one and poured himself a generous portion. Staring into Timon's eyes he drank, the koumiss dribbling down his chin. He upended the cup, allowing the last few drops to fall to the floor.

"Not the most palatable of drinks," he sneered, "But not one that will do me any harm."

"You see, Timon?" reproved Tomyra. "Parates wouldn't hurt me. You owe him an apology."

"I remain unconvinced." Timon frowned. "However, I'm willing to hear him out."

"What do you mean, hear me out?"

"You said you were a follower of the Light. Back in Ekbatana, remember? What exactly did you mean by that?"

Parates sat back down in his chair and settled himself with a smile. "I'm a follower of Ahura-Mazda," he said quietly. "The Light from heaven that banishes the darkness."

Timon nodded. "As I thought. I've made inquiries." He paused. "So you're opposed to Ahriman, the god of darkness and the Lie?"

Parates clapped his hands together softly then spread them wide, palms down. "Never speak that name."

Timon inclined his head in acquiescence. "As a follower of Ahura-Mazda you speak only the truth then?" His voice hardened. "In the name of your god, answer me this in truth...Do you seek to harm the lady Tomyra?"

Parates paused and looked at Tomyra then back to Timon. "On my honour, and in the name of my god, I do not seek to harm her."

Timon nodded again. "And did you send the lady Tomyra a gift of poisoned sweetmeats?"

Parates closed his eyes, his face screwing up as if in pain. "I did send a gift of sweetmeats, but I swear by my god that I did not put poison in them. Some other hand must have intervened between my house and your lady's."

"Whose hand?" asked Timon.

"Enough, Timon," interposed Tomyra. "Parates is my guest."

"Whose hand?" repeated Timon. "In the name of Ahura-Mazda, speak the truth."

Parates hesitated, his eyes flicking from Timon to Tomyra and back again. "In truth? I don't know for a certainty, I didn't see the act." He shrugged. "If I were to guess...this man Scolices."

"It could be," agreed Tomyra. "Scolices does hate me." She shivered and slipped a richly embroidered shawl over her shoulders. "My brother's hand reaches out from the grave."

Timon grunted. He crossed the small room and perched himself on the corner of the bed. "What of the note that came with the gift? Why put another's name if there was nothing to hide?"

"There was no note with it when it left my hand," said Parates quietly. "I sent a verbal message with the servant."

"Ah, yes...the boy Madoc."

Parates screwed up his forehead. "Who?"

"Madoc. The servant who delivered the poisoned sweetmeats," growled Timon. "Surely you remember him? The young Kelt who so conveniently died after making your delivery."

"Timon," snapped Tomyra. "You go too far. This man is my guest. I won't have you interrogate him so."

Parates shook his head. "I have had no one of that name in my employ."

"No, you were careful to use a servant of Ptolemy, not one of your own. Then you killed him so he couldn't implicate you." Timon grinned, a feral snarl that left his eyes hard and cold. "Deny it, Parates, in the name of your god of Truth."

Parates sat silently, staring down at the worn rug on the uneven wooden flooring. From beneath came the raucous shouts and singing of drunken men and from the open window wafted the sounds and smells of an army on the move. After several minutes, Parates stirred and looked up at Tomyra, a tired look in his eyes. "I swear to you, in the name of Ahura-Mazda that I did not kill this servant boy Madoc." He held up a hand as Timon opened his mouth. "Nor," Parates added, "Did I have him killed."

The merchant rose slowly to his feet and adjusted his robes. He bowed to Tomyra. "With your leave, lady, I will withdraw. It seems I have outstayed my welcome."

Tomyra also stood and held out her slim hand. "I'm sorry, Parates. Please call on me again. You're welcome any time." She flashed a hard look at Timon.

Parates clasped her hand briefly then, bowing again to Tomyra, left the room, accompanied by the maidservant.

Timon made a rude gesture at the closing door. "Good riddance," he grunted. "He may deny it, my lady, but he's guilty. His god notwithstanding." He turned to Tomyra with a smile. "Anyway, to happier things. I have good news..."

"Timon of Messa," Tomyra's voice was frigid with anger. "I have seldom seen such a display of ill manners to an invited guest. Your behaviour is a disgrace and if I were a man I would call you to account for it. As it is I shall ask my husband..."

"My lady!" broke in Timon. "You know I have only your safety in mind. That man is evil, he..."

"Enough! Among my people a guest is sacred. An insult offered to a guest is an insult offered to me." She turned her back on Timon. "You have my leave to go."

"My lady, you must know I..."

"Go!"

214

Timon blinked and opened his mouth to protest anew. He stared at Tomyra's rigid back and shut his mouth with an audible snap. He turned on his heel and stalked to the door of the bedchamber, pushing past the maidservant. Turning in the doorway he jerked his head in a taut semblance of a bow. "As you wish, my lady," he rasped before slamming the door behind him.

Timon emerged into the upstairs corridor and stood there, breathing hard. He gave an incoherent cry of rage and slammed his fist into a wall, rattling the nearby doors. He swore, holding his wrist then lifted his hand, scowling at his bruised and cut knuckles. He strode off down the corridor, pushing past the inn porter and disappearing down the darkened stairs.

When the sounds of Timon's footsteps faded, Parates emerged from the shadows in the corridor and stared after him, a smile slowly creasing his face.

# *Chapter 26*

P arates sat astride a glossy black fine-boned Arabian stallion, controlling the high-spirited beast with unconscious ease as his gaze scoured the wooded hills below him. The road from the hills disgorged into flat and featureless river plains in the distance. A cloud of dust marked the passage of the court, appearing to be merely a smudge on the landscape. Far to the south, another discolouration told of the presence of the king's army, marching north and west up the Tigris River.

*Another day, maybe two, before they meet and turn westward toward Babylon* thought Parates. *The wrong time of year to be arriving in the capital. Has no one told the king it will be hot and fever-filled in the summer?*

He sighed and turned his attention to the man beside him. "You have him?"

The man nodded and Parates pulled his horse's head round. "Take me to him."

The man nudged his horse, a brown gelding, down the rough track that led from the hilltop, back into the aspen forest that clothed the landscape. Green buds and newly unfurled leaves exploded along branches and twigs

216

scoured bare by winter storms. The air, fresh and clean, surged through their lungs, filling them with energy.

Parates grinned, despite his coming confrontation. *It really is too nice a day to kill someone.*

The path led down into a tangled forest, one that had not seen axe or fire for many years. The trees towered above them, beech and oak, gnarled and twisted roots gripping the leaf-strewn slopes. The horses slowed, picking their way carefully. Around them, the woods pulsed with new life, the air filled with bird song.

Parates sniffed, the odour of wood smoke tickling his nostrils. A few moments later, the path opened out into a small clearing. A dozen men sat around a small cooking fire or lounged against the tumbledown remnants of an old woodcutter's hut. They looked up as the horsemen entered the clearing, several of them uttering cries of greeting.

Parates dismounted and passed the reins to one of the men. He turned to one of the men by the ruined hut and raised an eyebrow enquiringly.

"Inside," grunted the man. "The little sniveller will be almost glad to see you, I think." He grinned and scratched his groin with a scarred and filthy hand.

Parates walked into the meagre shelter afforded by rickety walls and stared around at the debris strewn over the ground. A bundle of rags and leaves stirred in the corner and a pale face, streaked with grime, peered up at him.

"Parates," croaked the figure. "In the name of all the gods, why am I treated like this?"

Parates signalled to his men. "Get him up."

He waited while they hauled their captive onto his knees and brushed the filth off him with ungentle hands. They stepped back and watched with predatory grins on their faces. Parates looked around and shoved a segment of axe-hewn wood close to the prisoner. He sat down on it and stretched his legs out, staring at the unkempt captive. "Well, Scolices. Can you give me any reason to keep you alive?"

"Wha...what do you mean? What have I done?" asked Scolices, fear giving his voice a rise in pitch.

Parates inspected the other man silently, his hand stroking his short dark beard and an expectant expression in his eyes.

Scolices fidgeted, his tongue licking his lips nervously. He glanced into his captor's eyes then away again. "I...I don't know what you think I've done. I haven't done..." His voice trailed away.

"Poison," Parates flatly stated.

Scolices jerked his gaze round and stared at Parates. "Someone had to," he whined. "Besides, I thought you meant me to...talking about it like that."

"We were discussing possibilities, you fool. Poison is an excellent tool but it must be used properly." Parates massaged his temples with one hand. "One must prepare the ground first, carefully--not rush into it impetuously."

"I nearly succeeded."

"Really? I was under the impression both Nikometros and Tomyra still lived and were now on their guard."

Scolices shrugged. "I'll kill them next time."

"What makes you think there'll be a next time, Scolices? You have become a liability. Perhaps I should just have you killed right here and now. Who would miss you?"

Scolices blanched and licked his lips. "You would forget your vow?"

Parates contemplated the man in silence. From the forest came the distant hollow hammering of a woodpecker. At length, Parates shifted his weight and sighed. "Your dead chief laid a heavy burden on me. No, listen," Parates added when Scolices opened his mouth. "I made a promise and it's one I shall keep for I renounce the Lie." He brought his hands together softly before spreading them apart, palms down. "Yet your actions have forced me to skirt the truth closer than I would like. I haven't lied directly, not even to my enemies but I have misled. I fear Ahura-Mazda will turn his back on me."

"What do you mean?"

"I made an effort to get close to the woman, to earn her trust and gratitude and, despite your clumsy efforts, I succeeded. However, the Greek's friend, Timon, nearly undid it all. If his questions were a trifle more astute I would have been forced to kill him, and then her. I would probably be dead and, without me, you would have no hope of killing the Greek."

Scolices shook his head. "I don't understand. You kill but you won't lie to save your life? What nonsense is this?"

Parates regarded the other man coldly. "It's a matter of honour. I wouldn't expect you to understand."

He got to his feet and walked to the open side of the ruined hut and stood staring out at his men. They squatted around the smoky fire, talking and drinking. Blue wood smoke eddied and curled in the golden shafts of morning sunlight before rising through the sparse canopy of new leaves.

"Ahura-Mazda is the Light that banishes darkness," said Parates softly. "All who follow him renounce the Lie and attempt to live in honour." He glanced round at Scolices, who stood in the shadowed interior. "Yes, I kill when I have to...to defend my life, my honour, to pay a debt or to avenge a wrong. What man would not? Yet your actions brought me to the brink of a lie. It was only the fact that I couldn't be absolutely certain that you were the poisoner that allowed me to evade Timon's questions." Parates turned away again, shaking his head. "You make me feel unclean inside, before my god. I shall be asked to atone and I fear the price will be heavy."

"But you'll honour your promise?"

Parates whirled and crossed the leafmould-drifted floor of the hut in three strides. He gripped Scolices by the front of his tunic and shook the man before hurling him to the ground. "Do you understand nothing I have said?" he shouted. "I despise your dead master and you. Yet I made a promise and I will not break my word, though it means my death."

Scolices struggled to sit up, his pinioned arms hindering him. "Yes, yes, of course," he quavered. "I didn't doubt you. I only meant..." He broke off and looked up fearfully. "What am I...what do you mean to...?"

"I should kill you," said Parates flatly. "Yet I will not. I think you may yet be of some use."

Scolices sagged with relief then grinned and struggled to his feet, holding out his bound hands. "Of course, dear Parates. Tell me what to do."

# *Chapter 27*

Spring came late that year to the mountains that fed the streams then led into the Tigris and Euphrates Rivers. The snows were largely unmelted and the rivers low when Alexander's combined army and court forded the Tigris, the waters merely breasting the horses. Wagons and carts followed with scarcely a mishap. Children screamed with excitement and women and court eunuchs held fast nervously as the wagons lurched and rumbled through the swift waters of the shallows.

Nikometros, as befitted a favoured staff officer in the retinue of Perdikkas, the new Chiliarch, and most powerful man in the empire after Alexander, rode at the head of a unit of Cavalry. Beside him rode his aide-de-camp, Timon of Messa, grinning through a heavy beard as he accepted the salutes and cheers of the men.

The mood of the army rose when they neared Babylon, capital of the vast empire. The last of their battles were behind them; wounds suffered in the Kossaian campaign healing and loot jingled in their knapsacks. Soon they would enjoy the fleshpots of that ancient city, forgetting for a time the hard life of a soldier.

"Heady times, eh Timon?" commented Nikometros with a smile.

Timon grinned. "Aye, Niko. What a time to be alive and Macedonian. Nothing can stop Alexander now. Scarcely two months to rid the empire of the last opposition and he's ready for the nations to the west."

Nikometros' smile slipped. "Hush Timon. Don't tempt the gods. They're jealous of human achievement."

Timon snorted. "Human? You forget Alexander is styled a god." He looked around then leaned closer to his companion. "Seriously, Niko. Think on what the king has done these last twelve years and he's a young man yet. What kingdoms and lands will he conquer these next twelve?"

"They say he looks to Arabia next."

"What does he want with that? Just a hot desert and little else." Timon snorted with derision.

"Incense and spices though. Also, it leads to the southern lands--Afrik and beyond." Nikometros paused in thought for a few moments. "Ivory," he said pensively. "In Egypt I saw treasuries packed with ivory and gold that came from the south. Good slaves too and strange beasts. I swear there's an animal as tall as a tree that's all legs and neck. There was one in the menagerie at Thebes."

Timon gaped then let out a bellow of laughter and punched Nikometros lightly on the arm. "Good one, Niko! You almost had me there." Wiping his eyes he beckoned to Tirses, riding at the head of the small squad of Scythians. He leaned over and recounted the tale of the outrageous beast, struggling to maintain a straight face.

Tirses listened politely then glanced across at Nikometros. "Truly, sir?"

When Nikometros nodded, Tirses shook his head, an amazed expression on his face. "I shall look forward to seeing this marvellous beast, Timon. Thank you for telling me of it." He twitched the reins and guided his horse back to his command.

Timon stared after him with a look of disgust. "Idiot," he grunted. "Some people will believe anything." He turned toward the sound of rapidly approaching hooves from the north. "Hullo," he said, shading his eyes. "Who's this?"

A small body of horsemen approached the slowly moving cavalry detachment at a gallop. Tirses shouted a command and moved his squad up closer to his commander. The horsemen closed with Nikometros and drew rein, kicking up a small cloud of dust.

"Nikometros, well met!" cried the commander.

"Iolattos," Nikometros responded. "What are you doing here? Is the king near?"

Iolattos waved vaguely to the forested hills to the north. "Hunting. But he sends his orders. There's a level plain some fifty stadia to the west. We are commanded to set up camp there and await his coming."

Nikometros stared at the equerry, detecting an underlying current of excitement in the young man's voice. "What is it?"

Iolattos grinned. "Ambassadors from the whole world. There must be hundreds of them. They cooled their heels this winter, waiting for the king, waiting to bend their knee to him." The young man's excitement infected his horse and it shied violently, rearing. He fought it down again with an effort. "By the gods," he continued. There are embassies from Libya, Carthage, and Iberia. Even Kelts and Scyths. Ethiops and Etruscans too."

"The king already has loyal Scythians," growled Tirses. "What need has he of others?"

Iolattos raised an eyebrow but did not comment. He pointed back along the road to where the main body of the army marched, followed by a great straggling mass of the royal court. "Take your men forward, Nikometros and secure the area. I'll send riders to bring the army on with haste. The king wishes the camp to be set up to receive the ambassadors by dawn tomorrow." Iolattos saluted and dug his heels into his horse's sides. He, and his troop, galloped off down the road toward the approaching army.

Nikometros shouted out a command and, backed by the hurried orders of Timon and the other officers, had a detachment of cavalry thundering forward within minutes.

The road debouched into a broad flat flood plain set about with farms and herds of grazing cattle. Nikometros set his men to rapidly scouring the land for any dangers, spreading out in line abreast. By the time the sun crossed a twelfth part of the heavens, he turned the men back, feeling reasonably confident there was no danger to the court the presence of the army could not deter.

The main body of the army arrived soon after, taking up positions to form a vast square, into the centre of which straggled, over the next few hours, the immense baggage train of the court and associated camp followers.

Innumerable campfires erupted from the barrack lines and local grazing herds fell beneath axe and knife to feed the throngs. Tents were erected, latrines dug and the infrastructure of a minor city on the move set up. By nightfall the camp prostitutes were ministering to the needs of the soldiery, several infants were birthed and two separate murders discovered. Both assailants were summarily dealt with, their corpses mourned briefly by interested parties then cremated.

Alexander arrived several hours later, the quiet of the sleeping camp roused into a flurry of activity once more by the mere presence of the king. He washed fastidiously, removing the grime and blood of a successful hunt, changed his clothing, and immediately started a round of consultations with his generals and advisors.

A young squire roused Nikometros from his bed and, bidding a hurried farewell to Tomyra and his infant daughter Starissa, he hurried to the tent of the Chiliarch.

Perdikkas looked up when Nikometros entered. "Ah, Nikometros," he said. "I'm at my wits end. The king will receive the embassies tomorrow morning...this morning," he grimaced. "And now he wants every embassy escorted by a staff officer. Can you organise that?" Without waiting for a reply he turned to one of the court eunuchs and started issuing a string of commands concerning the reception tent and the furnishings.

Nikometros saluted and turned to one of the scribes writing at a nearby table. "You have a list of the embassies?"

The scribe broke off with a mutter of annoyance and handed Nikometros a sheet of paper. He scanned the list with a feeling of dismay. "All of these? There must be twenty or more. Where am I going to find twenty officers...and interpreters too, at this late hour?"

The scribe bestowed a smirk on the staff officer before bending to his task once more. Nikometros gave the man a sour look and hurried from the tent. Outside, he caught sight of Timon and Tirses and beckoned them over, rapidly explaining his problem.

Timon scanned the list. "Tirses and I can take the Scyths at least. I can explain procedures while Tirses can translate if there are any problems." He ran his finger down the names. "Bit tougher for you, Niko. Beggin' yer pardon but you aren't especially good at languages...ah, here. This lot will have had contact with the Greek colonies in Sicily and Italy. Romans...some minor tribe, so I hear, but warlike. With luck they'll speak a bit of Greek."

Nikometros nodded. "I thought also Bydos and Komon. They may know of others."

"No problem, Niko. I'll get back to the barracks and have a word with them." Timon glanced across the camp at the hurrying figures of soldiers and servants. "There's somebody else who may be able to help. Ho, Seleukos, sir, over here!" he called.

Seleukos sauntered over, his expression wary until he recognised Nikometros. Apprised of the situation he too scanned the list of embassies. "No great problem," he grinned. "I know a group of young officers keeping their heads down in the mess tent, hoping to avoid extra duties. This will be just the thing for them."

Nikometros moved through the camp toward the foreign embassies on the western fringes. The camp was awake and bursting with anticipation. Babble in a dozen tongues surrounded Nikometros as he walked. Macedonian troops, once the mainstay of the army, were less common now. Twelve years of warfare and attrition through battle and the manning of a myriad garrisons sprinkled through the conquered lands led to a lessening of their influence. Foreign eyes watched Nikometros - Persian, Mede, Egyptian, Hindu and a hundred lesser tribes. His hand strayed to his sword belt and he quickened his step.

The Roman embassy consisted of twelve tents, neatly arrayed in three rows of four and surrounded by a rough palisade of cut saplings. Two soldiers stood at the gate with long spears crossed to prevent entrance. A third man stood behind them and to one side. The light of a torch thrust into the soft pasture flickered and swayed. He strode forward with an upraised hand, shouting some unintelligible phrase.

"My name is Nikometros. I'm on the king's staff. I would like to talk to the ambassador." Nikometros waited but no sign of comprehension passed over the Roman's face. He cursed silently and tried again, using the Greek dialects more in use among traders rather than the classical style of his first attempt.

The Roman grimaced. "Why is it no one can speak Latin?" He sighed and beckoned Nikometros closer. "Well, Greek it must be then, but you have an atrocious accent."

Nikometros ground his teeth but repeated the introduction.

The Roman looked him up and down slowly then said, "The tribune Marcus Gracchus is asleep. Come back tomorrow." He turned on his heel and walked back to his spot by the torch.

"Tomorrow, my king will meet with your tribune," Nikometros grated, "It would be better for all concerned if the proper formalities were observed."

The Roman turned back and stared at Nikometros, considering. After a moment he nodded. "Wait here." He pushed through the gate and disappeared into the camp. Minutes passed.

Nikometros waited with growing impatience, walking up and down in front of the guards. Their eyes followed him ceaselessly, profound suspicion on their faces.

The gate creaked when the Roman officer emerged. He snapped a command to the guards and they came to attention, drawing their spears apart. He marched up to Nikometros. "What is your name and rank? I must know this if I am to present you to the tribune."

"My name is Nikometros, son of Leonnatos. I am a colonel on the staff of General Perdikkas, currently acting directly on my king's behalf."

"Very well, follow me."

"And you? Whom am I addressing?"

The officer turned. "Caius Valerius Gracchus. My rank is Praefectus."

"Gracchus?"

"The tribune is my uncle. Now if you will follow me."

Caius marched into the camp with Nikometros following. He walked between the rows of tents to a slightly larger one in the centre row. A single guard stood at the entrance and, as they approached, he swept the tent flap aside for them to enter.

The inside of the tent reflected an austere lifestyle. A narrow truckle bed occupied a far corner, the bedding rumpled and drooping to the bare ground. One small chest and another large one lay open in the other far corner. In the middle of the tent sat a lean, dark-complexioned man with short-cropped black hair. He sat on a folding stool behind a plain wooden table strewn with papers. Two oil lamps cast a flickering light over his plain linen tunic and purple-lined cloak.

Caius came to attention in front of the seated man and saluted by thrusting out his right arm then making a fist and bringing it sharply to his chest. He rapped out an introduction in Latin. "Tribune Marcus Gracchus, envoy of the senate and people of Rome--this is Nicomatrus..." Nikometros winced as another person murdered his name. "...Colonel on the staff of imperator Perdicus." Caius then turned toward Nikometros and, in a quieter voice, made the same introduction in Greek.

The tribune acknowledged his nephew's salute and introduction with a brief nod then gestured to a nearby stool. "Be seated Colonel Nicomatrus. How may I be of assistance?"

"Forgive the late hour, tribune," replied Nikometros. "I bring news that King Alexander will receive your embassy in the morning."

The tribune inclined his head in acquiescence. He contemplated Nikometros for a few moments. "I find it curious that a senior staff officer should call to deliver that news."

Nikometros smiled. "My duty was to organise the details for all the embassies. I chose to come to yours."

"Why?"

"You are direct, tribune. In truth, I've heard tales of the Romans. I wished to see for myself."

"And what did you hear?"

"That the Romans are disciplined and brave in war. I have at least seen the discipline."

Tribune Gracchus stared at his visitor, his face expressionless. "You think to see us at war?"

Nikometros smiled again. "Gods, no. Unless as allies. I sincerely hope that lasting bonds of friendship will be forged between our peoples tomorrow."

Gracchus shrugged. "I shall convey my report to the Senate. They will decide whether there is peace or war."

"Senate? I'm not sure I understand what that is. Is it the title for your king?"

"We have no king," said Gracchus with a sneer. "We exiled the last of them over a hundred years ago. We Romans rule ourselves, guided by the wisdom of the leading families."

Nikometros nodded. "I know the concept, though Macedonia has always been ruled by kings. Some of our neighbours to the south, such as the Athenians, rule by majority vote. They call it rule by the people, by the demos--democracy."

"A rabble," replied Gracchus. "The Athenians allow the least of men a say in the business of the state. We Romans at least limit it to those who have a stake in the future, the landowners."

Nikometros inclined his head but said nothing. After a few moments he turned the subject back to the preparations of the coming day. "The morning will start with sacrifices to the gods of all nations. Then the embassies will be called. I believe, if there is no complication, Rome will be called at about the noon hour."

"Why are we to be kept waiting? Do you think to insult us?"

"No, tribune, I assure you. There are many embassies and some must go first. There is no insult intended."

Gracchus grimaced, a sour look on his face but he nodded curtly. "Very well. Go on."

Nikometros hesitated. "Protocol has become quite complex since Alexander conquered Persia. He seeks to meld all the nations of the empire."

Gracchus raised an eyebrow but kept silent.

"The nations of the east and to the south will be required to do the prostration," went on Nikometros. "However, he has allowed a dispensation for the kingdoms of the west. Simple honours due to a king will be sufficient."

"We have no king," reminded Gracchus stiffly. "What constitutes 'honours'?"

"You advance when announced to a designated spot before the great throne, greet the king formally--I have the proper phrases--then drop to one knee and bow the head. Alexander will give you permission to rise. You do so and move to the prepared seating, where he will talk with you briefly. When you are dismissed you rise, bow, step back three paces then turn and walk away." Nikometros smiled. "I would be happy to practice with you if it will help."

Gracchus flushed and looked away, his nostrils flaring. "Your king asks too much of a free man of the Roman republic. I will depart without meeting him."

Caius coughed and stepped away from where he stood by the tent entrance. "Tribune, you must stay. It is imperative you discuss the Italian colonies..."

Gracchus waved him silent.

Nikometros frowned. "I really wouldn't advise departure, sir. It's no great thing, surely? You must have known an audience with Alexander would involve formalities."

"Formalities, yes," growled Gracchus. "I expect to deal with an honourable person respectfully, but it goes against my nature to fawn over a man who wields power by virtue of his birth. I respect only elected leaders."

Nikometros stared at the angry tribune, his forehead wrinkled in thought. "The kings of Macedonia are actually elected. Oh, it's true Alexander assumed the throne on the assassination of his father, Philip, but he could only be formally crowned after the army voted to accept him. If there had been another worthy contender, they may have voted him out."

"Truly?" asked Caius. "I never knew this."

"And if it's respect you look for then examine the last twelve years. Alexander has conquered every people he met. His military skill is without equal, yet he treats his former enemies with honour and justice. Surely his achievements allow a measure of respect when meeting him on a formal occasion?"

Gracchus thought for several minutes and then nodded slowly. "You have these required phrases?"

Nikometros drew a paper from the pouch at his belt and passed it across.

Gracchus took it and opened it out, tilting it to catch the flickering light from the oil lamps. "I will study it. You will have my decision before the audience. Now, Praefectus, see our guest out."

Nikometros got to his feet and saluted. "Until the morning, tribune." He turned and left the tent, Caius on his heels.

They walked in silence until outside the camp, when the young Roman put his hand out to delay Nikometros' departure. "My uncle will think on what you said, prattle about free Roman virtues awhile, but he'll be there tomorrow, Nicomatrus." He smiled. "For myself I wouldn't miss it. I've always wanted to see Alexander and the Macedonian army up close. I greatly desire to study how your army fights."

Nikometros grinned and clasped the Roman's arm. "Perhaps you can persuade your uncle to let you stay until the Arabian campaign. Then you'll see how we fight."

"We shall see," nodded Caius. "Until tomorrow then, Nicomatrus." He saluted, turned on his heel and marched back into his camp, leaving Nikometros to complete his preparations in the first cold light of the new day.

# *Chapter 28*

"Give us a song, Dienekes!"

The roar of drunken voices died down somewhat as a young man, naked to the waist and whose trailing chiton showed the marks of a less than steady hand on the wine cup, staggered to his feet. Lurching into the open space between the couches, he swept back long black hair and stared owlishly at the assembled feasters.

"Very..." he belched, "...well. Whash it to be? Shumfink shtirring or just a drinkink song?"

"Dionysos at Delos!"

"The Fall of Troy!"

"A love song..."

"Forget the song, bring out more wine..." bawled a young officer. With a laugh he hurled a crust of bread at Dienekes. His friends pulled him back down with renewed shouts for a song.

"Something bawdy!"

"Ask the king..."

Eyes turned to the reclining figure of Alexander. Though his skin was flushed and hair tousled, it was hard to detect any signs of drunkenness in the king, despite the quantities of unwatered wine drunk in the course of the evening. He rose up on one elbow and looked at the figure of Dienekes swaying in the middle of the vast state pavilion. His eyes unfocused for a moment then he clearly spoke into the silence. "Give us the passage from the Myrmidons," said Alexander. "Where the news of the death of Patroklos is brought to Achilles."

Dienekes opened his mouth then closed it with a snap as he recognised the significance of the passage. He looked around at his audience, licking his lips in agitation. Catching the eye of Ptolemy, who reclined beside Alexander, the young man raised an eyebrow in supplication. Ptolemy nodded and Dienekes shrugged, cleared his throat and drew a deep breath. The voice that emerged from the young man's throat was pure and controlled; no hint remained of his drunken slurring or unsteady limbs. He launched into song at the point where the news is first brought to Achilles, brooding in his tent outside Troy, that his friend and lover Patroklos had been slain by prince Hector.

All eyes turned toward the king, awaiting his reaction. Alexander, however, sank back down onto the couch and closed his eyes, a gentle smile on his face. Ptolemy leaned across and murmured in his ear, eliciting a nod. Seen only by those closest to him, a single tear ran down Alexander's cheek.

Nikometros sat to one side of the pavilion, some distance from the raised couches of Alexander and his senior officers and friends. Not as drunk as he had hoped to be at this point in the festivities, he kept a morose eye on his Roman companion.

The young praefect, Caius, sat upright on his couch, his back militarily straight and his face set in an expression of mixed horror and disgust. "This cannot be happening," he muttered beneath his breath. "Are these the conquerors of the world?"

Nikometros tipped his cup back again, savouring the rich dark wine. "Come now, Caius. Do you mean to tell me you Romans never feast and drink?"

Caius turned and regarded his tipsy companion. "Of course we do, but a feast of celebration is not an occasion for heavy drinking." He leaned forward, dropping his voice. "Unwatered wine, Nicomatrus, unwatered wine. It's madness to consume it in such quantities." He glanced around the pavilion, his eyes roaming over the dozens of scattered couches and their drunken occupants. "I notice your Persian guests absented themselves early, before the heavy drinking started."

Nikometros shrugged. "The Persian nobles can drink with the best of them but they seldom like to drink with Macedonians. Perhaps they don't like to reveal their inner selves in public."

"I don't blame them. This display borders on madness."

"Hush!" Nikometros' eyes flew wide and he gripped the young praefect's arm. "Keep your voice down. Allow the king some measure of relaxation after his last campaign."

Caius released his arm gently but firmly. "Agreed, Nicomatrus, but at least drink something less dangerous. I'm told you have very refreshing fruit drinks here in Persia. Why not them, or mixed with some wine if you must have it?"

Nikometros shook his head. "The water in the plains is dangerous. Men who aren't used to it die of the bloody flux. I nearly did so myself two years back. Even watered wine can bring disease. That's why the king drinks strong wine." He smiled, his eyes and ears drifting back to the song and the royal audience. "Besides," he added. "Macedonians are used to it. Most of us have imbibed since childhood."

Caius grunted. "If you say so." He tossed his head toward the singer and the rapt audience. "What's the significance of the song? Everyone seems shocked at Alexander's choice."

Nikometros looked around carefully then lowered his voice. "Alexander's boyhood friend and lover Hephaestion died recently. He always compared their friendship to that of Achilles and Patroklos."

Caius made a moue of distaste. "I was forgetting you Greeks had a taste for other men."

"Not all of us." Nikometros paused. "Besides, even I can see the point to it. A soldier cannot always marry so what better object of affection than the man fighting alongside you? The man who may save your life, if you mean something to him?"

The song finished and a thunder of applause rolled through the pavilion. Dienekes grinned and made exaggerated bows to the king and the cheering audience.

Alexander himself, tears still glistening in his eyes, leapt lightly over the low tables and embraced the young man then kissed him. "Nobly sung, Dienekes," exclaimed Alexander. "Your passion brought the tale alive." He clapped the singer on the shoulder and sent him back to his couch before turning slowly on his heel to regard his assembled guests. "Today is a day of great significance, my friends. Assembled before us were envoys and ambassadors from the entire world. Not only did we welcome princes of Hind and of the Asian lands to our east, but also peoples from the cold steppes of the north and the hot lands of the south, from Afrik, Libya and Carthage, Etruscans, Romans, Iberians, Kelts and others from lands of wonder and fable. They came to see for themselves the glory of our great Macedonian-Persian Empire."

"They came to see you, Alexander!" called out Ptolemy.

The pavilion erupted into a cacophony of cheers, the men drumming on the tables and couches with their fists. The noise threatened to become deafening.

Alexander stood in the middle, his arms outstretched, turning slowly as if to embrace them all. A radiant smile transformed his tanned and worn face, stripping away the years and cares. "I have a new venture," Alexander announced as the applause died away. "As you know, we're planning an expedition to Arabia. We need a safe sea route between Persia and my new capital at Alexandria in Egypt. Admiral Niarchos will lead the fleet south while I take the army overland, following him and establishing cities and ports as he searches out the route around Arabia to the Red Sea."

The room became silent.

He paused and lowered his arms, an intensity of longing replacing the smile on his face. "That expedition is but the start of greater things. The west beckons and I shall march into Libya and along the north coast of Afrik. With Carthage as our ally, Perdikkas will lead the armies to the Pillars of Hercules while I cross into Sicily and Italy and beyond. The Great Sea will become a lake within the Empire of a Macedonian world."

Alexander grinned and spoke into the hush. "You know me, fellow Macedonians. You followed Philip and I led you to victories beyond your dreams. I have never lost a battle and my armies are unconquered. I gave you gold and lands and power. Come with me, my friends, and we shall rule as gods over the entire world."

Silence followed for several seconds then Ptolemy stood, pushing back his couch. "I will follow wherever you lead, Alexander," he said simply.

As if releasing a pent-up storm of emotion, the men rose in a wave of cheering, stamping enthusiasm, crowding around their king, each eager to touch him and to share in his vision of the future.

Nikometros rose too, caught up by the soaring energy. He applauded and called out. Several minutes passed before he noticed the troubled face of Caius.

"This is not good, Nicomatrus," said the Roman quietly. "Your king means to subjugate my people."

Nikometros smiled uncertainly. "I don't think that's the case, Caius. He means to march through your country, but it has never been his way to attack a friendly people. He would rather have Rome as an ally than an enemy."

"And if Rome chooses not to ally herself?"

"Why wouldn't you?"

"Rome regards Italy as its area of influence. We have no need of Macedonia."

"Then why did you come? Why did Rome send your uncle as an envoy?"

"To find out your king's intent." Caius stood and straightened his formal robes. "I must convey this information to the tribune Gracchus immediately." He nodded his head and walked from the pavilion, threading through the excited crowd of partygoers.

Nikometros watched him go, a worried look on his face. After a moment he shrugged and turned back to the chattering crowd, seeking to fill his cup with some more of the rich, dark wine.

# *Chapter 29*

T
he land between the Tigris and Euphrates rivers stretched out flat and rich, the dark winter earth on either side of the Royal Road sprinkled liberally with budding shoots of the new wheat crop. The sky above blazed with the crisp blue of spring, the air still with winter's chill but bracing, invigorating the lungs and filling everyone with a lust for life. Birds sang in the blue vault of the sky and in the groves of trees and the strengthening sun promised hot days ahead.

Nikometros rode in the vanguard of the army, moving close to the king as he controlled his spirited stallion. His mood matched the day--crisp but lively--listening to the laughter and banter while Alexander talked with friends and generals about the coming expedition.

Behind them, stretching beyond the flat horizon, lumbered the vast entourage of the army and royal court. The army marched at ease, relaxed in the peaceful and subjugated surroundings. A low contented swell of sound enveloped it, speech and laughter rising and falling above the muted thunder of tens of thousands of feet.

A special detachment of the Companion Cavalry marched in full ceremonial panoply. Their expressions were severe and unsmiling, despite the glorious spring day. In their midst, steeped in costly incense and spices, resplendent in expensive garments and encased in rare woods and precious metals, lay the preserved body of Lord Hephaestion. He rode his catafalque in silence, on his last earthly journey before his spirit lifted in flames to the gods.

Further back, the women's court, together with another army of eunuchs, scribes, merchants, artisans and hangers-on, rolled slowly onward. The vast supply train brought up the rear, a myriad of wagons laden to bursting, toiling through the dust cloud kicked up by herds of cattle and horses; a city and surrounding countryside on the move.

In the distance, the long low black walls of Babylon had barely raised themselves over the horizon when the army made the last camp before entering the city. Alexander had his pavilion erected near the western borders of the camp, arranged on a low rise so he could sit at supper and look out toward the faint lights of Babylon twinkling in the still night.

From the west, a man rode toward them. He rode fast and hard, pushing his horse to a foaming lather. He passed fast through the guard posts and spurred on to the king's camp. Sliding from his trembling mount, he strode to the entrance of the pavilion and came to a halt, staring at Alexander and his friends.

Alexander looked up and grinned. "Niarchos! By the gods, I thought you with the fleet. Come in and have a cup of wine." The king rose to greet his admiral and friend, guiding him by one arm to a couch beside his.

Nikometros graciously gave up his place and moved back to share a couch with Seleukos.

"So, old friend," went on Alexander. "Tell me, are you in health?"

Niarchos nodded and sipped from his wine. "Yes Alexander. I'm well and the fleet is ready to sail. I had to come..." He hesitated and looked down.

Alexander frowned. "Niarchos, I know you too well. What's wrong?"

Niarchos put down his wine cup and rigidly sat up, gazing directly into his friend's face. "Alexander, the priests, the Chaldean astrologers..."

"What of them? Have they finished rebuilding the temple of Zeus-Bel? I gave them a fortune to do it."

"No Alexander, nowhere near it. But that isn't why I...Alexander, I've known you all my life, haven't I? We were boys together in Macedonia."

"Of course, but what has this to do with the priests?"

Niarchos pushed back grizzled hair with one hand, his eyes distraught. "I know your birth day, the very hour and place, Alexander. I asked them to read the stars for you. My friend, Babylon is unlucky for you now."

Alexander paused. "How unlucky?"

"They ask you not to enter the city but to march to the east again."

Alexander screwed up his brow in thought. "Not enter Babylon? I must, it's my capital city." He cocked his head on one side, his different coloured eyes searching his friend's face. "How far did you say they'd got with the temple?"

"Hardly past the foundations but what has that to do with their warning?"

Alexander laughed. "Everything. I warrant not all the money went to the temple. Now they're worried that I'll find them out so they try to warn me off."

Niarchos looked doubtful. "Possibly, yet they foretold my stars accurately enough before we went to India. They foretold honours, a good marriage and a trial by water. It all came true."

"Really? They predicted this, despite knowing you were admiral of my fleet and my good friend?" Alexander laughed again and embraced him.

"Forget these warnings. Eat and drink, my friend. Tomorrow we ride into Babylon together."

The Chaldean priests themselves arrived early the next day, just as the army struck camp. Alexander, warned of their arrival, met them on the road in his full parade armour. Gone was all trace of Persian influences; unsmiling, he met them as a Macedonian king and general, conqueror of their lands.

The priests came dressed in ceremonial robes, acolytes burning incense before them, and carrying the staffs of their authority. The head priest, his hair and full black beard curled and perfumed, bowed to the king and spoke quietly to him, the interpreter talking softly so only the king heard his words.

Presently, Alexander moved apart and spoke with the head priest alone. Only the interpreter heard his replies. He returned to his generals looking troubled. "They want us to march back to Susa until the end of summer."

Perdikkas made a rude noise. "What? Turn about just because they say so? Who do they think they are to dictate to you?"

Ptolemy shook his head. "If the gods say turn back...it would be foolhardy to go against them."

Niarchos nodded. "Aye, listen to them, Alexander. What have you got to lose? A few days trouble to turn this army around, but better that than risk ill luck."

"Their gods aren't our gods," snorted Perdikkas. "Take the omens yourself. Ask our own good Macedonian gods before meekly doing the will of foreign gods and their self-serving priests."

"You know as well as I do, Perdikkas, that the gods are the same," chided Alexander. "Bel, the god of these priests, is the same as our Zeus. I'm inclined to heed their warning, yet I desire to go to Babylon. Too much needs be done to waste half a year in Susa. I would take the omens but you know my priest, Aristander, is dead this past year. I trust no other."

Perdikkas sighed in exasperation and turned to Nikometros, who sat his horse beside him. "We have other priests...and priestesses. This young man is married to a priestess of the Land itself. Let her invoke her goddess and set your mind at rest. Then you can march into Babylon."

"I cannot wait out here much longer," Alexander snapped. "The eyes of the embassies are upon me. I cannot appear indecisive. Can you get your wife here quickly, Nikometros?"

Nikometros nodded and whirled his horse, plunging back along the crowded road toward the women's quarters.

The sun rose slowly, burning off morning dew. The army and court settled back into rest, though buzzing with rumour and question.

Alexander stood impassively, staring into the west, toward distant Babylon, his shadow shortening in front of him.

At last, a double beat of hooves signalled the arrival of the Scythian priestess. Tomyra slid from her mare and strode through the crowd around Alexander, while Nikometros held the reins of their horses. "You have need of my services, my lord?" she asked.

Alexander turned and nodded. "These Chaldean priests foretell great misfortune if I enter Babylon. They say the west is unpropitious and I should turn my face to the east again. What does your goddess say?"

"Not my goddess, my lord," murmured Tomyra. "The Great Goddess is Mother to us all." She raised her voice. "I will invoke the Goddess."

Tomyra drew her sacred willow sticks from a small pouch at her waist and, hitching her robes about her, squatted and threw the sticks onto the dusty road. She scrutinised them briefly, moved one or two and examined them again. With a slight shudder, she gathered them up, stood and faced the king. "Do not enter Babylon, Alexander, king of the Macedonians. Yet, if you must, enter with your back to the west. In this way you may avoid disaster."

Alexander frowned. "Enter with my back to the west? What do you mean?"

"Perhaps she means you should enter through the western Adad gate rather than the eastern Marduk gate," interposed Ptolemy.

"There's a problem with that," said Perdikkas. "If we try to go round the city there are huge swamps we would have to avoid. It'll take us days extra to traverse the distance."

Ptolemy shrugged. "Then we can enter from the north, through the Ishtar gate."

Alexander looked from Perdikkas to Ptolemy then back to Tomyra. "Well, priestess? Can we do that? Enter by the Ishtar gate?"

Tomyra nodded then, hesitating, shook her head. "No sire. If you enter the Ishtar gate from here it will be as if you are entering from the east. You must march your army north around the city and the swamps, approaching Babylon from the west. Then perhaps you can safely enter by the Adad gate."

Alexander thought for several moments and then scowled. "What sort of a fool would I look marching my whole army right around the city and swamp just to please these Chaldean priests?"

He thanked Tomyra and dismissed her then talked again with the Chaldean priests. They looked unhappy but bowed and withdrew to the city. Alexander marched westward with his army but, mindful of Tomyra's advice, bore north to camp just beyond the city limits, beside the Euphrates River. He sent the court on to Babylon, wanting the women to reach the comforts of the palace as quickly as possible. The king stood and looked at the great city, debating whether to take his army around the city like the priests wanted, or to defy Heaven by entering from the east.

Here, in the shade of willows, beside the wide expanse of the slowly moving Euphrates, more embassies came to him, including a few from Greece. He received them and listened politely though his attention strayed ever to the looming presence of Babylon. With the embassies came a small party of philosophers, including the sophist Anaxarchos, who had journeyed ahead of Alexander's army from Ekbatana to meet them.

Alexander welcomed them and spent the night in animated conversation. Anaxarchos reminded Alexander that modern Greek thinkers relied on reason for their decisions rather than relying on omens. Alexander listened and said nothing but, in the morning, made the decision to enter Babylon by the eastern Marduk gate in defiance of the omens.

# Chapter 30

lexander rode through the eastern Marduk gate of Babylon in the middle of the morning, his generals beside him and the Companion Cavalry drawn up in shining precision. The population of Babylon turned out to greet them, though their enthusiasm was tinged with curiosity. Most had caught wind of the Chaldean prophecies and came expecting wonders from the king who defied the gods. They were not disappointed.

As Alexander rode through the arch of the gate, a flock of ravens battled above him, filling the air with raucous cries. One fell dead in front of his horse, causing it to shy.

Then, as if to nullify the omens, good news arrived. Roxane, his young Sogdian queen, was with child. Alexander left the official welcoming ceremony, walked from the sacrificial altars to all the gods as soon as decency allowed and rode straight to the palace. He stayed within the harem an hour then left to make sacrifices for the health of the child--and to guarantee that it should be a boy child. Alexander announced the news to his friends simply and without fuss, asking them only to drink a toast to his child. He accepted their good wishes before retiring to his chambers for the night.

"Well," announced Peukestas, after the door closed behind the king. "This is good news indeed. It's high time the issue of the succession was settled."

"Don't be a fool," snapped Perdikkas. "This merely complicates matters. Do you want the Sogdian's brat as king?"

"I'd be careful what you say," remarked Ptolemy in a quiet voice. "Like it or not, the child is Alexander's. It's likely he'll make it his heir if it's male."

"And if it lives," muttered Perdikkas.

The others glanced toward the doors to the king's chambers then down at the intricately tiled floor. A silence fell over the group as they contemplated the full implications of the pregnancy--and of Perdikkas' words.

Nikometros coughed before speaking, in deference to his junior position. "Er...the king has other wives, doesn't he? Perhaps one of them..."

Peukestas nodded. "Indeed he does, young Nikometros. Especially the royal princess Stateira, daughter of Darius."

Perdikkas snorted. "A Persian princess. The king chose well there," he sneered. "Daughter of a coward. What a wonderful future king we have to look forward to if she ever begets a brat!"

"A pity he didn't marry a good Macedonian woman before he left. He'd have a twelve-year-old by now," said Seleukos. "A purebred Macedonian of good family. A leader we'd be proud to follow as Alexander's true heir."

"There are other purebred Macedonians..."

"Such as?" asked Ptolemy. "Yourself, I suppose?"

Perdikkas licked his lips, hesitated then he shrugged. "Alexander made me Chiliarch." He stared round at the ring of faces, varying degrees of uncertainty and hostility showing in their expressions. "Who doubts that Hephaestion was his heir in the absence of a child of his body? Well, he raised me to Hephaestion's position. He must mean me to be his heir."

"I wouldn't let Alexander hear this presumption," said Ptolemy. "What he gave, he can take away--and permanently."

Perdikkas smiled coldly. "The king's a realist. He knows he needs a stable government if his son is to inherit. I'd be honoured to serve as regent until he came of age."

"If he came of age," whispered Seleukos to Nikometros. "I wouldn't rate his chances highly."

Nikometros looked around the small group of army officers, aghast. "Gentlemen, it isn't seemly to discuss the king's heir in this manner. The king himself is...is still alive. I pray the gods give him many years yet. He's still young and in good health."

"Well said, young Nikometros," Ptolemy replied, nodding his approval.

"The apple falls close to the tree, it seems," commented Perdikkas dryly.

"Perhaps we should discuss it," Peukestas murmured. "The omens, after all..."

"Omens," laughed Perdikkas. "Superstitious nonsense. A man makes his own luck. Isn't that what Alexander has always said?"

"Even so. The Chaldean priests are well respected."

A chair scraped back, making heads turn toward a far corner of the room. Eumenes, a sulky expression on his face, got up and crossed the room. "Peukestas makes a good point. Many people believe the Chaldeans. Maybe some will act to fulfill the prophecies."

"What prophecies?" asked Perdikkas. "Nobody knows what the priests foretold, only that they gave a warning." He stared suspiciously at the effeminate looking Greek. "What do you know?"

Eumenes smiled smugly. "He sent for Peithagoras, the seer, this afternoon. When he returned from the harem. I happened to be nearby."

"And...?"

"Peithagoras didn't want to answer but in the end he said only that the omens foretold something very grave."

"I knew it!" cried Peukestas. "The parallel is there. Tell them, Ptolemy, you know him best. It's the story of Achilles and Patroklos all over again, isn't it?"

"Alexander has often thought of himself as another Achilles and Hephaestion as a Patroklos. What of it? It doesn't mean Alexander is doomed just because Achilles didn't long survive his friend."

"It makes you think, though."

"No, Peukestas, it does not," Ptolemy said firmly. "And you--and all you others..." He looked around the room. "You'd be well advised to cease this subversive talk. I've had enough of this. I bid you good night." He nodded to the assemblage then turned on his heel and strode from the room.

Perdikkas spoke into the silence after the door closed behind the king's half-brother. "So, we all know where he stands." He looked round at the others. "For myself, I make no plots nor look for any ill to befall the king. However..." he shrugged, "...we should be prepared should the unthinkable happen."

The meeting broke up a few minutes later and Nikometros left the room with the other young staff officer, Seleukos. They wandered out of the palace into the noisy streets of Babylon.

Seleukos stretched and ran his fingers through his long black locks. "Fancy sampling some of the night life?"

Nikometros hesitated then shook his head. "No, my wife is waiting for me. I don't like to leave her alone in a strange city."

Seleukos stared at his companion, a faint mocking smile on his lips. "You have too much promise to tie yourself down, Nikometros."

"Meaning?"

Seleukos shrugged. "General Perdikkas respects you. If you gave him half as much devotion as you give your woman, who knows the heights to which you might rise?"

Nikometros bristled. "I don't neglect my duties."

"No, but you don't give your all. Nikometros, there are troubled times ahead. You have a chance of greatness if you remember who has the power."

"The king has the power, Seleukos. I serve him."

"Oh, Nikometros," sighed the young staff officer. "You're being deliberately obtuse. Of course, Alexander has the power and long may he wield it." He stepped closer and dropped his voice to a whisper. "He won't always be king. And what if his only heir is an unproven child? Think on it, my friend." Seleukos clapped Nikometros on the shoulder and laughed. "Go to your woman then. I'll find myself a jug of wine and a willing wench." He turned and sauntered off down the darkened street towards the warm lights of the city.

Nikometros watched until the man disappeared in the shadows before turning and walking slowly along the outside of the palace walls to the gates of the Lesser Palace. He identified himself to the guards and wandered through courtyards and corridors toward his quarters.

Tomyra sat curled in a large cushioned chair, reading a book by the light of a bank of scented candles. A fire, blazing in the huge stone hearth, banished the chill of the spring night. Beside it sat the young nurse Petis, rocking Starissa in an antique wooden crib.

*My daughter too*, thought Nikometros.

He coughed and the girl looked round, startled. She scrambled to her feet and bobbed her head, blushing in the firelight. Nikometros waved her back down and crossed the room.

Tomyra looked up at him with a smile and, carefully smoothing the stitched pages of the book, placed it on a low table beside her. "I knew it was you. I've been waiting."

Nikometros smiled and stroked his wife's cheek. "What are you reading?"

"A book of stories written back in the time of a king called Kyros. The kings of Babylon conquered a people called the Jews and brought them here as slaves. Kyros freed them and returned them to their land, even though he was a Persian, not a Jew."

"Kyros eh? Then I must find you an account of Xenophon and the ten thousand. That is a story of another Kyros, though not a king like the greater Kyros. It's told mainly from the point of view of the Greeks in his employ."

Tomyra nodded. "I would like that." She patted the wide cushioned chair, moving her legs to one side. "Come and sit with me, Niko. There's something I must ask of you."

Nikometros sat, easing back in the soft pillows, his arm around his wife. "Ask then, my love," he said with a grin. "I can refuse you nothing."

Tomyra sat silently for a long time, staring at the fire and the nurse Petis rocking her child. "Niko," she said at last, her voice low and tense. "Niko, you must persuade the king to leave Babylon."

"What? Leave Babylon? Why?"

Tomyra shook her head. "Just make him leave, Niko. Please."

"You think I have the power to turn the king from his course?"

"Go to him, Niko. Remind him of who you are, tell him you come to him as his kinsman. He must leave or...or..."

"Or what, Tomyra? What did you see when you cast the sticks for him yesterday?"

Tomyra shuddered. "Don't ask, Niko."

His arm tightened around her. "I must if I am to persuade the king. What did you see?"

Tomyra stared at the fire and beyond it, her eyes unfocused then half closing. Her breath rattled in her throat before issuing forth as a hoarse whisper. "By water, by wine, by hand of man, the cord of life unravels in Babylon. Beyond lies a golden king. Many shall be sacrificed to him."

Nikometros' breath escaped in a hiss. He rose abruptly and moved away from the figure beside him.

The motion jostled Tomyra and her eyelids fluttered open. "Niko. Niko, what is it? What is the matter?"

"You prophesied about the Golden King again. I thought you said Alexander was the golden king."

Tomyra brought her slim hands up and massaged her temples. "I thought he was. Now I don't know. Perhaps another is, but this I know, Alexander mustn't stay in Babylon. The city is inimical to him."

Nikometros moved closer to his wife and knelt beside the chair.

The young girl, Petis, who sat wide-eyed and tense by the fire, relaxed and turned her attentions back to the child.

Nikometros took Tomyra's hand and stared into her dark eyes. "You said the cord of life unravels. Whose cord? The king's? Do you mean he may die?"

"The longer he stays in Babylon, the greater the danger."

Nikometros smiled. "Then don't worry, my love. Alexander plans only to stay a few months. The Arabian expedition will leave by midsummer."

"I will pray to the Goddess it isn't too long then." Tomyra turned and, gripping Nikometros' hand fiercely, added, "But better he leaves Babylon. Try, Niko, please."

# *Chapter 31*

A lexander energetically threw himself into work. Consumed as usual with an enthusiasm for the details of any project, he spent whole days and long evenings with architects, planning the great harbour at Babylon. Once the plans were drawn up to his satisfaction, he spent hours down at the site, watching the armies of labourers dredge rich river mud from the Euphrates, supervising the digging out of dark silt loam and interfering with the masons and carpenters as they constructed the new docking facilities. On more than one occasion he leapt down into muddy excavations to help some struggling labourer, or pushed aside a tradesman to correct faulty workmanship.

The finishing touches were put to the great fleet. Alexander consulted with Admiral Niarchos, planning the course of the expedition and the provisioning points. He met with priests, scribes and travellers from the countries along the route of the expedition, quizzing them about the tribes along the way, their methods of fighting, existing springs and wells, and suitable places to construct safe harbours. Everything was written down and copies made to be carried with the fleet and the accompanying armies.

The days grew warmer and Alexander took to bathing each evening in the great royal bathhouse beside the shaded and reed-strewn river. A series of lapis-lined pools fed cool crystal-clear water from upriver, the water plunging over shallow lips and golden fish shoaling around the bathers.

As the harbour and the fleet neared completion, Alexander's mind turned to other things, closer to his heart. Hephaestion, prepared and preserved by the skill of Egyptian embalmers, lay in state in the palace. Alexander visited the body often, sometimes staying beside it for an hour or more. He neglected himself once more and, for a while, the madness that consumed him at Ekbatana returned. Alexander threw himself into preparations for the funeral.

For two thousand paces the city wall came down and the rubble was used to construct a vast stone square. Within this, he had the pyre constructed, an enormous edifice over two hundred paces on a side. Wood and other flammables-- pitch and oils-- were collected and placed within the construction. Carvings, as fine as ever graced a palace, adorned each tier as it rose from the stony base, tapering as it went. Great carved friezes, depicting ships and warriors, hunting scenes and wild beasts, trophies of wars, garlands and rich cloths draped the sides. The great wooden construction contained a staircase so that the funeral bier could be taken to the top with dignity, rather than being hauled up the sides.

Nothing like this pyre existed in history or in imagination. Crowds came each day to gawk and crane their necks while it grew in size and magnificence. Among the crowds on these warm spring days, strolled Caius Valerius Gracchus, praefect of Rome, together with his uncle Marcus Gracchus, tribune and envoy of the Roman Republic to the court of Alexander.

Caius stared up at the swarms of workmen who hauled carved timbers up the sides of the vast funeral pyramid. "Incredible!" he breathed. "Such an ostentatious display of wealth."

Marcus Gracchus grunted. "Look well, praefect. You see before you an object lesson on the evils of a tyrant. Such wealth belongs to the people, to be disposed of for the common weal, not at the whims of a profligate panderer."

Caius looked around nervously. "Sir, it may not be wise to talk of such things out here." He caught the eye of a bearded Mede who scowled and made some unintelligible remark before turning away.

"Do you think any of this common rabble speaks or understands our pure Latin tongue?" The tribune shrugged. "Still, if it concerns you..." He walked off toward the stone columns of a nearby temple.

The two Romans stood beside a column several paces from the passersby on the street. They stood casually as if still engrossed in the spectacle of the construction, but continued to converse quietly.

"As I was saying," went on Marcus Gracchus, "Such criminal waste is just what I would expect of the man. This Alexander is no more than a despot, wielding almost unlimited power."

"I'm told he wasn't always so, sir. The evidence speaks of great military genius and a willingness to share the lot of common soldiers."

"Oh, I'm sure that was so, Caius. I, too, have read the reports. Yet you can see evidence that power and wealth have corrupted Alexander and his court." The tribune shook his head in disgust. "He lost what nobility he once had as a soldier. Now he's infinitely more dangerous."

"Dangerous, sir? In what way?"

Marcus Gracchus turned to his nephew with an expression of disbelief. "Are you blind, praefect? Deaf? You heard it from the despot's own mouth. He plans to invade Italy and subjugate our people."

"Er...well, yes sir...but, well, he plans an expedition to Arabia and North Africa. I talked with Nicomatrus. He assures me the des...Alexander seeks to have the Romans as allies."

"And you believe him? I'm sure this Nicomatrus is well connected--a relative of Alexander himself, I'm told, but he's still a relatively junior officer. Perhaps he even believes this tale. But do you really think he's privy to the king's Inner Council?" Marcus Gracchus straightened his toga, brushing dust from its folds. "No, Alexander will invade Italy and when he finds Rome opposing him, he'll try to destroy us."

Caius stood silently, digesting this thought. "Could he?" he said at last. "The Roman army is second to none."

"Face the facts, praefect. When Alexander crossed into Asia with a small Macedonian army, he would have been troublesome but no real threat had he faced Rome. Now, with the resources of an empire at his disposal, he could probably destroy us without a thought."

Caius thought then nodded slowly. "All right, sir. I bow to your knowledge. But, even if he could defeat us, would he choose to do so?"

A tearing noise and a chorus of shouting erupted from the construction site. The Romans looked up to see a cloud of dust where a huge ornate carving of an elephant lay in splintered ruins on the stone base. Already, teams of slaves rushed to clear away the destruction. Other teams ran forward with tackle to sway another great carving into the air.

"What do you mean, would he?"

"Alexander has a reputation for trusting people." Caius spoke slowly, struggling to find the right words. "He always tries diplomacy first and even when there is no recourse but war, he treats the defeated enemy with honour. Perhaps Rome could live at peace with Macedon."

Marcus Gracchus shook his head, his eyes steely. "Italy belongs to Rome. Will Alexander give up this westward expansion? I think not. Even if he did, it's Rome's destiny to rule all the lands of the Middle Sea. Inevitably, Rome and Macedon will collide."

"Then what is to be done, sir?"

"Alexander thinks himself a god. He forgets that he is mortal, like all other men." Marcus Gracchus stared into his nephew's eyes, holding him with the intensity of it. "He gives no thought to an heir. Instead, he surrounds himself with fierce wolves. Mark my words well. When he dies, his kingdom will be torn to pieces. His western dreams will be forgotten."

Caius frowned, tearing his gaze away from the tribune. "He...he is young yet, sir, barely past thirty. He may yet beget an heir."

"Then we must make sure that he never gets the chance to do so."

Caius licked his lips and looked nervously about him. The milling crowd of onlookers' attention remained fixed on the funeral pyre. A few glanced at the two Romans but evinced no interest in deciphering their strange language.

"You mean...?" Caius dropped his voice to a whisper. "Kill him?"

Marcus Gracchus said nothing, just stared at his nephew.

"It wouldn't be honourable," hissed Caius. "We're envoys, under a flag of truce."

"I am the envoy. You're merely an officer in my command. The survival of Rome is more important than any personal feelings of honour. That is why I shall return to Rome and present my report to the Senate while you seek to remove this obstacle to the supremacy of Rome."

"I?" Caius gulped, his face paling. "You want me to...to...?"

"You object to serving Rome?"

"I...no, sir." Caius turned away, breathing hard. "I wouldn't survive such an action."

"That's in the hands of the gods, praefect. However, you have my permission to seek an opportunity to carry out your mission in a way that maximises your chances rather than taking the first opportunity."

"I wouldn't know where to start."

"Must I think for you too? You already have an acquaintance with this Nicomatrus. Cultivate him, be seen with him, and befriend him. He already has access to the king. An opportunity will present itself." Marcus Gracchus drew himself up and stared down his hooked patrician nose. "When it does, Caius Valerius Gracchus, strike. Strike the tyrant for Rome and the good name of your family."

Caius drew himself to attention smartly, attracting a few curious looks from the bystanders. "Yes, tribune Gracchus. When Rome commands, I obey."

The tribune's craggy features softened and a small smile tried unsuccessfully to look natural on his face. "Good man. Write a letter to your mother this evening. I'll take it with me when I leave tomorrow."

# *Chapter 32*

T he sound of a flute soared in the warm spring night air, hung as if on beating wings then plunged like a stooping hawk. The notes died away in a trill evocative of cascading water. The old man took the instrument from quivering lips and bowed toward the audience.

Tomyra clapped her hands gleefully and turned to the others sitting around the small courtyard. "Didn't I say he played like a god? Didn't I, Niko?"

Nikometros rose to his feet and added his applause. "Indeed you did, my love." He fumbled in the pouch at his belt and took out a coin. He glanced at it, hesitated then flipped it toward the old man. Gold glinted briefly in the torchlight before a bony hand snatched it out of the air.

"Thank 'ee sir," quavered the old man. He stared at the coin and grinned, exposing blackened stumps of teeth. "Aye, thank 'ee honoured sir." He bobbed his head and withdrew.

"Gold, Niko?" Timon looked disgusted. "I admit he was good but silver would still be generous."

Bithyia nudged him in the ribs as she lay on the same broad couch with him. "Hush, husband," she whispered. "Niko's the host. His is the decision."

Nikometros laughed. "I thought it was silver when I took it out but it would appear mean if I searched for another. No matter. He'll eat well tonight."

"Drink more like it," commented Tirses. "Speaking of which..." He looked around for a servant, waggling his wine cup.

The Scythian warrior had at last succumbed to the growing heat of the coming Babylonian summer. With much grumbling and complaint, he had changed heavy felts and leather for cooler and thinner Persian dress. The gaily-coloured jacket and pantaloons he wore gave him an incongruously festive air, belying the fierce expression he determined to be proper for a warrior of his standing.

A servant hurried to his side and refilled the cup with dark wine. He offered a pitcher of iced water but Tirses waved it away. "No watered wine for me." He drank deeply and wiped his mouth on the sleeve of the soft linen jacket. Then he belched, before waving a hand in the air by way of apology.

"Be careful with the wine, old friend," admonished Nikometros. "It is good quality but this growing heat leads one easily to excess."

Tirses nodded, drinking again from his cup. "True but the water in Babylon isn't good. The natives seem to be able to drink it without ill effect but strangers die from it."

"Really?" asked Caius. "Is it that deadly, or is it that native Babylonians are nearer to their gods and thus their prayers are answered faster?"

"You cannot tell me these local gods are any stronger than Greek gods," growled Timon. "My prayers are answered well enough."

"Oh? What need have you of prayer, husband?" enquired Bithyia. She smiled sweetly and cocked her head on one side. "What have you been getting up to?"

Nikometros grinned when Timon flushed. "Seriously, Caius, some of the water here is dangerous. I believe it depends on where it comes from."

Caius nodded soberly. He picked up his cup of iced water and swirled it gently, staring into the clear liquid. "Everyone knows that Nicomatrus. Plains water can be deadly but mountain or spring water is usually pure. What I want to know is why?"

"Aye, and why should living in a place weaken the ill effects?" added Tirses.

"My mother's people believed that water close to people was worse than water from the mountains," said Tomyra slowly. She turned to Caius with a smile. "My mother was a Sauromantian priestess. She believed that some evil influence gets into the water from the bad thoughts of people."

"Interesting idea," commented Caius. "I don't know how you could be sure though."

"No, look," said Timon, getting to his feet. "This could be. Water that is standing, as in a pond or puddle is often bad, whereas swiftly moving water is usually potable." He started throwing his arms about in excitement. "Perhaps the motion of the water dislodges the evil influence."

Nikometros nodded. "Possible. I know that when the army camps it's better to draw water from upstream rather than downstream."

"That's because the water is muddier downstream," said Caius. "You can see the discolouration."

Timon and Nikometros laughed. "True," replied Nikometros. "And not just coloured by mud either--by horses and men also."

"Niko," reproved Tomyra. "I don't think we need to further discuss that avenue of thought."

Nikometros acquiesced with a smile and a nod. "Nonetheless, the water of the Euphrates upriver from Babylon is healthier than the water below the city. Even a day's travel downriver the water, though clear and sparkling, can induce flux." He shook his head. "I won't drink any water except pure spring water from the mountains. It's expensive to bring in but worth it. You need have no fear, Caius. Your water is safe."

Caius put down his cup and stared across at his host. "Romans do not 'fear', Nicomatrus. We reason and act accordingly."

"Of course," replied Nikometros hastily. "I implied nothing."

The conversation died away into awkward silence.

Timon lay back down on his couch with Bithyia and idly stroked her leg. He looked around at the other guests who sat or lay looking down at the floor or pretending great interest in the worked metal of their wine cups. He grimaced and cleared his throat. "It is good wine, Niko. Where do you get it from?"

Nikometros smiled his thanks at Timon. "Not a bad drop is it? It comes from Anatolia I believe. Parates has a monopoly on the imports of wine from that region and supplies most of the nobles in the north." Nikometros leaned down to pick up his own cup and missed the look of incredulity and fury on Timon's face. "In fact, he took advantage of the court moving south to open up a market in Babylon."

Timon struggled to his feet and threw his wine cup to the floor. It clattered and rolled, spilling a trail of red over the coloured tile floor. "Parates!" he shouted. "You buy from that son of a whore? Are you mad?"

Bithyia pushed herself upright, holding her swollen belly with one hand as she sought to restrain her husband with the other. "Timon, please," she cried, pulling at his arm.

Timon shrugged her off and strode over to Nikometros' couch and stared down at his host's startled face. "Have you taken leave of your senses, Niko? You know he tried to poison you."

Caius looked from one to the other then down at the pitcher of wine on a nearby table.

Tirses swore softly but fluently in Scythian, putting his cup down.

Tomyra flushed and sat up as Nikometros got to his feet, pushing Timon back from the couch.

"Timon, calm down," said Nikometros. "You've drunk too much."

"Then I'm lucky to be alive," snarled Timon, stepping forward to thrust his bearded face at his friend. "I suppose I should be thankful he hasn't poisoned this batch."

"Timon," Tomyra said in a voice trembling with anger. "I told you before, Parates shows himself a friend. I asked you to restrain yourself and not to insult my friends with your fanciful accusations. You will please apologise to my guests and sit down."

Timon glowered at Tomyra then looked away. He held himself stiffly at attention. "Lady, I would not willingly bring shame on you. But you are misled by this man. He seeks to harm you and Niko."

"Enough!" snapped Tomyra. She breathed hard then forced herself to relax. "Sit down, Timon...please."

Nikometros took his friend by the arm and half turned him toward his couch. "Come, Timon, please."

Caius watched the argument avidly. He turned to Tirses and spoke in a low voice. "Who is this Parates?"

Tirses wore a sour expression. "A Persian trader from the north borders. There was an attempt on the lady's life. Parates was implicated but it seems he wasn't actually involved."

Caius nodded toward Timon. "He still believes the man guilty."

Tirses shrugged. "I don't trust the man myself, for all our lady says. However, I'm content to watch and wait. Timon is more impulsive."

"This man Parates...he's in the city?"

"Indeed. Though he often calls on Nikometros and his lady."

Caius looked thoughtful. "You must point him out to me. It would be well to know the face of such a dangerous man."

"Come with me tomorrow and I'll show you him."

"You know where he's to be found?"

"Oh, yes. He owns a warehouse near the docks. His trade keeps him busy. It'll be easy to point him out unseen."

Caius nodded. "Poison, I think Timon said? I wonder where he obtained it?"

Tirses snorted. "The bugger only had it in his own warehouse. Arabian death weed. I gather it can be used to poison rats, so there was an excuse for him to have it."

"Indeed." Caius nodded again slowly. "Still, it makes you think." He looked back to where Timon, still angry, stood by his couch with Nikometros and Bithyia attempting to calm him.

"Come Timon," repeated Nikometros, bending to retrieve Timon's cup from under his couch. "Have some more wine. You can see for yourself it hasn't been poisoned." He signalled to a servant who hurried forward to fill the cup.

"Sit, husband," soothed Bithyia. She glanced over at Tomyra, who sat biting her lip and staring at Timon. She forced a laugh. "This lovely night puts me in mind of the nights we spent on patrol along the Oxus River. Remember how we argued half the night and spent the hours till dawn in sweet love?"

Timon grumbled but allowed himself to be persuaded onto the couch, sitting next to his wife. He took the cup from Nikometros and sipped, albeit reluctantly.

"I'm still waiting for an apology," said Tomyra in a cold voice.

Timon lowered his cup and stared across at her, open-mouthed.

Nikometros swung round, the smile falling uncertainly from his face. "My love," he said softly into the silence. "That isn't necessary."

"I think it is."

Timon erupted to his feet again with an oath. The cup went tumbling, splashing his robes and the floor. "Apology? To whom? The man isn't here." He stood with feet apart, hands knotted into fists, glaring around the courtyard. "Even if he was, I wouldn't," he grated.

Tomyra came to her feet and walked stiffly up to Timon. "Nevertheless, you will apologise. You insult me with your insinuations that I, as priestess of the Mother Goddess, cannot distinguish between a good man and an evil one."

"Lady, the truth speaks for itself. This man plays you for a fool."

Tomyra paled and she took a step back. She flicked her gaze to her husband. "Niko, you allow him to speak to me like this?"

Nikometros frowned. "Timon, calm down. Choose your words carefully, I beg you."

Timon rounded on his friend. "He fools your wife and he fools you, Niko. Gods, I cannot believe you can be so stupid as to fail to see..."

"Enough, Timon!" bellowed Nikometros. "You will hold your tongue."

"I speak the truth. Parates blinds you to his plans. Do you mean to just stand by while he murders you and your family?"

Nikometros swung his fist before he realised it. His knuckles clipped Timon's chin, rocking the soldier back on his feet. Timon's eyes flew wide in shock before he flushed scarlet. His hand swept down, dragging the short sword from its sheath.

Bithyia clung to his arm as he struggled to free his sword, screaming at him to stop.

The anger passed as rapidly as it came. Timon thrust his sword back and shrugged his wife off with an effort. He glowered at Nikometros then stepped back, coming to attention. "With your permission, sir, I will take my leave," he said expressionlessly.

Nikometros gave his friend an anguished look. "Timon..."

The old soldier saluted and turned on his heel, marching to the door. Nikometros gazed after him, a hand half raised in supplication. Bithyia glanced at Tomyra and Nikometros, flashed an uncertain smile, and hurried after her husband.

Nikometros let his hand fall to his side. He stared after his friend. "Timon," he whispered. "Timon, I'm sorry." His head dropped and he stood with shoulders slumped in the middle of the courtyard. After several minutes he turned to a silent Caius and Tirses. "My friends," he said tiredly. "I think I must ask you to excuse my lady and myself. I look forward to your company another time."

The two men rose and said a hurried and embarrassed farewell.

# Chapter 33

I n the darkness, while stars wheeled slowly toward a still distant dawn, men gathered to say farewell to Hephaestion. The great stone square around the funeral pyre filled with generals clad in their finest parade armour--steel and bronze and gold, gleaming in torchlight. Their breath smoked in the chill air. They waited at parade rest while junior officers filed in to take their places, followed by princes of the nations of the empire, bedecked in costly silks and jewels. Satraps came too, representing the far-flung provinces; mostly bearded Persians.

Priests wound into the open plaza, carrying effigies of the gods and piping a mournful dirge. Heralds entered, followed by army standard bearers, each representing a unit of the army. Musicians took their stations, bearing a variety of instruments--stringed, wind and percussion.

The square settled into a muted susurration of expectation. Sandals and boots scraped against stone, clothing rustled and armour chinked softly. Murmurs of voices rose and fell like the tides of a distant sea. Eyes turned toward the great edifice of the pyre rising into the darkness, the summit a vague outline against the starry night.

The ground shook with a steady tread and heads turned while a parade of twenty elephants, trunks entwined with the tails of the beast in front, wound in from the city entrance and took their places around the perimeter of the square. White tusks gleamed with gold, gaily coloured cloths hung down from their backs, almost to the ground, and the skin that showed was painted in bright reds and blues. Astride each elephant, legs firmly tucked behind the beast's great ears, sat dark-skinned mahouts from the valley of the Indus, their sole garment a snow-white loincloth. They controlled the massive animals by foot pressure, a gentle word and a heavy jewelled ankh.

Time passed. The first faint greying of dawn smudged the eastern horizon, carving the vast black walls of Babylon out of the night. The tops of the walls moved and heaved as the populace swarming over them strove for a sight of the unfolding spectacle. Across the broad Euphrates twinkled another star-strewn heaven, the orange firelights of the army encamped on the far shore forming strange constellations.

The king's Body Squires came, singing, bearing the body of Hephaestion, friend and lover of a god. Their footsteps on the flagstones set a slow cadence, matching that of the heavy beat of the heart of the one who led them.

Alexander, dressed simply in plain tunic and robe, his brow circled with a plain gold diadem, led the procession. He moved around to the front of the pyre, where a series of broad steps ascended into the heart of the structure. On either side of the stairs sat huge braziers and stacks of unlit torches.

The body, borne on its bier by a dozen young squires, moved up the stairs and into the edifice. Singers accompanied them and, for a while, their voices reached the waiting multitude, faint and muffled. At last they reached the topmost platform and set the body on its final resting place, high above the earth, its face turned to the heavens. The singers took up their places in the huge carved figures of sirens, high on the pyre, and lifted their voices in a great song of praise to the fallen hero. The song ended and the singers and bearers wound their way down the internal staircase. The priests moved forward, igniting torches one by one in the braziers, chanting blessings over each one.

The sky paled in the east, a greenish hue tingeing the firmament as the crowd of onlookers held their breath, eyes fixed on the still figure of Alexander, standing before the funeral pyre, eyes upturned as if seeking a final glimpse of his friend. He stirred, dragging his gaze away from where the body lay. He moved toward the pyre, taking a flaming torch from a priest and slowly ascended the steps.

At a silent signal, the mahouts uttered a soft cry and the elephants curled back their trunks, letting loose a tremendous blast of sound, a peal of trumpeting that crashed and echoed from the city walls.

Alexander threw the torch deep into the tinder dry centre. Flames leapt upward and his friends stepped closer, grasping torches and hurling them into the mounting fires. Two hundred feet of dry tinder caught and blazed, a roaring conflagration that ascended heavenward.

Air, sucked into the firestorm, tugged at the clothing of the watchers in the square, even as a mounting wave of heat threw them back, their faces reddened. The gigantic stepped pyramid of fire lurched, the immense wooden carvings, already ablaze, sagged inward. A gigantic carved eagle, wings spread with flaming feathers, crashed downward into the centre of the pyre, sending brilliant sparks blossoming into the dawn sky.

Flames engulfed Hephaestion in his coffin, alone at the top, adding the rich spices that permeated his body to the conflagration. A sculptured siren, superheated air moaning through its hollow interior, fell. A carved ship's prow joined it then, in a thunderous roar, the entire structure collapsed inward, a cloud of sparks billowing upward to replace the stars in the pale sky.

The sun rose through a blanket of thunderclouds on the distant horizon. The population of Babylon, the assembled army, officers and princes watched in silence as the funeral pyre burned slowly down to glowing embers and ash. At last, they stirred when the mounting breeze off the river, cool and moist on their fire-burnt faces, lifted the ash in a fine cloud, spreading it over the city.

Alexander, standing transfixed, shook slightly while his spirit returned from its communion with fire. He turned to his officers and crisply gave the order to dismiss.

With a sigh, the crowd moved back, dispersing with reluctance, caught up in the wonder of the spectacle.

Nikometros, his parade armour actually hot to the touch, his reddened face and limbs still glowing with heat, heard his name called. He turned and saw General Ptolemy beckoning. Stiffly, the dried sweat cracking and gritty in his joints, he moved, pushing through the crowd of onlookers intent on leaving the square.

"Nikometros," the general said. "There's someone here who travelled far to see you." He half turned and indicated a swarthy skinned young man beside him. The man smiled, white teeth showing in a luxurious curled and greased beard.

Nikometros looked blankly and without recognition at the stranger, taking in the fine silks and jewels and the ornamented scimitar by his side. He gave a small, courteous bow.

"May I present prince Mardesopryaxes of Pasargadae," went on Ptolemy. The general grinned. "Of course, you two have already met, so you need no real introduction."

"It's good to see you again, Nikometros of Macedon," said the prince, his teeth showing again in a friendly smile.

Nikometros frowned. "I...I fear you have me at a disadvantage, sire. I cannot recall..."

"I last saw you by the Oxus River, Nikometros," interrupted the prince. "You sent me south with dispatches. Remember?"

"I sent you south?" Nikometros frowned again as he struggled to recall the events of over a year before. "The only person I can remember taking dispatches south was...Mardes?" His eyes widened and he stared at the young man in front of him. "Mardes?" he repeated.

The prince nodded and laughed. "I looked somewhat different then." He preened, stroking his expensive garments. "Perhaps I should shave my beard and put on rags again."

"But you were in the auxiliary cavalry. Not a prince."

Mardes grinned again. "My father Artalaxes, may the Good God give him peace, was a nobleman, a prince of Pasargadae. I was only a younger son so I made my way where I could. I enlisted for adventure and, by the gods, I found it."

Nikometros shook his head then embraced Mardes, gripping him tightly. "It's good to see you, my friend. It really is. I didn't know what happened to you."

"A lot, as you can see." Mardes turned to General Ptolemy and gave a small nod of his head. "I delivered your report to the first Macedonian officer I could find, but what with one thing and another; it seems the message was delayed."

"That is so," agreed Ptolemy. "There was a small rebellion against a local garrison. It was quashed but your report was mislaid for several months. On top of that, circumstances changed for this young man so he was unable to follow up."

"Indeed," went on Mardes. "My father died while I was in Scythia." He bowed his head for a moment. "My older brother Astyges inherited the family estates and title but he chose to follow the rebellion. He died childless and the title and lands reverted to me." Mardes grinned. "I am now Prince Mardesopryaxes of Pasargadae, ruler of lands you must ride over for four days to reach the other side." He made an elaborate bow to a bemused Nikometros.

"Well," said Ptolemy. "I will leave you two to get reacquainted. Report to me at noon, Nikometros. We must get the funeral games underway." He saluted Prince Mardesopryaxes before striding off through the thinning crowd.

Nikometros shook his head, his smile breaking into a grin of delight. "By all the gods, it is good to see you Mardes...er, what should I call you? Mardesopr...I'm sorry."

Mardes maintained a neutral expression. "Mardesopryaxes. I'm usually addressed as Prince Mardesopryaxes, though 'Your Highness' will do." He struggled to maintain a straight face then burst out laughing. "If you could see your face, my dear Nikometros. Of course I'm joking. Just call me Mardes as usual."

Nikometros flushed then joined in the laughter. He clapped Mardes on the shoulder and drew him along toward the city. "Come and have some breakfast. I know Tomyra will be happy to see you."

"Tomyra is here? The priestess?"

"My wife now and mother to my daughter. A lot has happened since last we met. Come to breakfast and we can catch up on old times."

The two men moved off through thinning crowds toward the Lesser Palace.

Ahead of them, Alexander walked with a group of his friends, talking animatedly. As they passed one of the temples of Bel-Marduk, a group of priests hurried out and intercepted the royal party. Alexander shook his head, said something and walked on toward the Palace. The priests stood stunned, distress evident on their faces.

Nikometros accosted one of them as they approached but the priest just shook his head, muttering a few words in Persian.

Mardes asked a question then another while the priest started waving his hands about in agitation. After a few moments he turned back to Nikometros with an ashen face.

"What is it, Mardes? What's the matter?"

"The priests asked Alexander if they could re-kindle the sacred fires. He told them, no. Not until sundown."

Nikometros shrugged. "So what? The priests won't get their portion of the sacrifice until supper then. No great matter surely?" He stared at Mardes' expression. "Does this mean something in Babylon?"

"The temple fires are extinguished when the king dies."

Nikometros felt the hairs on the back of his neck prickle. "Alexander must know this. Surely they told him when he ordered them put out?"

"I would presume so, yet he chose to proceed." Mardes looked troubled. "My friend, in such ways the Fates guide our destiny and they aren't always kind or merciful."

# *Chapter 34*

T he funeral games lasted half a month. Alexander, oblivious to the superstitious mood of the populace and the more reasoning concern of his officers and friends, threw himself into the management of events. Always able to inspire loyalty and the desire to excel among his men, Alexander turned necessary military and naval exercises into competitive occasions. Ships raced on the broad Euphrates, the winners feted and garlanded. Swimmers crossed the river, others dove for prizes in the muddy waters near the harbour; while on land the army manoeuvred and exercised. Prizes were awarded for foot races, archery, javelin, wrestling and boxing.

The arts were not forgotten. Educated as a youth in arts and philosophy, Alexander added to his appreciation of history through the lands he conquered and the peoples he enfolded in his vision of a unified race. He lost himself for a while in the music of the kithara, his mind far away. He heaped praise on the winners and entertained them royally. But the plays affected him most. Thettalos, a renowned actor, often played for Alexander. This day he put on *The Myrmidons*.

Alexander listened, rapt. His eyes glazed, his lips moving soundlessly to the words as the ancient tale of heroism and tragedy played out. He embraced the actor with tears in his eyes afterward and awarded him a crown of gold.

A few days later, more embassies from Greece arrived. Nikometros watched from the rear ranks of the staff officers as the envoys arrived in the Great Hall of Audience in the Royal Palace. By using his position, he managed to include an invitation to Caius Valerius Gracchus, his newfound Roman friend. This was a perfect opportunity to introduce him to the complex politics of the Greek city-states.

The order in which the envoys were to speak caused a round of dissension before the audience got under way. The dominant politicians representing Athens and Thebes wanted to speak last. Many of the concerns being brought before Alexander consisted of complaints against other states. It was vital that one had the last word in order to refute ones opponent's lying accusations. In the end, Athens secured the final spot, the other envoys reluctantly allowing the supremacy of Athens in the covert struggle against Macedonian hegemony.

Alexander sat enthroned on a raised dais, dressed in purple robes and wearing the tall mitred crown of Persia. The envoys entered through huge doors and found themselves having to walk down a vast colonnaded aisle lined with dignitaries and princes of the nations of the Empire. Hundreds of eyes followed them in their long walk to the throne and the plain low stools set out for them.

After much bowing and formal phrases of greeting, the envoys seated themselves. There was a short pause before Alexander signalled his readiness and the first envoy, Dexileos of Thrace, rose to speak. He started off with a long obsequious speech of praise, followed by a request for justice against one of the leading families of Thrace.

Nikometros and Caius, standing well back in the crowd, to one side of the throne, had a good view of the proceedings and, thanks to the acoustics of the audience hall, could hear every word spoken in the centre without being overheard themselves.

"Thrace is a kingdom and this Dexileos will have sought redress from his king already," explained Nikometros. "Now he comes to Alexander for a ruling."

"The matter seems trivial," commented Caius. "I'm surprised your king even agreed to hear it."

"He agreed when he became Hegemon of Greece." Nikometros shrugged. "It's a kingly obligation."

Dexileos finished his speech and sat down. Alexander leaned to one side and conferred briefly with a scribe who recorded the proceedings. The scribe made a few extra notations.

The next envoy rose and introduced himself as Euboulides of Epirus. The speech resembled the last one except the subject of complaint struck closer to home. The speaker alluded to the high-handed actions of the Regent in Macedonia.

"Interesting," murmured Nikometros. "I wonder how he'll handle this."

"Is there a case?" asked Caius. "Surely he'll support his Regent."

"Not as simple as that." Nikometros looked around cautiously and drew back from the press of onlookers, pulling Caius with him behind one of the pillars. "His mother, the Queen Olympias, comes from Epirus. She hates the Regent Antipatros and will do anything to cause him trouble. I think this is another complaint that can be laid at her door."

The speaker's voice rose in pitch as he came to the climax of his speech. He struck a defiant pose and stood, awaiting a favourable decision. Alexander thanked him gravely and said a decision would be forthcoming after he talked to the Regent's envoy. An official announced the next speaker, leaving Euboulides to find his seat in embarrassed silence.

Another half dozen speakers followed in quick succession, the only common theme being the triviality of their petitions. Alexander listened patiently, interrupting from time to time to ask a pointed question or make some comment to his scribe. The audience became restive, fidgeting and shuffling despite the royal presence.

Petitioners from Macedon addressed the king next, pleading causes against the regent. Charges of bias were laid against his rule, accusing him of unjust taxation, and acting as if he were king, not Alexander.

"That last charge comes from Olympias, I'm sure," said Nikometros. "She is forever meddling in state affairs."

Endelus of Thebes rose and, with the skill of a trained orator, waited for complete silence before speaking. He praised Alexander, though not fulsomely as the previous speakers did then he went on to remind him that the gods looked favourably on one who tempered justice with mercy.

"What's he getting at?" muttered Nikometros.

"I was there at Chaeronea," said Endelus proudly. "And though your father won the day, yet did Thebes acquit itself with honour."

Alexander raised his head and stared at the old orator with interest.

"Chaeronea?" whispered Caius. "Where is that?"

"A battle in Boeotia," replied Nikometros. "Alexander and his father Philip met a combined force of Athenians and Thebans. The Athenians cut and ran but the Thebans held their ground and died. It was the last battle for the control of Greece."

"On that day," went on Endelus, "We Thebans faced your majesty in battle and, unlike some who fled the field, we stayed and fought."

Alexander inclined his head in agreement and glanced at the other envoys. A trace of a smile flitted across his face when he saw the thunderous expression on the features of the Athenian ambassador.

"The Sacred Band of Thebes made the ultimate sacrifice on that day," Endelus said solemnly. "Their bones lie buried still, where they fell, on the plains of Chaeronea." He fell silent.

Alexander stirred. "What is it you wish of me?"

"Grant that we may honour their memory in a lasting way," said Endelus. "We wish to raise a monument to the fallen on the site of the last stand."

Alexander stared at the envoy, considering. "I will think on it. Submit your plans for the monument to my clerk." He waved his hand in dismissal. The Theban bowed and resumed his seat, ignoring the angry looks of the Athenian ambassador.

Aischines of Athens, his nostrils flaring, clenched his hands and took several deep breaths before rising to his feet. He made a long speech praising Alexander and thanking the gods for his safe return from the distant parts of the Earth.

"Liar," muttered Nikometros. "He is of Demosthenes' party and hates Alexander."

"Who is this Demosthenes?"

"A self-important politician of Athens who can only elevate himself by dragging others down."

Caius nodded. "I know the type. Luckily they don't last long in Rome. We insist on honesty in our politics."

Nikometros raised an eyebrow but did not comment. "As I said, Demosthenes devoted his whole life to destroying Philip and after him, Alexander." He snorted, drawing a few curious looks from others in the audience. "Much good it's done him," Nikometros continued more softly.

"However, it's in his nature to envy what the gods have given other men. No doubt he will continue to make trouble."

"Why does your king not have him quietly killed then?"

"Assassination isn't Alexander's way. Oh, he'll kill where necessary but he always seeks a lawful means."

Aischines continued his speech of praise, laying on the compliments so thickly that even the Persians in the audience, long used to flattery, turned an askance eye on the man. When at length the Athenian came to an end, Alexander thanked him for his words and announced he intended them to take back a gift from him to Athens.

At a signal, the great doors at the end of the Audience Hall were thrown open and a huge wooden platform trundled in on greased wheels. Standing on the platform were two marble statues of young men, naked but painted in lifelike hues. Alexander waited until the statues arrived by the envoys then stood and gestured to them.

"See the statues of Harmodius and Aristogeiton, found in the palace at Susa. Knowing how much Athens values these statues, it is in my mind to restore them."

Caius nudged his companion. "Who are they?" he whispered.

"Harmodius and Aristogeiton," replied Nikometros with a moue of distaste. "They assassinated a tyrant nearly two hundred years ago and so of course are adulated by Athenians. The statues were looted by the Persian king Xerxes when he invaded Greece." Nikometros frowned. "I wonder why he's returning them now. Can't he see the significance?"

Caius shot him a questioning look.

"The Athenians believe Alexander is a tyrant. Why would he want to give them back statues of men who killed a tyrant? It might put ideas in their heads."

The Athenian ambassador was on his feet again, heaping more praise on Alexander. The king listened for a while then cut him off politely. He rose and walked away from the throne and out of a side door, escorted by his squires. The audience broke up into a horde of gossiping and speculating groups, drifting out into the corridors and courtyards of the palace.

Nikometros saw Perdikkas beckoning to him and walked over with Caius. Perdikkas nodded a greeting at the Roman.

"Nikometros," the general said. "Come to the Vine Room. The embassy has arrived from Macedonia...from the Regent. Alexander will see them in private." He glanced at Caius. "Bring him if you like." He turned and marched away, followed a moment later by Nikometros and Caius.

The Vine Room was a much smaller audience chamber closer to the royal quarters. Tastefully decorated with delicately painted vines and olive groves, it provided a more relaxed and informal setting. When Nikometros arrived, Alexander already sat on the ornate throne at one end of the room. Around him in a semi-circle, great padded couches stood on silver feet. Reclining and sitting on them were his close friends, Macedonian and Persian alike. Members of the Household, squires, lesser officers, court officials, scribes and eunuchs stood behind the throne.

Nikometros and Caius entered the room on the heels of Perdikkas and moved quickly to stand with the Household. Perdikkas moved with a quiet assurance to one of the couches and sat, exchanging a few quiet words with Alexander.

"This is what he calls private?" queried Caius in a hoarse whisper.

"Hush," motioned Nikometros. "Watch and learn."

The herald at the door announced the Macedonian envoy, representative of Antipatros, Regent of Macedonia. Heads turned as Kassandros, son of Antipatros walked in. A tall, red-haired man with a bushy red-gold beard, he hesitated on the threshold, looking across the room to the throne and half circle of couches. He frowned at the presence of Persians in the audience chamber, and at the mitred and robed king sitting among them. With a slight sneer he strutted across the floor, holding his head up high. He came to a halt just outside the ring of couches and gave a cursory bow, hardly more than a bob of the head.

"Damn fool thinks he's still in Macedon," growled Nikometros. "Has nobody told him the proper court etiquette?"

"My father Antipatros, Regent of Macedon and Greece, sends his greetings and well wishes to Alexander," announced Kassandros in a high-pitched voice.

"The fool's talking as if his father is king, not Alexander," muttered Nikometros.

Alexander nodded, his face carefully neutral. "I thank you for your father's greetings. You have dispatches from him?"

"Yes, Alexander." Kassandros clicked his fingers and one of his retinue hurried forward with a bundle of scrolls, sealed and bound. The man handed them to one of the king's scribes and scurried back to his place. "Further, Alexander," went on Kassandros, drawing hisses of disbelief from Ptolemy and Niarchos. "It has come to our ears that malicious lies are being spread."

"What?" whispered Caius. "Why do they hiss?"

"He's addressing him by name as if a friend. Everyone knows they detest each other."

"Lies?" queried the king. "Explain yourself."

Kassandros shrugged. "Various petitioners accuse my father of acting unjustly. This is nonsense. If they hold evidence they have only to present it at the proper time. Instead they come here, far away from any evidence, and tell their tales. It's all a pack of lies and, of course, you will dismiss it."

Alexander stared at Kassandros then waved a hand dismissively. "Please wait, Kassandros. I'll attend to this matter in a moment but first there are some other petitioners I must see."

Kassandros flushed scarlet but stepped back, biting his lip in fury when three Persians in long flowing robes stepped forward. They advanced to the foot of the dais and gracefully prostrated themselves before Alexander. Kassandros sneered, pointing at the Persians prostrate on the floor and addressing a remark to a companion.

Alexander frowned but kept his attention focused on the petitioners. He bid them rise then heard their plea, thanked them and dismissed them. Stepping down from the throne, Alexander darted swiftly through the couches and, before any could react, seized Kassandros by the hair and pulled the tall man down to his eye level.

Alexander stared into the other man's eyes, pale with fury. Kassandros read his death in them and blanched, his feet collapsing under him. Terror plastered over his features, the son of the regent gazed up at his king like a bird at a serpent.

"You have leave to go," said Alexander, releasing the man.

Kassandros staggered to his feet, clutching his robes about him. He turned and walked stiffly to the doors, every step seeming an eternity. He left behind him damp footprints, a reek of fear and urine and a rising tide of contempt.

"A fool," commented Nikometros to Caius as they walked from the emptying audience chamber a few minutes later. "A fool but a dangerous one."

"What will the king do, do you think? Send him home? Kill him?"

Nikometros shook his head. "Too dangerous. Antipatros is too powerful and controls the home army. If he thinks he or his sons are in danger he might rebel. No, the king will keep Kassandros here where he can keep an eye on him. Later, when General Krateros gets back to Macedon to take over the Regency...well, maybe then."

Caius stopped in his tracks. "A man with everything to lose," he muttered to himself. "Desperate and filled with hate. I must talk to him."

"I'm sorry," said Nikometros, turning back. "You said something?"

"No." Caius shook his head, catching up to his companion. "Nothing at all."

# *Chapter 35*

S ummer came and the heat increased daily. At a time when the kings of Persia would be enjoying cool mountain heights in Ekbatana, Alexander held his court in lowland Babylon, by the swamps of the Euphrates, attending to affairs of state and readying his army and fleet for the coming expedition.

Alexander rose at dawn most days, sacrificed to the gods in one of the myriad temples in the city, then spent the bulk of the day planning with his generals, meeting with his court officials or sitting in the throne room listening to petitions. No business was too great or too trivial for the king not to take an interest. He sat for hours at a time, breaking only for hurried meals or to snatch a cup of cooled wine or iced spring water. At dusk, he bathed in the cool pools fed by conduit from the river, enjoyed a light supper and sat up to midnight with friends.

Nikometros now commonly attended on the king. Perdikkas pushed him forward, giving him more vital duties, trusting him with greater secrets, using him in his play for power among the friends of Alexander. Consequently,

Nikometros often found himself with the other trusted officers of Alexander as he attended to state affairs.

This particular afternoon, the business concerned last minute preparations for the departure of the fleet. Niarchos fretted, worried that the last of the stores would not be found in time for the sailing in three weeks. Alexander, anxious to placate his old friend and admiral, issued a barrage of orders and sent officers and messengers scurrying to find the requisite items.

"Rope?" exclaimed Alexander. "Surely you have enough rope? You must have enough already to bind the whole city."

"And what do I do if I run out off the wastelands of Arabia?" asked Niarchos morosely. "I can't see us finding replacements in that stinking midden."

"Very well, you shall have as much as you need." Alexander looked around at his Council. "Well, where do we find it? The city is scoured clean."

"There are other cities," commented Eumenes. "Send to Susa or Ekbatana."

"We have no time. The fleet sails in three weeks."

"What about local supplies?" asked Ptolemy. "Fishermen on the river perhaps. If a thousand fishermen could each find a single coil..."

"Good. It's worth a try, Alexander," said Perdikkas. "I'll see to it." He beckoned Nikometros and gave him his orders. Nikometros in turn, hurried over to where Timon stood with the Household behind the throne.

"Timon, we must find rope and lots of it. Ask around the local fishermen. See if any will part with..."

"I heard the general, sir," interrupted Timon. "If you'll excuse me I'll attend to it." He turned to leave.

Nikometros flushed. "Timon..." He hesitated and lowered his voice. "Timon, why do you persist? I said I'm sorry if I offended you."

"You haven't offended me, sir," said Timon stiffly. "I'll take Antiphanes to help me...with your permission."

Nikometros nodded. "Do so then." He accepted the salutes of the two aides and turned back to the conference.

The meeting dealt with another dozen or so items, individuals being sent off on a variety of errands. The Household remained motionless behind the throne, attentive to the needs of the Great King. The court eunuchs kept their watchful eyes on the proceedings, sending for citron-water, perfumed towels and great ostrich-plumed fans to move the heavy moist air.

At last, Alexander pushed himself back and stretched, taking off the Mitra and running his fingers through sweat-dampened hair. "I think we need a break, gentlemen," he said, getting to his feet. "If you'll join me, we'll have some wine." He led the way into a cool inner room where servants immediately brought iced citron and wine.

Nikometros caught the eye of prince Mardesopryaxes, standing with the other Persian dignitaries and beckoned him over. They stood in the doorway of the inner room, sipping on draughts of watered wine and half-listening to the relaxed conversation within.

The Household relaxed too, the dignitaries drifting off to another room, leaving the eunuchs standing around in groups, chattering.

"I don't suppose you want to come back to the army," said Nikometros with a smile.

Mardes grinned. "Tempting, Niko, but my estates need me."

"How long will you stay in Babylon?"

"Not much longer. I'll see the fleet leave first."

"Make sure you come to dinner before you leave."

Mardes nodded. "I'd be delighted, Niko." He sipped his wine, idly gazing at the sight of the Great King arm-wrestling with one of his friends. He shook his head and smiled. "Not something I thought to see. Your king is a breath of fresh air in these stuffy halls."

"Your king too, Mardes."

"Yes, but thoroughly Macedonian for all he has adopted many Persian ways. He makes friends...and enemies." Mardes drank again, and then spoke around his cup, softly. "One hears things, Niko."

Nikometros looked up sharply. "What things? What have you heard?"

Mardes shrugged and stroked his lustrous black beard, teasing out the springy curls. "Nothing definite, Niko. If I knew anything I'd tell you."

Nikometros stared at his Persian friend a moment then nodded. "Let me know at once if you hear anything."

Mardes now paused and looked at Nikometros. "Why do you cultivate this man, Parates?"

"Parates? You've been talking to Timon."

"No, but I hear things aren't well between you."

Nikometros shrugged. "He's hot-tempered. We had a disagreement over the fellow but it'll blow over." His face clouded. "At least it would if Tomyra wasn't so dead set against him."

"He isn't a man to be trusted."

"Timon?" Nikometros lifted an eyebrow in surprise. "I'd trust him with my life."

"Parates," chided Mardes. "I've...made inquiries. He has a reputation in the north, my friend, and not an altogether savoury one."

"He's a merchant and in business, as in war, you make enemies. I found him to be honest and generous."

"I have no doubt he can appear so, Niko. But ask yourself, why should a merchant be so interested in a senior Macedonian officer?"

"I doubt there's any great secret there. He seeks patronage I'm sure, but he also has dealings with the Massegetae. He knows Tomyra."

Mardes gazed quizzically at Nikometros. "Or her brother, Areipithes?"

"He explained that. I believe him."

A motion in the corridor caught Nikometros' eye and he glimpsed a man in ragged clothes slip into the audience chamber. Nikometros started forward then turned when a hand gripped his arm. One of his aides passed a scroll and he looked down at it, hesitating.

A wailing started in the audience chamber, an ululating lamentation that raised the hair on Nikometros' neck. It gained in volume, a wordless howl of anguish echoing out into the corridors and catching the attention of the king and his friends.

"What in Hades?" breathed Nikometros, dropping the scroll. He ran forward and stopped at the entrance to the audience chamber, for a moment uncertain as to what was wrong.

Seated on the throne of the Great King, a look of crazed intentness on his face was the man dressed in ragged clothes. Around him the court eunuchs stood or knelt, lifting their arms and their voices to the heavens with every sign of grief.

Nikometros gaped at the man then at the eunuchs. From behind him came an exclamation of horror from Mardes. "Why don't they remove him?" asked Nikometros, moving forward once more.

"They...they cannot," stammered Mardes. "It would unman the kingdom if eunuchs freed the throne."

"Then by the gods, I will," roared Nikometros. He leapt forward, joined a moment later by two or three other officers. They hauled the man to his feet then hurled him sprawling to the marble floor of the hall. Nikometros whipped his sword out and pressed the point to the man's throat. The man looked up at the officers with a dazed expression. He blinked and ventured a hesitant smile.

Alexander walked into the chamber with his friends crowding around him. "What's going on?"

One of the officers stepped over to his monarch and saluted. "Sir, we found this man sitting on the throne." He glanced over at the eunuchs. "They weren't doing anything, sir, so we did. What do you want us to do with him? Kill him?"

The Persian dignitaries heard the commotion and joined the crowd around the throne. "Sire, you must," said one earnestly.

"Indeed, this is a dreadful omen, O Great One. You must avert heaven's wrath by putting him to death."

Alexander frowned. "Let him up." He waited until the man regained his footing and was dragged to face him. He stared into the man's vacant eyes. "Who are you? Who sent you?"

The man smiled, his eyes far off, but he said nothing.

"Kill him, Alexander," said Ptolemy. "It's necessary."

"Put him to the question," replied Alexander. "I must know if this was planned or if he acted alone." He watched as the man was hauled away. "Wait until I get there before questioning him."

Alexander turned back to the throne and the mob of people around it. "Come," he said. "We have work to do." He picked up a scroll and seated himself, calling for the next petitioner. Gradually, the room came back to a semblance of order while the king continued to conduct the business of the day as if nothing had happened.

# Chapter 36

U priver from Babylon, on the eastern bank, spread a huge walled area. The Persian idea of paradise encompassed a vast park and garden-- close-cropped meadows, orchards and small groves of trees throwing deep and cool shadows. Gravel paths wound between fountains, lakes and flowering plants and shrubs of all types. Dotted throughout this idyllic setting were small pavilions, open to the fresh river breezes. An army of groundskeepers, gardeners and servants kept the place in a constant state of readiness and near perfection. Yet, despite the array of humanity dedicated to preserving the paradise, one could walk all day among the flowers and trees, feed swans and water fowl on the lakes and listen to the peacocks calling in the groves without sighting a single person.

Alexander frequented this paradise from time to time but less so as the pressures of the upcoming expedition took hold. Rather than see its delights wasted, he encouraged his friends to use the facilities.

So it was that Nikometros and Tomyra found themselves in one of the pavilions while dusk fell on a hot, humid summer night. They sat side by side on a broad loving couch and looked out over a meadow toward a grove of trees. Small flashes of yellow-green light drifted over the foliage in the gathering darkness.

Nikometros slipped his arm around his wife's shoulder and leaned his head on her shoulder, savouring the scent of her hair. "We've come a long way in the last year or so, my love," he murmured.

Tomyra smiled and lifted her hand to caress her husband's clean-shaven cheek. "Yes, Niko, but we have further to go."

Nikometros sat up, his hand slipping away as he looked at Tomyra quizzically. "Do you speak generally or does...does the Goddess speak within you?"

Tomyra took his hand and raised it to her lips before speaking. "Both, dear Niko." She looked up at him. "We won't stay in Babylon, though we came for a purpose. The world turns on Babylon but your future...our future, lies elsewhere."

"Well of course. The army leaves in a few weeks and I'll go with it. You too. I won't leave you behind."

Tomyra smiled and turned back to contemplation of the dusk. "Do you remember the nights along the Oxus River, Niko? When my 'Owls' patrolled with your 'Lions'?"

Nikometros grinned and put his arm around Tomyra's shoulders again. "I remember nights alone with you in a small bivouac. I remember passion and fulfillment." He pushed back her long black hair with his free hand and kissed her ear tenderly.

"I wish I hadn't been a priestess. I could have gone with you openly and conceived in love."

"You always have my love."

"You know what I mean. I'd give anything for my first child to be ours together, made in love."

"Starissa is mine, Tomyra. Not of my body maybe, but of my heart."

"I know, Niko. I've seen you together." Tomyra sat silently, leaning up against her husband as darkness deepened outside the pavilion. At last, she put her hand out and stroked her husband's leg. "I would have another child, Niko. One of your body as well as your heart." She turned and kissed her husband, feeling passion swell and Niko's excitement rise.

He eased her back on to the broad couch and loosened her robes. He kissed her body, caressing smooth skin for long minutes before slipping out of his tunic. Darkness enfolded them as they joined and, for a time, they moved together in love. Clouds gathered on the western horizon and thunder grumbled in the distance.

Afterward, they lay together in the darkness. The moon rose golden behind the trees and the fireflies fled, unwilling to contest the power of her light. The breeze from the river, running before the thunderclouds, cooled the air, caressing their naked bodies.

Tomyra snuggled closer and drew her robes over them both. "There will be a child," she murmured softly.

Nikometros chuckled. "Is that the woman speaking or the Goddess?"

Tomyra smiled, unseen in the darkness. "The Goddess tells me I'll have another child. The woman wants it to come from this perfect time."

"Then let us hope. I'd like a son to raise. A strong son to take his place in Alexander's world empire."

"Yes, a man strong of limb and great of heart," laughed Tomyra. "We can name him for your father."

"Perhaps not a good idea, dear love. Not politic. But we shall find him a good name nonetheless. One that will become known."

They held each other close in the darkness until passion mounted once more. Then, throwing back the robe, they came together again, clothed only in golden moonlight.

"Just to make sure," panted Nikometros as he rolled off. "The boy must have stamina."

Tomyra drew her robe over them once more, feeling the cool of the night breezes. "I'm thirsty, Niko. Do we have wine?"

"I'll get you some." Nikometros kissed her and moved, pivoting to his feet. When he passed the opening of the wide doors to the meadow, he noted the first scudding clouds of the coming storm assaulting the moon-washed sky. He padded naked across the moonlit room; a shadow merging with the shapes of dimly discerned furniture. A few moments later he returned bearing two cups. He handed one to Tomyra then drank thirstily from his own.

Tomyra sat up and slipped her robe on before drinking. She sipped, savouring the wine, enjoying the lassitude and sense of wellbeing flowing through her. "I think I'll dismiss Petis. It's high time I took a hand in Starissa's upbringing."

Nikometros nodded. "I'd keep her on but I think it's a good idea for you to see more of her. She needs her mother."

"For a long time, I couldn't bring myself to love her, Niko. I must make up for the time I lost. She needs instruction in the ways of the Earth Mother."

"She's young yet, my love." Nikometros grinned. "It'll be a while before she can be schooled."

"It's never too soon to learn about the Goddess." Tomyra paused, considering. "I'll need Bithyia's help, even after the birth of her own child. We must heal the breach there."

A flicker of light lit up the room, followed by blackness and, several moments later, a ripple of thunder.

Nikometros frowned. "Timon is set against us, I fear. He considers himself slighted because you believe the words of Parates over his."

"I don't disbelieve him. Timon's an old and trusted friend but surely he must see that the Goddess would warn me if there was anything amiss with Parates?"

"Even I don't comprehend how the Goddess talks to you, love. How much less he." Nikometros sat down beside her again. "Explain it to him. Show him you value his friendship."

Tomyra nodded. "Yes. It's necessary. I'll do so tomorrow, when we return to the city." She fastened her robe and stood up. "Now, I'm hungry. Let us see what provisions were supplied."

Nikometros rose with her and, naked still, walked across to the tables along the far wall. "It's darker; the moon deserts us. We need a light. I'll fetch a lamp from the next room." He disappeared and returned a few moments later bearing a small earthenware lamp. The flame flickered in the cool breeze running before the storm, casting a warm buttery glow over their surroundings.

"Here," said Tomyra, handling platters of food. "Poultry, bread." She sniffed. "Goat's cheese." She arranged some onto a plate and walked back to the couch, Nikometros following with the lamp. "I suppose it's all right to eat it. No chance it was tampered with?"

"What, here?" replied Nikometros. "In the king's paradise? Not a chance. The place is well guarded and maintained by the most trusted servants." He cut off a hunk of bread with a knife and bit into it.

Sitting on the broad loving couch with the plate between them, they picked through the food and sipped from cups of wine. The lamp, set on a small side table, burned strongly, throwing Tomyra's robed body and Nikometros' naked one into sharp relief. Moths, attracted to the light, fluttered and spiralled to their deaths. Every now and then a large sphingid moth raced in from the darkness, battered at the flame for a moment before again seeking the coolness of the night. Lightning flickered outside, taunting the thunder.

"We have a problem with Tirses and his men, too," commented Nikometros around a mouthful of meat. "I think I'll have to send them back to Scythia."

"You cannot do that," objected Tomyra. "Parasades would kill them."

"Not if I send him word, explaining why."

Tomyra raised her eyebrows. "And why?"

"They're homesick. They're depressed and are drinking far too much. It's all I can do some days to get them out of bed in the morning. They neglect their duties, sitting around talking about the 'old days'." He shook his head. "For their own sakes, they must return home."

"Tirses won't go. He'll never leave your service. Some of the others, maybe, but not Tirses."

"Still, I think I must give them the chance."

A soft swishing noise from the darkness interrupted him. Something dark and swift passed between them, embedding itself in the upholstery of the couch. Nikometros stared down at the thin wooden shaft and the feathers of the flight, still vibrating from the impact. For a moment, no longer than two beats of his heart, incomprehension gripped him. Then with an inarticulate cry, he threw himself forward and over Tomyra, bearing her to the floor as the swishing noise came again, just before lancing pain gripped his leg.

Tomyra struggled to rise, her breath coming in whooping gasps. "What...what are you...doing, Niko?"

"Stay down!" Nikometros snapped. He glanced down at his leg, noting the arrow sticking into the calf. The point, gleaming redly in the lamplight, pierced the muscle, protruding through his leg. Blood ran in thick rivulets to the floor.

Nikometros scrambled deeper into the room, pushing Tomyra in front of him. He pulled the couch over, sheltering behind it, the plate shattering on the floor.

"You're unhurt?" he asked, running his eyes over her.

Tomyra nodded. "Bruised and startled," she said, a hesitant smile twitching her lips. "What is it, Niko? What happened?"

"Someone shot an arrow at us...two of them in fact." He drew his leg up to examine the wound, eliciting a gasp of shock from Tomyra. A shadow flicked across the room and a clatter told of another arrow seeking its mark.

"Three," he said grimly. Nikometros gripped the arrow tentatively and flexed it, testing the strength of the wood. He grimaced with the pain and let go of the shaft. He looked cautiously around the end of the couch and spied the knife lying among the shards of the earthenware platter. Throwing himself forward, he grabbed the knife as another arrow thumped into the couch beside him. He scrambled back into the cover of the upended couch, grunting with pain when the arrowhead scraped on the floor.

Nikometros gripped the arrow shaft again and sawed at the wood with the knife. Although not sharp, the blade scored a shallow groove. He put the knife down and taking a deep breath, flexed the shaft. A groan of pain escaped his lips when the sideways motion tore at his flesh. The wood snapped and the feathered end broke away in his hand. Gritting his teeth, Nikometros dragged the arrow forward, pulling the shaft through his calf muscle. Blood erupted anew when the arrow came free.

Tomyra mopped the blood with the edge of her robe then, ripping a napkin into strips, bound the wounds as tightly as she could. "It'll do for now, Niko," she whispered. She looked around the room at the flickering shadows cast by the oil lamp, and listened. Rolling peals of thunder drowned any other sound from outside the pavilion. "What can we do? Call for help? There must be servants somewhere around here."

"I'm sure there are," agreed Nikometros. "During the day. No, we cannot rely on outside help. We must do this ourselves."

Tomyra nodded. "How many do you think there are?"

"One archer. There was a pause between each shot. Maybe others."

"It's a Scythian arrow, Niko."

"I noticed."

"Where do you think they are now?"

"The grove is the only real cover but he could have crept closer in the darkness." Nikometros looked around the room. "I need a weapon."

"The knife?"

Nikometros snorted. "It would be hard to pierce his skin with that, let alone kill him." His eyes fell on the heavy drapes tied back at the edges of the open doorways. Across the top of the doorway, supporting the weighty material, stretched a polished wooden staff. "There." He pointed. "That will suffice."

"You'll be exposed if you try for it, Niko. I don't want to lose you now."

"Needs must, my love. If I move fast he may not expect it." He got to his knees and gathered his legs beneath him, his muscles tensed.

"Wait," hissed Tomyra. "Wait until he shoots again then move."

"Aye, but why should he shoot again if he cannot see us? No! Tomyra..."

Tomyra rose to her feet and darted for the interior door. An arrow hissed, thwacking into the folds of her robes. She stumbled then ran on, ducking into cover.

Frozen for a second, the hiss of the arrow released him. Nikometros dove for the drapes and pulled, swinging his whole weight on them. With a sharp crack, the wooden pole snapped and he fell to the floor, the drapes enveloping him. Pain careened up his leg as his wounds broke open again, blood soaking the bandages.

Nikometros fumbled for the wooden pole. He found the short end and rejected it, searching for the other fragment. He breathed a sigh of relief when his fingers found it. Wriggling from beneath the heavy folds of material, he eyed the room and the darkness outside, occasionally lit by white flashes of heavenly fire.

"Tomyra! Tomyra, are you all right?"

"I...I'm unhurt, Niko." She paused. "Be careful."

Nikometros did not answer, turning all his attention to the night and its hidden danger. He shifted, raising a fold of the drapes with the stick, hoping to draw another arrow. Nothing happened and he wriggled sideways into the cover of the wall. Stripping the drapes off, Nikometros sat up. He looked at the room again, noting the angles of the arrows in the couch. He nodded in satisfaction. "From the left. Then I must go to the right."

He got to his feet, leaning up against the wall and gripped the makeshift weapon tightly. Ignoring his injured leg, he waited until the next bolt of light before stepping out into the open doorway. He hesitated a moment then leapt to the right as an arrow zipped past his head. He landed on thick meadow grass and rolled. There was a crash of thunder above him and the first heavy drops of rain fell like ice water on his naked body. Quickly, he got to his feet and, crouching low, raced for the grove of trees, throwing himself to the ground under some bushes. He lay still, controlling his breathing and listening. In the pauses between rolls of thunder, the only sound was the splash of raindrops on the foliage. Nikometros gripped the wooden pole and crawled further into the grove, stopping every few paces to listen. Thunder became almost constant and flashes of light turned the night into a garish flickering day. Ahead, between the buttresses of an ancient banyan tree, something moved.

Nikometros crept closer, taking care not to disturb the leaf litter. Something unseen slithered away from his hand and he froze, the god's name gusting through his lips. The rain fell harder, drumming on the foliage and rim of bare earth around the banyan. He moved forward again, inching toward the place he had seen movement. Easing himself between two high buttress roots, he pulled himself upright against the bole of the tree and listened. Between peals of thunder, he discerned voices. Two men sat but an arm's length away and argued, their voices rose in recrimination and accusation. Nikometros strained to make out the words.

"...damn fool, I told you to let me..."

"It was my place to...I would kill..."

"...better to get close...with swords."

"...dangerous."

"What...do now?

There came a pause during which the roar of the rain dominated, the thunder slipping away to the east, even as brilliant flashes still lit the soaking landscape.

"Where's Caraxes?" asked one of the unseen voices.

A shrug, almost invisible in the night, preceded the answer. "Gone to the pavilion I suppose."

The first voice swore. "Find him. Help him."

"And you?"

"I'll follow. Someone must guard your back."

A bitter laugh.

Nikometros eased his head around the trunk of the tree, pushing aside a thin screen of pendulous roots hanging from one of the branches. In a flash of lightning, he saw two crouching men, one with a drawn sword, the other holding a Scythian double-curved bow and a half empty quiver of arrows.

Darkness descended and, when the light flared again a moment or two later, only the archer remained, standing at the edge of the canopy looking out through the driving rain at the dim flickering light of the pavilion. A shadow crossed the pavilion doorway and a thin cry pierced the rain and thunder.

Nikometros froze with shock then vaulted the high buttress root and threw himself at the remembered place of the archer. A flash showed him his aim was amiss but it was too late to correct the charge. He despairingly threw out his arm and, as he crashed to the ground, the wooden staff connected with the back of the man's legs. With a yell of fear the man fell back.

Lightning revealed a prostrate man a few feet from Nikometros. He scrambled to his knees and hurled himself forward. His hands scrabbled and found flailing limbs. A fist crashed into his ribs and he gasped, ripping at the man's clothing, seeking his throat. Fingers clawed at eyes and a knee brushed Nikometros' naked genitals. Nikometros gripped his staff and flailed it, connecting with something solid. The man screamed and struggled to get away. Nikometros struck again and missed, then again with more success.

The heavens blazed once, twice, a pause, and again.

Nikometros, on his knees, saw the man in front of him stumbling to his feet. He swung the knobbed end of his staff and felt a satisfying crack of wood on bone.

The man fell forward with a muffled groan and lay still.

Nikometros fumbled at the body, feeling for signs of life and finding none. He turned the body over and in the flickering of a distant discharge, brushed the curtain of blood from the man's face. A nearby bolt lit up the man's features.

"Scolices!" Nikometros sat back on his heels, a savage snarl contorting his face.

The deluge of rain faltered then eased to gusting showers. Another cry issued from the pavilion and Nikometros was on his feet again, racing out into the rain-slicked meadow.

Ahead, looming in the darkness flickered the dim glow of the oil lamp. Shadows obscured its light, moving. Closer, out in the rain swept night, a figure moved swiftly toward the pavilion, steel glinting in the light of the dying storm.

Nikometros ran on, desperate to intercept the figure before it reached the building, and knowing he could not. Despairing, he yelled inchoately and hurled his pole at the man. It fell short, skidding impotently on the wet grass.

The man stopped and turned, peering into the darkness at the naked man rushing toward him. He dropped into a crouch, the sword weaving small circles in front of him.

Nikometros tried to stop and his feet slid out from under him, dropping him to the slippery turf. He scrambled to his knees as the man stabbed forward, narrowly missing his face. He fell back and scrabbled sideways, the man advancing with a swagger and chopping downward, the blade slicing into wet earth.

Nikometros kicked out and connected with the man's leg.

The man grunted and swivelled, slashing out with his sword again.

Nikometros staggered to his feet and circled, leaping backward to avoid the man's blade. A crash of furniture from the pavilion distracted him and Nikometros turned his head back barely in time as the sword point nicked a thin furrow on his chest. Blood spilled, thinning rapidly in the rainwater coursing over his body.

The man grinned, his teeth showing dimly in the faint light. He ran forward, holding his sword out in front of him like a spear and forcing Nikometros to move backward.

Nikometros slipped and fell to one knee.

The man raised his sword high and leapt forward. With a cry, the man stumbled as his feet tangled on something lying on the ground. His feet flew out from under him, the discarded wooden staff on the ground scoring a wound on his leg as he fell over it. The man retained his grip on his sword, though it thumped to the ground beside him.

Nikometros hurled himself on the man, pinning his sword arm and lashing out with his fist.

The man grunted and raised his knee swiftly, cracking into the side of Nikometros' head. As Nikometros slipped off, his head reeling, the man freed his sword arm and forced himself to one knee. He grinned again and raised the sword, striking down at the naked body lying beneath him.

Nikometros rolled away as the blade descended, his fingers scrabbling for purchase on the wet grass. His hand closed around the staff and he pushed out with it, forcing it at the man thrusting down at him. He felt a shudder up his arm and into his shoulder and heard a strangled cry. The sword descended, turning and falling, the flat of the blade slapping against his naked belly.

The man slumped, his knees still on the ground but his body bent forward over Nikometros. He moved his head and coughed, a gout of blood spilling from his mouth.

Nikometros pushed himself away and the man fell onto his side. The body shuddered then stilled. Nikometros reached forward with one hand and ran his fingers up the staff to the jagged end ripped into the soft flesh of the man's throat. He felt the stickiness of fresh blood and wiped his hands on the grass before picking up the fallen sword and turning toward the pavilion.

All was silent inside. The rain fell softly on the roof, dripping into puddles under the eaves. The room lay in shambles, furniture overturned and smashed. Only the oil lamp burned undisturbed on its small side table.

Nikometros stood on the tiled floor, water, pink-tinged, pooling at his feet. The sting of his chest wound and the deeper throbbing pain of his calf barely impinged on his consciousness as he surveyed the room, a feeling of dread growing in him. "Tomyra," he called softly, then louder. "Tomyra!" Nikometros limped across the room, picking up the oil lamp as he passed. He paused in the doorway to the inner room and croaked out his wife's name again.

"T...Tomyra?"

"Niko, is that you?" Tomyra's voice, thin and hesitant, came from floor level.

Nikometros raised the lamp higher and peered into the shadows. For a moment, nothing made sense then, with an almost audible snap, everything became clear. The dark patches on the tile resolved into blood, the short, broad piece of metal became a stabbing sword and the fallen statuary, Tomyra.

Setting the lamp on the floor, Nikometros dropped to his knees and cradled his wife's head. A smear of blood marred her cheek and a swelling bruise threatened to close her right eye.

Her eyelids fluttered open and she smiled weakly. "I got mine, Niko. How about you?"

Nikometros nodded. "Both dead." He looked around. "Where is he?"

Tomyra pointed to a huge carved table across the room. "Over there, behind the table." She turned her eyes up at her husband. "Is he dead, Niko? Check him, will you?"

Nikometros gently lowered Tomyra to the floor again, pulling a cushion from a nearby chair for her head. Picking up the discarded sword, he padded over to the table and peered behind it. A man lay crumpled, face down, his hair a sticky mass of congealing blood. He leaned over and turned the body onto its back, revealing the left temple as a pulped cavity, fragments of skull sticking out through the mangled skin.

"Gods, Tomyra," said Nikometros. "What did you hit him with?"

"One of your gods, Niko. I'm not sure which one."

"Eh? What do you...oh, I see." Lying by the wall, a few paces from the body, lay a small marble statue of Apollo. Blood and hair spattered the base of the sculpture. Nikometros picked it up gingerly and set it on the table.

"Will he mind? Are there any purification rites we should perform?"

Nikometros smiled and returned to his wife's side. "Apollo is a gentleman. I'm sure he's delighted to save the life of a priestess of the Mother Goddess." He bent and picked her up, cradling her close. "If you like though, we can offer him a young kid by way of thanks."

He turned and walked outside into the night. The storm grumbled distantly and the air smelled fresh and clean. Silver moonlight poured from rents in the cloud cover, offering enough light for Nikometros as he carried Tomyra down the stone paved path toward the gates of paradise.

# *Chapter 37*

"**T**his is intolerable!" stormed Ptolemy. "That the life of a Macedonian officer and his family should be threatened by common cutthroats..." He broke off and glared around the room before turning to face Nikometros. His face softened. "And they tried to kill my son," he added in a whisper. "If this is a conspiracy, I'll find them all and have them executed for this." He approached Nikometros and clasped his shoulders firmly. "You're unhurt?"

"I've fared worse," replied Nikometros.

"There were three actual assassins, you say, and you killed them all?"

"No sir. That is, there were three but only two died. The one in the trees, the archer, was gone when the soldiers returned. He'll try again sir, I know it."

"Then we must ensure we catch him quickly. I wish you'd come to me immediately instead of waiting nearly a day."

"I'm sorry sir. My first thought was for my wife. I reported it to the captain of the guard at the gates but I...I didn't think you'd be interested in the affair."

"Not interested? Merciful gods, man, you're my son." Ptolemy gave him a hard look then he nodded. "You would know this man if you saw him again? You can describe him?"

"Yes sir. His name is Scolices, a Scythian of the Massegetae people. He bears a great hatred for my wife and myself."

"A Scythian? Not too many of them in Babylon. With luck he'll stand out." Ptolemy turned back to the papers on his table. "I'll draw up the necessary papers to have him arrested when he's found. Alexander will sign them today, I promise. In the meantime, your wife will remain under guard." He smiled wryly. "I cannot afford to keep you under guard. Nor would you agree to it if I ordered it so. However, I do insist that your man, Timon, accompany you everywhere. He's a good fighter and I'd feel better if he was with you."

"Yes sir, I'll ask him."

"Good man." Ptolemy nodded and dismissed Nikometros, who saluted and turned to leave. "Nikometros," added Ptolemy as his son reached the doorway, "Be careful."

Nikometros left the palace grounds and walked toward the lesser palace, his eyes watchful and his hand on the pommel of his sword. His left leg ached from the arrow wound but function remained largely unimpaired. He limped, favouring the injured leg until he caught himself doing so and then made an effort to ignore the pain. Reaching his own apartments, he hesitated, noting the presence of a squad of armed guards. He exchanged a few words with the guard commander then left and walked over to the nearby apartments of Timon and Bithyia.

Timon answered his knock, staring coldly at his commander. He made no move to invite Nikometros in.

"Timon, I need to talk to you. May I come in?"

"Bithyia is tired, sir. I'd rather you didn't."

"Then come outside and talk. Perhaps we could find a tavern."

"I don't want to leave her alone."

"Damn it, Timon. We must talk. If you won't ask me in then come out."

Timon stared for a long minute then shrugged. "As my commander wishes." He closed the door behind him and stepped out into the portico.

Nikometros sighed in exasperation but turned and led the way out of the lesser palace and into a street running down into the heart of Babylon. They walked in silence, their footsteps echoing off the brick and stone structures around them. The night was dark and overcast; the air heavy and humid, dim haloes forming around the flickering lights of the torches set on the street corners.

"You heard what happened last night?" asked Nikometros.

"Yes." Timon walked on in silence for a minute. "I...I'm glad you...I'm glad the attempt didn't succeed."

"Thank you, Timon. You should have seen Tomyra. She was magnificent." Nikometros grinned and half-turned toward his friend, his teeth visible in the torchlight. "She killed the man, you know."

"Indeed? I'm gratified. She wasn't injured then?"

"Nothing serious. Bruises, a few cuts. They'll heal."

They turned down a street that led toward the naval yards. The streets were busier here and the jostle of people and the growing hubbub forced them to walk closer together.

"How is Bithyia?" enquired Nikometros. "She's due soon?"

"The midwife says within days. I should be with her."

"I'm sorry to keep you from her, Timon. I promise you shall rejoin her soon."

"So where are we going? How about here, it looks decent enough." Timon indicated a busy tavern, a roar of laughter and conversation bursting from its door and open windows.

"No, not here. I had another place in mind. Just a bit further."

Timon looked quizzically at Nikometros but said nothing. They walked on, passing through the docks and into the quieter streets beyond. At last, Nikometros turned down a narrow street that ended in a tiny tavern. The surge of noise from the burgeoning humanity of the city dropped to a distant murmur. The lights of the tavern cast a mellow light over the stone-paved street, welcoming thirsty travellers.

"Here?" Timon asked. "Why this out of the way place?"

"It's quieter. We need to talk."

Nikometros led the way into the almost deserted tavern. He nodded at the barman and asked for a jug of wine. Accepting the pitcher of thin wine and two mugs he indicated a table in the far corner, deep in the shadows. Timon followed his commander and drew back one of the roughly fashioned high-backed chairs, preparatory to sitting down. He stopped in mid-action and stared into the shadows at the man sitting at the table.

"You!" Timon spat. He rounded on Nikometros. "You knew, didn't you? You knew he was here."

Nikometros nodded and set the wine on the table. "Yes, I knew. I invited Parates so we can settle this matter once and for all. Sit down Timon...please."

Timon scowled but reluctantly sat, drawing his chair away from the table. Nikometros smiled and poured wine into the two mugs, splashing more into Parates' mug.

Timon pushed his mug away. "I won't drink with him."

"Why not?" drawled Parates, leaning back in his chair. He sipped from his mug. "This may not be very good wine, certainly not up to the standards I'm used to, but you can be certain it isn't poisoned." He smiled at the furious expression on Timon's face.

"Please, Parates," soothed Nikometros. "Timon, no one will ask you to drink if you do not care to." He glanced from one to the other. "I want you to become...well, if not friends, then at least to tolerate one another."

Timon glowered in silence. Parates smiled and spread his hands. "Nikometros, I'm honoured to be considered your friend. I'd be only too happy to extend the hand of friendship to this worthy man."

"Thank you Parates," Nikometros said. "Timon, why do you feel such enmity toward Parates?"

"You really don't know?"

"I'm asking you."

"I don't trust him," said Timon. "He admits to friendship with that bastard Areipithes, he entertained Scolices and the poison which nearly claimed the life of Tomyra came from his warehouse."

"That's all?" asked Parates.

"That's not enough?" exploded Timon. He pushed back his chair and started to rise. "I'm not staying..."

"Timon." Nikometros grasped his friend's hand. "Please. Stay and hear me out." He waited until Timon subsided and reseated himself. "So," he went on. "There are three questions to be answered. The first is his friendship with Areipithes. Parates...?" He turned enquiringly to the Persian.

Parates shrugged. "I've told you already. I'm a merchant and a trader. I deal with many tribes along the borders. The Massegetae are known to me. I've dealt with Areipithes, I've done business with him...as I have with his father before him." Parates paused and steepled his hands in thought. "As for friendship with the man--well, apart from the fact that he's dead..." a small smile quirked his lips, "...he didn't treat me as a friend."

"The second point was entertaining Scolices," prompted Nikometros.

"The man was known to me as one of Areipithes' associates. He approached me on a business matter and I merely offered him hospitality as is my duty."

"And his business?" growled Timon.

"I regret we were interrupted before he could raise the matter," Parates observed. "I've said all this before, Nikometros, before the authorities."

"I know, Parates. Please bear with me. The third point was the poison."

"Arabian death weed has other uses. Some people use it to rid themselves of vermin. In any case, it can be found in many places. Most traders carry small amounts--I do myself." Parates leaned over the table. "However, I don't see how you can possibly know it came from my warehouse. And even if it did, anyone could have bought it."

Nikometros turned to Timon. "Parates has answered all three of your accusations reasonably."

Timon shifted uncomfortably. "He has a ready tongue, I'll admit. If I had but one of these doubts I'd be prepared to believe his story--but three? I don't believe in coincidences."

Nikometros sighed. "You believe in the gods, don't you, Timon?" Timon nodded and he went on. "Parates also believes. His god Ahura-Mazda is a god of truth." He turned to Parates.

"Parates, answer me this in the name of your god and as you follow the Light in truth--do you seek to harm, in any way, myself or my wife Tomyra?"

Parates sat silently and looked at Nikometros, then at Timon. He brought his hands together softly then spread them wide. "In the name of Ahura-Mazda and the truth for which he stands, I'm not trying to harm you or your wife."

"Words," sneered Timon. "I've heard some of the greatest liars swear by the gods."

"What of Tomyra?" Nikometros asked. "You've seen her power as a priestess, haven't you?" Timon nodded hesitantly. "You've seen true prophecy and heard the voice of the Mother Goddess speak through her?" Timon nodded again.

"Have you seen evidence that the Goddess protects her?"

"Yes," admitted Timon.

"Then will you believe her when she says that the Goddess speaks to her still and offers no warning about Parates?"

Timon frowned. "She says that? In truth?"

"She says that, Timon. No harm will come to her from Parates." Nikometros smiled encouragingly. "Won't you believe the Goddess?"

"Who am I to contradict the Goddess?" Timon said slowly. "I will accept the words of Tomyra."

"And will you also accept my hand of friendship?" asked Parates, extending his arm.

Timon hesitated then reached out and lightly brushed his fingertips with the other man.

"Excellent," Nikometros said with a grin. "Now," he added, raising his mug. "Let us drink to the future."

"Prosperity," said Parates. "And the fulfillment of our desires."

They drank, though Timon only sipped, screwing up his face at the thin, sour wine.

"Well, I must leave you now," said Parates, pushing back his chair. He dug into his purse and placed a coin on the table. "Allow me to offer my hospitality this time, my friends." He rose, bowed to Nikometros, then to Timon and exited the tavern.

Nikometros sat back and looked quizzically at his friend. "You mean it, Timon? You'll believe Tomyra?"

Timon grimaced then allowed a reluctant grin. "Aye, Niko. It was killing me to stay away. I still don't like him, you understand, but I'll give him the benefit of the doubt."

"Good man." Nikometros drained his cup and belched. "Come on then, let's go and tell Bithyia of your change of heart." He rose and moved toward the door, followed by Timon.

Outside, the humid air pressed close beneath the overcast sky. The lights of the city burned dully beyond the dark alleyway and the sounds of burgeoning humanity came muted to their ears.

Timon shook his head as he started up the alleyway. "Why in Hades did you choose this tavern, Niko? Apart from the quiet it has nothing else to recommend it."

"I didn't. Parates sent word that he wanted to make up with you and suggested we meet here."

Timon grunted. A shadow detached from the blackness of the alley and closed with him. Nikometros shouted an inarticulate warning and dragged his sword from its sheath. Timon whirled, meeting the shadow, staggering back with a cry. Light glinted dully on steel as the man leapt forward, arm upraised.

Nikometros strode forward then turned as he heard footsteps behind him. Without thinking, he met the sword thrust with his own, metal ringing loudly in the silent alley. The man grunted and swung again, pressing forward. Nikometros parried again, feeling out his opponent, judging his skill level. He feinted left, flicked the blade up toward the man's eyes, smiling to himself as the man flinched and stumbled back. He pressed forward and nearly died as another sword swept in from his right.

Throwing himself to the left, Nikometros crashed into the alley wall, the second man's sword ripping through his tunic. The first man immediately resumed his attack and together, they pressed Nikometros back towards the tavern. Lights came on in the houses along the alley and several shutters were thrown back as the inhabitants looked out. Light flooded the dark alley, allowing Nikometros to see his opponents clearly for the first time.

The men facing him hid enigmatically behind full beards. Their dark hair hung to their shoulders, only their bright eyes displaying any signs of emotion as they sought Nikometros' life. Now that he could see the men he fought, Nikometros recognised the differing quality of their sword skill. The second man was plainly a professional. He crouched, moving fluidly on the balls of his feet, his blade moving constantly, probing his quarry's defences. The first man who attacked him was just as plainly untutored in swordplay. He attacked rigidly and without imagination, boldly pressing forward seemingly without thought for his own safety.

Nikometros flicked a glance toward the entrance of the alley and caught a glimpse of Timon. The old Macedonian soldier's left arm hung by his side and it was all he could do to fight off the determined attack of his assailant. Nikometros abruptly launched himself at the amateur swordsman, the surprise making the man hesitate and step back. Nikometros stepped forward, whirled and slipped between the two men, narrowly avoiding the professional's blade. He ran to Timon's back and turned to face his foes again.

"You are hurt?" Nikometros slashed crossways, his sword blade making a double ring as it met his opponents' blades.

Timon gasped with exertion. "A scratch, Niko." He stumbled back, threatening to knock his friend off balance. "The fornicator's good though."

Nikometros felt himself tiring and knew help was needed if they were to survive this attack. He raised his voice and yelled, in passable if stilted Persian.

"Holla, good citizens. Call the city guard, I beg you."

313

There was little response, save a few shouts and the sound of more shutters thrown back. Timon grunted as his man slipped through his defence again, inflicting another minor wound.

The amateur grinned. "The guard won't save you." He pushed forward aggressively, forcing Nikometros to counter his attack. The other man moved sideways, flicking his blade out under Nikometros' guard. The sword tip scored a line along the underside of Nikometros' sword arm and into his chest.

Nikometros gasped with pain as the point glanced off a rib. He threw himself to the left, preventing the blade from penetrating further but distracting himself from the amateur's attack. The man swung down hard but misjudged the distance as Nikometros stumbled. Instead of a killing blow, his fist and pommel connected with Nikometros' shoulder, sending him reeling back against the alley wall. The amateur fell forwards, colliding with the professional as he moved in to finish his opponent off. Nikometros grimaced with pain and swapped his sword to his left hand, flexing his numb fingers.

The collision distracted Timon's opponent too and, as the man glanced sideways, the old soldier stabbed forward, into the man's arm. The sword fell with a clatter and the man backed away frantically, clutching at the dagger in his belt. Timon stepped over the fallen sword and, ignoring his disarmed opponent slashed at the back of one of the two men attacking Nikometros. The man swung round with a curse to defend himself.

Nikometros seized the opportunity and threw himself forward, crashing into the amateur and sending the man reeling backward. Nikometros followed, his sword back in his right hand, flickering and stabbing. He parried a high blow then ducked and thrust upward. The sword bit home and the man gasped, his sword dropping with a clangour. He stumbled back and collapsed; his face contorted and blood frothing from his mouth.

Nikometros turned back and saw Timon on his knees by the alley wall, his sword above his head, blocking repeated blows from his opponent. As he watched, the other man snatched up his sword again and joined in the attack. Nikometros yelled a battle paean, his anger rising, and threw himself forward just as Timon fell, clutching his chest. He stood over his friend and faced the two Persians.

Nikometros laughed bitterly as his anger flooded his mind. He gestured the men to attack and as one did, met the blow and turned it, stepped to the side and slashed at the other man. He turned back to the first, blocked, stabbed, blocked again. He ran forward, forcing the man back then turned and slashed, catching the man across the side.

Both men fell back a few paces, hesitated, and then ran from the alley, disappearing into the night. Nikometros watched them go, his breath coming in great whooping gasps and red spots dancing before his eyes. He shook his head, leaned over and threw up on the road.

Wiping his mouth, he stumbled back to Timon's body and dropped to his knees beside it, cradling his friend's head.

"Timon," he whispered. "Old friend..."

Timon's eyes fluttered open. "You stink of vomit, Niko." He gasped and held his side as a wave of pain gripped him. "Don't worry though, I'll take care..." The old soldier's head lolled.

Nikometros knelt, clutching his friend to him as shouts echoed and the tramp of feet announced the belated arrival of the city guard. Tears streamed from his eyes.

# *Chapter 38*

The Persian doctor withdrew his arms, bloody to the elbows, and held up a dark, shiny liver. He peered at the organ closely for several minutes before nodding in satisfaction. "Yes, it's as I thought. This man will live."

"Really?" said Nikometros, one eyebrow raised disdainfully. "You don't think you'd better examine your patient more closely? Look at his wounds, for instance?"

"Whatever for?" asked the doctor in some surprise. "The gods have spoken quite clearly through the sacrifice." He tossed the liver down onto the table by the eviscerated carcass of a lamb and wiped his hands perfunctorily on his robes. "Aside from the blow to his head, his wounds are ordinary. Keep them clean and he'll mend. If you can, get him out into fresh air away from the city smells for a while. Odiferous air makes wounds suppurate."

"And his head wound?"

"Watch him closely. If his mind wanders, you may need to sacrifice again. For the rest, clean air."

"The king invited me to join him sailing this afternoon. I'm sure I can take him with me."

"Sounds good," muttered Timon from his cot in the corner of the room. "I don't want to be any trouble though; perhaps you'd better ask the sacrifice."

The doctor shot his patient a dark look. "I'm sure you'll be no more trouble than usual." He put his knives away into a small leather bag, tying it up with a red cord. "I'll leave you now." He bowed to Nikometros, glared at Timon again and left the room.

"Charlatan," growled Timon. He started picking at the new scabs on his chest wound. "The damn thing's itching like Hades."

"Leave it alone, Timon. Let it mend." Nikometros called in a servant and ordered him to clear away the sacrificial mess on the table. "I'd better let the women know what's happening, I suppose."

"Idiot doctor," grunted Timon. "Why couldn't they just be here?"

Nikometros shrugged. "All doctors like things run their way." He left the room to find Tomyra and Bithyia and arrange for their presence on the king's ship that afternoon.

A fresh cool breeze blew from the north, carrying the small fleet of ships down river. The king's royal barge, its decking scrubbed white and its small triangular sail bowed out before the wind, led the other ships into a series of broad reed-lined waterways. Sailors tended the set of the sails, hauling on ropes and adjusting the angle to the following breeze as they moved into the sheltered canals. Alexander stood in the prow with his admiral Niarchos, pointing and gesticulating, talking animatedly. A few paces behind them a scribe scribbled furiously, making charts of the waterways and adding annotations.

Nikometros sat with Tomyra in the stern of the barge, leaning back against the padded deck rail and looking lazily out over the reeds. Timon and Bithyia sat on the other side, trying to relax. Timon's face was screwed up in pain, one hand clutching his side and wincing every time he moved. Bithyia fussed around her husband, adjusting cushions and mopping his sweaty brow, despite her swollen belly. She glanced across at Nikometros.

"Are you sure the king doesn't mind us here, Niko?"

Nikometros smiled and glanced forward. "Alexander's never one to mince words. If he didn't want us here, we wouldn't be here."

"He did seem a trifle upset when we boarded though," Timon gasped.

"That was because of the other night. He's most upset that his officers are attacked in the streets. He's issued arrest warrants and the city's being searched."

"I suppose it was Scolices again," asked Tomyra. "We'll never be safe until that man is dead."

"If he's in Babylon, the king's patrols will find him," replied Nikometros. "But I'm not sure he was behind the attack the other night."

"Oh?" Bithyia looked up, surprised. "Why not?"

"The attackers were Persian. The dead man, the one I killed is from the north, near the Scythian border, but he is Persian. I don't think Scolices could command the loyalty of such men."

"Besides," added Timon quietly. "Only one man knew we'd be there."

Nikometros looked his friend in the eye, willing his silence. "Exactly. We'll talk on this, my friend...later." He glanced at Tomyra but she was staring forward at Alexander.

"What's he doing?" she asked. "I mean, it's very pleasant out here, but why come out here into these reed beds?"

"He wants to expand the safe anchorage for his fleet," Nikometros explained. "I think he plans to have these channels dredged."

"He could just order it done. Why come out here himself?"

Nikometros chuckled. "Alexander believes in doing things for himself. He's a general and a king who leads, not just directs. I remember when we liberated Egypt he wanted to build a city in the north ..."

"The first of his many 'Alexandrias'," interrupted Timon.

"The point being that he didn't just order his architects to plan it out, he walked with a bag of flour over his shoulder and laid out the position of the streets, baths, libraries and palaces."

"So he does the same here." Tomyra nodded. "You have to admire his energy. A whole empire to govern and he still finds time to organise dredging for his ships." She leaned over the side and trailed a hand in the clear water. "Do you think we'll be able to bathe later, Niko? It's such a hot day and the water looks so inviting."

"When we get back to Babylon, my love. I wouldn't risk it here."

"Why not, Niko?" asked Bithyia. "I agree, a swim would be lovely."

Nikometros grimaced. "Look more closely," he said. He stood and looked out over the water, searching. After a few minutes he pointed. "There, that's why not."

Bithyia and Tomyra came across and stood beside him, shading their eyes against the reflective dazzle of sunlight on the rippling water. Timon eased himself up with a groan, and stared where Nikometros pointed.

"What?" Timon asked. "A crocodile?"

"Nothing so exciting," replied Nikometros with a laugh. He pointed again. "Smaller. See there, bobbing in the bow wave."

Tomyra screwed up her eyes and stared as the small object floated alongside then passed into the wake, being lost in the turbulence. "What was it?" she asked, puzzled.

"A turd," Timon said. "A human turd."

"A turd?" asked Tomyra. "What do you mean...oh!" She flushed with embarrassment.

"Where did it come from?" Bithyia asked. "This is a wilderness."

"Oh, the usual place, my dear," answered Timon, with a grin.

Bithyia rolled her eyes. "Men!" she muttered.

"No, really," said Tomyra. "You know what she meant."

Timon shrugged. "The city of course, where else?"

"But we're miles away."

"There are a lot of people in Babylon," observed Nikometros. "A lot of people produce a lot of...excrement. It's easier just to dump the lot in the river and let it all float away."

"But it's so insanitary," Tomyra protested.

"Same principle applies as when we set up camp," Nikometros said. "Always draw your water from upstream, never downstream."

"Well, I know I'm not swimming in this water," Tomyra said firmly.

After sailing many miles through a maze of slowly moving water channels, the barge anchored by a grassy islet. Alexander led the way ashore, scouting the boundaries of his little kingdom while servants and sailors started a fire, set out camp furnishings and prepared a meal. Nikometros and Bithyia carried Timon ashore and made him comfortable in the dappled shade of a willow where the cool breezes off the river could sooth his sweating body.

People from the other ships in the little fleet also came ashore. Nikometros was delighted to see Prince Mardesopryaxes disembark from one of the craft and called him over. The Persian prince brought with him a youth, clean-shaven and dressed in fine silks.

"Nikometros, may I present my youngest brother, Blepharaxes." He ushered the youth forward with a hand on the boy's shoulder.

The youth bowed his face solemn. "I am honoured," he said simply in flawless Greek. "I have heard of your exploits among the savages of Scythia."

Nikometros gave a small smile. "I'm delighted to meet you, Blepharaxes. May I, in turn, present my wife Tomyra--priestess of the Great Goddess."

Tomyra acknowledged the boy with a cool nod. "Savagery comes in many guises, as does civilised behaviour. At least that is what I have found among my people--the Scythians."

Blepharaxes blushed deeply and his mouth dropped open in horror. "Oh...oh, my lady...my apologies," he stammered. "I didn't mean to...to cause offence." He swallowed and took a deep breath, visibly collecting his thoughts. Bowing deeply once more, this time to Tomyra, he addressed her in formal tones.

"My lady Tomyra, I beg forgiveness for my crass comments. Though I offer up no excuse for my behaviour, I ask that you remember my extreme youth and, having no experience of the world to draw on, I rely solely on what my tutors impart to me. I can see that in this instance they are gravely mistaken."

"Bravely said," murmured Nikometros, in Scythian. "What do you think, Tomyra, give the lad another chance?"

Tomyra smiled and extended a slim hand to Blepharaxes. "There is nothing to forgive. How can any of us learn if we don't put ourselves in the path of knowledge?" She tugged on the youth's hand, drawing him aside. "Come and talk with me, there is much I would know about your people." As she walked off to the shade of a spreading willow tree, she beckoned to Bithyia. "This is my friend Bithyia. She too is Scythian."

Nikometros watched Tomyra and Bithyia strolling and talking with Blepharaxes. "A fine lad," he said. "I didn't know you had other brothers, Mardes. I thought your elder brother Astyges was the only one."

"Astyges and I were both sons of my father's wife. Blepharaxes is a son of one of his concubines. There are two others, barely walking, and of course, numerous daughters." Mardes waved a hand dismissively. "I sent for him to give him a taste of court life. It is in my mind to ask Alexander to let him remain behind in his service when I return home."

"I'd be happy to keep an eye on him," Nikometros said. "When do you return home?"

"Another week, maybe two," replied Mardes. "Alexander has set the date of the expedition for ten days hence. No point staying at court if the king isn't there, so I'll return to my lands. Plenty to keep me busy there."

"I'll be sorry to see you go. Perhaps you'll come back to Babylon when we return."

Mardes lifted an eyebrow. "Return? Surely the king will stay in the west, in his Macedonian homeland?"

"Hardly. Alexander views Persia as his home now. I know for a fact he intends to make Babylon his world capital."

Mardes inclined his head with a smile. "May the gods grant the king a swift and safe return to his people then."

"Indeed," agreed Nikometros. He turned, hearing his name called and saw Tomyra beckoning. Servants were serving up the noon meal. "Ah, lunch. Shall we?" He put his arm around his friend and started toward the others.

Mardes hung back. "A moment, Niko, I beg."

Nikometros stared at the prince's troubled face. "What's wrong?"

"It may be nothing." Mardes hesitated. "Your friend, the Roman..."

"Caius?"

"He keeps...what should I say...dubious company?"

Nikometros looked mystified. "I don't understand."

"He spends time...too much time, with Kassandros."

Nikometros frowned. "Why should that be a problem?" he asked cautiously.

"Kassandros hates Alexander. That's obvious for all to see. Add in a Roman who fears the king will subjugate his people and you have a dangerous combination."

"He could just be seeking information, Mardes. Caius is forever asking questions of anyone willing to talk to him."

"I hope so, my friend."

"You have seen them together? Do they behave suspiciously?"

"I haven't. One in my employ saw them with another man, two or three times in the last few days." Mardes shrugged. "He doesn't know this other man but he'll find out."

"Let me know when you do. I'm sure it's innocent enough but the king may need to know."

"I'll do so, never fear," replied Mardes. "Now," he added, rubbing his hands together. "You said something about lunch?"

Nikometros and Mardes rejoined the others in the shade of the trees where a great quantity of food and drink lay on trestle tables and on the springy turf. For a time, conversation lagged as all, commoners and nobility alike, assuaged their hunger pains. Afterward, they relaxed, in shade or sun, slept for a time or talked quietly. Nikometros lay on his belly on the short grass and watched tiny blue butterflies fluttering over the sward, feeding on nectar from minute white flowers that dotted the grass like stars in the heavens. The sailors and servants broke up into small groups and played dice or gossiped. Some of the Greeks, the king among them, swam or splashed in the shallows, oblivious or uncaring as to what else floated alongside them.

Timon rested quietly beneath the shade trees, a solicitous Bithyia at his side. As the day advanced, he developed a slight fever, his wounds reddening.

Tomyra drew Nikometros aside. "I don't like it, Niko. I fear his wounds are infected."

"Aye. He won't complain but I can see he's in pain."

"I'll feel better when we can get him back to the palace. I can treat him properly there."

They embarked in a warm mid-afternoon, turning their prows upriver to Babylon. Mardes and his young brother joined the king's barge. Facing into fitful breezes, the Assyrian shipmasters hauled down gaudy sails and unshipped great two-man oars. The sailors manned these amid joking and challenges.

As usual, Alexander made joy of necessity and organised races between the ship crews as they oared their way through reed-lined river channels. The king stood in the prow, took the helm or just strolled among the crew, joking and laughing with the sailors. He wore a battered sun-hat, worn and stained, with a purple ribbon, a symbol of his royal power.

Great trees grew alongside the river channels here; their arching canopies meeting above. The ships moved through great green caves of languid water then, bursting out into the sun once more, forged across pools covered with lily-pads, ablaze with white and yellow and pink flowers.

The stream broadened and the ships glided into calm waters. The wind, instead of a steady breeze from the north, gusted in flurries, whipping the tops of the trees. Great stone monuments and statues, crumbling and stained, loomed among the willows. Striding bulls and man-headed lions stared in stony disdain at the little fleet intruding on their endless silence.

Alexander ran to the side of the barge and leaned on the rail, staring eagerly at the enigmatic stonework. He turned to his Assyrian shipmaster. "What are they? Who built them?"

"Great King," rumbled the shipmaster. "They are the tombs of the ancient Assyrian kings. This is a burial ground."

A gust of wind answered his words, bending the trees and beating at the royal barge. Alexander's sun hat whisked overboard and its purple ribbon lofted into the air. It rippled and flew, lodging in the reeds beside a crumbling tomb.

The sailors stopped rowing and a groan of dread echoed through their ranks. One of the rowers, a young man, dropped his oar and dived overboard, swimming for the reeds. He unwound the purple ribbon, treading water, then after a moment's hesitation, wound it around his own head to leave both hands free for swimming. He swam back to the royal barge in a dreadful silence and handed it to the king.

Alexander thanked the man and turned away to take up his station in the prow, looking thoughtful. The rowers, under the urgings of the shipmaster, resumed their passage toward Babylon.

Nikometros turned to Mardes, noting the young Persian prince's stricken expression. "What? You look like you've seen your own death."

"Not mine," he whispered. "The king's."

Tomyra arrived and stood by the two men. "What does this mean, Mardes?"

Mardes turned his horrified face to Tomyra. "The king's diadem, his ribbon, his symbol of kingship, has gone from his head to a tomb and from there to another man's head. It's a most dreadful omen."

Nikometros turned and looked to where the young man had resumed his place at an oar. His fellows drew back from him, shunning him. "What if the king had the man killed? Like the madman on the throne. Would that avert the omen?"

"Possibly." Mardes nodded to where the shipmaster and one of the accompanying seers were obviously remonstrating with Alexander, entreating him to kill the young sailor.

Alexander refused, with an angry shake of his head. He beckoned the young man over and handed him something. The seer backed away and came toward the helm, shaking his head.

Nikometros accosted the seer, plucking at his sleeve. "What happened? What did the king say?"

The seer looked at the tall Greek officer with tears in his eyes. "He rewarded the man," he whispered in a tone of shocked disbelief. He wiped his tears away with his sleeve. "He won't execute the man to avert the omen. The king chooses to disregard all the warnings of the gods."

# *Chapter 39*

The embassy from Siwah returned. Sent months ago, during the madness of Alexander, to ask of Zeus-Ammon that Hephaestion be admitted as a god to the ranks of the immortals, men dreaded the return of the embassy. Alexander had emerged slowly and painfully from madness and many feared a relapse.

The king received the embassy in the Throne Room, surrounded by his Companions, generals and friends, who lounged on silver couches. The envoys entered, made obeisance to the Great King and ceremoniously unrolled papyrus containing Ammon's words.

The priest of Ammon at Siwah and friend of Nikometros, Ketherennoferptah cleared his throat and drew his wizened diminutive form erect. His voice, soft but commanding, penetrated to the corners of the huge reception room. "The god Ammon, all-high and all-mighty, sends greetings to his son Alexander, Pharaoh of Egypt, Great King of Persia, Hegemon of Greece. Know that Ammon is a jealous god and does not share the godhead lightly. The man Hephaestion is refused worship as a god but is accorded divine honours as a Hero. Ammon has spoken."

Ket rolled up the papyrus and retied the purple ribbon around it. With a bow he handed it to Alexander's secretary Eumenes and resumed his position with the other envoys.

For a long time Alexander remained lost in thought as silence enveloped the Throne Room. At last, he stirred and lifted his head to contemplate the priest of Ammon. "I have heard the words of my father Ammon, priest, and am content." He stood, the Companions and the rest of the court rising with him. "Let it be universally known that lord Hephaestion is proclaimed a divine hero. Let temples be erected in his name and prayers and sacrifices be offered to him as...as an averter of evil."

A buzz of comment broke out, and applause, scattered at first but quickly gathering strength, washed over the king.

Perdikkas leaned toward a smirking Eumenes. "Don't get too happy with the idea that your rival has been refused godhead," he whispered. "You're still going to have to use his name in all official documents from now on."

Eumenes' smile vanished.

Alexander dismissed the embassy with his thanks and ordered a great celebratory feast for that evening. "This good news has come at a most opportune time. The fleet leaves in five days' time and now lord Hephaestion can be invoked, with the gods, to bring a blessing on this venture. Let this feast be in honour of my admiral Niarchos, the greatest fleet the world has seen, and Hephaestion's elevation to heaven."

The meeting broke apart, Alexander conferring with his closest friends as he walked from the Throne Room. "Peukestas, make sure that sufficient funding goes out to the provinces. I want a temple to Hephaestion in every city before year's end."

Peukestas looked worried. "That will be a considerable drain on the treasury, Alexander, particularly as we are still outfitting the fleet. Perhaps we could start them in Babylon and say, Ekbatana and Persepolis, and wait until the new taxes are in?"

Alexander nodded impatiently. "Very well, but get them started. And don't skimp on the materials. Now, Ptolemy, Egypt was ever your love. See to the temple in Alexandria. I want it to be the talk of the civilised world."

"Of course, Alexander. No expense shall be spared. Egypt is a rich province."

The little group emerged from the shadowed palace into the sweltering heat of summer. The sun burned in a pale blue vault, the air rippling and distorting the great city that lay before them.

"It'll be good to get away from Babylon," Alexander said, flapping his tunic away from his sweating body. "Though I daresay Arabia will be just as hot."

"Probably," agreed Ptolemy. "Yet the desert heat is drier and not so enervating. This wet heat is dreadful. At least it will be cooler when we set sail."

Alexander laughed. "Not for you, Ptolemy. You'll march the army downriver. I'll watch you from the fleet until we reach the coast." He absentmindedly scratched a reddened mark on his arm.

"Hurt yourself, Alexander?" enquired Eumenes solicitously. "Shall I send for a doctor?"

Alexander glared at the effete Greek until he dropped his gaze. "No doctors." He shrugged. "It's only an insect bite."

The feast started at sunset. As the sun dipped below the western horizon, Alexander offered up the sacrifice to Herakles, dedicating the feast to the hero-god, and to Hephaestion. He washed the blood from his arms and, donning a clean robe, led the guests into the dining area.

The night was fine, the stars blazing in the skies above the open courtyard and the great open cooking fires only added to the sweltering heat of the summer evening. Servants pried whole ox carcasses off the cooking slabs, the well-cooked flesh sizzling and crackling in the juices and gravies. With a flourish they sliced them open before the assembled feasters, eliciting cries of wonder and praise as roasted hogs were drawn out of the oxen. These in turn were cut open to reveal sheep, then poultry and fish, packed one within the other.

The smoking meats were carved and laid in great platters before the guests, together with mountains of vegetables and steaming hills of cooked grains - the new water-grains from the east. Bread was brought in huge baskets, hot and fresh from the ovens, and plenty of drink. Wine, beers, citron and spring water from the king's own stores flowed like minor rivers.

Nikometros reclined on a couch near Seleukos and prince Mardesopryaxes. Timon was absent, his wounds causing him sufficient trouble to warrant an early night. Women were excluded from these feasts by custom. It was not deemed seemly that they attend festivities when men drank, often to excess.

Everyone ate their fill, though the heat of the Babylonian night depressed appetite and fostered thirst. Initially, the wine was well watered but after the food had been cleared, people started drinking the wine neat. Voices grew louder, more argumentative, more discordant.

The young men, officers new to their station and eager to be noticed, began to pledge toasts to the king. He answered each one with a smile and drank the toast. As the night progressed, Alexander grew flushed, his eyes bright, his greying blond hair plastered with sweat.

Nikometros sipped his wine and looked around at the other guests. His gaze slipped over a small knot of men standing in the shadows behind the king, hesitated, then returned. He frowned when he recognised Caius, the Roman praefect and Kassandros, son of the Macedonian Regent.

"Who is that with Kassandros? Do you know them?"

Mardes stared then nodded. "That young man with the fair hair is the man my spies told me about. I don't know who he is."

Seleukos turned his attention from the officer reclining on the other side of him. "That is Iollas, the king's cupbearer. The other young men are squires. Why?"

"I was wondering why Kassandros sought him out."

Seleukos shrugged. "Iollas is brother to Kassandros. No doubt he bears messages from home."

"Brother?" Nikometros half raised himself and stared at the group of men, talking quietly but animatedly behind the king. He glanced at Mardes, catching his troubled look.

"You think there's something significant in that?" asked Seleukos. "Iollas is trusted, has been for years. You may be sure the king knows already if there's even the slightest suspicion."

Nikometros sank back down onto his couch and picked up his wine cup again. "You're probably right."

The noise grew in volume, cut off raggedly while several dancers and musicians ran in and lined up in front of the king. When silence fell at last, a young man, almost feminine in beauty stepped forward and, in a high, clear voice, dedicated their dance to Alexander.

Mardes nudged Nikometros. "By all the gods," he murmured. "We're in for a rare treat. That's Bagoas, the king's boy."

"Bagoas? Who is he?" Nikometros peered over the couches toward the open space where the dancers were arranging themselves.

The musicians started, flutes and tinkling cymbals in a martial beat.

"Come now, Nikometros. All this time in Alexander's court and you don't know about Bagoas?" He laughed quietly. "You must truly only have eyes for women, not boys."

"Only one woman, my friend."

Mardes shook his head. "My preference lies with women too, but I can appreciate the extraordinary beauty of Bagoas. He was the Great King Darius' before, you know. Now he's Alexander's shadow."

"I really don't know why you Persians feel you must cut your boys," interjected Seleukos. "Oh, I know emasculation preserves the beauty but from what I heard, eunuchs close to the throne are nothing but trouble."

"It's true that the predecessor of Darius met his end at the hands of a eunuch," Mardes replied. "Oddly enough, that eunuch's name was Bagoas too. However, it's an old custom and I daresay won't be changed anytime soon." He smiled at the earnest young officer. "What of yourself, Seleukos? Are you a lover of boys?"

Seleukos shook his head. "No, not particularly. Though like you, I can appreciate male beauty." He craned his neck to watch the dancers. "I say, look at that!"

The dancers, eight in all, were dressed in helmets and short kilts or trousers. Four, obviously meant to represent the Greek army, stood at attention with mock swords and shields. The other four, led by Bagoas, stood in for the Persians, armed with scimitars.

With a wail, flutes erupted into a frenzied skirl, rising and falling. The dancers flowed, moving forward, offering graceful blows at the others, the cymbals crashing as mock swords met mock shields. They swirled, advancing and retreating, every eye caught by the beauty and grace. The music changed, becoming slower, more languid. The dancers laid aside their weapons and moved closer, offering friendship and love. As the dance ended, the dancers paired off, Greek and Persian, sinking to the floor in a loving embrace.

Applause erupted from the onlookers, with cheers and not a few invitations from the guests on the nearer couches.

Alexander rose to his feet, a trifle unsteadily and beckoned to Bagoas, a great grin on his face. He embraced the young man and, amid further cheering, kissed him tenderly. Turning, his arm around the youth, Alexander led him back to his couch and pledged a toast to Bagoas. Together, they drank from the king's gold cup.

The drinking resumed, followed by bawdy humour. Music started up again, falling into the rhythm of old Macedonian drinking songs.

Alexander listened for a while, his foot tapping out the beat, and one hand holding his wine cup, the other stroking Bagoas' hair. At last he put down his cup and got to his feet. "A komos!"

Bagoas discreetly slipped away, disappearing back into the palace.

A cheer went up and a rough line formed behind the king. The music rose, men stamped and bawled out the words of songs, any they could remember, while the line lurched and weaved about the courtyard. Guests snapped off branches from the vines growing along the walls and fashioned them into wreaths. The line of dancing men wound itself between the remains of the cooking fires, threading between couches and empty amphorae of wine. Unwatered wine worked its way on the heads and feet of men and the komos ground to a halt, the dancers breaking up into swaying groups or collapsing onto couches. The festivities broke up shortly after and the guests dispersed.

Alexander went into the palace but returned some minutes later. He wore a fresh wool robe and his hair was tied back and plastered down with orange-water. He called to his friends. "Medios is having a small supper party. Come and join me."

Ptolemy walked over unsteadily and put his hand on Alexander's arm. "Do you think you should? You look a bit feverish."

"It's nothing. Just a touch of the sun. I'm not going for long--come on, it'll be fun."

He walked off, leaving Ptolemy shaking his head. Several other friends gathered round, persuading Ptolemy and at last he gave up with a laugh, following Alexander.

Nikometros plucked at Seleukos' arm. "Who is this Medios? I haven't seen him around court."

"A nobody. A junior officer under Admiral Niarchos."

Medios welcomed his guests, expected and unexpected, into a modest house. About twenty men lay on couches around the walls of the largest room, leaving an open space in the middle so everyone could see everyone else. Talk was subdued at first but as men continued to drink thirstily in the oppressive Babylonian night, the conversation grew livelier.

Talk turned to Alexander's boyhood and the early years of his reign. He praised his friends for their loyalty and steadfastness. "What better friends could a man have?" he cried. "Even those of you who came later have proven themselves true friends." He threw out his arms as if to embrace everyone present. "A toast. I will drink a toast to you all!"

Servants brought in the wine in a great beaker, cooled in snow and beaded with condensation in the hot, humid air.

"By the gods," chuckled Seleukos. "That's truly a huge cup. A cup of Herakles at the feast of Herakles."

Alexander got to his feet and accepted the beaker, holding it aloft in both hands. "To love!" he cried.

"To love!" echoed his friends.

Alexander lifted it to his lips and sipped. He hesitated a moment and Nikometros, seated only two couches away from his king, saw him shiver and break out in goose flesh on his bare arms. Then the king lifted the cup and drank deeply, turning slowly to face all his friends as his throat worked convulsively. The cup continued to tip and several young men burst into cheers and cries of encouragement.

Alexander drained the last of the cold wine and lifted the cup aloft in a salute. "To love!" he cried again. "To you all, my belov...aah!" Alexander dropped the cup and staggered, holding a hand to his side. He swayed while his friends looked on in horror then his eyes rolled up and he started to collapse.

Ptolemy leapt forward, followed closely by Nikometros, catching their king and laying him on his couch. Alexander turned an ashen face to Ptolemy and muttered something. Ptolemy leaned closer, gesturing furiously to the others to keep quiet.

"I...I will be..." Alexander repeated in a hoarse whisper. "Take me back to the palace. I just need to rest."

Ptolemy and Nikometros, together with a handful of other guests, escorted Alexander back to his rooms. Bagoas was waiting, having been alerted by the squires and took charge of his monarch without a word. They left him sleeping beneath a thin coverlet on a bed by the open pool.

"What happened?" asked Nikometros. "Is the king ill?"

"You were there," Ptolemy said. "He drank the wine and collapsed."

"Poisoned?" asked a young man.

"Don't be a fool," replied Perdikkas. "He'd be dead already if he'd been poisoned."

"Then what?"

Ptolemy shrugged. "It's a hot night and that wine was frigid. No wonder it hurt him. He'll be all right tomorrow, you wait and see."

Nikometros excused himself and hurried home in the first light of dawn. As he went he thought back over the omens surrounding the king. *How did Tomyra's prophecy go,* he thought. *"By water, by wine, by hand of man..."* He shivered, despite the warmth of the night.

# Chapter 40

Timon grumbled a good deal before at last consenting to remain in bed under care.

His wounds were inflamed and hot to the touch.

Nikometros used his influence to have his friend installed in one of the many apartments of the main palace, not far from the king's suite. Here, in rooms open to the river, with pools to bathe in and ornamental ponds stocked with fish that swam beneath lily pads in golden shoals, Timon could escape the heat. Within a day or two his wounds started healing, the incipient fever abating. By the third day after the river cruise, he felt well enough to entertain company.

"I'm happy to see you well again," Tomyra said, her body held stiffly formal. "I was worried."

"Thank you," said Timon, with a smile.

An awkward silence followed, until Mardes stepped in and deflected attention away from their strained friendship. "I say, Timon, these rooms are truly magnificent, aren't they? I must look into building some like this back home."

"You have a river palace too?" asked Bithyia. "Tell us about it."

"Oh, nothing much to speak of," said Mardes. "The estate is somewhat rundown and in need of attention. The palace itself is on a hillside but there is a small river close by. I was thinking I could build a modest summerhouse on its banks."

"Well, let us know when you build it," Nikometros grinned. "We'll definitely come and try it out for you."

The conversation faltered again while Timon and Tomyra struggled to maintain a polite façade while the cause of their estrangement still rankled.

"Er...you got permission to use these rooms from the king himself, I understand, Niko," said Mardes.

Nikometros nodded. He looked around at the uncomfortable expressions and hurried to explain. "Yes. The king was most forthcoming. When he heard the problem he suggested these rooms himself."

"And how is the king? Recovered from his party?"

Nikometros frowned. "His fever is worse. He won't stop working and give his body time to heal."

"Worse?" asked Mardes. "But I saw him yesterday coming back from offering the sacrifice. He looked fine then."

"He was. He went to another party that night and came home with a fever again. The next morning...this morning, he had to be carried in a litter to make the sacrifice. Then he spent the whole day in planning with Niarchos." Nikometros shook his head. "The fever is higher this evening. Despite the heat, he lies wrapped in blankets, shivering, or else bathing in cold pools."

"This sounds more than just a reaction to an excess of cold wine," rumbled Timon. "Has he seen a doctor?"

"He refuses to see one. He remembers Glaukios in Ekbatana."

"The king must leave Babylon," Tomyra said in a low voice. "He must heed the warnings of the gods."

"No doubt, my love, but try to convince him of that."

"Willingly, Niko. You just get me in to see him and I'll convince him."

"I can try, I suppose, but I don't hold out much hope."

"What of the other matter, Niko," put in Mardes. "Have you told the king?"

"What? About Kassandros? Yes, I mentioned it to Perdikkas."

"What did he say?"

"Not much," Nikometros said with a grimace. "He didn't think it was important. He knows Kassandros from his youth and thinks he's a blow-hard, rather than a real danger."

"Even with the Roman?"

"He says the Roman is one man, far from home with no real friends. What can he do?"

"Come Niko," remonstrated Mardes. "You don't believe that."

"No, I don't," agreed Nikometros. "I'm only telling you what Perdikkas said." He walked over to a small table and poured iced citron into several small cups. "I'll wait a day or two. If nothing happens to Kassandros or Caius, I'll try to speak directly to the king." He passed the cups out to his friends, then lifted his and drank.

"From what you've told me, my love," Tomyra said. "It may be too late."

"Too late?" Timon stared at her. "What do you mean?"

"Only that Iollas, the king's cupbearer is brother to Kassandros and by chance, the king falls ill after drinking wine no doubt served by Iollas."

"Iollas is trusted," said Nikometros uneasily. "Anyway, he could have poisoned the king's wine any time. Why now?"

"The Regency." Mardes nodded, a troubled smile on his face. "Their father Antipatros is Regent of Macedon. Alexander has just sent his trusted general Krateros back to Macedon to become Regent in his place. If Alexander dies, Antipatros will defy Krateros and hang on to power, maybe even increase it. That's enough of a motive."

"And the Roman?" Bithyia asked. "Where does he fit in?"

"When Alexander pushes west he'll meet and subjugate the Romans," said Timon. "He has no love for Alexander either."

"So, what can we do?" asked Nikometros.

Mardes considered the problem. "Probably very little at the moment. You've voiced your concerns to Perdikkas. Hopefully he'll pass them on to Alexander. If not, I'd wait a couple of days and talk to Ptolemy."

"It could just be a fever. Babylon was never a healthy place for foreigners."

Mardes laughed. "Don't let the king hear you say that. He's trying very hard to become a native."

The others joined in the laughter and Bithyia took advantage of the moment to lead the others in to a light supper. The conversation turned to lighter matters for a while, Tomyra entertaining them with stories of Starissa. After the supper, the ladies excused themselves to go and see the child, while the men talked over wine.

"Have you told Tomyra about the attack the other night?" asked Timon.

Nikometros looked startled. "Of course! How could I not...I mean, your wounds...oh, you mean about Parates?"

"Exactly. Have you told her about Parates' complicity?"

"Possible complicity. We cannot prove it."

Timon made a rude noise. "Who else knew we were going to be there?"

"Could you have been followed?" Mardes asked.

"Possibly," replied Nikometros, "but it would have been a great coincidence. I was in the palace before crossing to the lesser palace to find Timon. The guards would not have admitted any unauthorized people, so unless these thugs happened upon us in the street, no, I would say we weren't followed."

"You're sure the motive wasn't robbery?"

"They were Persians..."

"Even Persians can be robbers," interposed Mardes with a grin.

"...and their equipment was good. The man I killed had money in his purse. I wouldn't say his motive was robbery."

"Then I'd say Parates must stand high in your suspicions," said Mardes. "Have you confronted him?"

Nikometros shook his head. "No, he's disappeared and no one can tell me where he is."

"The actions of a man with something to hide," growled Timon.

"So, what will you do now?" asked Mardes.

"Not much we can do," replied Nikometros. "Stay on guard. Keep looking for him."

"And tell Tomyra," added Timon.

"I'm not sure that's a good idea. Not at present, anyway."

Timon set his jaw. "You've got to tell, Tomyra. Immediately."

"Tell me what?"

Nikometros and Timon swung round to see Tomyra standing in the doorway, Bithyia beside her with Starissa in her arms.

Nikometros sighed and got up, crossing over to his wife. He took his daughter from Bithyia and held her close, chucking her under her chin.

"Tell me what, Niko?" asked Tomyra again. "What's this about?"

"Parates."

Tomyra turned an angry glare at Timon. "I suppose you've been filling my husband's head with your suspicions and innuendoes again. I thought we'd agreed to stop that."

"Niko," growled Timon. "Tell her."

"I'm not going to stay and hear that man slandered again. Give me Starissa, Niko. I'm going home."

"Tomyra, wait." Nikometros hung onto his child and walked back to his couch. "Answer me one question and you can leave."

Tomyra stared at her husband, her lips thin and nostrils flared. "Ask then."

Nikometros paused, searching for the right words. "Tomyra, answer me as a priestess of the Great Goddess, not as a woman or as my wife. Can you do this?"

Tomyra glared at him a moment longer then dropped her gaze. "I can," she said, a tinge of curiosity showing through.

"Has the Goddess intimated to you in any way that Parates is to be trusted?"

The silence dragged out. Starissa squirmed in Nikometros' arms and fought to be released.

Mardes went over and took the child who stared up at his dark face. With a gurgling smile she reached up and pulled at his beard.

"No," replied Tomyra at last. "In truth, the Goddess has told me nothing either way."

Nikometros nodded slowly. "I know you miss your lands and your people, my love. I know too that Parates was a link with this past but he wasn't what he seemed."

"Go on."

"Only one person knew where Timon and I would be the other night when we were attacked."

"Parates," whispered Tomyra.

Nikometros nodded.

"Scolices I can understand, Niko, but why Parates? What harm have we ever done him?"

341

"Who can know what hurt, real or imagined, motivates him? I do know that we must guard against him. I intend to see Peukestas tomorrow and ask him to issue an arrest warrant. Alexander will sign it, I'm sure."

Tomyra nodded. "I feel so foolish. I didn't think I could be fooled so easily." She looked at Timon and flushed. "Forgive me, Timon. I've done you a great wrong."

Timon lowered his head in embarrassment, answering gruffly. "Nonsense, lady. He's a smooth talker. No doubt he'd fool me too, if I were in your place."

"But he didn't, Timon. That's the point." Tomyra advanced and put her arms around the old soldier. "I thank you, my trusted and loyal friend."

Nikometros coughed and hid a grin. "Well, fortune is smiling on us at last. A few more days and we can all be shed of this city. Timon and I march with the army, and the ladies have been granted passage on the fleet downriver, at least to the coast." He smiled at his friends. "All we need to make it perfect is for Mardes to be coming with us."

Mardes smiled and handed Starissa back to her mother. "I regret I cannot do that, my friends. However, when Alexander returns in triumph, I'll come back to Babylon to see you."

# *Chapter 41*

A lexander postponed the departure of the fleet next morning. Too weak to walk or ride, he was carried to the sacrifice and afterward conducted such business as was urgent from a couch beside his pool. In the afternoon he became tired and was carried over the river to the royal gardens, the King's Paradise, where he lay in the cool shade of the trees, listening only to the gentle sigh of the breezes and the splash of fountains. As night fell, the fever increased. He was carried back to the palace, to the Royal Bedchamber, where he spent the night in fitful sleep.

Days passed and the king became visibly weaker. His generals, Perdikkas, Ptolemy and Peukestas, did what they could to relieve the king of any non-essential business, diverting petitioners and court officials. Alexander insisted on seeing Niarchos and Perdikkas every day though, discussing details of the fleet and army. Medios often came, just to gossip or to play at knucklebones. The king was always glad to see him, though he looked drawn and tired when he left.

Kassandros stayed away from the court, not venturing from his lodgings. The Roman praefect, too, forsook the court and ventured out into the surrounding countryside, seemingly no longer interested in what went on in Babylon. Iollas, the king's cupbearer and brother of Kassandros, remained close to the king; ever ready with wine or cold spring water when Alexander thirsted.

Nikometros decided to call on Ptolemy.

"I'm concerned, sir. The king is sick and...and...I fear it may not be just a fever."

Ptolemy looked up from his paperwork and stared searchingly at his son. "If not a fever, then what?"

Nikometros looked away, his hand straying to the amulet of the Goddess circling his left arm. He took a deep breath and looked back at the general. "I think the king has been poisoned."

Ptolemy pushed the chair back from the desk and stared at Nikometros. "By whom?"

"Iollas, the king's cupbearer, and Caius Gracchus the Roman."

"And why?"

"Kassandros, brother to Iollas, hates the king. The Roman fears what will happen to his people if Alexander invades Italy."

"You've seen them together?"

"Yes sir."

"How often did you see them together?" asked Ptolemy.

"Only once sir. At the feast of Herakles, but Mardes--prince Mardesopryaxes, has seen them together on two other occasions."

"When?"

"About three weeks ago and just the other..."

"Three weeks!" Ptolemy stared at his son. "You suspected these men of plotting to kill our king and you waited three weeks before reporting it?"

"Sir, the prince only saw Kassandros and the Roman with another man. It was not until a few days ago that he confirmed the identity of that man as Iollas."

"Even so, Nikometros," Ptolemy said with ice in his voice. "I would know why you wait so long to report it?"

"I did, sir, to Perdikkas, about three days ago."

Ptolemy sat silent for a few moments. "Perdikkas?" he muttered. "Why hasn't he said anything?" He stared at Nikometros again. "You're certain he understood?"

"Yes sir. He said something about them being brothers and having much to talk about."

"No doubt," Ptolemy remarked dryly. "However, Perdikkas is aware of the omens and the mood of the populace. It does no good to ignore these things." He tapped his fingers on the arm of his chair, his rugged, lined face creased with worry. He nodded and rose to his feet. "We shall tell the king ourselves."

Ptolemy led the way across the palace to the river suites and approached the squires on guard outside the king's rooms. He talked quietly to them for a few moments then waited while his message was conveyed to the king. Minutes later, the squire returned and opened the door, ushering them inside.

Alexander lay, wan and pale, on a couch beside the pool, a single linen sheet draped over him. Medios sat beside him, in the middle of a long and involved tale when Nikometros and Ptolemy entered. He looked up and grinned, beckoning Ptolemy over.

"I say, Ptolemy old chap, listen to this." He turned back to Alexander. "As I was saying, it was at this point the girl turned to him in front of all the guests and said, as cool as you like, 'I'd rather marry your horse. At least he has brains as well as being well hung.'" Medios broke into guffaws of laughter, slapping his knees and nudging Alexander.

The king smiled politely but made no comment.

Ptolemy took advantage of a lull in the mirth as Medios drew breath, to interpose. "Alexander, I must talk with you. Alone."

The king looked up at Ptolemy with curiosity. He glanced across at Nikometros, then back at Medios. "Leave us Medios."

Medios frowned then got up and made an exaggerated bow to Alexander. "Your word is my command. I'll return later."

"He means well, but he's awfully tiring," murmured Alexander after the door closed on Medios. "What was it you wanted to say?"

Ptolemy looked around and saw a figure sitting on an embroidered cushion, leaning against a wall in the shadows. The figure, a youth in his late teens or perhaps early twenties, watched Alexander, an attentive expression on his beautiful face.

"What about Bagoas?"

Alexander smiled at the youth. "Bagoas stays. There is nothing you cannot say in front of him."

Ptolemy nodded. "Nikometros has something you should hear."

Nikometros saluted his king and gave a succinct outline of his suspicions. When he finished, Ptolemy added that Perdikkas had been told but had apparently done nothing.

Alexander thought for a moment. "Neither will I."

"Alexander, you must do something," remonstrated Ptolemy. "There is a very real danger here." He hesitated. "This illness..."

"This is but a slight fever. It will pass with good care." He smiled again at Bagoas. "I'm in good hands."

"I don't doubt it. However, not to arrest Kassandros is..."

"...to know exactly where the danger lies," finished Alexander. "Think on it, Ptolemy. His father Antipatros rules Greece in all but name. Arrest his eldest son and I cast doubts on his loyalty too. Remember the lesson of Philotas and Parmenion. The whole western empire could rise in revolt." He paused, panting for breath.

Bagoas moved quickly to the king's side and lifted Alexander's head. He wiped the sweat from his damp forehead and lifted a silver cup of fresh cold water to the king's lips.

"Thank you, Bagoas." Alexander coughed and beckoned Ptolemy closer. "Wait until Krateros takes over the Regency and Antipatros comes out to Asia. Then there'll be a reckoning."

"And his brother Iollas, your cupbearer?"

"Loyal, I'm sure of it. Gods, Ptolemy! He's had ample opportunity over the years."

"What of the Roman praefect, Caius Gracchus?" Nikometros asked.

Alexander's eyes turned flinty. "He's being watched. I'll take him with me when we move west. I'm most curious to see if Romans are the fighters they claim to be."

"Is there nothing we can say to change your mind, Alexander?" asked Ptolemy. "In truth, you look terrible. Won't you see a doctor?"

Alexander frowned. "No doctors," he snapped. "Now if you're finished, I think I'll rest." He sank back into his pillow and closed his eyes.

Ptolemy saluted and walked toward the door.

Nikometros started to follow then turned back. "Sir," he said tentatively. "There is an alternative." He saw Alexander's eyes flicker open. "My wife Tomyra is a priestess, as you know, sir. She's well versed in the healing arts of prayer and herbs. Allow her to minister to you."

Alexander shook his head weakly. "Thank you for the kind thought, Nikometros but I don't want it said I'm so ill I need a physician, even one as beautiful as your wife."

"With respect, sir, people believe this already. I'm sure she could affect a cure rapidly if you let her." He smiled. "You can always dismiss her if you change your mind."

Alexander thought on it for several minutes, his chest rising and falling under the thin sheet. He looked at Bagoas, his eyes locked on the youth's. Bagoas gave a very slight nod and Alexander smiled weakly. "Bully," he whispered. To Nikometros he said, "Very well. You may send for her."

Nikometros grinned. "I'll be back as soon as I can." He ran from the room, startling the squires on duty outside the king's apartments. He crossed the palace to his own suite of river rooms and burst in on Tomyra. "Tomyra! Pack your herbs and whatever else you need. The king has sent for you to cure him."

Tomyra looked up from the rug by the pool where she played with Starissa. "What are you saying, Niko?"

Nikometros stopped and grinned again. "I've just come from the king. Alexander agreed to let you try to cure him of the fever."

"How did he get that idea?"

"I told him of course. He doesn't want a doctor but I told him you're a priestess and could heal all sorts of things. He agreed, so get your things."

Tomyra picked up Starissa and walked over to the child's cot. She settled her daughter then turned and walked up to Nikometros, lifting her gaze to his as she approached.

Nikometros' smile faltered as he caught the flash of fire in her eyes.

"Let me see if I understand you, husband," she said. "You have volunteered my services as a healer to the king?"

"Yes, that's right." Nikometros frowned. "What's the matter?"

"You ask me to heal the king despite the gods telling us plainly he'll die? The old Assyrian gods in the graveyard of former kings, Bel-Marduk and other gods here in Babylon, and even the Great Goddess herself have foretold death and disaster and you want me heal him?"

"Yes, I want you to try, Tomyra. Alexander is our king."

"If the gods foretell his death and I heal him, am I not acting in opposition to the gods? Perhaps even god-cursed?"

"Tomyra, love." Nikometros took his wife by the shoulders and drew her close.

Tomyra shrugged free sharply and stepped back, glaring.

Nikometros grimaced. "But you warned the king of his danger outside Babylon. Does that warning not mean you were trying to avert his death?"

"Don't be a fool, Niko. It isn't the same. The gods wouldn't send us omens, wouldn't warn us through sacrifices or divination if they didn't want us to try and avert the danger."

"You confuse me, Tomyra. Why, then, can't you take action now?"

"The gods warned Alexander of the consequences of a certain course of action--entering Babylon. He chose to ignore those warnings. If the gods now act against him should I battle the gods?"

"No. No, of course not," said Nikometros, aghast. "But what do I tell the king? I told him you would."

"Then, dear husband, you must explain to him why I cannot."

"I can't go to the king and tell him the gods want him dead. He would..." Nikometros broke off, his eyes wandering as he grappled with a thought. He snapped his fingers suddenly and whirled back to face Tomyra. "What if it isn't the gods that are killing him?"

Tomyra frowned. "What do you mean by that, Niko?"

"There are men that wish Alexander dead. Kassandros for instance." Nikometros paced about in excitement. "He has motive and opportunity perhaps, through his brother Iollas, the king's cupbearer. And the Roman, Caius. He would benefit if the king died."

"How does this make a difference?"

"If men seek to encompass Alexander's death, then the warnings of the gods may still be heeded. If he asks you to heal him, isn't he seeking to avoid his fate?"

"Hmm. This bears thinking on." Tomyra turned away and stared around the room, finally letting her gaze rest on Starissa, sleeping in her cot by the pool.

"If it's from the gods, you cannot succeed," went on Nikometros. "But if it's from man, you may actually be doing the will of the gods."

"I'll ask the Goddess," Tomyra said quietly. She knelt beside her daughter's cot and bent her head in silence. After several minutes, during which Nikometros struggled to contain his impatience, she looked up. "The Goddess won't answer me direct. All I hear are the words of her prophecy...'by water, by wine, by hand of man'."

"There you have it then," cried Nikometros. "By hand of man! It couldn't be plainer. How else do wine and water get to the king but by the hand of a man? The gods are still warning us, telling us we can act to save the king."

Tomyra continued to kneel in silence, her gaze fixed on the sleeping child. "Perhaps you're right, Niko," she whispered. "Yet it feels like I'm defying the gods." She rose to her feet and walked slowly over to the door. She called out to her servants to come and watch Starissa then gathered together several items from her carved wooden chests. "Very well, Niko," she said as she tied the neck of her leather purse. "Let us go and challenge the gods."

Nikometros and Tomyra crossed to the royal suite and were admitted to the king's bedchamber by Ptolemy.

Alexander had donned a fine wool robe and sat on the edge of the couch, half-supported by Bagoas. When Tomyra entered the room, Alexander straightened and stood, advancing to meet her. "Welcome, Tomyra, daughter of Spargises," he said with a smile. "Your husband assures me you can make me feel better."

Tomyra flashed her husband a hard look then bobbed in a quick curtsey. "That is in the hands of the gods."

"Of course. I keep telling everyone it's this infernal heat. If I could just get cool and get a bit of rest, I'd be fine."

"May I examine you, sir?"

Alexander looked surprised then nodded. He moved back to the couch and sat down.

Tomyra took his right hand and examined the palm for a few moments. She pursed her lips, a small frown flitting over her face. "You have made the choice of Achilles," she murmured.

Alexander said nothing but smiled.

Next she rested the tips of her fingers on the king's wrist, frowning as she picked up a small tremor. Running her hand up the king's arm, she paused at the hot, inflamed insect bite. "This must be cleansed." She peered into his different coloured eyes. "Your right eye is grey yet your left eye appears almost black, sir," she noted. "The pupil is much larger. Have you suffered a blow to the head?"

"Some time ago. It was nothing, for I survived."

Tomyra leaned forward and smelt the king's breath, noting that despite the sweat beading on his forehead, an indefinable fragrance clung to him. "I can prescribe an infusion of herbs that will strengthen your blood and purify it. It tastes foul but you must drink a cupful three times a day."

Alexander cocked his head to one side and smiled up at Tomyra. "What herbs do you use?"

"Would you recognise them if I told you?" Tomyra countered.

"No, probably not." Alexander gave a weak grin. "Tell Bagoas though. He knows a lot more about these things."

Tomyra nodded and moved off to one side with the eunuch. She started to describe the course of treatment, open her packages of herbs and jotting down instructions on a scrap of paper.

Ptolemy smiled and cracked the knuckles of his hands. "Very good, Alexander. It's about time you came to your senses."

Alexander grinned. "You always were the sensible one, weren't you?"

# Chapter 42

C hafing at the postponement of the Arabian expedition, the army became restless. A number of small incidents indicated falling morale, so Ptolemy, together with some of the other senior army officers, led detachments out into the countryside and put them through gruelling manoeuvres. They returned to Babylon two days later, tired but content in their abilities. Ptolemy washed the grime from his body and donned clean clothes before hurrying to the king's suite, anxious to check on his friend's health.

Alexander was not there. The squires let the general into the bedchamber, where he found Tomyra and Bagoas carefully preparing another batch of medicine, the air pungent with aromatic herbs and ingredients less discernible.

"My lord Ptolemy," said Tomyra, turning to him with a smile. "You are welcome."

"Thank you lady." He nodded, smiling at Bagoas, who withdrew to the far end of the room.

The eunuch busied himself with the herbs though he watched Tomyra and Ptolemy sidelong through his long eyelashes.

"How is Alexander?" Ptolemy asked.

"Responding nicely," replied Tomyra. "He's gained some strength but he's impatient to resume his life." She smiled ruefully. "He insisted on riding to the sacrifice this morning and conducts business again in the main hall."

"That is indeed good news. I can tell you I was worried about him."

"He isn't out of danger yet." Tomyra paused, folding her hands in front of her as she sought the right words. "He...he has a fire inside him. He seeks to do so much, so soon, that I fear he will consume himself."

Ptolemy nodded. "That was ever Alexander's way. He isn't content unless he excels. He drives himself to succeed where lesser men give up."

A commotion in the hallway outside the apartments caused the two of them to swing round, breaking off their conversation. One of the squires on guard detail threw open the doors. "It's the k...king, sir," he stuttered in agitation. "He's..."

Alexander stumbled through the doorway, half supported by the other squire and Nikometros. Behind them crowded half a dozen others.

Ptolemy rushed over and helped Alexander to the couch by the pool.

Nikometros and the squires hushed the hubbub and started shepherding the concerned courtiers toward the doors.

Tomyra beckoned to Bagoas and together they stripped Alexander's sweat-soaked robe from him and helped him into a clean one. The king's body shook and his teeth chattered, fresh sweat breaking out on his brow.

"I...I'll...'ll be...fine," he gasped. "I just got up a bit s...soon."

Ptolemy rounded on Nikometros as he shut the door, finally cutting off the clamour in the hallway. "What happened?" he snapped. "I thought the king improved."

"He was," Nikometros replied tersely. "He conducted business all afternoon and showed just normal tiredness, nothing more. He broke for a rest and a drink..."

"A drink?" Tomyra asked, turning from the bedside. "You didn't let him drink wine?"

"Of course not. Water only, chilled but not too cold."

Ptolemy nodded. "What then?"

"He resumed business but a short time later his bowels cramped and he broke out into a sweat. He made it to the privy but collapsed as he came out. We brought him back."

"The water," said Tomyra grimly. "It must be. Did you see which pitcher he drank from, Niko?"

Nikometros nodded. "Yes. I know because he remarked on the fine painting on the outside of it. It was a new one."

"Can you bring it to me, Niko? It's important."

Nikometros stared at his wife then nodded and left the room.

Tomyra and Ptolemy turned back to where Alexander lay on the bed. The king shook as if lying on ice, his arms clutching the sheet to his body, his eyes wide but vacant. After a few minutes he started to relax. He let the sheet slip down and lay panting. Moments later he moaned and started thrashing his limbs about, breaking into a new sweat.

"This is bad," muttered Tomyra. "Bagoas, restrain him as best you can. Don't let him hurt himself."

Bagoas glanced at Tomyra reproachfully but held his king firmly but gently, wiping the sweat from his face.

Alexander lapsed into uncontrollable shivering again.

The door opened and Nikometros strode in, clutching an elegantly worked pitcher. He handed it to his wife who held it up and sniffed. Her nose wrinkled.

"There's a faint smell of decay," she said softly. "This isn't spring water." She hurried to the table and selected a clean bowl, pouring the water into it. The water swirled clear but with tiny grey flecks that settled slowly. "Look, there's a residue." She slipped her fingers into the water and rubbed at the grey slime on the bottom of the bowl. Lifting her fingers from the bowl she sniffed again. "Faugh! Something died in this water." Tomyra wiped her hand on a cloth.

"How did he come by this water?" asked Ptolemy. "Who gave it to him?"

Nikometros frowned. "It was there on the table when the king came in from business. I supposed the king's cupbearer..."

"Iollas," grunted Ptolemy. "Who else had access to the room?"

"The squires on duty, slaves. Perhaps a court official or two."

"I'll have enquiries made," Ptolemy said grimly. "However, I don't think we'll find out." He looked over to where Alexander lay on his couch, his limbs shaking with fever. "What are his chances?"

"This morning--good," Tomyra replied. "Now," she shrugged. "His life hangs in the balance. I'll do my best. Pray to your gods that he has a strong constitution."

Ptolemy called in the squires and oversaw while they moved Alexander to the formal bedchamber.

Tomyra dosed the king with potions and left him in the care of Bagoas, withdrawing to the shadowed far end of the room with Nikometros and Ptolemy. "The next day or two will tell. He must be watched, guarded even. The tainted water has injured his intestines. That means he's to drink boiled spring water only, no wine, no citron. I'll prepare a healing tonic for the morning."

Ptolemy nodded. "I'll set the squires to guard him." He looked around the chamber. "The room is large enough, I can get four of five in here comfortably enough."

Tomyra shook her head. "Not in here, outside. He must have quiet. It's vital he sleeps."

"Very well then, outside in the hallway. No man will be admitted alone to see the king."

"Don't let any food or drink into the chamber unless it comes from me," went on Tomyra. "I'll put my mark on it, see?" She scratched a symbol on a cup.

"Who watches the king then?" asked Nikometros. "There must be somebody here in case he needs anything in the night."

Tomyra turned her gaze toward the bed with the still figure of Alexander lying on the coverlets. Bagoas sat on the edge of the bed, dipping a napkin in cool water and gently wiping the sweat from his master's face and limbs.

"I think he's in good hands."

Nikometros saw the dark circles beneath the eunuch's eyes; the taut and stretched look to his face. "He's dropping from exhaustion. He must have relief."

"He insists," replied Tomyra. "However, I'll relieve him at midnight."

Ptolemy went outside to leave detailed instructions with the captain of the squires. He helped the captain arrange the guard roster and made sure every man understood that no one was to enter or leave the room alone except Bagoas, Tomyra, Nikometros or himself.

The captain looked troubled. "Er, sir...I cannot tell someone like, well...General Perdikkas they cannot come in."

"Of course not, captain," replied Ptolemy. "Who said anything about keeping them out? You admit them, but you make sure you're with them at all times. Don't allow them to give the king anything. Don't leave them alone with the king--for any reason. Say it's on his doctor's express orders. Understand?"

"Yes, sir," said the captain.

"One more thing, captain. If anyone seeks admittance, you're to send word to me immediately...before letting them in."

Ptolemy re-entered the bedchamber and motioned Tomyra and Nikometros to follow him out. "I think I've set up sufficient safeguards but you can never be sure. Tomyra, if you would watch the king after midnight? And Nikometros, I'd appreciate it if you could be here before dawn tomorrow. Bring your loyal Scythians. I need people around the king I can trust."

Nikometros raised his eyebrows in surprise. "You'd trust Scythians above Macedonians?" He glanced at his wife anxiously. "I'm sorry, Tomyra. You know what I mean."

Ptolemy nodded and lowered his voice so the guard outside Alexander's bedchamber could not hear. "Your Scythians have proven their loyalty...to you and the king. Most Macedonians would die for Alexander but family feuds and distrust have a way of surfacing in times of trouble. A man loyal to the king may find he has other loyalties...given the right incentive." He turned and walked away.

Nikometros and Tomyra exited the palace and returned to their apartments where, for a while, they enjoyed the company of their daughter and sought to forget the troubles crowding in on them. After Starissa was put to bed, they had a meal sent in and whiled away the time in conversation, watching the fireflies winking in the shrubberies in the summer dusk.

Later, Tomyra rose and stretched. "I think I'll go back now."

"Stay a while longer," Nikometros pleaded. "It's not yet midnight."

"I know but I think I should. Bagoas must be very tired." Tomyra kissed her husband. "I'll see you at dawn."

She crossed the dark courtyards, her way lit by an avenue of flickering torches. Deep shadows moved by the old buildings and she wrapped her cloak tighter about her, despite the hot, humid night. All about her the palace grounds lay silent, though she knew that hundreds of people were still up, watching, waiting, fearing the impossible.

The squires outside the king's Bedchamber were alert and challenged Tomyra when she approached.

She knew one of the young men, Andremedon, and drew him aside before she entered. "All is well?"

Andremedon shrugged. "Yes, my lady. But I only came on duty an hour ago. Before that a bunch of 'igher-ups arrived...Perdikkas, Peukestas, Eumenes...people like that."

"They were admitted?"

"Well, couldn't keep 'em out, could they? Don't worry, they 'ad someone with 'em at all times."

Tomyra smiled. "And since you came on duty?"

"All quiet. The king's fancy boy, beggin' yer pardon, ma'am," Andremedon jerked a thumb over his shoulder toward the bedchamber. "'E came out and wanted more spring water. The servants brought it. Aside from that, nothin'."

Tomyra frowned. "But there's water in there..." She broke off and smiled at the young man. "Thank you, Andremedon," Tomyra said, touching the young man's arm. "I'll go in now."

Andremedon opened the door for Tomyra and stood back, allowing her to enter before shutting it quietly behind her.

The bedchamber lay shadowed and quiet, though the air carried a sour smell of sweat and sickness. Tomyra moved toward the bed where Bagoas sat, wan and hollow-eyed, his hand gently stroking Alexander's sweat-matted hair.

"How is he?" Tomyra whispered.

"The fever has abated," replied Bagoas, his voice trembling with fatigue. "He rests easier, my lady."

"You had better get some rest yourself, Bagoas."

The eunuch shook his head. "I'll be all right. I must be here for my master. What if he should wake and need something?"

"I'll watch him and wake you if you're needed."

Bagoas stared into Tomyra's eyes then looked away, nodding. "Just for a few moments then, while he sleeps." He lurched upright and stumbled across the room to where a cot lay by a wall, almost lost in the shadows. "Just for a little while," he repeated, slumping onto the bed. "Wake me in..." Bagoas collapsed, unconscious.

Tomyra crossed to the cot and gently eased the youth's legs onto the bed, arranging his limbs. She walked back to the king's bed and smoothed the bedding, checking her patient's temperature with the back of her wrist. She nodded, permitting herself a small smile.

"The gods may yet grant you life, King of Macedon," she whispered.

Tomyra picked up the cup of water beside the bed and sniffed it. She dipped a finger into it and touched her tongue with a drop.

"Nothing wrong with it," she murmured to herself. "But why didn't he use my water pitchers?" Picking up the open pitcher she carried it across the room and set it down next to the door. Selecting a new pitcher from a straw-packed chest, she carefully examined the seal. Satisfied it was unbroken; she cracked the seal and tasted the water before placing it within easy reach on the bedside table.

Wandering from the bedside, she checked on the sleeping Bagoas before looking around the room. She discovered a low table set out as if an altar in one corner. Candles burned low on the table, fitfully illuminating a score of figurines. Picking one up, Tomyra recognised it as a likeness of Hephaestion, carved from ivory. Others gleamed golden, some in bronze and copper or darkly polished wood, marble or stone. She handled one of some whitish stone, flecked and mottled with veins of green. In the flickering candlelight the green discolouration seemed to move and flow over the figure's surface. She replaced it, her lips curling in distaste.

Turning from the altar, Tomyra made her way to a cushioned chair and settled herself comfortably to keep watch. Nothing moved in the bedchamber save for the laboured rise and fall of the king's chest, his breath rasping in his throat. Tomyra's eyes drooped but she caught herself and got up to walk around a bit. She poured a cup of water from the king's pitcher then sat down again. Tiredness again swept over her.

Abruptly, Tomyra jerked upright in a room that had become much darker. The candles on the altar were puddles of cooling wax. Tomyra cursed and hurried across to the bed. Alexander lay in sleep, breathing more comfortably. She felt his forehead and smiled in relief. Checking the water pitcher she saw it was still cold so she poured herself another draught, sprinkling some on her face and neck before sitting down again.

Tomyra's thoughts wandered and she considered her life and its changes. In her mind's eye she saw her homeland; the high cold plains, rolling seas of grass and mile after mile of whispering pine forest. She smelled the pungent earth, churned up by a thousand hooves, tasted the thrill of the chase, racing through the river thickets after wild boar, heard the rumble of the tribe's wagons on the move, the excited cries of children, and the clash of arms.

The shadowed room closed around her and Tomyra saw herself in one of the many shrines dedicated to the Great Goddess. She moved in the Dance of Greeting, heard the responses from the maidens consecrated to the virgin priestess of the Earth Mother, felt the pull of the robes against her as she bent to the sacrifice.

As the blood gushed onto the hard-beaten earth floor she heard the voice of the Goddess, rising and falling in a formless susurration. Gradually, she distinguished words and she struggled to discern their meaning.

"Why...do...you...fight...me?" came the voice in a sibilant, halting whisper. "It...is...his...time."

"Great Mother," gasped Tomyra. "I am your servant."

"No...no...longer...my...child."

Horror gripped Tomyra's heart as she felt the divine presence withdrawing, ebbing and draining from her soul. "No!" she sobbed. "Don't leave me."

"Tomyra...Tomyra...Tomyra, wake up." She felt her maidens pulling at her, drawing her back from the sacrifice, even as the Goddess left her. Her eyes flew open and she looked about her, her heart hammering.

Nikometros stood beside her, his hand clutching her shoulder, shaking her. "Tomyra," he called again. "Wake up!" He strode across to Alexander's bed and stared down at the king.

Tomyra staggered to her feet, her mind gradually taking in the cold grey light of dawn filtering through the open windows. She saw her husband standing by the bed and walked over to him. "Niko," she whispered. "What are you doing here? It cannot be...how can it be dawn already?"

"You slept, Tomyra," Nikometros said, his voice flat and empty. "And while you slept..." He pointed at Alexander.

Tomyra closed her eyes and shook her head. "I wasn't asleep, Niko. The Goddess, she spoke to me."

"If you say so, Tomyra, but the damage is done either way."

Alexander lay sprawled on the bed, a great purple stain on his robe and on the pillows beside his head. His eyes stared up at the ceiling and his mouth worked convulsively. "We must...march east," the king muttered. "I must see Encircling Ocean...I must see the end." He thrashed his limbs, sweat breaking out and rapidly soaking his sheets. He groaned loudly and sat up, pointing toward a corner of the room. "Don't harm it," he commanded. He cocked his head as if listening. "The snake. The gods have sent it." He collapsed back onto the bed and laid there, eyes closed and breathing heavily.

"He's delirious," Tomyra said. "He shouldn't be, his health was improving."

Nikometros picked up the cup, and then upended it with a curse. A dribble of dark wine splashed onto the table.

"Who gave him wine?"

"That's impossible," said Tomyra. "He had only water. I checked it myself."

Nikometros pointed to the wine stains. "Someone got wine to him."

Presently Ptolemy arrived. They sent for fresh bed linen and a clean robe and cleaned the king before settling him back into the bed.

Alexander's delirium slowly waned into muttered incoherence, and then he slept.

Tomyra woke Bagoas and suffered his silent but reproachful look. In the presence of the men, Bagoas lapsed once more into silence.

Alexander woke as the sun rose above the black walls of Babylon. He opened his eyes and looked about him, his eyes moving from person to person until they lit on the worried face of Bagoas. "Bagoas," he whispered, giving the young man a radiant smile. "I had the strangest dream."

"My lord," interposed Nikometros. "Who brought you the wine? Can you remember?"

Alexander shook his head slightly and coughed. "I was thirsty, so thirsty. I woke and it was there."

"Rest my lord Iskander," murmured Bagoas, his eyes bright with tears. "You are very ill."

Alexander smiled. "I'll be better now, you'll see. Help me up; I must make the morning sacrifice." He struggled up onto one elbow, supported by Bagoas. He swung his legs over the side of the bed and clutched his chest, a look of agony on his face. A stifled groan ripped out of him and he doubled over in a paroxysm of coughing.

Bagoas, assisted by Tomyra and Nikometros, eased Alexander back onto the bed and propped him up with pillows. Bagoas took a clean cloth and wiped bright red arterial blood from Alexander's chin.

The king looked up at him with a forced smile, fighting for breath. "Perhaps I won't make the sacrifice this morning, after all." He leaned back on the pillows and closed his eyes.

Ptolemy beckoned Nikometros back out of earshot. "I must summon the other generals," he said grimly. "Alexander is dying."

# Chapter 43

"Alexander, this has gone too far," Peukestas remonstrated. "Let us bring in a doctor."

Alexander, pale beneath his tan, fluttered his hand in dismissal. "No doctors," he gasped. "I've told you. Don't raise the subject again." He closed his eyes and drifted into semi-sleep.

Peukestas turned away, a mix of emotions warring for supremacy. "Ptolemy," he muttered. "Back me up."

Ptolemy shook his head and signed to the eunuchs of the bedchamber to rearrange the bed clothing.

Alexander now lay in the formal King's Bed, where once Darius had slept. Built for a giant, the bed measured nine feet by six and dwarfed the dying king. The eunuchs fluffed the pillows and propped Alexander up into a half sitting position. Behind the carved headboard with its hunting motif, Bagoas gently waved an ostrich plume fan, moving the still air of the chamber over the sleeping king.

Their efforts roused Alexander. He opened his eyes and signed Peukestas closer. "Order the army to assemble," he whispered. "Commanders and above...in the courtyard."

Peukestas went out and presently there came the growing sounds of men trooping into the palace grounds.

Alexander laid unmoving, eyes closed, his breath rasping. Around him the generals and staff officers withdrew from his immediate presence and talked quietly.

Peukestas returned, with the news that most of the officers were assembled. "A lot of the ranks have come too. They have heard rumours."

"What will happen, sir?" asked one of the body squires. "I mean, what if..." The young man's voice broke off in a sob.

"Control yourself, Andremedon," hissed Perdikkas. He glanced over his shoulder at the bed. "He'll hear you."

"All the same," Eumenes murmured. "It pays to think ahead."

"You mean, what will happen to the king's secretary when the king no longer requires a secretary?" jeered Seleukos.

Perdikkas grinned at Eumenes' fury. "I imagine you'll find some other avenue for your...ah, talents."

"Gentlemen, please," said Nikometros quietly. "This is not seemly. We should be more concerned with helping the king."

"Helping him do what?" Seleukos asked. "He's dying well enough without our help. I think your wife has seen to that."

Nikometros paled. "What are you implying, sir?"

Perdikkas stepped between the young men, sending Seleukos a meaningful glance. "Nothing, Nikometros, I assure you. It's obvious that the gods have set a term to Alexander's life. No blame falls to your wife. In fact, I thank her for her efforts."

Nikometros, his face a stiff mask, stepped back, accepting the general's words with a nod.

Ptolemy plucked at the young man's sleeve. "Don't blame yourself...or your wife. The gods will not be denied."

The morning advanced and the men waiting beside Alexander's bed grew tired, sending out for food and drink. The king's rasping breath waxed and waned as he struggled, sweat beading on his body as the heat of the day increased.

At last, Perdikkas stepped up to the bed and put his hand on Alexander's shoulder. "Alexander, the men are still waiting for orders in the courtyard. Should I send them away?"

The king's eyes opened and he shook his head, rocking it weakly on the pillows. "Let...let them in. Everyone."

Perdikkas looked around at the others, his eyebrows knotted in perplexity. "Let them in? How? The room is too small."

Ptolemy pointed to a small door at the far end of the room. "Let them in through there. They can file past the bed and out of the main doors." When Perdikkas hesitated, Ptolemy added softly, "Go on, man, the men deserve to see him one last time."

Perdikkas nodded. "Peithon, Leonnatos," he beckoned to two of the staff officers. "See to it. Get the men organised and see them through."

The officers left on the double, throwing the doors wide.

A few minutes later, the first soldiers entered through the small door. They advanced hesitantly, and then under the direction of Peithon, walked in single file past the bed.

Alexander, as the first man approached, drew himself into a sitting position and turned to face the soldier. "Dienorus," Alexander whispered.

The soldier gaped, his eyes wet with tears. He stumbled past the bed, ushered out by the other staff officers. The next man approached.

367

Alexander greeted the first few by name, officer and enlisted man alike. Presently he lapsed into silence, though he continued to acknowledge each man by a look or a vague tremor of his fingers.

The men filed by slowly, several hundred, officers and ranks. The morning turned past the noon hour and still they came. Alexander drew on reserves of strength and remained upright, pressed back into his pillows, the only sounds being the shuffling tread of the men and the ragged intake of each breath the king made.

Many openly wept, and several hardened troopers, veterans of a lifetime of rapine and slaughter, broke down as they left the Bedchamber.

"He knew me," bawled one, tears streaming down his scarred and bearded face.

"I could see it in his eyes," sobbed another. "He thanked me."

At last, the procession thinned and ceased. The doors closed, shutting off the tide of grief and unrest from outside the palace. Stillness fell over the room, even as the last rays of afternoon sunlight streamed through the window onto the rumpled and sweat-stained sheets of the bed.

Alexander sank back, his face grey and hollowed. He closed his eyes and his breathing faltered and ceased.

Ptolemy, closest to the bed, gasped in horror and strode to the bedside. He grasped Alexander's shoulder and shook it. "No. Alexander, no!"

The king's eyes fluttered open and he stared vacantly up. "Bagoas?" Alexander whispered. "Where is Bagoas?" He feebly licked his dry and cracked lips.

"Here, lord." The king's eunuch slipped forward from his position behind the bed. He smoothed a damp cloth over Alexander's face and arms, wiping away the stale sweat.

"Ah...feels good."

Bagoas held Alexander's head up off the pillows and poured a little water from a cup onto his parched lips. Alexander coughed, spilling the water. Bagoas set the cup down and, dipping a napkin in the water, squeezed a dribble into the king's mouth.

"Thank you, Bagoas." The king closed his eyes and drifted into an uneasy sleep, his breathing laboured but regular.

Perdikkas ushered two men forward. The men, garbed in long flowing robes and wearing expressions of terror, reluctantly advanced to the side of the bed. "Go on then," growled Perdikkas. "Examine him."

"Who in Hades are these?" asked Peukestas.

"Doctors. It's probably too late to do any good, but if there's any chance, we should take it."

The doctors timidly put their hands on the king, resting their fingers lightly on his wrist, bending their ears to his chest. After a few moments they exchanged a scared glance and turned to face Perdikkas.

"Well? Can you save him?"

"It...it's c...complicated," stuttered one. "We sh...should have been called days ago."

The other one gave a nervous smile. "I can prescribe a tea," he said. "Perhaps with a regimen of fasting and exercise..."

Peukestas snorted. "This is ridiculous. The time for doctors is over." He looked around at the others. "I'm going to the temple of Serapis to petition the god. Who will come with me?" He looked at Ptolemy, who shook his head. Most of the other officers did likewise but Leonnatos and Peithon agreed to accompany the general.

"Very well, then," muttered Peukestas. "I'll spend the night in prayer at the temple and bring the oracular utterance to you in the morning. It's the least I can do for my king and my friend." He pushed through the crowded chamber.

Perdikkas dismissed the doctors and ordered lamps to be lit against the deepening dusk. He had chairs brought in, together with food and wine and Alexander's friends and generals settled down to the long death watch.

The night passed slowly and silently. The usual noises of palace and city faded to a watchful uncertainty, the stars in the heavens steadily wheeling above the palace where a god lay dying.

Toward dawn, Alexander stirred. He drew a deep ragged breath and started coughing violently, spraying a fine speckle of bright blood over the sheets. His eyes opened and wandered round the room, finally alighting on Perdikkas. His hand twitched then beckoned to his general.

Perdikkas sat on the edge of the bed, his craggy face set in a mask of concern. "Alexander. I'm here. What would you have me do?"

Alexander opened his mouth but could form no words. He fumbled with the royal ring for a moment then pulled it off his hand and passed it across to Perdikkas. The king closed his eyes again.

Perdikkas got up and faced the room. He held up Alexander's ring with a triumphant expression. "He gives me his ring of authority."

Ptolemy made a disgusted noise. "All it means is he deputises you to act for him during his illness. It's no more than that."

"Nonsense," broke in Seleukos. "He handed over his ring. He clearly nominates Perdikkas his successor."

Chairs scraped as officers leapt to their feet, their voices rising in argument.

"What about the baby?" asked one of the squires. "Roxane is pregnant. Surely her babe will inherit."

"Yes," said another. "Alexander's son must succeed him."

"And what if it's a girl?" asked Nikometros, getting caught up in the excitement.

"Gentlemen!" Perdikkas' voice cut through the babble. "This is all irrelevant. Of course, Alexander's blood will succeed him, but for now he's named me as regent, to hold the kingdom in trust."

"Name you?" growled Ptolemy. "I didn't hear him name you. He only gave you his ring and who knows what he meant by that." He planted his fists on his hips and stared round the room. "No, if there is any man worthy to succeed Alexander...or act as Regent...it's Krateros. Do you forget he's even now on his way to Macedon to assume the Regency of Greece?"

Niarchos pushed his way to the front. Silent in his grief he felt emboldened to speak. "Aye, let Alexander himself tell us his wishes. Ask him what he wants."

A chorus of agreement arose and Perdikkas scowled. "Very well, I'll ask him. Keep quiet."

The general bent over the bed and gently shook Alexander. When the eyes opened, unfocused in a face devoid of expression, Perdikkas asked his question. "Alexander, to whom do you leave your kingdom?"

The king drew a shuddering breath and moved his lips, a whistling rattle escaping his throat.

Perdikkas, leaning close over Alexander's mouth, smiled. He turned, his face triumphant. "He says, 'Hoti to kratisto'--to the best."

Ptolemy's face darkened. He turned aside to Nikometros and lowered his voice. "Kratisto or Kratero, I wonder. To the best or to Krateros?"

With the dawn came Peukestas, together with a coterie of close friends, tired from their vigil at the temple of Serapis. He entered the bedchamber and looked around at the assembled officers, noting the strain and suspicion evident between them. "What has happened?" he asked. "Alexander...?"

"Still lives," Seleukos said dryly. "He has named no successor but leaves my lord Perdikkas as Regent."

Perdikkas beckoned to Peukestas. "What did the god say? Should we move him to the temple?"

Peukestas shook his head. "The god said it were better that he stay here."

"My lords," came a quiet voice. Heads turned toward the bed where Andremedon knelt, his hands holding the king's. Alexander's breath came in great laboured gasps, the fluid in his lungs bubbling and rattling in his throat. "He goes, my lords," the squire sobbed.

Peukestas pushed through to the bed. He stared down at his dying king then dropped to his knees. "Alexander, where do you wish to be buried?"

Alexander's hand rose toward the morning sunlight breaking through the curtained windows. "Ammon," he wheezed, before falling back into his torturous breathing.

Perdikkas joined Peukestas beside the bed. "You are a god, Alexander. When do you wish to be worshipped?"

Alexander opened his eyes and looked up at his general. Gradually his breathing eased and he smiled. "When...you're...happy." He shut his eyes and sank back into the pillow. His breathing cycled slower and shallower for a time and then ceased.

Every man in the room held their breath, eyes fixed on their king.

Ptolemy reached over and placed his hand over his friend's heart. After a moment he stepped back and straightened, tears streaming from his eyes. "Alexander is dead."

# Chapter 44

Perdikkas and Peukestas stared at each other in shock. Everyone in the room, despite Alexander's protracted illness, wore stunned or grief-stricken expressions.

The squire Andremedon put his hands to his face and sobbed.

Bagoas, standing on the far side of the bed, his face contorted in an agony of grief, threw himself onto Alexander's body with a wail of anguish.

The sound, ripped from a breaking heart, sent Andremedon stumbling back. He cried out and ran for the door of the bedchamber, bursting through it and pushing past the throng of servants, eunuchs and officials crowding the corridors of the palace. He ran until he found the army, still clogging the forecourt of the palace.

A great swell of grief rose from the army. A surge of wordless anguish and panic rose from a thousand throats. Men pushed and shoved, some to get out of the forecourt, others to go in to the palace and see for themselves.

Inside the death chamber, the generals heard the swelling panic and reacted instantly. Training and experience precipitated them out the door, racing for the courtyard to stem the rising chaos.

Perdikkas burst into the courtyard and shoved his way to a raised platform at one end. He grabbed a trumpeter and pushed him onto the platform. "Sound the call to Assembly. Quickly, you fool."

The herald put the trumpet to his lips and sounded a long quavering note. The milling mass of armed men hesitated, heads turning to see what was happening. The herald blew again, more confidently, calling the men to Assembly. Training took hold and with a deal of grumbling and shoving, the Macedonian army and its auxiliaries formed ranks. The Persian levies formed up too, but moved toward the edge of the courtyard, fingering their weapons and looking askance at their erstwhile comrades. Slowly, the noise died as they awaited some announcement from their officers.

"Too bloody slowly," muttered Ptolemy. "Has discipline disintegrated so fast?"

"Look at the Persians," commented Nikometros. "They're on the verge of mutiny. If someone doesn't reassure them quickly there'll be bloodshed."

Perdikkas waited patiently for complete quiet before signalling to Peukestas.

The satrap of Persia, though Macedonian, had adopted the dress and customs of his Persian subjects. A tall, imposing man with the full beard of the noble Persian, he smoothed his robes and composed his face. He stepped to the front of the platform and addressed the Persians in their own language. "Noble lords and esteemed warriors, it is with a heavy heart that I stand before you today. Our beloved Great King, Alexander son of Philip lies dead. Great is our grief yet we have no cause for concern. The Kingship passes on and in due course, the successor to the Great Alexander will be named. In the meantime, go about your life as always. You are dismissed."

The listening Persians visibly relaxed, sheathing their weapons and moving toward the exits.

The Macedonians, straining to understand a foreign language started muttering. A soldier near the front yelled out a rough translation, his words repeated and shouted across the courtyard. The muttering swelled to a roar of displeasure.

"What do you mean, 'name a successor'," an officer called out. "In Macedon we choose our king."

"That's right! It's the law. The king only reigns with the permission of the army."

"The bastards are trying to cut us out. Kill them!"

Perdikkas took his place at the front of the platform and held up his arms for silence. As the sounds of fury died away he started speaking softly, conversationally, in the gutter patois of the common soldier, forcing them to listen. "Men of Macedon, we've all lost the greatest king that ever ruled the earth, the bravest warrior, the noblest man to walk this world since the gods themselves left us. We each of us bear an enormous burden of grief."

A low moan rose from the army as the misery and anguish in thousands of hearts found expression.

"Remember though, that you're men favoured above all other generations. You've known Alexander, you're part of his army, and you've shared in his everlasting glory. It is to you, his Macedonians, that he's left the mastery of half the world. Show that you're the men of courage that Alexander believed in. Go back to your camp. Wait there for further orders. Be assured that all things will be done according to law, Macedonian law."

The army broke up into small groups, individuals, and started to leave the forecourt. Perdikkas watched them go then turned and left the platform, followed by the other generals, the bodyguard and staff officers.

Within the city, the priests quenched the temple fires for the second time in just over a month. A tide of lamentation swept over Babylon, many genuinely grieving the strange young conqueror, others going through the forms of grief, voicing the ritual phrases and hoping fervently that a successor would be named soon, before serious trouble erupted.

Orders went out to the army, to the officers and senior veterans, to attend an assembly in the great audience hall, where matters pertaining to the succession would be heard. They came, by the thousand, filling the hall, packing it so full that the doors had to be closed. Latecomers and those not invited stood in the courtyards outside, cursing and feeding the rumours. Inside, on the dais around the vacant throne, stood the generals and staff officers.

Nikometros looked out on the crowded hall, his heart hammering. He nudged his neighbour, an older staff officer named Peithon. "Gods, I've never seen so many men in a room."

"Impressive sight," drawled Peithon with a smile. "Damned dangerous too. Better keep your wits about you, young Nikometros...and your hand close to your sword."

"What's going to be decided today, have you heard?"

"The succession, of course. Maybe something about those responsible for his death."

"What do you mean?"

Peithon essayed a quick grin. "Don't worry, no one blames your wife. She tried to save him at least. No, it's Kassandros they suspect."

"They have him?"

"No. He and his brother Iollas fled immediately. A guilty action. They'll be caught and tried...if they aren't killed on the spot." Peithon turned and gave Nikometros a curious stare. "You knew the other one didn't you? The Roman."

"Caius Gracchus? What about him?"

"He's under house arrest." Peithon chuckled. "Made no attempt to leave the city. He just waited to be arrested."

A trumpet sounded, calling the assembly to order.

Perdikkas advanced to the empty throne. His hand caressed the purple robe draped over the back of the throne then lifted the royal ring above his head. "Alexander handed me his ring, his authority, before he died." Perdikkas turned and placed the ring on the throne, beside the royal diadem. "It is for you to choose on whom to bestow it."

Walking casually to the edge of the dais, Perdikkas surveyed the vast audience hall in silence for several long moments. "Roxane, the legitimate wife of Alexander, is five months with child," he announced. "We pray it will be a boy. If it is, it must first be born, and then raised until it comes of age. Only then can the child of Alexander become king. The question before you today is not who succeeds Alexander, but rather who do you want to rule you in the meantime?"

"There is another choice!" Heads turned as Niarchos strode out of the crowd. Alexander's admiral of the fleet, a lean weather-beaten Cretan, stepped up onto the dais beside Perdikkas. In a loud voice used to giving commands above the scream of gale winds, Niarchos addressed the assembly. "Have you forgotten Alexander has another child? What of Queen Stateira? This noble-born princess is the daughter of Darius. Remember how, at Susa, Alexander married her and made her his queen? Well, she too is with child."

He let this news sink in, letting the roar of conversation die away before continuing. "We all know the way Alexander did things. Without doubt he would have weighed the two boys carefully before deciding the best one to succeed him. Well, he didn't live to make his choice, so we must do it for him. I vote for Stateira's child, she has the right of rank."

Perdikkas swung round on Niarchos, his face darkening with anger. "What in Hades are you doing?" he hissed. "This isn't the time to argue which child will inherit. That choice is years away. We must settle the issue of the Regency."

"This is ridiculous," growled Ptolemy. He turned to Nikometros. "This isn't what Alexander would want. Help me here."

Nikometros called for attention to no effect. He walked up alongside Perdikkas and called again. "Hear me, men of Macedon!" He waited for the hubbub to die down. "A discussion of the inheritance is pointless at this time. Neither child is born, nor do we know the sex of the children. If only one is a boy then he must inherit. And what if the child is sickly?"

Perdikkas nodded and clapped Nikometros on the shoulder. "Thank you Nikometros," he murmured. "Someone with a bit of sense at last."

Nikometros stared at the general then turned back to the assembly, raising his hands. "No, what the heir, whoever he is, needs most is someone to act for him. However, instead of a single Regent I move that we appoint a Council of Regents. The power is too much for a single man."

Ptolemy joined his son. "Well said. A council, not a single Regent."

Perdikkas raised his voice in scorn. "And just who do you propose for this council? You and your cronies, I suppose?"

"There is one man that Alexander trusted above all others," Ptolemy said. "He trusted him so much that he sent him to govern Macedon for him--I speak of General Krateros. Surely this trusted general would be the logical choice to head the Council?"

"Krateros?" stormed Perdikkas. "He isn't even here. How can he take control when he's only halfway home?"

"Perhaps Alexander named him his heir," interposed Ptolemy. "Tell us yourself, Perdikkas. Did you mishear Alexander? Did he say Krateros rather than kratisto?"

The audience hall erupted into violent argument, men forming into factions and acrimoniously debating the relative merits of the candidates.

"Forget Krateros!" yelled Aristonous, one of the Bodyguard. "Alexander gave his ring to Perdikkas. He meant him to be the Regent."

Shouts of agreement drowned out the opposing views and a chant gradually took hold of the emotion-ridden men. "Perdikkas, Perdikkas!"

Perdikkas smiled triumphantly and moved toward the throne. As he reached out to pick up the ring he hesitated and looked across at the hostile faces on the dais. "Well," he muttered. "Will any of you support me?"

Aristonous and Seleukos stepped forward but before they could say anything another voice shouted from the floor of the hall.

"Give Perdikkas the ring and he'll keep it. The heirs aren't even born yet." A red-faced man shouldered his way through the crowd toward the dais. As he advanced, cheers arose around him and hands reached out to clap him on the back. "We only have the word of the generals that Alexander even gave him the ring in the first place. All they are after is power and what goes with it." The red-faced man turned to face the assembly. "Have you forgotten the treasury?"

The soldiers growled and surged forward, an avaricious gleam in their eyes.

"Who is that?" hissed Perdikkas.

Seleukos stared incredulously. "Meleagros, a commander of the phalanx, an infantry officer, for god's sake. Who in Hades is he to start poking his nose in?"

Perdikkas shouted for order, reminding the assembly they were soldiers of Alexander, not a mob. "Furthermore," he added. "This is a lawful assembly. Any man has the right to be heard, but let it be done in a seemly manner."

"Then why are we talking about unborn heirs and Regents?" called another voice from the crowd. "There is among us the very blood of Alexander. I say his brother should inherit."

Nikometros turned to Ptolemy. "He's talking about you, sir. You too are a son of Philip."

Ptolemy shook his head. "I? Egypt is all I want." He hesitated, a gleam of excitement in his eye. "But yes, by the gods, it could be." He made a hesitant step forward.

"Who are you talking about?" yelled a young man at the edge of the dais. "Alexander had no legitimate brothers."

"You're too young to remember," the voice shouted. A man, an old scarred veteran struggled free and pushed to the front. "I'm talking about Arridaios, legitimate son of Philip by his lawful wife Philinna."

"Arridaios! You must be joking, he's a halfwit."

"Besides, he's in Macedon!"

"No, no," the veteran disagreed. "He's here in Babylon. And if he once was a halfwit..." The man shrugged. "...he seems to have outgrown it. Why, not more than a month ago I saw him with Alexander at the morning sacrifice. He looked healthy enough then."

The mob, fickle as ever, began to call for Arridaios.

Meleagros slipped away into the crowd.

Perdikkas swore softly and turned to Seleukos, appealing for his help. "Call for Roxane's child again," he hissed. "Quickly, before they set their minds on Arridaios. I can persuade them but it'll be better if someone else calls for it."

Seleukos nodded. "Men," he started to say. "We do indeed need the blood of Alexander to rule us..."

Peithon interrupted him, striding angrily to the edge of the platform. "Are you fools?" he shouted. "This Arridaios is a halfwit. Everyone knows he was dropped on his head as an infant and has never grown up." He laughed. "Yes, what a great king he would make. He drools, he shits himself and he plays with dolls. Do you really want an idiot for a king?"

"Shame on you, sir!" called the old veteran. "He's Alexander's brother. We cannot go far wrong with him as king."

"Yes, Arridaios!" yelled another. "Arridaios, Arridaios, Arridaios!"

Perdikkas pulled Peithon back, his face contorted with rage. "You imbecile! Now they want him more. I could have persuaded them but you called them fools." He listened to the chanting grow louder and looked around at the others on the dais, biting his lip. He stepped forward, shouting for order.

The men continued yelling their support for Arridaios, drowning out Perdikkas.

Perdikkas stepped back, frowning and turned to Seleukos. "What can I do?" he muttered. "I must do something."

The shouting died down at the far end of the hall before suddenly increasing in volume and exuberance.

Meleagros appeared, dragging behind him a short, stout man with black hair and beard. He pushed through the crowd, grinning and triumphantly scrambled onto the dais with the other man. Panting, he turned to the mob of soldiers. "Behold your king!" He pushed the dark-haired man in front of him and stood with his hands on the man's shoulders. "This is the lawful son of King Philip of Macedon, the brother of the Great Alexander--your King."

"It's true," called a soldier in the front ranks. "Why, he's the spitting image of the old king. Good for you, sir! Long live King Arridaios!"

Perdikkas caught hold of Meleagros and spun him around. "You unmitigated fool!" he yelled. "This is no king."

Ptolemy joined the fracas. "This is a farce," he said angrily. "We should be honouring the memory of Alexander by choosing a successor wisely. Instead, you've shamed us all."

Peukestas, Seleukos and Nikometros all joined in, their voices rising in anger.

Arridaios edged away, a frightened look on his bearded face. He bolted for the back of the dais but Meleagros lunged and caught him.

A roar went up from the watching army and Meleagros shouldered his way past the generals dragging Arridaios with him. "Don't run!" Meleagros hissed. "Just stand there and try to look like a king."

Arridaios shook his head, tears forming in his eyes. "I don't want to. I'm frightened. Why can't I just go back to my rooms? I want my breakfast."

Meleagros cursed, struggling to hold the reluctant man without seeming to coerce him. He looked around for inspiration and spotted the purple robe of state draped over the back of the throne. "How would you like a wonderful purple robe? It belonged to Alexander and King Philip before him. Now it is yours."

Arridaios' eyes grew wide, his face splitting into a drooling grin. "Yes, I'd like that. If I had on Alexander's robe no one would be nasty to me."

Meleagros snatched the robe off the throne and dropped it over Arridaios' shoulders. He turned the man once more to face the army and proclaimed. "See, your king--King Philip Arridaios. Long may he reign!"

A tremendous cheer went up from the soldiers, those with spears drumming them on the tile floor; others stamped and clapped, raising a cacophony of sound.

Ptolemy turned away disgusted. "What a ridiculous figure the man cuts," he sneered. "Alexander should have had him smothered."

Perdikkas, already angry, lost control. He threw himself at Meleagros and tried to wrestle him away from Philip Arridaios. A number of junior officers attempted to separate the two whereupon the Companions, standing nearby watching the developing situation with incredulity, drew their swords with a whisper of steel. They shook their weapons and lofted a piercing battle paean. Immediately the soldiers drew weapons and the mass of men started to divide into factions poised for bloodshed.

382

Meleagros paled, clinging to the trembling figure of Philip Arridaios. He racked his brains for inspiration as a new clamour filled the Audience hall. The squires pushed in through the crowd, some fifty strong and scrambled up on the dais. They stared at the mob of soldiers, their hair shorn close and ragged, and their eyes red from weeping.

"How can you betray Alexander like this?" yelled one of the squires. "While his body lies unburied?"

Meleagros smirked and pushed Philip Arridaios ahead of him. "The squires speak the truth. Alexander lies unburied. The burial of a king is the sacred duty of his successor. You have chosen your king already. Will you stand by him?"

The clamour died down as men turned to hear this new argument.

"Come with me," Meleagros urged. "Come with your king, Philip Arridaios of Macedon, as he performs his sacred duty of entombing his predecessor." He jumped down from the dais and strode toward the doors, Philip Arridaios stumbling along behind him, clutching his purple robe.

After a moment's pause, the army surged after him, cheering and shouting.

"Dear gods," cried Ptolemy. "If they secure the body, nothing will stop them. We must do something."

"Follow me!" said Perdikkas. He dashed for the rear of the hall, heading for the corridor that led straight to the king's apartments.

A few minutes later, Perdikkas and his followers burst into the bedchamber, the roar of the approaching mob already loud in the hallways outside the apartments. The body of Alexander lay on the bed, Bagoas sitting beside him, his face a mask of grief. The bedclothes, rumpled and sweat stained from the death had been changed and smoothed. Alexander's face, pale and hollow, lay in peace, his unruly hair combed and dampened in place.

Nikometros, arriving on the heels of the generals, stared at the body of his king. "He has lain for hours in this heat," he muttered. "Yet he...he looks as if he sleeps."

"Huh," grunted Seleukos. "Not even a whiff of decay. Are you sure he's dead?"

"Of course he is," Perdikkas snapped. "Quickly now. We must barricade the room."

The squires and the Companions that accompanied them hastened to drag furniture across the room, piling it against the door. The generals, Perdikkas, Peukestas, Ptolemy and Niarchos; stood by the bed, their swords drawn. Seleukos and Nikometros flanked them, with the squires and Companions standing by the barricade.

The tramp of feet and shouting outside the room died down and the door shuddered as the soldiers heaved against it. Furniture shifted and crashed to the floor, the doors pushing apart, revealing soldiers in armour standing several rows deep outside the bedchamber. Spears stabbed through the gap, sending the defenders reeling back. The soldiers pushed again and with a grinding screech the doors flew open, spilling men into the room.

"Fall back, lads," rapped Perdikkas. "Swords out but defend only."

The squires and companions withdrew until their legs touched the bed, crowding against the generals and staff officers. Others worked their way around it until Alexander lay inside an island sea of men.

For a moment the mob of soldiers stood uncertainly by the jumble of furniture near the doors. They stared at the resolute men around the bed. Then, reluctantly, they stumbled forward, impelled by the pressure of their comrades. With a yell, several men threw their spears before charging forward, dragging their swords out.

A spear glanced off Perdikkas' helmet, sending him reeling. Another hit one of the Companions. The man clutched his thigh and went down, cursing.

Bagoas threw himself onto the body of Alexander as the spears flew, taking a grazing cut on his arm. One of the squires picked up a spear and threw it back into the mob of attackers. A man screamed and fell.

Swords clashed and Nikometros found himself face to face with a sweating Macedonian. He tried to parry the savage blows of his opponent but felt a reluctance to retaliate. "I...don't want...to fight you," Nikometros panted.

His opponent grunted in reply and pressed home his attack, forcing Nikometros back.

Ptolemy grappled with a man trying to stab into the defenders with his spear, throwing him back. "Stop!" he bellowed.

Men hesitated, glancing sideways at the general.

"Are we beasts to fight over the corpse of one of our own, or are we men?" he asked. "What are we fighting about?"

"We're here to bury the king," yelled a voice from the back.

"Where is he?" asked another, more quietly. "What have you done with him?"

"Come and see then," replied Niarchos. "Give way there, lads," he added, motioning the defenders to step aside. "Look at your king."

The soldiers stood silently, taking in the sight of their Great King Alexander, lying dead on the bed before them. Some wept openly, and most put up their weapons.

"What are we to do, sirs?" asked an old grizzled veteran. "The king needs burying proper-like. It's what we came here to do, but we don't want no bloodshed, do we boys?" He looked around at his fellows. "How about it, sirs? A truce while we figures out what to do? You is outnumbered after all."

Perdikkas nodded. "A truce is acceptable but the body must not be touched in the meantime. Do you agree?"

"Don't listen to him," Meleagros snarled. "He's only seeking some advantage. Don't forget who your king is." He pushed a pale and trembling man forward. "You promised to stand by him."

"That's true," agreed the old veteran. "And so's we shall but we needs to parley, not fight. These 'ere are our comrades." He turned back to face Perdikkas. "We won't touch the body whiles we talk."

"Good man," said Perdikkas with a grim smile. "I, for my part, promise you the body of our king will be taken to Macedon and buried in the royal burial ground at Pella. It will be shown all the honours due it and interred in its rightful place."

Meleagros, hearing the mutterings of approval from the soldiers around him, gave up his efforts to take possession of the king's body. He scowled at the assembled men. "Can we trust them, though?"

"Send for a black goat," Perdikkas said. "We sacrifice to Hecate. We'll bind ourselves with a sworn statement."

The goat entered, bleating with fear, dragged by one of the young courtiers.

Perdikkas drew his dagger and, pulling its head back, slit its throat. The goat struggled and kicked, spraying its blood over the floor and those standing nearby. One of the squires held a bowl to catch the blood.

Perdikkas dipped his fingers into the hot blood and lifted his hand high, while the young squire held out the bowl to the others. The general swore an old and colourful oath, binding himself in the most horrific way to honour the terms of the truce. "Swear as I did," Perdikkas said quietly.

One by one, the generals, followed by the officers and commanders and then the common soldiers, came forward and dipped their fingers in the blood, swearing the oath.

"Good," Ptolemy said as the last of the men present swore. "Officers of Colonel rank and above to the Conference Room. We have things to discuss."

As the men started filing from the room, servants ran in with bandages and water to take care of the wounded.

Peukestas signalled to Nikometros. "Send for the embalmers, son. Let them prepare the body for burial."

# Chapter 45

D ays passed, the city of Babylon seething with rumours and intrigue. The army of Alexander split reluctantly into two wary camps--the infantry of Meleagros camped around and within the palace, the cavalry of Perdikkas in the royal parks adjacent. This atmosphere of distrust engendered a rise in crime within the city, bands of thugs roamed the streets with impunity, raping, looting and generally causing mischief.

Despite the dangers, Nikometros felt impelled to move his family out of the lesser palace and into lodgings within the city. Not being able to watch constantly within the palace grounds because of his cavalry connections, he was reluctant to trust his loved ones to the dubious attentions of the infantry phalanx.

The generals, too, moved out of the palace grounds. Perdikkas stayed close to the source of his power, the cavalry, bivouacking in the royal park. Ptolemy, Peukestas, Eumenes and other senior officers stayed with wealthy Persian friends in the city.

Nikometros and Tomyra found lodgings at one of the better taverns, having the money to rent a suite of rooms for themselves, Starissa and her nurses. However, space was at a premium, there being many staff officers and court officials uprooted from their normal lives.

Thus, Timon and Bithyia lodged at another tavern close by. As Bithyia neared her time, Timon was reluctant to leave her or to put her to undue exertion, so Nikometros and Tomyra left their daughter in the care of her nurses and visited their friends.

Tirses and Berinax joined them, having something urgent to discuss. They gathered in an upstairs room in the tavern, where Bithyia could relax on a cushioned couch.

"Menares reports to me that he and the other 'Lions' wish to return to Scythia," stated Tirses. "They've already sent word home and received a reply."

"But that'll be suicide!" Timon said. "Do they have a death wish?"

Tirses shook his head. "No, my friend, though a year ago I would have agreed with you. It seems even Parasades can change his mind."

"Can he be trusted?" asked Nikometros. "He may just kill them when they return."

"Again, no," Tirses said. "He gives his word as chief of the Massegetae and swears an oath on the Mother Goddess that he will allow them back."

"Why do they want to return?" Bithyia asked. "I thought they swore to follow lord Nikometros into permanent exile."

Tirses shrugged. "Things change. When we left Scythia it was an adventure and they had great pride in being 'Lions'. Now...?"

"Now they're disillusioned and long for home," growled Berinax, completing his friend's statement. "Forgive me, lord," he nodded at Nikometros, "But in Scythia people looked up to them as the chosen men of the great barbarian war leader. Here, the lord Nikometros is but one of many, and not of the highest. They feel let down."

"Also, they feel their oath to serve Alexander ceased with his death," added Tirses.

"Ingrates," muttered Timon.

"It's true," Nikometros said quietly. "I don't blame them. All they have of Scythia is what they carry with them."

"So who wants to return?" asked Tomyra.

"Berinax and I will remain here in my lord's service," Tirses said firmly. "The others want to return and intend to set out immediately, providing lord Nikometros will give his permission."

"What if he doesn't?" asked Tomyra.

"Then they will wait awhile but go anyway. They would feel bad though."

"Gods preserve us," Timon muttered. "We wouldn't want that."

Nikometros smiled. "Very well. They have my permission...and my blessing. I'll pray that Parasades keeps his word."

"Thank you," Tirses said, rising. "I'll convey your words to Menares at once. Berinax?"

Berinax got up and followed Tirses to the door.

Tomyra put down her cup and stood also. "Wait. I'll accompany you." She turned to Nikometros. "I'd better check on Starissa. I don't like leaving her alone too long with the city in this state. Bithyia, I'm sorry. I'll return in the morning."

"She isn't alone, my love," Nikometros replied. "The nurses are with her and are devoted to her service." He smiled. "However, I agree. I'll come with you."

"No, stay, Niko. I know you and Timon have things to discuss. Tirses will see me home."

Tirses nodded. "With my life, sir."

Tomyra and her bodyguard left.

Bithyia retired to her bedroom mildly complaining of backaches while Nikometros and Timon settled back with their wine.

"It's hard to believe discipline could break down so fast," said Timon. "Less than a week and we're back to the lawless times before Philip's accession." He grinned. "I don't suppose you can remember those, Niko?"

"No. And nor can you. You aren't that old."

Timon shook his head. "I can remember my father talking of them, though. Bad times."

"It won't be that bad. The generals will get things sorted soon."

"Maybe if they wanted the same thing. As it is they're all pulling in different directions. They'll pull this empire apart if they're not careful."

"I know what you mean. Perdikkas wants to be another Alexander. Ptolemy just wants to retire to Egypt but can't stand the thought of Perdikkas in power. Peukestas wants an end to the fighting. He's happy enough in Persia. The gods alone know what will happen when General Krateros confronts Antipatros in Macedon. Eumenes? Well, I'm not sure what he wants...aside from power."

"And Meleagros?"

"That joke? He's nothing but a jumped-up phalanx commander and not a very good one at that."

"He controls the infantry though."

"Only because he controls that half-wit Arridaios. That can't last. Sooner or later the infantry will come to their senses."

"So what will you do, Niko? Who do you support?"

Nikometros sank back in his chair, a thoughtful look on his face. "See what happens, I suppose. I'm on Perdikkas' staff though I'm not sure that's where I want to be." He sipped from his cup, his eyes unfocused, staring at the wall. "I'd like to return home to Macedon but there'll be civil war there soon. I don't want to take my family into that. I can't go back to Scythia either, though I think Tomyra would like to."

"What about your father? Would Ptolemy find a place for you?"

"Possibly. Egypt is an interesting place, Timon. Easily defensible, rich, and best of all, the people love us Macedonians." Nikometros smiled. "You know, that might be..."

The sound of running feet and shouting interrupted him. The door burst open and Berinax stumbled in, gasping and clutching his side. Blood soaked his tunic and welled through his fingers, spattering the wooden floorboards.

Nikometros and Timon leapt to their feet, wine cups flying, and caught Berinax as he collapsed.

"My lady," the Scythian gasped, blood trickling from the corner of his mouth. "She...she's been..." Berinax slumped, his eyes rolling back in his head.

Nikometros shook the man, his own eyes wide and staring. "What? What has happened?" A sound behind him made him turn, his hand fumbling for his sword. Bithyia stood in the doorway to the bedroom, her mouth open with horror.

"What has happened to Tomyra?" she whispered. "And Starissa?"

Timon lowered Berinax to the floor and crossed to his wife, taking her in his arms. "We don't know, but we'll find out."

Nikometros stood and stared at his friend. "Stay here, Timon. Look after Bithyia." He turned and ran from the room, crashing down the stairs and through the main room of the tavern, sending patrons flying and stumbling out of his path. He raced through the streets, sword in hand. Pedestrians fled from the wild-eyed man and shouts of alarm rose in his wake.

Nikometros arrived outside his lodgings to find a small crowd gathered. He pushed through to where a Scythian crouched over the body of a man on the roadway.

He looked up as Nikometros grasped him by the shoulder. "My...my lord," stuttered the man. "It's Menares, he's dead."

"What happened?" Nikometros looked around at the curious faces then at the entrance to the tavern. He took a step away from the Scythians. "Where is she? Where are my wife and daughter?" He stumbled toward the doorway.

"My lord," said the Scythian, rising to his feet. "They've gone. They..."

Nikometros rounded on him. "Gone? Where have they gone?" He paused and peered closely at the man. "Eraxes, isn't it? Where have they gone, Eraxes?"

"We were set upon in the street. Several men." Eraxes hung his head. "They...they took the priestess, my lord. And your daughter."

"And you didn't defend her?"

Eraxes nodded and held out his arm. Blood oozed sluggishly from a rent in his chest. "We arrived too late to prevent them, lord. They already had them. Menares died in vain."

Nikometros looked at the body on the roadway. Already, the bystanders were moving away, having lost interest now that the excitement was over. "Where is Tirses?" he asked. "Tirses swore to protect her."

"Wounded, my lord, but he follows, with Loces. He bade me stay here until help arrived. Berinax went to find you. He did find you, lord?"

"Where did they go?"

Eraxes pointed down the street toward the docks. "Er, shall I find the other Scythians, my lord? We could pursue them."

"Yes, do that," muttered Nikometros.

Behind him, Eraxes hovered uncertainly. "I'll just go then," he muttered to himself. He turned and hurried away in the opposite direction, leaving the body of his friend to be found by the next passing guard patrol.

Nikometros stepped over the body of Menares and pushed past a couple of men still gawking at the scene. Breaking into a run, he raced down the uneven street toward the lower city, his face contorted in a fierce snarl and his sword at the ready. He ran through the darkened streets, heading down toward the docks and the warehouses crowded with the supplies of the aborted Arabian expedition. He came to the main thoroughfare paralleling the river and stopped, searching the darkness for a hint of his quarry. The road lay in shadowed silence, broken only by the snarling of dogs over some morsel of food and the soft slap of the water against the docks. He felt a great burst of despair wash over him and he threw back his head and howled.

"Tomyra!"

Dark shadows detached from the inkiness of the warehouses and flitted across the road as the echoes of the cry died away. One figure gripped Nikometros' sword arm as the other hurled itself onto his back, hand searching to silence the man.

Nikometros staggered and fell to one knee, struggling to free his sword arm. He yelled again, incoherently, and hit out at the man hanging onto his back. The man grunted in pain.

"My lord," gasped the man. "Be quiet, I beg you!"

"Tirses?" Nikometros stopped struggling and sat down hard on the stone paving of the road.

The dark figures let go of Nikometros and squatted beside him. "Niko," Tirses said quietly. "It's very important that you keep quiet and listen."

"Where is Tomyra? My daughter?" Nikometros pushed himself to his knees, his sword scraping on the road.

Tirses pushed him down again with a curse. "Loces, control him. Sit on him if you have to." He gripped Nikometros tightly and brought his face close to his commander's. "Niko. If you don't keep quiet, Tomyra could die."

Nikometros ceased his struggling at once. "Go on," he said.

"We pursued them to a street near here, Niko. They turned on us and disarmed us. They wanted us to carry a message to you."

Nikometros looked at Tirses in silence for a few moments, then shrugged loose of the man's grip. "What's the message?"

"They said, 'Tomyra and your daughter are alive and unhurt. If you want to see them continue that way you must come alone to a place of their choosing at a time of their choosing.'"

"And where is this place?"

"They didn't say. You're to return to your lodgings and they'll send word."

"If you hadn't stopped me, Tirses, I might have attracted their attention and be with them right now."

"Dead more like, and your family too." Tirses shrugged, the gesture almost lost in the darkness. "At least if you wait you might be able to come up with some sort of plan."

"I don't need a plan," Nikometros said bleakly, getting to his feet. "I'll meet them wherever they want."

# Chapter 46

"I have men scouring the waterfront right now," Ptolemy said. "Rest assured, Nikometros, we'll find your wife and daughter."

"I'm not sure that's best, sir," replied Nikometros quietly. "If the kidnappers are found they may panic and kill my family. They said they would contact me."

"Nonsense. You must take the initiative." Perdikkas looked disapprovingly. He sat rocked back in a carved chair with his booted heels resting on a table covered with documents. The chair tipped as he moved, a leg sinking into the soft earth inside the tent and he hurriedly lowered his legs. "You cannot let these brigands dictate to you."

Nikometros walked to the opening of the tent and looked out. Outside the immediate vicinity of the general's tent, the royal park brimmed over with cavalry, horses tethered in lines hard by the tents. Mess halls dispensed food but a few strides from latrine trenches; armourers filling the air with clamour next to camp followers. He frowned and turned back to the two generals.

"This cannot continue, sir." Nikometros waved his hand vaguely, encompassing the whole park. "We're vulnerable here."

"Do you think I don't know that?" snapped Perdikkas. "But as long as that bastard Meleagros controls the half-wit, there's little we can do."

"The longer you leave him in control, the more entrenched he'll get," Ptolemy said. He covered a smile with one hand, though his eyes twinkled. "They tell me Meleagros calls himself Chiliarch these days. I thought that was your title, Perdikkas."

"It is," Perdikkas replied. "However, Alexander himself gave me this in front of you all." He held up Alexander's royal ring. "This gives me more power than any self-proclaimed title."

"Maybe, but the cavalry is still outnumbered five to one. The infantry follow the new...faugh, I cannot call him king! This puppet of Meleagros."

Voices raised in argument intruded.

Nikometros walked to the tent entrance and looked out, seeking the cause of the disturbance. A squad of about a hundred infantrymen stood arguing by the roped off area around the tent. A small group of squires stood between the foot soldiers and the general's tent, nervously fingering their swords.

One of the squires turned and ran back to Perdikkas' tent, brandishing a piece of paper. He burst into the tent, pushing Nikometros to one side and executing a hurried salute. "Sir, the rebels are outside. They have a royal warrant for your arrest."

Ptolemy grabbed the paper and scanned it quickly before passing it to Perdikkas. "That's what it says."

Perdikkas read it out loud. "Treason, eh?" he snorted, when he finished. "Well, we'll see about that." He got up and buckled on his sword belt.

"Sir, is that wise?" asked Nikometros. "I can raise the guard with a shout and I'm sure the squires can hold them for the few minutes it would take for them to arrive."

"That's right, sir," agreed the squire. "We can hold them."

Perdikkas smiled at Nikometros and clapped the squire on the shoulder. "No need. I'll talk to Meleagros' men." He tossed back his hair and squared his shoulders before marching out to meet the infantry squad.

Perdikkas walked out past the squires and stood alone in front of the soldiers sent to arrest him. He paused, unconcernedly looking at his fingernails before he began quietly to speak. Greeting the officer in charge by name, he reviewed the last campaign they had fought in together against the Kossaians. "You know, Alkestas," Perdikkas went on, addressing his remarks directly at the infantry officer. "Alexander spoke highly of you after that campaign." He shook his head, frowning. "I wonder what Alexander would think of you now, disgracing yourselves like this. You know, as well as I, that Alexander's half-witted brother has been used before as an object of intrigue." He lowered his voice confidentially, the other officer leaning closer to hear him. "Most kings would have killed him, but what did Alexander do? He cared for him, knowing he was an innocent, incapable of anything but childish pursuits. And you want to make him king? I'm amazed that Alexander's men would come to me as servants of Meleagros, doing his bidding. You know this arrest warrant comes from Meleagros--a man Alexander wouldn't trust with senior command, knowing his character too well."

Perdikkas paused and yawned, looking disinterestedly at the shuffling soldiers. "Well," he said at last. "You disgust me. In truth I imagine you disgust yourselves. You're dismissed." He turned his back and sauntered toward his tent.

Alkestas flushed and looked around at his men. None would meet his eye. They milled around and stared at the ground.

The officer's shoulders slumped. "About turn," he rapped. "We're going home, lads."

The squires grinned and they, together with other cavalrymen who had gathered to find out what was happening, gave Perdikkas a cheer.

He returned the grins, feeling very pleased with himself.

"Nicely done," murmured Ptolemy as Perdikkas entered the tent. "Alexander could scarcely have done it better."

"Nonsense. Alexander would have had them eating out of his hand. Nonetheless, it will suffice." He clapped his hands together, becoming serious once more. "Now, to business. It's become too dangerous here. I'm going to move the cavalry out of the city."

"Won't that provoke Meleagros, sir?" Nikometros asked.

"Exactly." Perdikkas smiled. "We'll put a bit of pressure on the bastard, invest the city, and cut off his supplies. That'll bring him to the bargaining table."

By early afternoon, the cavalry vacated the city, setting up camp to the north of the city outside the main gates and refusing admission to the supply wagons. Refugees, both from inside and outside the city went unmolested. Country people, fearing the ravages of war, sought sanctuary within Babylon, whereas the inhabitants of the city, afraid of famine, poured out of the city.

Two days later, at sunrise, envoys from Meleagros left the Ishtar Gate for Perdikkas' camp. Eumenes led the delegation. A lean, austere man in his fifties, he inclined toward intellectual pursuits rather than military deeds and had held the position of Secretary under Alexander, despite his enmity with Hephaestion. Fiercely devoted to the Royal House of Macedon, he willingly acceded to Meleagros' pleas to intercede with Perdikkas and the other generals.

Nikometros commanded the squad entrusted with bringing the delegation safely through the camp. His thoughts though, were elsewhere. Two sleepless days without word from the kidnappers had brought his nerves to breaking point.

Eumenes entered the large tent pitched in the shade of tall palm trees. The sides of the tent were folded back admitting cooling breezes on what promised to be another baking hot summer day. He looked around as he entered, nodding with approval at the simple furnishings so reminiscent of Alexander's campaigns. A bed, a chair, a trestle table and a couple of chests set on dry swept soil. Several other chairs were set out for the envoys.

Perdikkas rose to greet Eumenes, warmly grasping his forearms. "Welcome Eumenes. I wondered how long it would be before Meleagros remembered you."

Eumenes inclined his head with a smile. "Thank you Perdikkas." He nodded at the other officers before accepting a chair and a cup of wine.

Perdikkas waited until Eumenes had refreshed himself before opening the negotiations. "What does he want?" he asked bluntly.

"Meleagros, Chiliarch and Protector; and King Philip Arridaios send their greetings. They would seek reconciliation between the cavalry regiments and the rest of the army. They ask also that you raise the siege and allow supplies back into the city."

"We're all interested in reconciliation," Perdikkas said. "But what does Meleagros offer in return for my lifting the siege?"

"Forgiveness, my lord," Eumenes replied with a wry smile. "He's willing to overlook your treason and welcome you as a loyal officer of King Philip...under his command of course."

Perdikkas let out a great guffaw of laughter, slapping his knee. "Tell him that I'm willing to reconcile and end the siege only when Meleagros and his accomplices have given themselves up for trial." He sobered and stared hard at Eumenes. "You have my word that I won't harm Arridaios."

Eumenes coughed delicately and sipped his wine. "We seem to be at an impasse then. Shall I convey your terms to Meleagros or do we negotiate?"

"You have the authority?"

"Oh, I'm sure that we can reach mutually acceptable terms with a little effort. It would be better to end this quickly, my lord Perdikkas."

Several hours of discussion followed. Gradually the terms of a peace settlement filtered out of the argument and rhetoric, both sides giving a little, accepting and rejecting ideas put forward by the negotiators. By sunset, agreement was reached.

"Very well," Perdikkas proclaimed to the waiting generals. "Here are the terms of the truce. The siege is lifted. I recognise King Philip Arridaios' claim to the throne and accept Meleagros as joint commander of the army. Krateros will be appointed the guardian of the king and Antipatros will stay on as Regent of Macedon. I will remain as Chiliarch of Asia." He scrawled the terms on a piece of paper, signed it and handed it to Eumenes.

Eumenes nodded then silently left the tent to ride back to the city.

When he was out of earshot, Peukestas turned on Perdikkas angrily. "Have you taken leave of your senses? You would offer that man a share of the command?"

"A dangerous course," added Ptolemy.

"Of course it's dangerous," Perdikkas replied. "But not as dangerous as allowing Meleagros and his cronies sole access to the King. Yes, I'll call him that...for now. The last thing I want is for the army to disintegrate into chaos. We all lose then."

"But to share your command with a commoner?"

"Can you think of a better way to winkle him out of the city? He won't refuse that bait."

# *Chapter 47*

Meleagros and King Philip Arridaios rode out of the city the next morning to meet with Perdikkas. Behind them marched representatives of the infantry to the music of trumpets and flutes, eager to make their peace with the cavalry. They drew themselves up opposite the Companion Cavalry, who sat resplendent in parade armour, controlling their high-spirited mounts.

The King rode out into the space between the two bodies of men and, dismounting, embraced Perdikkas.

The general smiled and joked, giving every appearance of enjoyment. Meleagros followed, eager to make his peace too, but Perdikkas' embrace was formal and restrained. "One other thing remains," Perdikkas said. "It's an ancient custom of Macedon to exorcise the evil of discord by a sacrifice to Hecate. I propose that the entire army assembles on the plain tomorrow for the ceremony of Purification. Then we can put all this behind us."

The meeting broke up shortly thereafter and the troops were dismissed. Most drifted back into the city, seeking refreshment after hours of marching and standing in the hot sun.

Nikometros went with them, eager to find out how the search for Tomyra and Starissa progressed. The streets of Babylon teemed with life, the citizenry in an almost festive mood, relieved that civil war had been averted. Nikometros pushed through the jostling crowds toward the inn where Timon and Bithyia lived. As he turned into the street, a hand plucked at his sleeve. He turned to see a pleasant-faced young Persian man regarding him.

"Nikometros?" the young man asked. "Please follow me."

"Is this about Tomyra...my wife?" Nikometros demanded. He grabbed the young man roughly. "Where is she?"

The young man pushed Nikometros away. "If you want to see her, follow." He shrugged. "If not, it's all the same to me." He turned and started walking away.

"Wait!" Nikometros hurried after the man and fell into step beside him.

The two men moved at a leisurely pace down toward the waterfront in almost complete silence. The young man refused to answer any questions, replying only with grunts or monosyllabic references to the desired direction of their travel.

Nikometros looked about him carefully and thought he recognised the area from the other night. Few soldiers frequented this area and the men they passed, sailors, stevedores and beggars all turned and looked at the out-of-place Macedonian officer gleaming in his burnished parade armour.

At length they turned down an alleyway between two large warehouses. Sounds from the city came distantly and even the closer cries of the dockworkers and boat crews seemed muffled by the looming buildings.

The young Persian stopped by a small door set into one of the warehouses. "In there." He gestured for Nikometros to precede him.

"After you," Nikometros replied. He stood back, his face wary.

The young man smiled and opened the door, stepping through into relative darkness after the sunny streets.

Nikometros followed, hand on his sword hilt, looking around cautiously. Rows of bales and lines of stacked barrels stood out like silent sentinels in the dimness of the warehouse, their contents filling the air with a musty, spicy aroma. Scampering and squeaking told of an ongoing rodent problem. Nikometros' eyes flicked to a movement in the middle of a wide-open space on the warehouse floor and he gasped, taking a few steps forward. Cross-legged on the dusty floorboards, in a pool of sunlight thrown by a high window, sat Parates. In front of him a small child lay, kicking and gurgling with delight as the man dangled a brightly coloured cloth toy.

"Starissa!" Nikometros said. He moved forward, his eyes fixed on the child, unaware of others in the room until his arms were pinioned from behind.

Two men swiftly bound his arms and forced him to kneel on the floor. One removed his sword and sent it spinning into a corner, shards of reflected sunlight flashing like falling gold pieces. Two others stood by the door, swords in hand.

Parates signalled to the two men by the door. "Keep watch outside. Make sure we aren't disturbed."

The two men hesitated, glancing into the darkened interior of the warehouse before obeying their leader.

Parates got to his feet slowly and stepped around the child. He looked down at Nikometros with a sad expression. "I don't expect you to believe me, Nikometros son of Leonnatos, but it gives me no pleasure to see you like this. In the months I have known you, I have come to respect and...even like you. Were it not for my sworn word, I would not bring you to this."

"Where is my wife, Parates?"

"She's here." Parates turned and beckoned and two figures moved from the shadows between the bales.

Tomyra stumbled forward, pushed by a tall thin man behind. Her hands tied behind her back threw her off balance and the gag in her mouth prevented her from crying out. She turned a dishevelled face toward Nikometros, her eyes bright with unshed tears, hair dirty and plastered with sweat. Her thin linen robes, cooler in the summer heat than her woollen Scythian ones, were dirty and torn. Her cloak hung awry, fastened by a solitary enamelled gold brooch.

The thin man thrust her forward, laughing as she tripped and fell, sprawling headlong onto the floor. He emerged from the shadows completely and walked past Tomyra toward her husband. He stood over the kneeling soldier, a triumphant grin on his face.

"Scolices," Nikometros said flatly.

"At last," Scolices hissed. "Now I'll fulfill my promise to my chief. I'll enjoy killing you." He stepped forward and backhanded Nikometros, the savage blow sending him crashing to the floor.

Nikometros shook his head dazedly and struggled to his feet, blood trickling from the corner of his mouth. "Let my wife and child go."

"Of course," interposed Parates. "They'll be released as soon as it's safe. We don't war on women and children."

"It didn't stop you before. You tried to poison Tomyra."

Parates spread his arms wide in an exaggerated shrug. "An unfortunate mistake. I'm glad there was no lasting hurt."

"Stay out of this, Parates," Scolices snarled. "My lord's anger was with both the Greek and the bitch, Tomyra. They must both die. In fact, I'm of a mind to eliminate the whole family, seeing as we have the child as well."

Parates frowned. "That wasn't the agreement we came to. I agreed to help you kidnap the woman and child as bait on the understanding that only the Greek was to be killed."

"Then you misunderstood."

"Perhaps you misunderstand your position, Scolices. You're a guest in my country. It's my resources, my men you used for your scheming. If I choose to deny you this woman, you have no say in the matter." He turned and walked over to Tomyra, drawing his dagger. He reached behind her and sliced through the rope binding her. "Don't be concerned for your child, Tomyra."

"You think to deny me?" muttered Scolices. "I have bought your men." He glanced around the dim warehouse and nodded toward the two men standing guard behind Nikometros.

At once, one of them leapt at the young man leaning against the wall by the door and knocked him down with a swift blow. When the young man groaned, trying to rise, the attacker stepped close and kicked him under the jaw. The young man's head snapped back and he collapsed untidily by the wall.

The commotion made Parates turn, dagger in hand, only to be met by the other guard. The man, his own dagger drawn, ducked under Parates' arm, taking advantage of his unexpected attack. The man's dagger flashed in the sunlight and Parates staggered back with a low cry, dropping his weapon.

Tomyra reacted instantly to her release and the attack on Parates. She dropped to the floor, rolled and scrambled to her feet. She dived toward her child and scooping Starissa up, raced for the shadows, her robes flapping and threatening to trip her.

Scolices roared with rage and leapt after her.

Nikometros threw himself headlong and collided with Scolices' legs, sending the Scythian tumbling. By the time he regained his feet, Tomyra and her daughter had disappeared behind the bales and barrels.

Scolices turned on Nikometros with a scream and hauled him to his knees by his hair. Whipping his dagger out, he thrust it towards Nikometros' face, slicing through one cheek. The bloodletting steadied Scolices and he drew his arm back, breathing heavily, staring at his victim. Without turning, he called out to Tomyra. "Come out, bitch! Come out or your man dies."

"No, Tomyra!" Nikometros shouted. "He'll kill..." He choked as Scolices reversed his dagger and rammed it into his throat. His hair ripped, leaving Scolices clutching a handful of blond strands when Nikometros collapsed on the floor, gagging and gasping.

"Wait!" Tomyra called from the shadows. "Don't harm him further. I'll come out."

Scolices grinned and aimed a swift kick at the fallen man before he turned to face the shadowed bales. Slowly a figure walked out into the brighter area in the middle of the floor. Scolices gaped, his eyes wide.

Tomyra walked slowly out into view, her head held high. Gone was her cloak and loose-fitting robe. She stood naked before them, long raven hair framing her delicate features, small breasts high and thrusting, firm belly showing hardly a trace of her recent pregnancy and childbirth, her sex hidden by a thatch of dark curls.

Nikometros stared at his wife and groaned in anguish.

Parates sat clutching his wounded side, his only reaction a raised eyebrow.

The guards ogled and uttered short grunts of appreciation.

Scolices stared too, his mouth hanging open. He took a step forward. "By all the gods and goddesses of Scythia and Persia both," he breathed. "You think to offer yourself to spare your man?" A lascivious smirk took hold of his face. "Well, you're a whore and a fallen priestess after all. You've probably given yourself to many men by now. What's one more?" He moved closer, his eyes flicking over her naked body, his tongue moistening his lips.

Tomyra lowered her head, her face burning. "Please," she whispered. "Spare my husband."

Scolices laughed. "Let's see how good you are first. No doubt my men would like to enjoy your charms too before I..."

Tomyra's head snapped up and she leapt forward, a foot connecting hard with Scolices' midriff. He staggered back, dropping his blade with a clatter, his breath hacking out painfully. She fell back onto her hands, gathered her legs beneath her and, almost without a pause, launched herself at the guard standing over Parates.

The man gaped, his arms rising in defence but too slowly. The top of Tomyra's head cracked into his face and he fell backward over Parates, howling with pain.

Tomyra fell to her knees, shaking her head to clear it, struggling to her feet to meet the threat from the other guard.

Parates scrabbled in the dust for his fallen dagger, found it and, with a cry of pain, threw himself on the guard rolling on the floor. The man held his broken nose with one blood-soaked hand and tried to clear the tears streaming from his eyes with the other. Parates knocked him backward, his dagger rising and falling. The guard's screams choked off.

The second guard moved swiftly after an initial hesitation, striding to Scolices' assistance, helping the winded man up. Scolices scowled, his breath still coming in painful gasps, and shook off the man's arm. "Get her," he wheezed. "Kill the bitch."

The guard hefted his dagger and cautiously approached Tomyra as she regained her feet. He dropped into a crouch and moved forward, his dagger weaving and probing.

Tomyra retreated slowly, leaping back when the man struck at her.

Scolices watched his man close with Tomyra, clutching his midriff. He nodded in satisfaction as the tip of the man's dagger ripped a thin line across the naked woman's arm. Then he turned to look at his enemy, Nikometros.

The Greek was on one knee and, as Scolices stepped toward him, he lurched to his feet, almost overbalancing as he fought to keep his balance with his arms tied to his sides.

With a contemptuous sneer, Scolices pushed Nikometros hard, laughing as he fell again. Striding past, he opened the door of the warehouse and leaned out, scanning the alleyway. "Tissernes, Merraces, get in here!" Scolices waited to make sure the two men sent out earlier were coming before turning back into the dim warehouse.

The second guard, a grim smile on his face, slowly forced Tomyra backward toward the shadows of the bales. Crisscrossed streaks of blood laced her arms and breasts where she could not evade the guard's dagger. She glanced desperately around her, searching for some weapon.

Parates, blood streaming from his chest wound, sat slumped beside the corpse of the man he had killed. He lifted his head weakly and stared at the naked woman and the armed man as if uncertain as to their identities. He coughed, sending a gout of blood over his chin. With an effort he pushed himself upright and stood swaying, his bloody dagger dangling from his fingertips. "T...Tomyra," he croaked, the effort forcing new freshets of blood from his mouth. Parates frowned in concentration and swung his arm, tossing the dagger toward her, falling to the floor with a crash as he overbalanced. The dagger fell several feet short of Tomyra and to one side.

The clatter of the dagger distracted the guard and his head turned toward the sound for an instant.

Tomyra did not hesitate, throwing herself to the side, hands scrabbling for the weapon. She got her hands to it and rolled, even as the guard lunged forward, stabbing down. Tomyra rolled again, fetching up hard against a bale of cloth.

The man's dagger swung again but he misjudged his strike, slamming the blade into the bale.

Tomyra heaved upward, grappling with the man as he relinquished his dagger and groped for her, his hands slipping on her blood-slicked body.

The man rapidly bore her down, one hand effortlessly gripping her dagger hand as his other found her neck.

Her free hand scrabbled, trying ineffectually to pull his hand from her throat then reaching for his eyes. Her knee slammed up toward his groin but he deflected her attempts, grunting as the blows impacted his thigh.

The man grinned while Tomyra's strength failed, his hand tightening its grip on her throat. He leered at the naked woman in his grip, leaning closer, pushing himself against her.

Tomyra's eyes rolled up, her limbs started to shake. *Mother, help me*, she silently pled. Her free hand fell from the man's face, plucked at his clothing before falling to her belly. She felt his manhood pushing hard toward her and her mind fled back to her ordeal with Dimurthes. *No! Never again!* She lunged, gripping the man's testicles through the thin cloth of his trousers. With the last of her strength she squeezed and twisted, seeking to rip the hated Serratae chieftain's parts from him.

The man screamed, his voice rapidly escalating in volume and pitch. He let go of Tomyra and collapsed, his hands clutching himself in agony.

Tomyra leaned against the bale, drawing painful gasps through her bruised throat. She looked down at the man at her feet and her lips drew back in a snarl of anger and hurt. Dropping to her knees, she plunged her dagger into the whimpering man's throat, cutting off his cries.

Nikometros staggered to his feet when Scolices came back into the warehouse. He glanced toward his wife anxiously then dragged his attention back to the man advancing on him. He strained at the ropes encircling his chest and arms, feeling them stretch slightly but not enough to free his arms. Searching, he spotted the dagger dropped by Scolices and started toward it.

Scolices saw the dagger a moment later and snarled in rage, drawing his short sword. He ran after his enemy with a shout.

Nikometros dropped to his knees and strained sideways, his fingers scrabbling at the dagger on the floor. His fingertips grasped it as Scolices swung his sword. He swayed back, the blade arcing past his face to embed itself into the wooden floor. Nikometros rose with difficulty, stepping backward, his hand finally managing to grip the dagger firmly. He thrust it forward as far as he could and turned his side toward the Scythian.

Scolices hefted his sword and advanced on Nikometros with a grin. "You think to fight me with that, Greek?" He flicked his sword forward and batted the dagger blade aside. The guard behind him roared with pain and Scolices stepped back a pace and risked a quick glance. He turned back with a scowl. "Enough. Time to end this." Scolices slashed at Nikometros, forcing him to lurch backward. Stepping swiftly after him, Scolices slashed downward, feeling his blade strike home.

Nikometros saw the blade descending and swayed to one side. A moment later a blow to his chest armour preceded an arc of pain searing across his left arm, followed a moment later by a surge of blood. He staggered back and fell even as the severed ropes loosened about him. Fighting the agony in his left arm, Nikometros swung with his right and slammed the dagger into Scolices' thigh when the man stepped forward to finish his fallen enemy.

Scolices howled and staggered back, clutching the dagger embedded in his leg.

A shaft of light briefly illuminated the warehouse when the door crashed back. The two guards, Tissernes and Merraces, entered at a run. Tissernes tripped over the supine body of the young man, his newly drawn sword flying from his grasp. Merraces leapt to avoid his fallen comrade and found himself looking at a nude woman crouched over the body of a dying man. He gaped at the sight of a naked woman covered in blood and hesitated.

With a scream, Tomyra launched herself at Merraces, her long black hair flying and the sunlight glinting redly off the blood-smeared dagger. She crashed into the man and carried him to the floor, yelling and stabbing.

Nikometros flung himself at Tissernes' dropped sword and scooped it up, rolling awkwardly before staggering to his feet, agony blossoming afresh in his arm. A wave of light-headedness swept over him and he tried to raise his left hand to his face. Unable to lift his arm, he looked aghast at his blood-soaked tunic and the blood spattering the floor beneath him. Dragging his eyes away from his wound he saw Tissernes before him. With a surge of red-hot rage, he swung the sword upward and round, pivoted on his heel and slashed downward, the blade biting deep into the base of the Persian's neck.

Tissernes thumped to the floor.

Scolices gripped the dagger in his thigh and, gritting his teeth, pulled it out. Blood spurted, soaking his leg. He glanced at Tomyra and Merraces wrestling for their lives, then back to Nikometros in time to see him deliver the deathblow to Tissernes. Staring at his enemy's back he tightened his grip on the bloody dagger in his left hand and the sword in his right. He nodded, a grim smile on his face, and moved quietly forward.

Nikometros looked down at the bloody corpse of Tissernes but saw nothing. Black spots swam before his eyes. He swayed on his feet, his heartbeat loud in his ears, drowning out the creak of floorboards behind him.

"Nikometros," whispered a voice in his head.

"Nikometros," someone said just behind him.

"Nikometros!" shouted a thin voice from a distance.

He turned, swinging fast, his sword arcing across even as he lost consciousness and fell sideways to the floor. He only glimpsed Scolices behind him; the Scythian's sword falling like a thunderbolt.

# *Chapter 48*

Morning sunlight streamed through an open window of the lesser palace, falling in warm shafts over the figure lying in the rumpled bed. Hidden from view behind the headboard of the bed sat an old slave, his hand tugging rhythmically on a tasselled rope, swinging the ostrich-plumed fan fixed above the bed. The man in the bed opened his eyes and stared about him without moving, taking in the figure of a grizzled soldier standing looking out of the window and a young woman playing with a child by the bed. He smiled and struggled to raise himself. "Tomyra," he whispered.

The woman turned with a cry of joy, the child staring up curiously. "Niko! You're awake. Timon, look! My lord awakens!"

The old soldier turned, his teeth showing white in the greying profusion of his beard. He strode to the bedside and gripped Nikometros' right hand like a vice. "Thank the gods!"

Nikometros winced and almost cried out as a wave of pain washed over him. His vision greyed and he slumped back on the pillows.

"Careful, Timon!" cried Tomyra. "He's weak yet."

Nikometros forced his eyelids open and gazed at his wife. "What happened?" he whispered. "Why am I so weak?"

"You lost a lot of blood, my love. The doctors thought you might die but I knew you wouldn't." Tomyra smiled. "Your time is not yet."

"I remember...I think there was a fight...or did I dream?"

"There was a fight, my love. In the warehouse. You fought Scolices and saved all our lives."

Nikometros nodded weakly. "I seem to remember you fighting too, though for some reason my memory is of you nak..."

"Hush, Niko," interposed Tomyra hurriedly. She flushed and glanced at Timon. "That's between us."

Nikometros lay quietly, drinking in the sight of his wife. "Between us, Tomyra." He essayed a faint smile. "Agreed."

"It was a near tragedy though, from what I hear," Timon said. "A pity the City Guard couldn't have arrived a bit sooner. They might have caught Parates too then we could all rest easy."

"I don't think you need worry about Parates," Tomyra replied. "He was badly wounded and may not survive." She hesitated. "Besides, he did save our lives. I'm glad he got away."

"I think I remember," Nikometros whispered. "He called out a warning to me. Scolices attacked me but I survived. I don't know how though. I turned, glimpsed his sword coming at me...and that's the last I remember. I would guess you killed him, Tomyra."

"No, you did. I was still fighting the man on the floor." Tomyra shook her head and smiled up at Timon. "You should have seen it, Timon. Scolices was in his downswing, moments from killing Niko then Niko turns, pivots on his heel, his sword arcing round and catching Scolices in the inner thigh. I never saw blood gush so mightily."

Timon nodded, stroking his beard. "The great artery in the leg. A lucky stroke."

"Lucky or not, it sufficed. Scolices went down as if pole-axed and bled to death before he could even try to rise. Niko collapsed also and I thought he was dead too. Covered in blood but most of it from Scolices." Tomyra grinned and took her husband's right hand in hers. "I should have had more faith in the Mother."

"And Starissa is unharmed?"

"Yes, Niko. The Mother looks after her too."

Nikometros lay back with a smile on his face and looked from Tomyra to Timon.

The old soldier stooped and picked up Starissa, setting the child on the sheets beside her father.

Starissa stared at the pale, tousled man in the bed with wide eyes for several long moments before venturing a shy smile. She reached out tentatively and grasped one of Nikometros' fingers in a chubby fist.

"What it is to have children," Nikometros whispered. "I can feel the future in her...oh, gods, Timon. I was forgetting." The smile slipped from his face to be replaced by a frown of anxiety. "What of Bithyia? How is she?"

Timon grinned. "She's fine, Niko." He preened, looking smug. "In fact, you're looking at the proud father of a baby boy. You can tell he's going to grow up to become a redoubtable warrior." Timon laughed. "Why, already he's practicing horrendous war cries to terrify his enemies."

Nikometros disentangled his hand from Starissa's fist and reached out to touch Timon. "I'm overjoyed, old friend. You must bring him to see me when I'm stronger, Bithyia too, I miss her."

A soft rapping came at the door of the bedroom. A moment later it opened and two heavily bearded men peered in, their faces breaking into grins of delight at the sight of an awake Nikometros.

"Mardes! Tirses!" Nikometros struggled to prop himself on his right elbow as his two friends entered. "It's good to see you." He tried to move his left arm to greet them but failed, collapsing back with a puzzled frown. "My arm. Why can't I move it?" He reached across with his right hand to pick at the bandages.

Tomyra restrained her husband. "Leave it, Niko." She hesitated, biting her lip. "Niko. Your wound was severe. The muscles and tendons were cut to the bone. The doctors say you won't lose your arm but you may...you may not regain full use of it."

"I'll be a cripple," Nikometros said flatly.

"Never a cripple," Mardes said. "Merely a wound of honour. Many warriors bear the wounds of battle for all to see."

"Besides which," added Timon. "Great fighter though you are, I think your talents as a leader will be more important."

"Always my leader," Tirses said. "Gods, Nikometros! I arrived with the Guard. The warehouse looked like a slaughterhouse. It's hard to credit how a captive man and a woman could wreak such destruction. I was only glad to be there to render such assistance..." Tirses blushed and looked down at the floor. "My lady, I thank the gods I wore my cloak that day, despite the heat."

"Eh?" Timon frowned, looking from Tirses to Tomyra. "What am I missing? What's the significance of your cloak?"

Tomyra smiled. "Nothing you need be concerned about, Timon." She reached out to the Scythian warrior. "You have my thanks again, Tirses." Giving him a quizzical look she added, "You'll stay then, rather than return to Scythia with the others?"

"Yes, lady. The others will wait until both of you are recovered, before they bid you farewell. For myself, I'll always serve the Lion, whether he be of Scythia, Persia or Macedon."

"I wish I could remain too," Mardes said. "I must take my young brother back to my estates, but I'll try to return to Babylon in a few months. I hope you'll still be here."

"I think we will, dear Mardes," Tomyra replied. "It'll be a while before Niko can take up his duties again."

"Speaking of which," Nikometros said. "I presume Perdikkas was told. I'm still technically on his staff."

"He knows," Timon replied. "Though he has rather more to occupy his mind at present. He's trying to govern an empire after all."

Nikometros nodded. "How is he coping with Meleagros? I know he can't stand the man."

Timon looked away. "He has no problems there," he muttered.

"Good. The last thing we need is a civil war. I'm sorry I missed the Purification Ceremony though. I heard they were to have the trained elephants to give the Royal Salute. Ever since Hephaestion's funeral I've wanted to see elephants again."

Timon coughed and turned away from the bed. "You didn't miss much, Niko. Nothing you would have wanted to see." Below his breath he muttered, "I wish to all the gods I hadn't seen it either." He stood silently staring out the window while Nikometros looked puzzled.

Tomyra filled the awkward silence by tidying up the bedclothes and pouring wine for the visitors. After a few inconsequential comments about general matters and the city gossip, Mardes and Tirses excused themselves, promising to return the next day.

When they left, Nikometros looked at Tomyra and at Timon, still staring out the window. "What? There's something you aren't telling me."

"Leave it for now, Niko, please," Tomyra said. "You're still very weak. You need your rest."

Timon turned from the window and nodded. "I'll leave you too. I should be getting back to Bithyia." He walked to the door and was reaching for the handle when it opened.

"May I see the patient?" Ptolemy asked. He looked past Timon to where Nikometros lay on the bed. "Ah, good. I see you're awake at last, Nikometros. I need to talk to you." He put a hand on Timon's shoulder. "Stay a moment, if you would, Timon."

"Good morning, sir," Nikometros said, a smile of pleasure creasing his pale features. "It is good to see you."

"And you, lad. The doctors tell me you'll be up and about again within a few days but that you must be careful of your arm for a while." Ptolemy smiled at Tomyra. "I'll look to you, dear lady, to see he does as he's told."

Tomyra smiled and dipped in a small curtsey. "Indeed, lord Ptolemy. I will do my best."

Nikometros glanced at Timon. "Sir," he said to Ptolemy, "something happened at the Ceremony of Purification, but they won't tell me what. What happened?"

Ptolemy's smile vanished. He stared at the man in the bed for a long while before answering. "You would have found out eventually. No doubt your family and friends sought to spare you but I won't.

"The army, both cavalry and infantry, met on the field outside the Nitokris Gate," Ptolemy said, his voice cold and detached. "All was done with great ceremony, the sacrifice of the finest wolfhound from the royal kennels. The omens were bad. The victim did not go consenting and to make matters worse, the King..." Ptolemy snorted derisively. "The King disgraced himself by trying to stop the sacrifice. It took place; the field was purified and the army entered."

Timon grimaced but remained silent.

"Oh, it was a glorious sight," went on Ptolemy. "No doubt about it. The armour polished, weapons sharpened. The walls of Babylon made up one side of a giant square, the infantry one side, the cavalry another and the royal elephants the fourth."

Ptolemy broke off and walked to the window, breathing in the warm summer air, heady with the scents of perfumed shrubs. "You missed the elephants in India, lad, though you saw them briefly in the darkness when we cremated Hephaestion. They paint them, you know, scarlet, ochre or green; and drape them with rich silks threaded with gold. They made the feet red with henna...a custom for occasions such as this. The mahouts ride on their necks, richly attired and looking like kings. They are there to control the great beasts, make them do their bidding."

"Sounds fabulous, sir," Nikometros said.

"Yes, it was...then. Nobody expected what happened next, except those of us privy to the plans. The ceremony called for the army to give the paean of rejoicing and then to march off the field. Instead, the pipers played advance and the cavalry advanced on the infantry." Ptolemy allowed himself a small smile. "Scared the livers out of them! I shouldn't laugh though. It demonstrates just how much discipline has decayed since..."

Nikometros smiled with him but he felt a deep surge of something wrong and waited for Ptolemy to finish the story.

"Anyway, King Philip called out loudly for the army to surrender the mutineers--he had been carefully coached by Perdikkas--and, after a bit of confusion, they did. About thirty of them. They bound them and turned them over to the cavalry, throwing them on the ground."

"Meleagros too?" asked Nikometros.

"No. We were waiting for him to object, but he kept quiet." Ptolemy paused for a few seconds before resuming his narration. "The pipes sounded again and the elephants answered with a great crashing roll of sound. They moved forward at a run, squealing, their great ears flapping. Then they reached the men lying helpless on the ground." Ptolemy paused again and looked directly at Nikometros. "The screaming didn't last long. When it was over, the elephants moved away and the army sang the paean before dismissing."

Nikometros looked sick. "Who thought up that idea?"

"Perdikkas. He takes his position very seriously and Meleagros was in the way."

"But Meleagros wasn't...he didn't die?"

"Not then. He fled the field and sought sanctuary at the altar of Marduk. Little good it did him. Perdikkas' assassins found him at dusk and killed him."

"And you...you can live with this, sir?" Nikometros asked quietly.

"Gods, no!" barked Ptolemy. "Don't you know me better than that, lad? It was necessary; that's the most that can be said for it, but it wasn't Alexander's way. He would have handled it in a more seemly fashion."

"So what will you do, sir?"

"I cannot remain here, under Perdikkas. I'll leave for Egypt tomorrow." Ptolemy's eyes crinkled at the edges and his gaze softened. "I like Egypt, I felt safe there. Alexander loved it too."

Nikometros nodded. "I'll be sorry to lose you, sir. I've enjoyed your company these past months."

Ptolemy glanced at Tomyra and Timon then at Nikometros. He lowered his voice. "Then come to Egypt. There'll always be a place for you."

"I'd like that. What do you think, Tomyra?"

"Your decision, my husband. I'll follow you anywhere."

"What of Perdikkas?" Nikometros asked. "Will he just let me go?"

Ptolemy sat down on the edge of the bed. "There is another small service you can render, lad, if you're willing to stay in Babylon awhile. You remember the old Egyptian Ket?"

"Ketherennoferptah!" Tomyra cried, clapping her hands. "I haven't seen him in a long time. How is he?"

"He's back in Egypt at the moment, making arrangements. They concern you too, should you be willing. Though I must warn you, there's an element of danger."

Nikometros gave a vague lop-sided shrug, the muscles on his left side not responding well. "Life has an element of danger. You intrigue me, sir."

Ptolemy smiled. "Just as in life men stayed close to Alexander, drawing on his fire and energy, so too in death. Perdikkas is already benefiting from being the custodian of Alexander's body. When it is properly embalmed and everything in readiness, he plans to take the body back to Macedon and inter it with the ancient kings of Macedon. You know why?"

"To honour him?" Tomyra ventured.

"Yes, but for another reason also."

"A king buries his predecessor," Timon said slowly. "He seeks the kingship."

"I don't intend to let him do that," Ptolemy said.

"You want to be king?" Nikometros asked. "I didn't think you were interested."

"Not the whole kingdom, only Egypt. You remember, Nikometros. You were with Alexander and I in Egypt. You were at Siwah when the god Ammon claimed Alexander as his son. Alexander was pharaoh in Egypt. I mean to take him there and bury him in a tomb befitting a pharaoh."

"And by burying him, proclaiming yourself pharaoh after him," Timon said.

"That too," Ptolemy said equably. "However, I believe it's what Alexander himself would want. Ket believes it too; else he wouldn't help me. He's in Alexander's city of Alexandria now, making plans for a glorious golden tomb and temple for his worship. Think of it, a king in a gold coffin carved with his features and laid in a golden tomb for eternity, bringing prosperity to all who worship at his shrine."

"The Golden King," Tomyra whispered. "It's the prophecy."

Nikometros felt a shiver of awe at her words. "How...what is my part in this?"

"The body, when it leaves for Macedon, will be accompanied by enormous riches as burial gifts. A large armed guard will go with it. Now, if I'm to...ah...persuade them to part with this prize, without bloodshed if possible, I must have an advantage. That's where you come in. Perdikkas trusts you; I believe you can be made commander of this funeral procession without too much trouble. The men love you. They'll follow you if you lead them into Egypt."

Nikometros lay still, trying to digest this possible future. He looked up at his wife and his friend.

"Follow the Golden King, Niko," Tomyra stated. "It is fated."

"Aye, Niko," rumbled Timon. "What else is there for you here? Would you follow a man like Perdikkas or like Ptolemy?"

"You know as well as I, Nikometros..." Ptolemy said softly. "...that an illegitimate son cannot inherit, but I have need of a talented soldier, one trained under Alexander. Come to Egypt, my son. My army needs a trusted and experienced general."

Nikometros grinned. He leaned forward and gripped Ptolemy's hand tightly. "You have one, sir. I will bring Alexander to you in Egypt."

# *Postscript*

A lexander's funeral cart was reckoned one of the wonders of its age. The embalmed body, encased in gold and precious stones lay in a richly worked temple of expensive carved woods and was transported in a great wagon that required sixty-four mules to pull it.

It left Babylon over a year after Alexander's death and moved slowly through the Persian Empire toward Hellespont and Macedon. Crowds lined the route, eager to catch a glimpse of the Golden King.

As it passed through Syria, Ptolemy met the procession with his army. Without bloodshed, he persuaded the escort to part with their charge and escorted the embalmed body in its golden temple, south into Egypt. Ptolemy installed Alexander temporarily in the Egyptian city of Memphis while his tomb and temple were completed in Alexandria. When it was ready, the body of Alexander was laid to rest amid great ceremony and rejoicing.

Nikometros fulfilled his promise by delivering Alexander's body to Egypt. He became General of the Egyptian army and, though he never fully recovered the use of his left arm, lived a full and successful life, defending Egypt against its enemies for many years.

Tomyra went on to have the son conceived in Babylon's Paradise, as well as several others. The power of the Goddess left her as she had foreseen, but it soon became evident that the power had transferred to her daughter Starissa.

Starissa became a priestess of the Egyptian goddess, Isis. The worship of Isis altered somewhat under her aegis, taking on overtones of Greek and Scythian customs.

Timon and Bithyia stayed close. Timon retired from active military life a few years after moving to Egypt and he took on a new role as tutor to Nikometros' first-born son, as well as his own. Bithyia bore no other children. She channelled her energies into guarding the new priestess of the Mother Goddess.

Tirses remained faithful until his death nearly ten years later. He was killed in battle while protecting his general's back. He was entombed with honour in the family tomb in Alexandria.

Parates disappeared, though a trader and entrepreneur somewhat reminiscent of the man emerged a few years later in northern Persia, along the borders of Scythia. Here, the similarity ends, however, as this new trader openly followed the teachings of Ahura-Mazda and was known to be fair and honest in all his dealings.

Caius Valerius Gracchus, the Roman praefect, remained under house arrest in Babylon. Eventually, Perdikkas brought him to trial as an accomplice but Caius evaded justice by falling on his sword.

The Empire disintegrated after Alexander's death. His successors reverted to the old pattern of tribal and family squabbles that marked the early history of Macedon.

Roxane, the Sogdian, bore a son who became Alexander the Fourth. She immediately set about killing off her chief rival, Stateira, Alexander's queen, and her unborn child. The young Alexander and Philip Arridaios became joint kings, ruled by the Regents.

Krateros died early and Kassandros took the throne in Macedon. Philip Arridaios was murdered by Alexander the Great's mother, Olympias, who was in turn murdered by Kassandros. Kassandros also murdered Roxane and Alexander seven years later.

Ptolemy reigned in Egypt, his dynasty ending three hundred years later when Rome conquered Egypt and Cleopatra (Ptolemy's descendant) committed suicide.

Perdikkas attempted to recover Alexander's body but failed and his officers killed him. One of his officers, Seleukos, eventually became king in Babylon and left his kingdom to his son Antiochus.

Another general, Antigonus the satrap of Phrygia, also carved himself out a kingdom, as did other officers such as Eumenes and Leonnatos.

Peukestas was satisfied to remain as a satrap of Persia. He allied himself with various generals and kings if he perceived them to have genuine Macedonian interests, eventually joining with Eumenes against Antigonus and was defeated. He retired from public life and apparently lived to a ripe old age.

Following Alexander's death and the dissolution of his empire, the proposed invasion of Europe never took place. Rome grew in power and eventually conquered the scattered remnants of Alexander's empire. The world would be a very different place if Rome had been conquered by Macedon.

If you enjoyed this author's book, then please place a review up at the site of purchase, and any social media sites you frequent!

**You can find ALL our books up on our website at:**

*https://www.writers-exchange.com*

**All our Historical Novels:**

*https://www.writers-exchange.com/category/genres/historical/*

**All Max's Books:**

*https://www.writers-exchange.com/max-overton/*

# *About the Author*

**M**ax Overton has travelled extensively and lived in many places around the world--including Malaysia, India, Germany, England, Jamaica, New Zealand, USA and Australia. Trained in the biological sciences in New Zealand and Australia, he has worked within the scientific field for many years, but now concentrates on writing. While predominantly a writer of historical fiction (Scarab: Books 1 - 6 of the Amarnan Kings; the Scythian Trilogy; the Demon Series; Ascension), he also writes in other genres (A Cry of Shadows, the Glass Trilogy, Haunted Trail, Sequestered) and draws on true life (Adventures of a Small Game Hunter in Jamaica, We Came From Königsberg). Max also maintains an interest in butterflies, photography, the paranormal and other aspects of Fortean Studies.

Most of his other published books are available at Writers Exchange E-Publishing, https://www.writers-exchange.com/Max-Overton/ and all his books may be viewed on his website: http://www.maxovertonauthor.com/

Max's book covers are all designed and created by Julie Napier, and other examples of her art and photography may be viewed at www.julienapier.com

# If you want to read more about books by this author, they are listed on the following pages...

# A Cry of Shadows
{Paranormal Murder Mystery}

Australian Professor Ian Delaney is single-minded in his determination to prove his theory that one can discover the moment that the life force leaves the body. After succumbing to the temptation to kill a girl under scientifically controlled conditions, he takes an offer of work in St Louis, hoping to leave the undiscovered crime behind him.

In America, Wayne Richardson seeks revenge by killing his ex-girlfriend, believing it will give him the upper hand, a means to seize control following their breakup. Wayne quickly discovers that he enjoys killing and begins to seek out young women who resemble his dead ex-girlfriend.

Ian and Wayne meet and, when Ian recognizes the symptoms of violent delusion, he employs Wayne to help him further his research. Despite the police closing in, the two killers manage to evade identification time and time again as the death toll rises in their wake.

The detective in charge of the case, John Barnes, is frantic, willing to try anything to catch his killer. With time running out, he searches desperately for answers before another body is found...or the culprit slips into the woodwork for good.

Publisher: https://www.writers-exchange.com/a-cry-of-shadows/

# Adventures of a Small Game Hunter in Jamaica
{Biography}

An eleven-year-old boy is plucked from boarding school in England and transported to the tropical paradise of Jamaica where he's free to study his one great love--butterflies. He discovers that Jamaica has a wealth of these wonderful insects and sets about making a collection of as many as he can find. Along the way, he has adventures with other creatures, from hummingbirds to vultures, from iguanas to black widow spiders. Through it all runs the promise of the legendary Homerus swallowtail, Jamaica's national butterfly.

Other activities intrude, like school, boxing and swimming lessons, but he manages to inveigle his parents into taking him to strange and sometimes dangerous places, all in the name of butterfly collecting. He meets scientists and Rastafarians, teachers, small boys and the ordinary people living on the tropical isle, and even discovers butterflies that shouldn't exist in Jamaica.

Author Max Overton was that young boy. He counted himself fortunate to have lived in Jamaica in an age very different from the present one. Max still has some of the butterflies he collected half a century or more ago, and each one releases a flood of memories whenever he opens the box and gazes at their tattered and fading wings. These memories have become stories-- stories of the Adventures of a Small Game Hunter in Jamaica.

Publisher:     https://www.writers-exchange.com/adventures-of-a-small-game-hunter/

# Ascension Series, A Novel of Nazi Germany
{Historical: Holocaust}

*Before he fully realized the diabolical cruelties of the National Socialist German Worker's Party, Konrad Wengler had committed atrocities against his own people, the Jews, out of fear of both his faith and his heritage. But after he witnesses firsthand the concentration camps, the corruption, the inhuman malevolence of the Nazi war machine and the propaganda aimed at annihilating an entire race, he knows he must find a way to turn the tide and become the savior his people desperately need.*

## Book 1: Ascension

*Being a Jew in Germany can be a dangerous thing...*

Fear prompts Konrad Wengler to put his faith aside and try desperately to forget his heritage. After fighting in the Great War, he's wounded and turns instead to law enforcement in his tiny Bavarian hometown. There, he falls under the spell of the fledgling Nazi Party. He joins the Party in patriotic fervour and becomes a Lieutenant of Police and Schutzstaffel (SS).

In the course of his duties as policeman, Konrad offends a powerful Nazi official who starts an SS investigation. War breaks out. When he joins the Police Battalions, he's sent to Poland and witnesses there firsthand the atrocities being committed upon his fellow Jews.

Unknown to Konrad, the SS investigators have discovered his origins and follow him into Poland. Arrested and sent to Mauthausen Concentration Camp, Konrad is forced to face what it means to be a Jew and fight for survival. Will his friends on the outside, his wife and lawyer, be enough to counter the might of the Nazi machine?

Publisher: https://www.writers-exchange.com/ascension/

## Book 2: Maelstrom

*Never underestimate the enemy...*

Konrad Wengler survived his brush with the death camps of Nazi Germany. Now, reinstated as a police officer in his Bavarian hometown despite being a Jew, he throws himself back into his work, seeking to uncover evidence that will remove a corrupt Nazi party official.

The Gestapo have their own agenda and, despite orders from above to eliminate this troublesome Jewish policeman, they hide Konrad in the Totenkopf (Death's Head) Division of the Waffen-SS. In a fight to survive in the snowy wastes of Russia while the tide of war turns against Germany, Konrad experiences tank battles, ghetto clearances, partisans, and death camps (this time as a guard), as well as the fierce battles where his Division is badly outnumbered and on the defence.

Through it all, Konrad strives to live by his conscience and resist taking part in the atrocities happening all around him. He still thinks of himself as a policeman, but his desire to bring the corrupt Nazi official to justice seems far removed from his present reality. If he is to find the necessary evidence against his enemy, he must first *survive...*

Publisher: https://www.writers-exchange.com/maelstrom/

## Book 3: Dämmerung

Konrad Wengler is captured and sent from one Soviet prison camp to another. Even hearing the war has come to an end makes no difference until he's arrested as a Nazi Party member. In jail, Konrad refuses to defend himself for things he's guilty and should be punished for. Will his be an eye-for-an-eye life sentence, or leniency in regard of the good he tried to do once he learned the truth?

Publisher: https://www.writers-exchange.com/dammerung/

# Fall of the House of Ramesses Series, A Novel of Ancient Egypt

{Historical: Ancient Egypt}

*Egypt was at the height of its powers in the days of Ramesses the Great, a young king who confidently predicted his House would last for a Thousand Years. Sixty years later, he was still on the throne. One by one, his heirs had died and the survivors had become old men. When Ramesses at last died, he left a stagnant kingdom and his throne to an old man--Merenptah. What followed laid the groundwork for a nation ripped apart by civil war.*

## Book 1: Merenptah

The House of Ramesses is in the hands of an old man. King Merenptah wants to leave the kingdom to his younger son, Seti, but northern tribes in Egypt rebel and join forces with the Sea Peoples, invading from the north. In the south, the king's eldest son Messuwy is angered at being passed over in favour of the younger son...and plots to rid himself of his father and brother.

Publisher: https://www.writers-exchange.com/merenptah/

## Book 2: Seti

After only nine years on the throne, Merenptah is dead and his son Seti is king in his place. He rules from the northern city of Men-nefer, while his elder brother Messuwy, convinced the throne is his by right, plots rebellion in the south.

The kingdoms are tipped into bloody civil war, with brother fighting against brother for the throne of a united Egypt. On one side is Messuwy, now crowned as King Amenmesse and his ruthless General Sethi; on the other, young King Seti and his wife Tausret. But other men are weighing up the chances of wresting the throne from both brothers and becoming king in their place. Under the onslaught of conflict, the House of Ramesses begins to crumble...

Publisher: https://www.writers-exchange.com/seti/

## Book 3: Tausret

The House of Ramesses falters as Tausret relinquishes the throne upon the death of her husband, King Seti. Amenmesse's young son Siptah will become king until her infant son is old enough to rule. Tausret, as Regent, and the king's uncle, Chancellor Bay, hold tight to the reins of power and vie for complete control of the kingdoms. Assassination changes the balance of power, and, seeing his chance, Chancellor Bay attempts a coup...

Tausret's troubles mount as she also faces a challenge from Setnakhte, an aging son of the Great Ramesses who believes Seti was the last legitimate king. If Setnakhte gets his way, he will destroy the House of Ramesses and set up his own dynasty of kings.

Publisher: https://www.writers-exchange.com/tausret/

# Glass Trilogy
{Paranormal Thriller}

*Delve deep into the mysteries of Aboriginal mythology, present day UFO activity and pure science that surround the continent of Australia, from its barren deserts to the depths of its rainforest and even deeper into its mysterious mountains. Along the way, love, greed, murder, and mystery abound while the secrets of mankind and the ultimate answer to 'what happens now?' just might be answered.*

**GLASS HOUSE, Book 1**: The mysteries of Australia may just hold the answers mankind has been searching for millennium to find. When Doctor James Hay, a university scientist who studies the paranormal mysteries in Australia, finds an obelisk of carved volcanic rock on sacred Aboriginal land in northern Queensland, he realizes it may hold the answers he's been seeking. A respected elder of the Aboriginal people instructs James to take up the gauntlet and follow his heart. Along with his old friend and award-winning writer Spencer, Samantha Louis, her cameraman, and two of James' Aboriginal students, James embarks on a life-changing quest for the truth. Publisher: https://www.writers-exchange.com/glass-house/

**A GLASS DARKLY, Book 2:** A dead volcano called Glass Mountain in Northern California seems harmless...but is it really?

Andromeda Jones, a physicist, knows her missing sister Samantha is somehow tied up with the new job Andromeda herself has been offered to work with a team in constructing Vox Dei, a machine that's been ostensibly built to eliminate wars. But what is its true nature, and who's pulling the strings?

When the experiment spins out of control, dark powers are unleashed and the danger to mankind unfolds relentlessly. Strange, evil shadows are using the Vox Dei and Andromeda's sister Samantha to get through to our world, knowing the time is near when Earth's final destiny will be decided.

Federal forces are aware of something amiss, so, to rescue her sibling, Andromeda agrees to go on a dangerous mission and soon finds herself entangled in a web of professional jealousy, political betrayal, and flat-out greed.

Publisher: https://www.writers-exchange.com/a-glass-darkly/

**LOOKING GLASS, Book 3:** Samantha and James Hay have been advised that their missing daughter Gaia have been located in ancient Australia. Dr. Xanatuo, an alien scientist who, along with a lost tribe of Neanderthals and other beings working to help mankind, has discovered a way to send them back in time to be reunited with Gaia. Ernie, the old Aboriginal tracker and leader of the Neanderthals, along with friends Ratana and Nathan and characters from the first two books of the trilogy, will accompany them. This team of intrepid adventurers have another mission for the journey, along with aiding the Hayes' quest, which is paramount to changing a terrible wrong which exists in the present time.

Publisher: https://www.writers-exchange.com/looking-glass/

# Haunted Trail A Tale of Wickedness & Moral Turpitude

{Western: Paranormal}

Ned Abernathy is a hot-tempered young cowboy in the small town of Hammond's Bluff in 1876. In a drunken argument with his best friend Billy over a girl, he guns him down. Ned flees and wanders the plains, forests and hills of the Dakota Territories, certain that every man's hand is against him.

Horse rustlers, marauding Indians, killers, gold prospectors and French trappers cross his path and lead to complications, as do persistent apparitions of what Ned believes is the ghost of his friend Billy, come to accuse him of murder. He finds love and loses it. Determined not to do the same when he discovers gold in the Black Hills, he ruthlessly defends his newfound wealth against greedy men. In the process, he comes to terms with who he is and what he's done. But there are other ghosts in his past that he needs to confront. Returning to Hammond's Bluff, Ned stumbles into a shocking surprise awaiting him at the end of his haunted trail.

Publisher: https://www.writers-exchange.com/haunted-trail/

Amazon: https://amzn.to/3AUyIqv

# Hyksos Series, A Novel of Ancient Egypt

*The power of the kings of the Middle Kingdom have been failing for some time, having lost control of the Nile Delta to a series of Canaanite kings who ruled from the northern city of Avaris.*
*Into this mix came the Kings of Amurri, Lebanon and Syria bent on subduing the whole of Egypt. These kings were known as the Hyksos, and they dealt a devastating blow to the peoples of the Nile Delta and Valley.*

## Book 1: Avaris

When Arimawat and his son Harrubaal fled from Urubek, the king of Hattush, to the court of the King of Avaris, King Sheshi welcomed the refugees. One of Arimawat's first tasks for King Shesi is to sail south to the Land of Kush and fetch Princess Tati, who will become Sheshi's queen. Arimawat and Harrubaal perform creditably, but their actions have far-reaching consequences.

On the return journey, Harrubaal falls in love with Kemi, the daughter of the Southern Egyptian king. As a reward for Harrubaal's work, Sheshi secures the hand of the princess for the young Canaanite prince. Unfortunately for the peace of the realm, Sheshi lusts after Princess Kemi too, and his actions threaten the stability of his kingdom...

Publisher: https://www.writers-exchange.com/avaris/
Amazon: https://amzn.to/3Zs3RK3

## Book 2: Conquest

The Hyksos invade the Delta using the new weapons of bronze and chariots, things of which the Egyptians have no knowledge. They rout the Delta forces, and in the south, the unconquered kings ready their armies to defend their lands. Meanwhile in Avaris, Merybaal, the son of Harrubaal and Kemi, strives to defend his family in a city conquered by the Hyksos.

Elements of the Delta army that refuse to surrender continue the fight for their homeland, and new kings proclaim themselves as the inheritors of the failed kings of Avaris. One of these is Amenre, grandson of Merybaal, but he is forced into hiding as the Hyksos sweep all before them, bringing their terror to the kingdom of the Nile valley. Driven south in disarray, the survivors of the Egyptian army seek leaders who can resist the enemy...

Publisher: https://www.writers-exchange.com/conquest/

Amazon: https://amzn.to/3OItEc0

## Book 3: Two Cities

The Hyksos drive south into the Nile Valley, sweeping all resistance aside. Bebi and Sobekhotep, grandsons of Harrubaal, assume command of the loyal Egyptian army and strive to stem the flood of Hyksos conquest. But even the cities of the south are divided against themselves.

Abdju, an old capital city of Egypt reasserts itself, putting forward a line of kings of its own, and soon the city is at war with Waset, the southern capital of the Nile Valley, as the two cities fight for supremacy in the face of the advancing northern enemy. Caught up in the turmoil of warring nations, the ordinary people of Egypt must fight for their own survival as well as that of their kingdom.

Publisher: https://www.writers-exchange.com/two-cities/

Amazon: https://amzn.to/3D10lia

## Book 4: Possessor of All

The Hyksos, themselves beset by intrigue and division, push down into southern Egypt. The short-lived kingdom of Abdju collapses, leaving Nebiryraw the undisputed king of the south ruling from the city of Waset.

An uneasy truce between north and south enables both sides to strengthen their positions.

Khayan seizes power over the Hyksos kingdom and turns his gaze toward Waset, determined to conquer Egypt finally. Meanwhile, the family of King Nebiryraw looks to the future and starts securing their own advantage, weakening the southern kingdom. In the face of renewed tensions, the delicate peace cannot last...

Publisher: https://www.writers-exchange.com/possessor-of-all/

## Book 5: War in the South

Intrigue and rebellion rule in Egypt's southern kingdom as the house of King Nebiryraw tears itself apart. King succeeds king, but none of them look capable of defending the south, let alone reclaiming the north. Taking advantage of this, King Khayan of the Hyksos launches his assault on Waset, but rebellions in the north delay his victory.

The fall of Waset brings about a change of leadership. Apophis takes command of the Hyksos forces, and Rahotep brings together a small army to challenge the might of the Hyksos, knowing that the fate of Egypt hangs on the coming battle.

Publisher: https://www.writers-exchange.com/war-in-the-south/

## Book 6: Between the Wars

Rahotep leads his Egyptian army to victory, and Apophis withdraws the Hyksos army northward. An uneasy peace settles over the Nile valley. Rebellions in the north keep the Hyksos king from striking back at Rahotep, while internal strife between the Hyksos nobility and generals threatens to rip their empire apart.

War is coming to Egypt once more, and the successors of Rahotep start preparing for it, using the very weapons that the Hyksos introduced--bronze weapons and the war chariot. King Ahmose repudiates the peace treaty, and Apophis of the Hyksos prepares to destroy his enemies at last. Bloody warfare returns to Egypt...

Publisher: https://www.writers-exchange.com/between-the-wars/

## Book 7: Sons of Tao

War breaks out between the Hyksos invaders and native Egyptians determined to rid themselves of their presence. King Seqenenre Tao launches an attack on King Apophis but the Hyksos strike back savagely. It is only when his sons Kamose and Ahmose carry the war to the Hyksos that the Egyptians really start to hope they can succeed.

Kamose battles fiercely, but only when his younger brother Ahmose assumes the throne is there real success. Faced with an ignominious defeat, a Hyksos general overthrows Apophis and becomes king, but then he faces a resurgent Egyptian king determined to rid his land of the Hyksos invader...

Publisher: https://www.writers-exchange.com/sons-of-tao/

# Kadesh, A Novel of Ancient Egypt

Holding the key to strategic military advantage, Kadesh is a jewel city that distant lands covet. Ramesses II of Egypt and Muwatalli II of Hatti believe they're chosen by the gods to claim ascendancy to Kadesh. When the two meet in the largest chariot battle ever fought, not just the fate of empires will be decided but also the lives of citizens helplessly caught up in the greedy ambition of kings.

Publisher: https://www.writers-exchange.com/kadesh/

# Scythian Trilogy
## {Historical}

*Captured by the warlike, tribal Scythians who bicker amongst themselves and bitterly resent outside interference, a fiercely loyal captain in Alexander the Great's Companion Cavalry Nikometros and his men are to be sacrificed to the Mother Goddess. Lucky chance--and the timely intervention of Tomyra, priestess and daughter of the Massegetae chieftain--allows him to defeat the Champion. With their immediate survival secured, acceptance into the tribe...and escape...is complicated by the captain's growing feelings for Tomyra--death to any who touch her--and the chief's son Areipithes who not only detests Nikometros and wants to have him killed or banished but intends to murder his own father and take over the tribe.*

**LION OF SCYTHIA, Book 1:** Alexander the Great has conquered the Persian Empire and is marching eastward to India. In his wake he leaves small groups of soldiers to govern great tracts of land and diverse peoples. Nikometros is one young cavalry captain left behind in the lands of the fierce, nomadic Scythian horsemen. Captured after an ambush, Nikometros must fight for his life and the lives of his surviving men. Even as he seeks an opportunity to escape, he finds himself bound by a debt of loyalty to the chief...and his own developing love for the young priestess.
Publisher: https://www.writers-exchange.com/lion-of-scythia/

**THE GOLDEN KING, Book 2:** The chief of the tribe of nomadic Scythian horsemen is dead, killed by his son's treachery. The priestess, lover of the young cavalry officer, Nikometros, is carried off into the mountains. Nikometros and his friends set off in hard pursuit.

Death rides with them. By the time they return, the tribes are at war. Nikometros must choose between attempting to become chief himself or leaving the people he's come to love and respect to return to his duty as an army officer in the Empire of Alexander.

Winner of the 2005 EPIC Ebook Awards.

Publisher: https://www.writers-exchange.com/the-golden-king/

**FUNERAL IN BABYLON, Book 3:** Alexander the Great has returned from India and set up his court in Babylon. Nikometros and a band of loyal Scythians journey deep into the heart of Persia to join the Royal court. Nikometros finds himself embroiled in the intrigues and wars of kings, generals, and merchant adventurers as he strives to provide a safe haven for his lover and friends. With the fate of an Empire hanging in the balance, Death walks beside Nikometros as events precipitate a Funeral in Babylon...

Winner of the 2006 EPIC Ebook Awards.

Publisher: https://www.writers-exchange.com/funeral-in-babylon/

# Sequestered
# By Max Overton and Jim Darley
{Action/Thriller}

Storing carbon dioxide underground as a means of removing a greenhouse gas responsible for global warming has made James Matternicht a fabulously wealthy man. For 15 years, the Carbon Capture and Sequestration Facility at Rushing River in Oregon's hinterland has been operating without a problem...or has it?

When mysterious documents arrive on her desk that purport to show the Facility is leaking, reporter Annaliese Winton investigates. Together with a government geologist, Matt Morrison, she uncovers a morass of corruption and deceit that now threatens the safety of her community and the entire northwest coast of America.

Liquid carbon dioxide, stored at the critical point under great pressure, is a tremendously dangerous substance, and millions of tonnes of it are sequestered in the rock strata below Rushing River. All it would take is a crack in the overlying rock and the whole pressurized mass could erupt with disastrous consequences. And that crack has always existed there...

Recipient of the Life Award (Literature for the Environment):

 "There are only two kinds of people: conservationists and suicides. To qualify for this Award, your book needs to value the wonderful world of nature, to recognize that we are merely one species out of millions, and that we have a responsibility to cherish and maintain our small planet."

Awarded from http://bobswriting.com/life/

Publisher: https://www.writers-exchange.com/sequestered/

# Strong is the Ma'at of Re, A Novel of Ancient Egypt

{Historical: Ancient Egypt}

*In Ancient Egypt, C1200 BCE, bitter contention and resentment, secret coups and assassination attempts may decide the fate of those who would become legends...by any means necessary.*

## Book 1: The King

That *he* is descended from Ramesses the Great fills Ramesses III with obscene pride. Elevated to the throne following a coup led by his father Setnakhte during the troubled days of Queen Tausret, Ramesses III sets about creating an Egypt that reflects the glory days of Ramesses the Great. He takes on his predecessor's throne name, names his sons after the sons of Ramesses and pushes them toward similar duties. Most of all, he thirsts after conquests like those of his hero grandfather.

Ramesses III assumes the throne name of Usermaatre, translated as "Strong is the Ma'at of Re" and endeavours to live up to the sentiment. He fights foreign foes, as had Ramesses the Great; he builds temples throughout the Two Lands, as had Ramesses the Great, and he looks forward to a long, illustrious life on the throne of Egypt, as had Ramesses the Great.

Alas, his reign is not meant to be. Ramesses III faces troubles at home--troubles that threaten the stability of Egypt and his own throne. The struggles for power between his wives, his sons, and even the priests of Amun, together with a treasury drained of its wealth, all force Ramesses III to question his success as the scion of a legend.

Publisher: https://www.writers-exchange.com/the-king/

## Book 2: The Heirs

Tiye, the first wife of Ramesses III, has grown so used to being the mother of the Heir she can no longer bear to see that prized title pass to the son of a rival wife. Her eldest sons have died and the one left wants to step down and devote his life to the priesthood. Then the son of the king's sister/wife, also named Ramesses, will become Crown Prince and all Tiye's ambitions will lie in ruins.

Ramesses III struggles to enrich Egypt by seeking the wealth of the Land of Punt. He dispatches an expedition to the fabled southern land but years pass before the expedition returns. In the meantime, Tiye has a new hope: A last son she dotes on. Plague sweeps through Egypt, killing princes and princesses alike and lessening her options, and now Tiye must undergo the added indignity of having her daughter married off to the hated Crown Prince.

All Tiye's hopes are pinned on this last son of hers, but Ramesses III refuses to consider him as a potential successor, despite the Crown Prince's failing health. Unless Tiye can change the king's mind through charm or coercion, her sons will forever be excluded from the throne of Egypt. Publisher: https://www.writers-exchange.com/the-heirs/

## Book 3: Taweret

The reign of Ramesses III is failing and even the gods seem to be turning their eyes away from Egypt. When the sun hides its face, crops suffer, throwing the country into famine. Tomb workers go on strike. To avert further disaster, Crown Prince Ramesses acts on his father's behalf.

The rivalry between Ramesses III's wives--commoner Tiye and sister/wife Queen Tyti--also comes to a head. Tiye resents not being made queen and can't abide that her sons have been passed over. She plots to put her own spoiled son Pentaweret on the throne.

The eventual strength of the Ma'at of Re hangs in the balance. Will the rule of Egypt be decided by fate, gods...or treason?

Publisher: https://www.writers-exchange.com/the-one-of-taweret/

# The Amarnan Kings Series, A Novel of Ancient Egypt

{Historical: Ancient Egypt}

*Set in Egypt of the 14th century B.C.E. and piecing together a mosaic of the reigns of the five Amarnan kings, threaded through by the memories of princess Beketaten-Scarab, a tapestry unfolds of the royal figures lost in the mists of antiquity.*

**SCARAB - AKHENATEN, Book 1:** A chance discovery in Syria reveals answers to the mystery of the ancient Egyptian sun-king, the heretic Akhenaten and his beautiful wife Nefertiti. Inscriptions in the tomb of his sister Beketaten, otherwise known as Scarab, tell a story of life and death, intrigue and warfare, in and around the golden court of the kings of the glorious 18th dynasty.

The narrative of a young girl growing up at the centre of momentous events--the abolition of the gods, foreign invasion, and the fall of a once-great family--reveals who Tutankhamen's parents really were, what happened to Nefertiti, and other events lost to history in the great destruction that followed the fall of the Aten heresy.

Publisher: https://www.writers-exchange.com/scarab/

**SCARAB- SMENKHKARE, Book 2:** King Akhenaten, distraught at the rebellion and exile of his beloved wife Nefertiti, withdraws from public life, content to leave the affairs of Egypt in the hands of his younger half-brother Smenkhkare. When Smenkhkare disappears on a hunting expedition, his sister Beketaten, known as Scarab, is forced to flee for her life.

Finding refuge among her mother's people, the Khabiru, Scarab has resigned herself to a life in exile...until she hears that her brother Smenkhkare is still alive. He is raising an army in Nubia to overthrow Ay and reclaim his throne. Scarab hurries south to join him as he confronts Ay and General Horemheb outside the gates of Thebes.

Publisher: https://www.writers-exchange.com/scarab2/

**SCARAB - TUTANKHAMEN, Book 3:** Scarab and her brother Smenkhkare are in exile in Nubia but are gathering an army to wrest control of Egypt from the boy king Tutankhamen and his controlling uncle, Ay. Meanwhile, the kingdoms are beset by internal troubles while the Amorites are pressing hard against the northern borders. Generals Horemheb and Paramessu must fight a war on two fronts while deciding where their loyalties lie--with the former king Smenkhkare or with the new young king in Thebes.

Smenkhkare and Scarab march on Thebes with their native army to meet the legions of Tutankhamen on the plains outside the city gates. As two brothers battle for supremacy and the throne of the Two Kingdoms, the fate of Egypt and the 18th dynasty hangs in the balance.

Finalist in 2013's Eppie Awards.

Publisher: https://www.writers-exchange.com/scarab3/

**SCARAB - AY, Book 4:** Tutankhamen is dead and his grieving widow tries to rule alone, but her grandfather Ay has not destroyed the former kings just so he can be pushed aside. Presenting the Queen and General Horemheb with a fait accompli, the old Vizier assumes the throne of Egypt and rules with a hand of hardened bronze. His adopted son, Nakhtmin, will rule after him and stamp out the last remnants of loyalty to the former kings.

Scarab was sister to three kings and will not give in to the usurper and his son. She battles against Ay and his legions under the command of General Horemheb and aided by desert tribesmen and the gods of Egypt themselves. The final confrontation will come in the rich lands of the Nile delta where the future of Egypt will at last be decided.

Publisher: https://www.writers-exchange.com/scarab4/

**SCARAB - HOREMHEB, Book 5:** General Horemheb has taken control after the death of Ay and Nakhtmin. Forcing Scarab to marry him, he ascends the throne of Egypt. The Two Kingdoms settle into an uneasy peace as Horemheb proceeds to stamp out all traces of the former kings. He also persecutes the Khabiru tribesmen who were reluctant to help him seize power. Scarab escapes into the desert, where she is content to wait until Egypt needs her.

A holy man emerges from the desert and demands that Horemheb release the Khabiru so they may worship his god. Scarab recognises the holy man and supports him in his efforts to free his people. The gods of Egypt and of the Khabiru are invoked and disaster sweeps down on the Two Kingdoms as the Khabiru flee with Scarab and the holy man. Horemheb and his army pursue them to the shores of the Great Sea, where a natural event...or the very hand of God...alters the course of Egyptian history.
Publisher: https://www.writers-exchange.com/scarab5/

**SCARAB - DESCENDANT, Book 6:** Three thousand years after the reigns of the Amarnan Kings, the archaeologists who discovered the inscriptions in Syria journey to Egypt to find the tomb of Smenkhkare and his sister Scarab and the fabulous treasure they believe is there. Unscrupulous men and religious fanatics also seek the tomb, either to plunder it or to destroy it. Can the gods of Egypt protect their own, or will the ancients rely on modern day men and women of science?
Publisher: https://www.writers-exchange.com/scarab6/

# The Pyramid Builders, A Novel of Ancient Egypt
{Historical: Ancient Egypt}

*The third dynasty of the Old Kingdom of Egypt saw an extraordinary development of building techniques, from the simple structures of mud brick at the end of the second dynasty to the towering pyramids of the fourth dynasty. Just how these massive structures were built has long been a matter of conjecture, but history is made up of the lives and actions of individuals; kings and architects, scribes and priests, soldiers and artisans, even common labourers, and so the story of the Pyramid Builders unfolded over the course of more than a century. This is that story...*

## Book 1: Djoser

King Khasekhemwy has two sons, Djoser and Imhotep, but their destinies are very different. One will become king and the other his architect and the power behind the throne. Together, they plan to build something new, a great tomb that will be the wonder of the world. But not all is peaceful within the kingdoms of Egypt. Djoser's son Sekhemkhet will inherit the throne, but there are others that seek power and set their plans in motion, and they care nothing for the architectural ambitions of their king.

Ordinary men and women inhabit Djoser's Egypt too, living their own lives, dreaming of power or simple happiness, but sometimes these dreams do not harmonise with the plans of kings...

Publisher: https://www.writers-exchange.com/djoser/

## Book 2: Sekhemkhet

Sekhemkhet faces the daunting prospect of following on from the glories of his father's achievement. He desires an even bigger pyramid than that of Djoser and orders Imhotep and Den to build it. However, the king finds it easier to build a tomb than to raise heirs to follow him on the throne, and a cousin seeks to take advantage of Sekhemkhet's precarious position and challenge the king.

Not all is well within Den's family. He is married, but love from an unexpected source threatens to destroy the success he has so laboriously built up. Will he sacrifice love for ambition, or can he find a way to have both?

Publisher: https://www.writers-exchange.com/sekhemkhet/

## Book 3: Khaba

The throne of Egypt has passed to Khaba, an old man who seeks only to secure his family's position. Construction of a pyramid tomb is a secondary consideration, and the fortunes of those who desire to build them languish as he refuses further innovations. It is left to his grandson and heir, Huni, to dream of greater architectural glories.

Architect Den has achieved love, but at the cost of ambition. He and his burgeoning family struggle to survive, his relatives seeking out love of their own even as they look for opportunities to further their careers. The promise of a return to fulfilment is offered, but will they be able to grasp it?

Publisher: https://www.writers-exchange.com/khaba/

## Book 4: Huni

Like a breath of fresh air after a generation of stagnation, Huni becomes king and sets about reorganising Egypt. He divides the land into administrative regions under governors and devises a way to bring the blessings of the gods to all men--he will build small pyramids up and down the length of the river, reserving a simple tomb for himself.

Even as Den and his sons build for the king, his twin daughters threaten to tear down the king's future. One falls in love with the heir to the throne, while the other seeks the heir's death. Which one succeeds will determine the fortunes of their extended family.

Publisher: https://www.writers-exchange.com/huni/

## Book 5: Sneferu

The kings of Egypt are turning from the worship of all gods to raising the sun god Re above them all. Rather than a stepped pyramid for the spirit of the king to ascend to the undying stars, they seek a representation of the beneficent rays of the sun in a smooth-sided pyramid. This brings with it a host of new problems to be overcome by the king's architects. Meanwhile, the king takes several wives and has many sons who vie for power, using murder to achieve their ends.

Den is old and passes the title of architect on to his son Khepankh and grandson Djer, but they make mistakes as they try to learn new techniques of building massive pyramids. Their mistakes threaten to be their undoing, but they find a way to build true and strong, and a new talent arises from a union between Den's family and the heir to the throne.

Publisher: https://www.writers-exchange.com/sneferu/

## Book 6: Khufu

Khufu is excited by the pyramids of his father Sneferu and wants to build a great one that will eclipse everything else ever built. The Great Pyramid presents unique challenges that must be overcome if the pyramid is to be built. Architect Hemiunu finds solutions, but even he relies on help from Rait, a woman of great talent. She must battle prejudice even from her own father if she is to achieve ultimate success.

The sons of Khufu vie for power. Their actions will lead to wars between nations, and call into question who has the right to sit on the throne of Egypt. Meanwhile, the family of Den have taken to sailing and trade and find the fabled land of Punt where discoveries will affect the lives of kings yet unborn.

Publisher: https://www.writers-exchange.com/khufu/

## Book 7: Djedefre

Djedefre becomes king, with his brother Hordjedef his principal adviser. Breaking with tradition, the king appoints Rait as his architect, gambling that she will be up to the task of building a pyramid. An earthquake damages the Sphinx, and is seen as an omen of the gods' disfavour, but the king makes a decision that might avert disaster, though many view it as added blasphemy. Concerned for the future, those close to the king plot to remove him.

The king's heir is put aside, and a struggle for power breaks out, leading to deadly strife between the brothers Baka and Setka. Death and exile follow, with consequences that threaten Egypt's future.

Publisher: https://www.writers-exchange.com/djedefre/

## Book 8: Khafre

Khafre seizes control and takes the throne of his brother, while his nephew Baka flees to Amurru with his uncle Hordjedef. The new king wants a pyramid as big as his father's, appointing a conventional male architect. However, he has cause to regret his decision, bringing back Rait when things go wrong. Others passed over for the position seek to hurt Rait and violate her daughter Neferit.

The head of the Sphinx is rebuilt, with Khafre's features replacing the damaged face of the god Inpu. Hordjedef quarrels with exiled Baka and returns to Egypt, pleading for forgiveness, but as Khafre sickens, Baka seeks revenge. The heir, Menkaure, must battle for the throne of Egypt when his father Khafre dies.

Publisher: https://www.writers-exchange.com/khafre/

## Book 9: Menkaure

Menkaure meets Baka in battle and defeats him. Baka returns to Amurru, but Menkaure's reign is beset by troubles at home and abroad. Although Menkaure's pyramid is rising swiftly, the king falls sick with the 'shaking fever', for which there is no cure. Only a medicine brought back from Punt seems to hold out hope, but Shepseskaf assumes the power of regent, ruling in place of his sick father.

An ambitious army officer by the name of Userkaf takes command of the northern army, and he is deeply devoted to the god Re, allying his family with the priests of Iunu. Neferit's daughter Peseshet strives to become a physician in the face of opposition from the medical fraternity.


## Book 10: Shepseskaf

Menkaure's health continues to decline and Shepseskaf must now become king. He strives to finish his father's pyramid, but desires something simpler for himself, forsaking the pyramid form. Others desire power in Egypt--the king's sister Khentkaus wants to be king; Userkaf, now a General, dares to think of greater things; and even the priests of Re and Ptah look to increase their status. Shepseskaf's heir dies, and the king must not only rescue his family's future but must fight off Egypt's enemies at home and abroad.

In Amurru, Baka dies, and his son Bauefre desires the throne of Egypt. He leads an army south against Shepseskaf and Userkaf in a final battle.

# TULPA
## {Paranormal Thriller}

*From the rainforests of tropical Australia to the cane fields and communities of the North Queensland coastal strip, a horror is unleashed by those foolishly playing with unknown forces...*

A fairy story to amuse small children leads four bored teenagers and a young university student in a North Queensland town to becoming interested in an ancient Tibetan technique for creating a life form. When their seemingly harmless experiment sets free terror and death, the teenagers are soon fighting to contain a menace that reproduces exponentially.

The police are helpless to end the horror. Aided by two old game hunters, a student of the paranormal and a few small children, the teenagers must find a way of destroying what they unintentionally released. But how can they stop beings that can escape into an alternate reality when threatened?

Publisher: https://www.writers-exchange.com/TULPA/

# We Came From Konigsberg
{Historical: Holocaust}

Based on a true story gleaned from the memories of family members sixty years after the events, from photographs and documents, and from published works of nonfiction describing the times and events described in the narrative, *We Came From Konigsberg* is set in January 1945.

The Soviet Army is poised for the final push through East Prussia and Poland to Berlin. Elisabet Daeker and her five young sons are in Königsberg, East Prussia and have heard the shocking stories of Russian atrocities. They're desperate to escape to the perceived safety of Germany. To survive, Elisabet faces hardships endured at the hands of Nazi hardliners, of Soviet troops bent on rape, pillage and murder, and of Allied cruelty in the Occupied Zones of post-war Germany.

Winner of the 2014 EPIC Ebook Awards.

Publisher: https://www.writers-exchange.com/we-came-from-konigsberg/

## You can find ALL our books up on our website at:

*https://www.writers-exchange.com*

## All our Historical Novels:

*https://www.writers-exchange.com/category/genres/historical/*

## All Max's Books:

*https://www.writers-exchange.com/max-overton/*

www.ingramcontent.com/pod-product-compliance
Lightning Source LLC
Chambersburg PA
CBHW071340020726
47502CB00001B/181